Fair Are the Meadows

Books by Lauraine Snelling

Home to Green Creek

Land of Dreams
At Morning's Light
Fair Are the Meadows

Leah's Garden

The Seeds of Change
A Time to Bloom
Fields of Bounty
A Season of Harvest

Under Northern Skies

The Promise of Dawn
A Breath of Hope
A Season of Grace
A Song of Joy

Song of Blessing

To Everything a Season
A Harvest of Hope
Streams of Mercy
From This Day Forward

Red River of the North

An Untamed Land
A New Day Rising
A Land to Call Home
The Reapers' Song
Tender Mercies
Blessing in Disguise

Return to Red River

A Dream to Follow
Believing the Dream
More Than a Dream

Daughters of Blessing

A Promise for Ellie
Sophie's Dilemma
A Touch of Grace
Rebecca's Reward

Home to Blessing

A Measure of Mercy
No Distance Too Far
A Heart for Home

Wild West Wind

Valley of Dreams
Whispers in the Wind
A Place to Belong

Dakotah Treasures

Ruby • *Pearl*
Opal • *Amethyst*

Secret Refuge

Daughter of Twin Oaks
Sisters of the Confederacy
The Long Way Home

A Blessing to Cherish
An Untamed Heart

HOME TO GREEN CREEK · 3

FAIR ARE THE MEADOWS

LAURAINE SNELLING

with Kiersti Giron

BETHANYHOUSE
a division of Baker Publishing Group
Minneapolis, Minnesota

Published by Bethany House Publishers
Minneapolis, Minnesota
BethanyHouse.com

Bethany House Publishers is a division of
Baker Publishing Group, Grand Rapids, Michigan

Printed in the United States of America

Library of Congress Cataloging-in-Publication Data
Names: Snelling, Lauraine author | Giron, Kiersti author
Title: Fair are the meadows / Lauraine Snelling with Kiersti Giron.
Description: Minneapolis, Minnesota : Bethany House Publishers, a division of Baker Publishing Group, 2026. | Series: Home to Green Creek ; 3
Identifiers: LCCN 2026000147 | ISBN 9780764243547 paperback | ISBN 9780764247064 cloth | ISBN 9780764247071 large print | ISBN 9781493455461 ebook
Subjects: LCGFT: Fiction | Christian fiction | Romance fiction | Novels
Classification: LCC PS3569.N39 F35 2026
LC record available at https://lccn.loc.gov/2026000147

Scripture quotations are from the King James Version of the Bible.

Cover design by Dan Thornberg, Design Source Creative Services
Image of woman by Leonardo Baldini / Arcangel Images

Published in association with Books & Such Literary Management, www.booksandsuch.com.

Baker Publishing Group publications use paper produced from sustainable forestry practices and postconsumer waste whenever possible.

26 27 28 29 30 31 32 7 6 5 4 3 2 1

The Home to Green Creek series
is dedicated to both sides of my family,
those who emigrated to America
and those who remained in Norway.

One

Green Creek, Iowa, May 1891

Why was she so nervous?

Helen drew a deep breath, buttoning the bodice of her best, dove-gray dress. She had sung for weddings before, so why the flutter in her middle now? Perhaps because all those attending would be so near and dear to her that she wanted to do her best? But no, that should set her more at ease, not less.

Or was it that Ødger Gunderson would accompany her on his guitar? She squashed that thought like a stubborn mosquito.

"Miss Stenerson! Are you ready?" An eager tapping came at her door.

"Almost." Helen pinned on her brooch, checked her softly upswept blond hair in her little bureau mirror, then opened the door to greet Ruthie. "Don't you look nice."

"I heard you singing. You sounded pretty as—as a cardinal."

"Why, thank you." Helen smiled down at her seven-year-old student—now almost part of her family, after these two years living in Forsberg House. "I was just practicing the hymn Maya and Eben asked me to sing for the wedding."

"We're almost ready to go. Come on." Ruthie flew ahead of

Helen down the stairs. "I like to hear the meadowlark sing too. Mr. JJ is building a birdhouse for lots of birds, each room . . ." She paused and glanced back, scrunching her face up. "Sort of like a boardinghouse. He said the birds would eat lots of the bugs. Do you think the birds could eat all the mosquitoes too?"

Helen rolled her eyes. "Would that God would have it so." Gently she nudged Ruthie's shoulder ahead of her down the stairs. "Come on, we'd better hurry."

"Ja, we better." The little girl clattered down the rest of the stairs.

Helen smiled and followed, Ruthie's joy lifting her own heart. Why should she be self-conscious on such a day? *Forgive me, Father.* Maya had been through so much heartache last year, losing her husband and then her first baby. But little Torvald, who had lost his mother, had been an unexpected gift—as had Eben.

And now, they were all ready to celebrate a wedding.

An hour later, Helen and Amalia stood in the guest bedroom of Eben and Maya's new home, built on a low hill on the north side of the Miller property, which neighbored that of Forsberg House. Amalia pinned wildflowers in Maya's light brown hair while Helen held nine-month-old Torvald, who squirmed and reached for his mother as if he sensed something was different today.

"Are you nervous?" Amalia asked her cousin.

"Not really." With a soft smile, Maya fingered the lace at the neck of her light blue lawn dress, the first color she'd worn since her first husband died at sea last March. "Just . . . so thankful."

"It was a lovely idea, to have the wedding here at your new home." Bouncing Torvald on her hip, Helen stepped to the window and peered out at the guests beginning to arrive below. The room still smelled of new wood, though the house-raising had been late last fall.

"I can hardly believe I won't be coming back to the boardinghouse after this." Maya glanced about the little room with full eyes. "And yet, somehow this house already feels like mine. Mine and Eben's."

"And so it is."

"Did you know that JJ made us a rope bed for a wedding present? That man is so good to everyone. You *all* are so good to us."

Helen shared a secret grin with Amalia. Somehow they had managed to keep the quilt for Maya and Eben a secret also. When Maya went over to the Miller house, Amalia had sat down at the sewing machine and treadled away. Eben's mother, meanwhile, had sewn sheets and had enough duck and goose feathers to make two pillows. The newlyweds would lack nothing as they set up housekeeping.

Amalia added a last sprig of pale blue-violet Sweet William to Maya's hair and then stepped back. "There. You're beautiful."

Torvald crowed and lunged toward his mother. They all laughed.

"He thinks so too." Helen handed the baby over with a smile.

"Perhaps I'd better nurse him once more before the ceremony, so he doesn't make a fuss in the middle." Maya kissed her adopted son's fine blond hair.

"Probably a good idea. Just try not to let him muss your dress." Amalia tickled Torvald's chubby foot. "Let us know when you're finished."

Helen and Amalia slipped downstairs to the large parlor at the front of the house, where the crowd was gathering. Only close family and friends, but they already nearly filled the chairs that Absalom and Erik, Amalia's brother, had helped Eben set up yesterday. Eben's brother, Lawrence, and his family, along with his sisters and their families who lived a bit farther away, visited with his parents. Absalom's father, Magistrate Karlsson, stood leaning on his brass-headed cane and chatting with the boarders from Forsberg House who better knew Maya and Eben—JJ, Amos, and the Rykavyk brothers, who had worked with Eben on the threshing team last summer.

And of course, Ødger Gunderson, Maya's brother, who had come with her from Norway last year after her husband died right before their voyage.

Ødger approached Helen now, a smile on his blond-bearded face, guitar case in his hand. "God dag, Miss Stenerson. Are you ready for our song?"

Our song—what a nice ring that had. Helen smiled back, willing away the butterflies in her middle. "I believe so. I do love the hymn they chose."

"Ja. So do I." Ødger's broad shoulders rose and fell with a sigh as he surveyed the sunshine-filled room, the wide wooden planks of the floor, the broad stone fireplace. "My heart is full today, to see this joy for my sister."

Helen's chest tightened. Seeing Maya go through such grief last year must have hurt Ødger deeply. "I can imagine."

Rev. Larsen, the elderly minister from Green Creek, stood near the hearth in his best cassock, a smile wreathing his gentle face. "Ladies and gentlemen, if you would all take your seats, I believe we are about ready."

Amalia, who had slipped upstairs again, came down carrying Torvald. She gave the reverend a nod and sat next to Absalom. Torvald, bouncing on her lap in his short dress, chewed on his fist.

The reverend beckoned Eben forward. He came to stand before the fireplace, towering over the reverend and looking a bit stiff in starched collar and dark gray suit rather than his usual farm clothes and suspenders. Yet the smile on his gentle face near to outshone the sun outside. In the front row, Mr. and Mrs. Miller clasped hands, and a hush fell over the gathering.

Off to the side, Ødger plucked a soft tune on his guitar. Ruthie and Thomasina, the orphan girl from Chicago who had landed at Forsberg House last summer after stowing away on the train, emerged from the hallway by the stairs. They both wore new dresses, Ruthie's robin's-egg blue and Thomi's a deep rose, and held baskets of flowers. Behind them came Maya, carrying a bouquet of violets, Sweet William, and columbine, her flower-crowned head held like a queen.

Helen glanced at Eben, and the look on his face brought a lump to her throat.

Maya stopped on the other side of the reverend, facing Eben, while the little girls sat down next to Absalom and Amalia. Ødger played a few last notes, then stopped.

Rev. Larsen beamed over the gathering. "Dear friends, we have come together in the presence of God to witness the marriage of Eben Hiram Miller and Maya Anne Bredesen, to surround them with our prayers, and to share in their joy. Let us enter into this celebration confident that, through the Holy Spirit, Christ is present with us now also. We pray that this couple may fulfill God's purpose for the whole of their lives."

After handing her bouquet to Ruthie, Maya clasped Eben's hands, looking up into his eyes with such trust Helen found her own vision blurring with tears. The ceremony was simple, since Maya was a widow, but the couple spoke their vows with such conviction that more than Mrs. Miller sat wiping their eyes.

At last the reverend nodded to Helen and Ødger, and she stepped forward while he sounded the opening chords on his guitar.

Straightening her shoulders, Helen gazed out the front window toward the rolling green fields of spring and began to sing.

"Love divine, all love excelling,
Joy of heaven to earth come down!
Fix in us Thy humble dwelling,
All Thy faithful mercies crown."

Her heart lifted as her voice soared, the melody carrying her upward as music always did.

"Jesus, Thou art all compassion,
Pure, unbounded love Thou art;
Visit us with Thy salvation,
Enter every trembling heart!"

On the next verse, Ødger joined in, his rich baritone harmonizing with her soprano, then finally they invited everyone to join them as they finished the hymn. Once, Helen glanced over and saw Ødger's gray-blue eyes fixed intently on her. Ears warming, she refocused on little Torvald bouncing on Amalia's lap.

As the hymn concluded and Helen sat back down, Rev. Larsen led Eben and Maya through exchanging rings, then looked out over the gathering once more.

"Eben and Maya, by their promises before God and in the presence of this assembly, have joined themselves to one another as husband and wife. Those whom God has joined together let no one separate." He raised his arms in blessing. "Now may the Lord bless you and keep you, make His face shine upon you and be gracious to you." Lowering his arms, he beamed. "Eben, you may now kiss your bride."

Eben gazed down at Maya and cupped one hand to her cheek, as if asking her permission. Smiling, she lifted her face to him, and he kissed her with gentle promise.

Applause broke out, and Torvald squealed, setting everyone to laughing.

Mrs. Miller and Amalia took charge then, ordering young Hank and Ned Miller, Eben's nephew, to help the men set up tables outside. Helen helped spread white cloths and unload the bounty of food all the women had brought, including a frosted wedding cake lovingly crafted by Mrs. Miller. Everyone feasted, laughed, talked, and passed Torvald around to cuddle, till at last the slanting rays of afternoon sun proclaimed time to get home for chores.

"Amalia said you are keeping Torvald tonight?" Helen asked Mrs. Miller as she helped clear the tables.

"Going to try to." Mrs. Miller chuckled. "Thought it would be nice for them to have one night of privacy on their own—and Maya says he's started sleeping through the night most nights. She'll nurse him just before I take him, and we've got plenty of fresh milk from our cows. But we'll see how it goes." She lowered her voice. "Have they told you about the chivaree?"

"The what?"

Mrs. Miller shook her head, suppressing a smile as Eben and Maya strolled near, hand in hand. "Amalia can tell you about it," she whispered.

"What's a chivaree?" Helen asked Amalia as they headed back to the boardinghouse, the men to the barn for chores and women to the house to get a simple supper on for the boarders who hadn't attended the wedding.

"Ah, that was new to me too." Amalia tied an apron on over her Sunday dress. "I had to ask Mrs. Miller to explain it to me. It's some American custom where the friends and family of the bride and groom go over to their house the night of their wedding and wake them up with all sorts of racket."

Helen felt her eyebrows rise high. "I've never heard of such a thing."

"Ja, well, Mrs. Miller said it's more a tradition out in the country. You grew up in the city, didn't you?"

"Yes, well, mostly." And before living with her aunt in Cincinnati, she certainly wouldn't have known anything about rural wedding customs. But she wasn't ready to tell Amalia about that earliest part of her life. "What a curious idea, though."

"Ja, I'm rather glad no one gave us a chivaree. But then, Absalom's father sent us to that lovely hotel for our wedding night. Would you slice the bread, please?"

"Will we be joining in this—chivaree?" Helen fetched a loaf of sourdough from the breadbox.

"I think so. Eben's brother is heading it up—apparently it's usually the bride's brother, but of course it's all as new to Ødger as to you and me."

Some hours later, Helen, Amalia, Absalom, Erik, and Ødger crept across the dark fields between the Forsberg House and Miller properties, toting various bundles, including two protesting hens in a crate. Hank, Thomi, and Ruthie trailed along behind, buzzing with excitement over being allowed to stay up so late.

"I feel as if we are plotting some crime," Ødger whispered, tiptoeing alongside her.

Helen giggled softly. "I know what you mean."

They climbed the low hill leading to Eben and Maya's home, the moon rising silvery over the fields. A small crowd had gathered below the bedroom window, where one light burned. Eben's brother, Lawrence, stood whispering to his sisters' husbands and a few other friends, along with Eben's parents.

"Here." Lawrence passed out pots and pans and ladles, handing a large cowbell to Ødger.

"What do we do?" Ødger asked.

"Shh. Just make a bunch of noise when I give the signal. You'll see."

Once everyone had some noisemaker, Lawrence lifted his lantern and yelled, "Chivaree!"

Noise exploded around them, whoops and hollers, ladles and spoons banging on pots and pans and an old washtub. Ødger had seemingly lost his hesitation and clanged the cowbell with abandon.

A rustle at the window, and Eben's head and nightshirted shoulders stuck out. "Why in thunder are all you rascals makin' that racket?" But he grinned. Maya poked her head under his arm, her cheeks flushed.

"Chivaree! Chivaree!" Lawrence and his brothers-in-law yelled. "Give us a kiss!"

Now Eben reddened. The hollers increased till Maya stood on tiptoe and pecked her husband's cheek, bringing renewed whoops.

Absalom looped his arm around Amalia, grinning, and gave her a smooch on the cheek too. She slapped at his chest, laughing.

"Now you gotta entertain us, if you want to be let alone," someone hollered.

"All right, all right." Eben lifted his hands. "Ma left some cookies and lemonade downstairs. Help yourselves."

The merrymakers crowded into the downstairs of the house, where the newlyweds briefly joined them, flushed and smiling, till the refreshments had been demolished. Then the noisy crowd presented gifts to the bride and groom—Amalia and Absalom bestowed the two clucking chickens, Hank gave a lovely framed drawing of the new house, and Ruthie held out a squirming gray kitten, one of Magpie's spring litter, whom she'd been clutching against her chest the whole time. Mrs. Miller unfurled a beautiful braided rag rug, while Helen gave a set of dish towels she'd been embroidering with wildflowers since the winter.

"At least this makes up somewhat for routin' us outa bed." Eben hugged his wife to his side. "We thank you kindly. Now you varmints go home and leave us alone." He gave another good-natured grin, but a note of authority rang in his voice also. "My wife and me want to get some sleep."

After more laughter and teasing, the crowd finally dispersed.

"Well, that was quite a commotion." Ødger blew out a breath as they headed back through the cooling night, his now-muffled cowbell in hand. He'd be spending the night at the boardinghouse tonight rather than the magistrate's home in Decorah.

"Definitely." Helen shook her head and chuckled. "I'm not sure I'd want a chivaree done for me." She clamped her lips closed—she hadn't really meant to say that. And she knew quite well there lay little chance of her ever being a bride. She'd missed her chance for that.

Usually that knowledge came with a measure of acceptance. But tonight, thinking of Eben and Maya's happy, flustered faces, something deep within her ached.

Two

Miss Stenerson, what's this?"

At Ruthie's question, Helen looked up from sifting through her trunk for summer clothes. With the weather warming at the end of May, Helen wanted to get out her cooler blouses and skirts in time to iron them for the last two weeks of school. She'd let Ruthie and Thomi come in to see her "pretty things," as they put it.

She hadn't often invited the little girls into her room, needing to preserve the quiet of her own space after the days of constantly answering questions from three dozen children ranging in age from five to sixteen. But Amalia wasn't feeling well this Saturday morning—the reason for which she'd confided in Helen some weeks ago—and had gone to lie down, so hopefully digging through Helen's big trunk would keep the girls quietly entertained for a while.

Now Helen lowered her armful of skirts and bent closer to see what Ruthie held up toward the window's natural light.

A delicate gold bracelet, too small for Ruthie's slender seven-year-old wrist. It caught the sunbeams with a sharp glint, making Helen blink—both at the light and the memories.

"I believe this was mine when I was little, perhaps even a baby."

Helen took the bracelet from Ruthie, feeling the fragility of the slim band in her fingers. She ran her thumb over the engraved letters, almost too small to read.

Ruthie leaned her blond-braided head against Helen's shoulder. "Primrose," she read. "That isn't your name."

"No." Helen's fingers tightened slightly on the bracelet. "Perhaps it was my mother's."

"You don't know your mother's name?" Ruthie's brow furrowed.

"No. I mean, yes, of course I do." Old memories tiptoed at the edges of her brain, but Helen pushed them away, as she usually did. "It was Adelaide. But she may have had a nickname I didn't know about." Or had the nickname been Helen's own? And why did it bother her so much that she didn't know? Helen closed her hand around the bracelet and pushed it back away under the stack of childhood journals and sheet music in the far corner of her trunk. "I'm almost finished, so let's put the rest of these things away."

"You have nice jewelry." Thomi peeked into a small, carved wooden box. "How come you never wear any of it?"

"Sometimes I do." Helen touched the cameo at her neck. "I wear this brooch almost every day. My aunt gave it to me, and it has a photograph of her and my uncle in it."

"I wish I had something like that. I have a little photograph of my papa. I'd put that inside. Now I just keep it in my drawer," Thomi said. Slowly, she handed the box to Helen to be tucked away. "There's a real pretty necklace in there. Why don't you ever wear that?"

"I don't think it's quite appropriate for a schoolteacher." Helen's high collar suddenly felt too tight. Why had she let the little girls dig through her things with such freedom? She tried to latch the box, found it wouldn't close, and opened it to see that part of the chain of the garnet and jet necklace had gotten caught in the hinge. She worked it free, biting her bottom lip. The necklace was too ornate for her taste, but it had been her mother's—long ago. Aunt

Ophelia had given it to Helen when she turned twenty-one, and not wanting to offend the gracious woman who had largely raised her, Helen kept it safe. She worked the chain free with a little jerk and clicked the box closed.

"Come." She tucked the box into a different corner of the trunk and laid a stack of her winter woolens atop it, drawing a breath to steady herself. "Let's go down and see about getting dinner on for Tante Amalia, if she's still resting."

"Is Tante Malia sick?" Ruthie picked at a chip in the corner of Helen's trunk.

Helen glanced at the little girl, her irritation softening. "No, just tired." At some point perhaps Amalia would tell Ruthie her special news, but that wasn't Helen's place. "We should let her rest, don't you think? You girls are getting to be such capable young ladies in the kitchen."

Ruthie's grin peeked out again. "Ja."

They crept softly down the boardinghouse stairs and past the closed door of Amalia and Absalom's room, between the front hall and the kitchen. Still quiet in there—perhaps Amalia had fallen asleep. Heading into the kitchen, Helen hoped the nap would do her friend good, hard as she worked keeping this boardinghouse going for all of them. Certainly not what the brave young woman had signed up for when she and her parents left Norway for America more than two years ago. Both Amalia's and Ruthie's parents had died of cholera aboard ship, thrusting Ruthie into Amalia's care as her guardian by the dying mother's request—and Amalia into the role of trustee of Forsberg House, till Ruthie came of age. Amalia had shouldered the unexpected responsibility with all her heart, though it hadn't always been easy, but marrying Absalom last spring had certainly helped ease her load and grow her joy.

"What's cooking for dinner? Beans?" Thomi reached for the lid on the pot at the back of the stove.

"Careful." Helen held out her hand to halt the child, then handed her a dish towel. "It's hot."

Thomi, who had grown three inches since arriving at Forsberg House last summer, lifted the cast-iron lid cautiously, as Amalia had taught. "Yep. Beans."

Helen took the lid from her. "I'll stir and season them while you girls set the table and get the bread. The men will be in soon."

She tasted the beans, fragrant with chunks of ham, then added salt and pepper. They tasted better than the beans her mother used to make—almost all they'd eaten for much of her early childhood. Helen shook her head. Why were these memories crowding in all of a sudden?

"I'm tired of beans."

Helen whispered the words into her bowl, swinging her five-year-old legs beneath the rickety table. She picked with her fingernail at a bit of dried food stuck to the table's edge.

"What did you say?"

Helen started at the snap in her mother's voice, but she looked up and met her gaze, her small chin jutting out with surprising boldness. "I don't like beans anymore."

Her mother stared at her a moment, strings of hair falling about her face, her slender chest rising and falling with quick breaths, eyes reddening. "Fine, then." Her mother had snatched the pot off the stove with her bare hands, hurled it out the door into the yard, muddy with melting snow. The beans hit the slushy dirt with a sickening splat. The pot rolled till it hit their narrow, broken-down fence with a clang.

Helen sat frozen in her chair, hands gripping the seat, tears also frozen in her eyes, too scared to trickle onto her cheeks.

Her mother stared out at the mess, then back at Helen. Dazedly she lifted her reddened hands to cover her face and sank to the dirty floor of their one-room cabin, sobbing. She stayed crumpled there in a heap till she fell asleep.

Helen gazed at the cold lump of beans in her bowl, another lump choking her throat.

She never complained about beans again.

"Table is set!" Ruthie spoke nearly at her elbow.

Helen started, almost dropping the wooden spoon. She caught the handle just before it disappeared into the bubbling, fragrant beans and set it on the saucer Amalia kept by the stove for that purpose. "All right—thank you, girls." Steadying herself, she drew a breath of relief to hear Amalia coming through the door.

"Goodness, I didn't mean to sleep so long." Amalia yawned and tied on her apron. "Mange takk for your help."

"Of course." Helen smiled and turned. "Feeling better?"

"Ja, guess I just needed a lie-down." Amalia gave the subtle rounding beneath her apron a gentle smooth.

Helen hid a smile. Soon the reason for Amalia's fatigue would be obvious to everyone. "You barely ever take time to sit down, much less lie down. Shall I slice the bread?"

"Nei, takk, I can do the rest. But if you'd go out and ring the bell to let the men know dinner is almost ready? I told Absalom, he's working on a case in the parlor, but Ødger and Erik are still in the fields. Hank might be with them, or in the garden. JJ's in the barn."

Helen nodded, stepping back from the stove. She opened the kitchen door and headed out onto the back porch, her shoulders relaxing at the fresh May breeze on her face, the noontime sun so bright she blinked and lifted her hand to shade her eyes, gazing across the boardinghouse garden to the fields beyond their home.

Home. The word hit her suddenly, halting her for a moment as she reached for the dinner bell rope. When had this place become home to her? Strange, that a room on the second floor of a boardinghouse, shared with so many others, should feel more like a place she belonged than almost any other she'd had. More than the various shacks and, yes, even boardinghouses where she and her mother had lived—or more camped than lived—through her early childhood. More than Aunt Ophelia's opulent dwelling in Cincinnati. Helen had been happy there, safe and cared for, even loved, but—home? No, Ohio was no longer that, even if it had once been.

But here, at Forsberg House in the little town of Green Creek, she had found a place to belong. Helping Amalia with various tasks about the kitchen, knowing her assistance was never expected but always appreciated . . . assisting the children with their schoolwork . . . grading papers in the evenings by the parlor fire . . . sharing big, noisy meals at the spreading dining table.

And most of all, the people—Amalia, Ruthie, Thomi. Absalom, Hank, JJ, and Amos. They had become family to her, nearer and dearer than any she had yet living, except Aunt Ophelia.

Thank you, Father. For this place, these people. She sent the simple prayer winging heavenward as she tugged the rope, setting the bell JJ had hung beside the back door to clanging.

"Hey, Miss Stenerson." Hank came loping from the garden before she even turned to head back inside. He yanked off his tattered straw hat and wiped his wrist across his dirt-smeared young forehead. "I sure am ready for dinner."

She smiled at the lanky lad, shooting taller every week it seemed, especially since he turned twelve. "When aren't you?"

Hank splashed water on his face and hands from the pump on the back porch. "I was practicin' that poem you give me for the program, out there while I been hoein'."

Helen bit back a correction of his grammar. Hank, another of the orphans who had found shelter at Forsberg House, had come so far this past year to even be attending school at all. "I look forward to hearing your progress on it."

He sent a grin over his shoulder, then headed into the kitchen, the screen door slapping behind him.

Helen shook her head with a chuckle, then glanced back toward the fields to make sure the men had heard the dinner bell. Sure enough, two figures made their way through the rows of tenderly sprouting corn toward the boardinghouse, hoes on their shoulders. Helen turned to go back inside, then hesitated and turned back, trying to think of a reason to delay so she could meet them before they came in.

Or rather, so she could meet Ødger. Perhaps even talk to him a moment.

Her cheeks burned with mortification at the thought. What was she doing? A sedate and serious schoolma'am who shouldn't have thoughts of young men at all by her current teaching contract, not to mention . . . well, other reasons. And much less of her friend's cousin, a seminary student just starting to find his footing here in America. They hadn't seen Ødger as much this winter, since he had lived with the magistrate, Absalom's father, all this year while he studied at Luther College in Decorah. Helen, though, saw him most Sunday mornings before church, as he had started helping Rev. Larsen with the morning services for which she played the piano. And come spring, he'd begun coming out to the boardinghouse every weekend again to help with fieldwork.

Of course, they'd also played and sung together for the wedding . . .

That memory flipped her stomach a bit, but she set her shoulders and opened the screen door to go back inside. She wouldn't let herself fall into such foolishness. Though she couldn't keep from one last peek over her shoulder—and saw Erik heading into the barn with the tools, while Ødger climbed the back steps, heading straight toward her.

"God dag." He grinned, lighting his clear blue-gray eyes, then immediately switched into English. "I thought that bell would never ring. The sun is hot today."

Helen's heart pattered, and she let the screen door slip from her fingers despite herself. The shine in those eyes, the cheerful strength in that voice. Ødger's determination to master the new language in her summer classes last year had first impressed Helen about this young man—even before she noticed his broad shoulders and neatly trimmed golden beard and mustache. And the way his low, rumbling laugh reminded her of the pleasant hum of bumblebees . . . *stop it.* She clenched her fingers in her apron and smiled at him. "You sound like Hank. He practically made it from the garden to here in one leap."

He chuckled. "Working in the hot sun gives hunger to us all." Ødger crossed the porch with long strides and pumped water to splash on his face, droplets catching on his thick crop of tawny hair and dampening the sleeves of his blue work shirt, rolled up to expose the tanned muscles of his forearms.

Helen darted her eyes away, pressing one hand to her waistband to still the flutters there. "How goes the fieldwork?"

"Very good." Ødger scrubbed his face with the towel Amalia kept there. "Erik says the rains have come just right this spring. Thanks be to God." He stepped up to the door and smiled down at her.

"And your studies?" She shouldn't just keep him standing out here. She wanted to keep him standing out here. "When does your semester at Luther College end?"

"We have three more weeks." He sighed. "Though I fear I will need another full year to complete my seminary degree. I still struggle with the language, it holds me back."

"You have made such progress." Helen met his eyes.

"Maybe so. But having conversation and wrestling theological tomes—and writing about them—are very different." His grin returned. "But what about you? When do you finish the school year?"

"Two weeks." At the stomp of boots, Helen glanced over to see Amalia's brother, Erik, climbing the steps, JJ right behind him. She held the screen door open wide again. "Please, come in, gentlemen. I know you are hungry."

Erik dipped his head, as quiet as Ødger was willing to talk, and let JJ take his turn at the pump ahead of him while Ødger followed Helen inside. He headed into the dining room as Helen helped Amalia serve bowls of hot beans, the little girls carrying platters of bread and butter and cheese, bowls of jam, pickles, and canned fruit back and forth.

Chatter and laughter rose with the steam from the bowls as they sat around the long dining table, Absalom at one end with Amalia beside him, JJ at the other, telling a story that made Ruthie and Thomi erupt into giggles.

Helen slipped into her usual place between Amalia and the little girls, with most of the men, including the railroad and construction workers, on the other side of the table. Today, Ødger happened to sit right across from her, sending a glad tingle mixed with dismay through her. How was she to concentrate on acting normally and properly with those smiling blue-gray eyes in her view every time she looked up from her bowl?

Silence fell as Absalom began the traditional Norwegian blessing, and Helen drew a grateful breath. Closing her eyes, she bowed her head and brought her wayward thoughts back to the familiar words.

"I Jesu navn, går vi til bords, å spise og drikke på ditt ord. Deg Gud til ære, oss til gavn. Så får vi mat i Jesu navn."

Helen whispered the amen, a measure of peace seeping into her heart, and spread her napkin on her lap, smiling at Thomi doing the same. Helen had first learned that prayer when she arrived at Aunt Ophelia's, whose husband had been Norwegian, and it always brought back the sense of relief and safety she'd found in living there.

"So, Erik." Asgar Rykavyk, one of the construction workers who'd lived here at the boardinghouse nearly the two years Helen had, slathered butter on a slice of sourdough bread and dipped it into his beans. "Tell us of your adventures out west."

Erik swallowed his bite of soup and glanced at Amalia. He'd

only recently returned from working on the railroad since the fall, attempting to find his place in the world again after being released from prison in New York. "It was, well, broadening." He cleared his throat. "Saw a lot of open spaces, big skies. Tall mountains too, near as steep as ours back in Norge."

"I hear they have mighty cold winters," put in Eivor, Asgar's brother.

"Ja." Erik nodded. "Winter back home is cold, but out in Wyoming, we got caught in a blizzard, cold and wind like I'd never seen before. Our railcar was stranded for several days, we had to burn most of the wooden seats to keep alive."

Helen glanced at Amalia, who sat motionless beside her, staring at her brother. Clearly she had yet to hear this much from him herself.

Erik caught his sister's eye himself and seemed to check his words. "But I made it back safe and sound, as you can see." He cracked a smile, which always seemed an effort for him, still. "Also saw some interesting sights—buffalo, for one thing."

Helen paused her spoon. "I thought most of the buffalo had been exterminated by settlers trying to destroy the Indians' way of life."

Erik's eyes sobered again. "Ja, that's mostly true. But there's one small herd still in the Pelican Valley. One Sunday, a friend and I made a trip to see them. We had made friends with a young Crow man, and he guided us."

"What an experience." Ødger leaned in closer. "You must tell us more, cousin."

"What do they look like?" Ruthie piped up.

"Like great, woolly cattle. Their heads are huge, with beards and horns, and they have humped backs. The young look much like brown, furry calves, though."

"I wish I could go west and see a buffalo." Thomi's voice came softer than usual, more wistful. "And find my papa."

Helen met Amalia's eyes as her friend rose to take bowls to the kitchen for refills. Helen pushed back her chair and followed.

"We've still had no word from Thomi's father, nor her grandparents in Italy." Amalia spoke low, ladling soup. "I don't know how much longer to let her keep her hopes up."

"Can you stop her from hoping?" Helen held out another bowl for refilling. Thomi's father had supposedly gone to California when he left his daughter at a Chicago children's home, from whence she'd stowed away on a train disguised as a boy—till she got thrown off the train and ended up at Forsberg House.

Amalia sighed. "Probably not. But . . . I hate to see that look in her eyes."

Helen bit her lip and headed back into the dining room, a steaming bowl for a Rykavyk brother in each hand.

They all had something to weigh their hearts, some hope that might never be realized. Setting down Eivor's bowl, she caught Ødger's gaze across the table and her hand stuttered a bit, splashing out a drop of hot soup onto her thumb. Helen clamped back an exclamation and tucked her hand into her apron, avoiding those piercing eyes as she sat back down.

Was Ødger looking at her more than usual today? If so, she couldn't let that progress. Much as her heart might leap at the thought. She couldn't let a man care for her again . . . or she for him, even aside from her teaching contract.

It wasn't worth the inevitable pain.

THREE

"Tante Malia? Are you all right?"

Amalia dragged her eyelids open, blinking at the bright morning light through the window of her and Absalom's room downstairs.

Ruthie's worried face peered into hers. Beyond the cracked bedroom door, footsteps sounded on the stairs, boarders' voices in the hall.

"Uff da." Amalia flung the covers back and her feet over the edge of the bed, sitting up. Her head felt thick and foggy, her mouth dry. "What time is it?"

"I'm not sure." Ruthie's voice came small. "But Hank and JJ already finished the chores, and I fed the chickens and picked the eggs."

Amalia rubbed her bleary eyes to better see the small clock on the bedside table, then her eyes widened. "Half past six! How could I have slept so late?" She surged to her feet, then flailed and caught at the bedpost, squeezing her eyes against the sudden rush of dizziness.

"Tante Malia! What's wrong?"

"It's all right, den lille. I'm fine." Amalia sat back on the bed till her vision cleared. She'd had some morning nausea in the early weeks of her pregnancy, but since then she'd felt fine. Now her body must have let down after the rush of the wedding.

"But you don't seem fine." Ruthie's chin quivered, and she twisted her apron skirt between her fists. "And—and what about earlier this spring, when you kept throwing up? I thought you were better now, but . . . but . . ."

"Oh, Ruthie." She'd thought she hid that from the little girl. Amalia ran her hand down Ruthie's calico sleeve and unclenched one of her small hands to squeeze it. An inner nudge prompted her next words. "I didn't realize you've been worried about me. Did it remind you of when your mor was sick?" And died, of cholera.

Ruthie buried her face in the quilt. Her tumbled braids jerked with a quick nod.

Amalia's eyes stung. "Come here, den lille."

Keeping her face averted, Ruthie climbed up onto the bed next to Amalia, heedless of her chore dress, and burrowed her head into Amalia's shoulder. Amalia shifted to slip her arm beneath the little girl and cuddled her close.

"That makes sense it would remind you of your mor, to see me not feeling well." She spoke softly into Ruthie's hair. "But I don't have cholera. I promise."

"You sure?" Ruthie twisted to see Amalia's face, leaning her head back.

"Ja, very sure. I am quite well, but I may need to rest a bit more. So it's a good thing I have a big girl like you to help around here, isn't it?"

Ruthie stared into Amalia's eyes a moment, her blue ones solemn, then gave a small nod.

"Good. Mange takk." Amalia kissed her cheek. "Then why don't you go help Mr. JJ in the kitchen? I'll be right there to get breakfast on—it's a good thing I put oatmeal to cook overnight. Then you need to get ready for school." As Ruthie ran off, Amalia smiled and sighed, then ran her hand over her gently growing belly.

This baby was already changing things. She would have to tell Ruthie and the other children soon.

But before she told anyone else, she needed to share her news with Maya.

A few hours later, kneeling between the rows Erik had furrowed, Amalia plucked stubborn weeds from between barely sprouting lettuce and carrots, careful not to disturb the growing roots. She breathed deep of the scent of damp earth and growing things, then glanced over at her cousin.

A couple of rows over from Amalia, Maya knelt, planting bush beans. Torvald crawled around her in his newly shortened frock, hands and knees brown with dirt, baby babble making them smile. Far beyond, Erik and Eben drove the team pulling the corn planter through the fields.

"Your garden is coming along. How many more rows of beans do you want?"

Amalia bent her head from side to side to ease the kinks in her neck. "At least six more. I want to can lots of beans this year." They always did, but this year she was especially mindful of stocking the pantry well over the summer, since the baby would come near the beginning of autumn. Her chest tightened a bit when she thought of feeding the boardinghouse crew three times a day in late pregnancy, or with a newborn. *Do not worry about tomorrow* flitted through her mind, and she drew a breath. *Ja, Lord. Help me to remember that. And . . . please show me how to tell Maya about the baby. I don't want to hurt her.*

"Takk for your help today. Tomorrow we will come over and help you." Amalia stood and stepped over the rows to join Maya. "Are you glad to be sharing the big Miller garden this year?"

"Ja, it would have been too much to prepare and plant a separate one by our house, with getting married so late in the spring.

And it's nice to work together on the big garden. But Eben did plant a few herbs and flowers near my kitchen this week. He is so good to me."

Amalia smiled. "As well he should be." She bent down to tug at a stray weed.

Maya reached to snag Torvald's gown as he dug chubby fingers into the ground where she'd just planted. "Nei, min lille. Those seeds need to grow." She picked him up and plopped him back on all fours facing the opposite direction. Torvald chortled and immediately set off crawling toward Amalia, who knelt to face him.

"You keep your mor busy, don't you, den lille?" Amalia trotted her fingers across the dirt toward the baby, then tickled his dimpled hand.

He paused and gazed up at her, drooly grin showing four teeth.

"He does for certain. But you know about that, with the girls and Hank keeping you on your toes." Maya wiped her forehead under her sunbonnet.

"They are getting so grown-up that it seems they help more than create work most days. I can't believe Thomasina is almost ten."

"Well, one day you'll have your own little ones crawling around." Maya lunged forward to catch Torvald's fist just before he crammed a fat earthworm in his mouth. "Nei, dirty."

Amalia's pulse sped a bit. "Actually . . . I've been wanting to talk to you about that."

"What do you mean?" Brushing off Torvald's grimy fist, Maya glanced at her, then paused. "What is it?"

Amalia ran her tongue over her teeth. *Lord, give me the words. Help me not to hurt her.* "About little ones. I'm already, well, that is . . ." She smoothed her hand over the subtle bump growing beneath her dress.

Light broke over Maya's face, and she reached across Torvald to clasp Amalia's hands. "You are with child?"

"Ja." Amalia let out a breath. "I've known for a few months now."

"But that is wonderful. Why did you wait so long to tell me?" Maya squeezed Amalia's hands, then released her. "I was rather worried earlier this spring, you looked a bit peaked, but then you seemed better."

"I didn't have the morning sickness as bad as you did, or I couldn't have kept it hidden this long. And you didn't see me rush for our washbasin some mornings." Amalia grimaced, then met her cousin's eyes. "I wanted to tell you sooner, and I should have—I'm sorry. But you were so busy getting ready for the wedding, and I just wasn't sure how you would feel, after . . . Jakob."

The smile on Maya's face faded. She glanced down, watching Torvald examining a sow bug between his chubby thumb and forefinger.

"You've been through so much, kjære Maya." Amalia's throat tightened, and she wondered if they both were thinking of another time she had called her cousin that endearment, when she laid Maya's tiny, born-too-soon son in her arms last August. "I couldn't bear to think of adding to your pain."

"You wouldn't do that." Maya looked back at her, lips tipped in a faint smile, though tears shimmered in her gray-blue eyes. "The pain is there, regardless. But it does grow more gentle with time, as Mrs. Miller told me it would. And you have only ever sought to ease my sorrow." She swiped a finger under one eye. "My heart has a place that will always hurt for wee Jakob, but Torvald helps so much. I can never thank the Lord enough for the family He has given me, though I'll always miss the ones I lost." She smiled broader now. "And I could never *not* be happy for you, my cousin. You have done so much for me, and I know you have been waiting for your own little one well over a year now. When are you due?"

"Late September, I think. More or less."

"Good. That gives us plenty of time to prepare—though autumn will be here before we know it. Does the magistrate know?"

"Absalom told him, ja. He can hardly wait for his first grandchild. And Mrs. Miller knows, I told her first."

"That is good. She was such a support to me, last summer."

Quiet fell over both of them again, and Amalia bit her lip as she tossed a few more weeds on the pile, then paused, crouching, to tie a loosened bootlace. Whatever Maya said, Amalia's condition couldn't help but prick pain to her cousin's heart, remembering her pregnancy this time last year. "Have you and Eben ever talked about . . . having more children?" She glanced up at her cousin.

Maya tucked back a strand of loosened hair into her sunbonnet, leaving a smear of dirt on her cheek. "A little. Dr. Armitage says there's no reason I couldn't, just because I lost a baby—many women do, and go on to have other healthy children." The doctor had helped Maya last August when she lost her baby—and nearly her life. As if remembering how he'd then brought newborn, orphaned Torvald to her to nurse—and mend more than one broken heart—Maya lifted her adopted son into her arms and cuddled him against her shoulder. "But my monthlies haven't even come back yet, with nursing Torvald. And I'm not in any hurry. I know the doctor is right, but . . ." She sucked a small breath. "I'm still afraid."

"I don't doubt it." Amalia pushed to her feet, blinking at a slight dizziness in the beating sun. Her vision cleared after a few seconds, and she caressed her growing middle, feeling the faint flutter within that always made her heart skip a beat. "I'm afraid myself, at times, and I haven't been through what you have."

"But you watched it."

"Ja." Amalia sighed. Memories from Maya's too-early labor and birth last year flickered at the edges of her mind, much as she tried to shut them out. The anguished cries, the blood-soaked sheets, the tiny, still form in the box JJ carved . . . *Please, Lord. Let that not happen again.* Amalia shook herself and peered up at the sun. "It's nearly noontime. We'd best get dinner on for the men."

That night Absalom worked late, not returning to the boardinghouse till Amalia was finishing the supper dishes. As she wiped the last plates and set them in the cupboard, Absalom's tired step came on the back porch.

Amalia glanced over her shoulder to greet him. "There you are. Have you been dealing with that hearing all day?" He'd just wrapped up a lengthy trial the previous week, so she'd hoped he would be home earlier this week.

"No, actually. It wrapped up this morning." Absalom thumped the leather satchel he used to carry important briefs to and from the office onto a kitchen chair and sat down on another with a sigh. "But then a new case came in, some recent immigrants who have arrived in town and needed help figuring out a land deed."

"Well, they were in good hands with you."

He stepped behind her to kiss her hair, then circled her waist with his arms, resting his hands on her expanding middle. "How were you and our little one today?"

"Fine—though I slept in today and gave Ruthie a bit of a fright." She told him about it, reaching into the cast-iron warming oven at the top where she'd kept Absalom's plate.

"I'm glad you realized why she was upset. Mange takk." He took the plate from her with a weary smile, bowed his head for a silent grace, then dug in to the ham, baked beans, and new asparagus, tender young spears that had sprouted back again in the garden after they planted the perennials last year.

She poured him a glass of milk, then one for herself, sitting down across from him. The clock ticked, the boardinghouse a welcome quiet for the two of them after the bustle all day long.

"I finally told Maya." Amalia took a sip of her milk. Mrs. Miller had urged her to drink plenty for the baby.

Absalom's brows rose beneath his mop of dark curls. "I'm glad. How did she take it?"

"We had a good talk. She is glad for us."

"I knew she would be."

"I know . . . I just hadn't known how to tell her before. But I'm grateful she knows now."

"You won't be able to hide it too much longer." Absalom grinned at her when she slapped a napkin at him, then scraped his fork around the plate once more. "That hit the spot. Mange takk, wife." He squeezed her hand on his shoulder as she took his plate, his eyes smiling up at her.

Amalia frowned. "What spot?" Still so many American idioms she didn't understand.

Absalom chuckled and scrubbed a hand through his curls. "I've no idea."

They slipped into bed together a bit later, the late spring breeze cool through their open window. She snuggled her back against her husband's chest for warmth, curling against him. Absalom laid his arm over her, and over their baby.

So many new unknowns ahead of them this year. But they would face them together, by God's grace.

Four

"I don't think I kin do this, Miz Stenerson."

Helen looked up from retying Minnie Nygard's hair ribbon for the school program to meet Hank's wide-eyed gaze. The boy had turned pale under his brown work-tan, a sheen of perspiration on his upper lip—not surprising in the warmth of the schoolhouse this early June evening, but he leaned on the corner of her teacher's desk, shoved to the side to clear space for the program tonight, as if he might actually faint.

"Go sit with the others, Minnie." Helen patted the little girl's shoulder and sent her toward the front row of chairs where the younger classes gathered, then motioned Hank toward the corner behind the flag by the blackboard, the most privacy they could get. "What's wrong, Hank?"

"That ol' poem." Hank pulled at his collar, stiffer and whiter than any she'd ever seen on him, above his new brown suit, which Amalia had made with room to grow. "I can't do it, I know I can't."

"Just take a breath, right now. In—and out. That's it." Helen laid a gentle hand on his shoulder. "You've done so well in all our practices. I think this is just a touch of stage fright."

"It's different doin' it just for you or the other kids, and doin' it for that whole passel o' people out there." Hank scrubbed his hand through his shock of brown hair, ruining the slicked-back brushing Amalia had insisted on before they left the boardinghouse. "All those folks'll just see they were right, and I don't belong in school at all."

Helen sighed. So they were back to this again. "Hank." She waited till he met her eyes with his reluctant brown ones. "We've talked about this, so many times. You have just as much right to be here as any student in this school. You're brighter than many of them, in fact. I know not everyone in this town has always seen it that way." Her middle twisted, remembering the malicious gossip a few boys had repeated from their parents about the "waifs and vagrants" taken in by the boardinghouse. "But those ugly voices aren't the majority. And they don't speak the truth—they never have."

Hank stared at the floor. Did he believe her words? Could he?

Helen pressed her fingertips together, resisting the urge to hug the twelve-year-old boy before her. Hank wouldn't take kindly to that. She loved all her students, did her best to invest in them all equally. But something about this boy . . . how friendless and starved she knew his early years had been, the uphill battle getting him to believe they at Forsberg House truly loved and wanted him . . . her heart ached for him. *Lord, give me the right words.* "Perhaps you need to just not think about yourself right now at all, Hank."

He huffed and lifted his head to glare at her. "Don't know how I'm s'posed to do that."

"Why did you choose your poem? Do you remember?"

Hank jiggled one shoulder. "'Cause I liked the story you told us about it. How those soldiers followed orders and were heroes for it, even though they got killed. You said it was an accidental tragedy."

"A tragic accident, yes. During the Crimean War, just about thirty years ago."

"An' I liked how it sounded, I guess. The 'Half a league, half a league, half a league onward' an' all that."

"And you've learned to recite it beautifully. Why do you think people write poems, when it comes to it?"

"I dunno." Hank glanced over Helen's shoulder toward the filling schoolroom, the rising murmur of voices as families seated themselves. "To make folks miserable?"

Helen swallowed a chuckle and resisted the urge to follow his glance. She should be out there, greeting parents, making sure all the other students were ready for their parts. But at this moment—here was where she needed to be. She'd worked for nearly two years to get Hank to stay in school, to like school, to accept that he belonged in school. She couldn't just let him give up right now.

"I think people write poems because sometimes, poetry says what nothing else can properly say. If Alfred, Lord Tennyson hadn't written this poem about that little group of soldiers from the Light Brigade, people might have already forgotten them."

Hank swiveled his head to meet her gaze. "That wouldn't be right."

"I agree. But because he did, in words that capture our imaginations and gallop through our brains, they will be remembered for generations, perhaps long after our own lifetimes. As long as people continue to read and memorize—and recite—this poem. You can share that with the families today—tell those young men's story, to honor them. Will you do that?"

He stared at her a moment longer, then gave a quick jerk with his head. "I guess so."

"Good." Helen let out a breath and gave his arm a squeeze. "Now, go take your seat with the rest of the upper grades. I must make sure Sammy Larsen hasn't untied half the hair ribbons of the primer class girls yet."

She hurried away, her gray taffeta skirt bustling, her heart beating a *Thank you, Father* beneath her starched white blouse. Now, to get through the rest of the night—and pray Hank wouldn't lose his nerve again before the end of the program. Helen smiled and greeted parents, directed elderly guests to the best seats, checked in with the mothers in charge of refreshments. She separated Sammy and another little boy from a tussle on the front bench, calmed the tears of a little girl who couldn't see her mother, and reminded the older ones who was carrying the flag.

Out of the corner of her eye, she saw the rest of the boardinghouse contingent arrive—Absalom had dropped her and the children off earlier. Now he and Amalia and JJ filed in, followed by Erik, Maya, and Ødger.

Helen's pulse picked up a bit at the sight of Ødger's broad shoulders and neatly trimmed beard. His gaze darted around the room, seemingly searching until he met her eyes, then he grinned and nodded at her.

She nodded back, trying to school her answering smile to be demure and proper, not the beam that wanted to break free at seeing him. Oh, she must stop this. She turned to answer a question from Ruthie, grateful for the opportunity to shield her face.

"Yes, it is nearly time to start." Helen drew a steadying breath, willing her cheeks to cool as she checked the schoolroom clock. "Take your seat, Ruthie, and make sure Thomi is ready." She trusted steady little Ruthie to keep Thomasina on track, even though Thomi was older.

Helen shooed a few students back into their places, coaxing out one five-year-old who had gone to sit with his parents and finally leading him by the hand. She was about to head to the front to open the program when a muffled scuffle from the second row caught her ear. She glanced over to see Thomi glaring red-faced at Bertram Flinch, a cowlicked boy who had tangled with the feisty little girl before. Ruthie, on Thomi's other side, scowled at Bertram too. Helen bit the side of her tongue. She should have made sure those two weren't seated near each other, but it was a bit too late for it now. Helen raised a brow at them, and Bertram spread his hands with an angelic expression while Thomi lifted her chin and folded her arms, seemingly subsiding. With a shake of her head, Helen sent up a silent prayer for no more squabbles and stepped to the cleared space before the rows of desks as a few latecomers filed into the back of the schoolroom.

"Good evening, everyone." She clasped her hands before her with a smile. "Welcome to our end-of-the-year school program." Applause scattered across the room. Someone gave a muffled cheer—was that Ødger? Surely not. Helen focused on Maya and Eben, smiling halfway back with Torvald bouncing on Eben's knee. "It is such a privilege for me to teach these boys and girls of yours each year, and this last has been no exception. I know you will enjoy seeing their exhibition of what they have learned through recitation, mathematical exercises, geography, and more. But first, I have asked Reverend Larsen to lead us in an opening prayer."

The elderly minister rose from the corner where she'd directed him and shuffled to the front, beaming over the crowded room as if it were his beloved congregation—as indeed in large part it was. Rev. Larsen's step came slower this last year or so, his eyesight weaker, his voice sometimes on the quavery side. But he loved his people, and they loved him.

"Thank you, Miss Stenerson. Shall we pray?" The minister, his head glistening under the sparse white hairs neatly brushed over it, closed his eyes. "Heavenly Father, how grateful we are for each one of these children, the gifts thou hast given them, and our dear Miss Stenerson's faithful tutelage of them through another year. Bless this gathering tonight, and each one of us who goes from here to thy service, following thy will, and knowing ever deeper thy love within our hearts. In the name of Christ Jesus we pray, Amen."

"Amen" came the rumbling chorus. Her own heart quieted, Helen smiled at Rev. Larsen as he made his halting way to his seat, then stepped back to the front.

"Thank you, Reverend. And now, we will open our program by singing 'The Star-Spangled Banner.'"

After that came recitations and mental arithmetic exercises, then Helen cleared her throat. "And now, something new for us this year, ladies and gentlemen: a geography bee from our second- and third-reader students. Please welcome Thomasina Benetti, Ned and Lisa Miller, Arne Larsen, Elsie and Anna Nygard, and Bertram and Archie Flinch." The audience clapped hard, a few more whoops sounding, probably from proud fathers.

The students lined up in two lines, the Nygard and Flinch siblings on one side, the other four facing them.

Helen stepped into the middle. "First, an easy question to begin with: What is the capital of the United States?"

Archie jerked up his hand. "Washington, DC."

"Very good. Next, for a country dear to many in our community: the capital of Norway?"

Thomi's hand shot up. "Oslo!"

"Excellent." Helen continued on, the questions getting more and more difficult, moving from the capitals of countries to states, languages, and even imports and exports. One by one, students sat down for answering incorrectly, leaving only Thomi and Bertram facing each other.

"For our last two contestants, I will question you one at a time—Bertram first, since you won the last round. And so, your last question: What are the chief exports of Italy to the rest of the world?"

The boy fidgeted, reddened.

"Do you need another moment?" Helen prompted.

"Well—well, my pa says Italians only bring anarchy an' the Mafia and take away Americans' jobs," Bertram blurted.

Helen's ears tingled. The room fell silent. Thomi's eyes widened, her small face turning red, then white.

"That is not the answer to the question, Bertram." Helen enunciated each word with precision. "Do you care to try again?"

His face now redder than Thomi's had been, Bertram shook his head and shuffled to his seat, chin nonetheless at a defiant tilt.

Helen drew a breath and turned back to face Thomi, meeting the little girl's eyes. "Thomasina. What unique contributions does Italy share with the rest of the world?"

For a moment she thought Thomi wasn't going to respond. The child's usual bravado seemed fled, and her eyes darted from one corner of the schoolroom to the other for a moment, as if she herself might flee—as she had fled the children's home in Chicago, as she had at first tried to flee the boardinghouse when Amos brought her there, kicked off the train for stowing away. As her own family had fled unrest in Italy when Thomi was just a wee thing.

But then her dark brown eyes locked with Helen's, and Thomi lifted her pointed chin. "Italy's chief exports to the world," she said, her voice barely shaken, "include raw silk, olive oil, and wine. Italy is also starting to produce and export manufactured goods from its iron and steel."

"That is correct." Helen drew a breath and smiled at the little girl, then turned to the crowd. "Ladies and gentlemen, it gives me great pleasure to declare Miss Thomasina Benetti the winner of our inaugural Green Creek Geography Bee."

The applause came hard and fast. Thomi gave a quick bow, then skittered back to her seat, where Ruthie clasped her hand. Bertram slouched down in his seat and ignored her.

The older students' recitations came next, passing in a near-blur—and then, before she knew it, it was Hank's turn. She second-guessed her decision to let him go last as the boy slowly approached the front of the schoolroom, lit by flickering kerosene lamps buzzed by curious moths as darkness had now fully fallen. She'd thought "The Charge of the Light Brigade" would be a stirring conclusion to the evening—but what was she thinking, to leave the near-finale of the program on Hank's uncertain shoulders? They would finish with one more song afterward . . . but still.

Hank's face paled in the lamplight again as he stood there, his collar stiff nearly to his ears, his shoulders still boy-slim under the new brown suit coat. His eyes searched the schoolroom, much as Thomi's had—these two young ones alone in the world and friendless, till Amalia and Forsberg House had sheltered them. Small wonder they still hesitated to trust whether Green Creek, or the world, would truly make them welcome.

Then Hank's shoulders shifted back a bit, and his chin lifted, a steadiness coming into his eyes as they locked onto something at the back of the room.

Helen glanced to follow his gaze and saw Amalia had risen from the back row, standing quiet but looking straight at Hank, smiling and nodding.

Hank cleared his throat. "'The Charge of the Light Brigade.' By Alfred, Lord Tennyson." He hesitated again, his jaw working.

Helen held her breath. *Help him, Lord. Help him remember the words—help him know he can do this.*

"Half a league, half a league,
Half a league onward,
All in the valley of Death
Rode the six hundred."

Hank's voice, thin and tremulous at first, strengthened.

"'Forward, the Light Brigade!
Charge for the guns!' he said.
Into the valley of Death
Rode the six hundred."

As the drama of the poem built, Hank seemed to forget the crowd. He rose slightly on his toes, voice fluctuating, hands moving with the drama of the story.

"Cannon to right of them,
Cannon to left of them,
Cannon in front of them
Volleyed and thundered . . ."

Helen watched him, tears in her eyes.

"When can their glory fade?
O the wild charge they made!
All the world wondered."

Hank paused, his eyes shifting to encompass the whole audience, who sat quiet, stunned, listening.

"Honour the charge they made!
Honour the Light Brigade,
Noble six hundred!"

He stopped, swallowed, gave a stiff little bow. Stepped back. The room erupted in applause and cheers. Hank ducked his head, reddened. Hurried back to his seat.

Feeling a bit shaky, Helen stepped back to the center and drew a breath. "Thank you, Hank, for that stirring conclusion to our recitations. And now, to close our program, I want to invite all of our students to come forward and lead us in singing 'America.'"

The students scrambled forward and filed into place, Helen stepping to the side to lead them. With the added voices of the parents and families rising with the familiar words, she let her voice carry strong and clear, soaring above the childish chorus.

"My country! 'tis of thee,
Sweet land of liberty;
Of thee I sing . . ."

Gazing at the rows of dear young faces, her voice suddenly caught, and she had to steady it. So many of these children, or their parents, had come from far countries to this one. Often through much hardship, and still facing prejudice in this land, as they'd seen reflected even tonight. She would need to follow up on what had happened with Bertram. Yet as they sang together, they showed a picture of what America could be—the beauty of "out of many, one"— many nations, languages, and cultures, bringing their hard work and giftings to benefit the whole.

"Long may our land be bright,
With freedom's holy light,
Protect us by Thy might,
Great God, our King."

It was over. Chatter and laughter rose as parents extricated themselves from small desks and joined their children, giving hugs, tousling hair, patting backs. They gathered at the long table where mothers served cookies, lemonade, and water from the school well outside.

Helen smiled, greeted, thanked parents. Hugged little ones and handed out embellished paper rewards of merit to individual students, all with a brief handwritten note acknowledging the child's achievements this year.

"Congratulations on a wonderful program, Miss Stenerson."

Helen looked up from handing a reward of merit to Lisa Miller for her excellent penmanship into Ødger's smiling, bearded face. "Thank you—or should I say, mange takk?" She smiled back, trying for a light tone to cover the tremble in her middle at his nearness. With the packed crowd, the sleeve of his jacket nearly touched her elbow.

He chuckled. "It was your classes in this very room last summer that finally helped me make progress with my English. Though many mistakes I still have, ja?"

"You have made such progress indeed." Helen glanced about at the milling families, the students darting to and fro amid the crowd, expending their suppressed energy now the program had concluded. "As have all these children. It's a privilege to be their teacher. I often feel I merely have the job of drawing out the giftings and intelligence that are already there."

"Your job is not as easy as you make it sound, I think." Ødger met her gaze, his eyes sobering. "I saw a bit of that tonight. The geography—what did you call it?"

"The geography bee. And yes—I didn't see that coming, though perhaps I should have." She sighed, touching the cameo at her neck. "I wish we all could remember we are largely a nation of immigrants, wherever we hail from."

"Some people are always quick to forget—no matter where we are." Ødger's eyes crinkled with a smile again. "Yet people like you keep the light shining, welcome for all."

Helen swallowed and tried to think what to say. Sammy and Arne's parents came up to thank her, and Ødger stepped politely away. By the time Helen turned back to look for him after most of the parents had dispersed, Ødger was gone.

She sighed, gazing at the emptying schoolroom, littered with cookie crumbs, dirt tracked from the schoolyard, and a few forgotten rewards of merit.

The evening had gone extraordinarily well—despite a hiccup here and there. The memory of Hank's recitation still stirred her heart and made her smile.

Another year finished, and successfully overall, by the grace of God.

Now to fill the summer. What would these next months bring?

FIVE

"Well, last exam of the year. Congratulations, Mr. Gunderson."

Ødger handed his closely written papers across the massive carved desk to Professor Amundson. "Thank you, sir. I have learned much in your classes."

The professor flipped through the pages and stroked his silver goatee with a keen glance at Ødger. "And you have made much progress this year. I know it cannot have been easy, adjusting to a new land and language while also taking seminary-level classes."

Ødger cracked a half grin. "I'm afraid I may have forgotten some rules of grammar amid Luther's arguments on predestination."

Professor Amundson chuckled. "If this semester is any guide, the insight of your ideas shines through the grammar."

Ødger's ears warmed. He wasn't sure how to take such praise. "Mange takk."

The older man added Ødger's exam to the stack of other papers on his desk. Behind them in the classroom, the remaining students filed out into the hall, eager to begin summer break. But Professor Amundson folded his slender hands on the desk and looked at Ødger. "We should be thinking about your plans for next year."

Ødger nodded. "I know I still have a couple of classes to finish." While he'd only had a year of studies left at the School of Mission and Theology back home in Stavanger when they left for America, transferring to Luther College and his emerging grasp of English had set him back a bit. The college wasn't even officially a seminary any longer, but since it was run by the Lutheran church and intended to prepare students for ministry, his professors had worked out a way for him to finish his divinity degree.

"Yes, but that is easily managed, perhaps could even be done by correspondence." The professor steepled his fingers.

"Correspondence, sir?" Ødger frowned. Why would that be necessary, when he lived right here in Decorah with the magistrate?

"Indeed. You see, seminaries are beginning to encourage students to spend a year of training in the field—a sort of apprenticeship, as it were, to a pastor in ministry somewhere, working at an actual church. I'd like to see you find a place to complete your training in this practical manner. I've already written to two possible churches, about you and a few other promising students."

Ødger swallowed. The thought of diving into actual ministry sent a thrill through his veins, and he warmed with gratitude to think this professor had taken such an interest in him to already be seeking out churches. But—to leave Green Creek, leave his family? Not to mention a certain young woman. . . . He blinked Helen Stenerson's blue eyes and blond coiffure from his mind. "How far away, sir?"

"Likely still here in Iowa. But not necessarily. We'll have to see what the response is." Professor Amundson stood and extended his hand. "You have a passion for ministry and the things of God that does my heart good to see, young man. I thank the Lord for bringing you to our shores—and our college."

"Thank you." Ødger gripped his hand, then unsure what else to say, tucked his school satchel under his arm and hurried out of the classroom.

Striding down the second-floor hallway of the elegant main building, newly rebuilt after it burned two years ago—a rebuilding he'd had a strong hand in, last summer and fall, till the rededication in October—he drew a long breath, grateful for the still-cool air inside, though outside the early June sun shone hot. The whole summer stretched before him, filled with work of a different sort. He would continue as part of the construction crew here, building new faculty buildings and student dormitories to surround the main building, set to even have electric lighting and steam heating, from what he'd heard.

In late summer, he'd thought to rejoin Eben's threshing crew, as he had last year, but if he were to go minister in another town, perhaps that wouldn't be possible. Ødger rubbed the side of his neatly trimmed beard. *So many changes, Father. Please show me your path amid them all.*

And what of Helen Stenerson? More and more, his eyes and heart drew to her whenever they were in the same company. She seemed to enjoy his presence as well, yet at times he sensed her putting a distance between them. Why was that? Or did he just imagine it?

True, her role as schoolteacher and his lack of an established ministry, yet, could raise some obstacles. But surely nothing insurmountable.

Stop getting ahead of yourself, man. The lady may have no interest in a stubborn Norwegian.

Heading toward the stairs that led down to the first floor, he suddenly paused at the distant hum of an organ. Must be the one in the chapel, which he'd often heard during evening prayers. The soothing swells had rolled over him in the early fall when he'd been aching over Maya's losses and struggling to follow his professors' words in class, calmed him before the first semester's exams, lifted his heart with Advent music at Christmastime. He rubbed his ear a moment, debating, then turned and hurried down a different hallway toward the sound. He'd enjoy the music once more before the next few months kept him mostly outside this building's walls.

Softly creaking open the dark wooden door of the chapel, he peered in, the organ swelling louder in his ears. He drew a deep breath, his shoulders relaxing at the music as they always did. Shutting the door behind him, Ødger padded quietly down the narrow aisleway—then his feet stuttered to a stop.

Instead of one of the usual male students who plied the organ's pedals during chapel, a young woman sat there, her light brown curls swept up on the back of her head, her fingers flying over the keys.

Who could she be? Luther College didn't admit women. Someone's wife, perhaps?

Well, no matter whether the player were male or female—she was gifted, even more so than some of the students he'd heard play. Ødger slipped into a pew and sat back to enjoy the music.

The surging harmonies of Bach's Prelude and Fugue in G washed over him, silencing everything else, and he closed his eyes, carried back to their small stone church in Norway where he and Maya and the rest of their siblings had grown up, where first their onkel and then Ødger himself had played the organ for services. Onkel Kristoff had given Ødger his guitar too, had taught him all he knew about music. His chest ached, missing the older man. His onkel's heart for music and the things of God had been a gentling influence on Ødger in his youth, when he wrestled between the high spirits that sometimes got him into trouble and a growing tug toward the ministry.

His far had scoffed at first when Ødger told him he wanted to be a pastor, after he heard a visiting missionary telling stories of God's work on the African continent. "You'd best learn to keep yourself out of trouble at home before you try going to another land to tell folks how to live," he'd growled.

But that wasn't what Ødger wanted to do—tell folks how to

live. It was the growing sense of the greatness and love of God, far bigger than his father's rather narrow understanding of religion, that had begun to capture his heart. The stories of Christ in the Gospels, how He cut to the heart of matters in His dialogues and parables, leaving the hypocritically religious nonplussed. The way He constantly reached out to the forgotten and despised on the margins, the sinners, the unclean, the foreigners . . . and told them they belonged, even when those in power said otherwise.

That was what called to Ødger, even as a high-spirited teen. Not that his scrapes were anything serious—a tussle in the schoolyard, teasing the girls at school or his cousins and siblings at home. Though they always came to him when in trouble themselves, as did the children of the village, especially when any bullies were involved. His mouth quirked at how he'd once gotten a particular bully his comeuppance, a scheme involving the village water fountain and a ball of string.

Onkel Kristoff had talked to him after that, while showing him some new chords on the guitar. Told him about Christ's way of returning good for evil, and something about coals of fire. And Ødger had listened, as he somehow always did to his onkel in a way he couldn't seem to with his far, the words sinking deep into his heart like seeds awaiting the sun.

Perhaps his onkel's own life experience had lent extra depth and measure to his wisdom. His wife, their tante Anne, had struggled mentally, often sinking into a depression that kept her bedridden weeks at a time. Onkel Kristoff always cared for her without complaint, loved and prayed for her faithfully, though the patient lines about his eyes spoke of suffering—even if Ødger hadn't fully realized it as a boy.

He opened his own eyes with a long breath, suddenly realizing the music had stopped.

And found the young woman on the organ bench had turned and sat looking at him, an amused smile playing about her lips.

Ødger's scalp heated as he pushed to his feet, scooting out the pew. "I'm sorry. I did not mean to intrude." He started to back away down the aisle.

"Please." She stood and gestured with a graceful hand. "No need to apologize. My father said I could practice here a bit, now classes are mostly finished."

"Your father?"

She smiled. "I'm Lena Amundson."

"Ah!" Ødger felt his eyebrows lift. "So—Professor Amundson. Your father has been one of my favorite teachers this year. The way he can open up Luther and Calvin and make them seem alive today . . ." He shook his head and cracked a half smile. "He is a great man."

"Thank you." She tipped her head. "And you are?"

"Ah." Where were his manners? He strode down the aisle and made a slight bow. "Ødger Gunderson. I came from Norway last spring."

She nodded. "I thought perhaps. Velkomst."

Ødger grinned and shrugged. He knew his accent still was quite noticeable, but he tried not to let it bother him. At least he could make conversation in English pretty well now.

"You play very well. Bach's Prelude and Fugue in G, correct?"

"Indeed. You know organ music?" She gestured behind her at the magnificent instrument.

"Ja." Slipping his hands into his pockets, Ødger tipped his head back to gaze up at the pipes soaring toward the ceiling. "I used to play, in our church back in Norge."

"Really." She gazed at him a moment, then stood and gestured to the bench. "Would you like to try this one?"

Ødger stared at her, despite the leap in his gut at her words. He hadn't touched any instrument but his guitar since leaving home in Norge—hadn't had time to miss it, really, but suddenly his fingers ached for the touch of the ivory keys. "You are serious?"

Miss Amundson laughed, a chuckling tinkle. "Certainly. I don't think anyone would object—and if they do, I'll set them right."

Did being a professor's daughter really give her such privilege? Or did her assured confidence merely project that it was so?

Ødger hesitated once more, then gave in to the organ's tug. He strode up the few steps toward the platform and slid onto the bench, his hands caressing the keys, their touch so familiar—yet it seemed a lifetime since he played in that small stone church at home. His throat suddenly ached for his parents, for their other siblings. He could almost imagine Maya and her first husband, Einar, sitting a few rows behind while he played.

He pressed keys and pedals, feet pumping stiffly at first, hands more used to hammer and nails than ivory keys now. He played a few scales, then began the first movement of Bach's Trio Sonata No. 6 in G major, his fingers tripping lightly over the lower and middle keyboards. Not too difficult a piece, and the skipping melody lifted his heart as his hands and feet warmed to the familiar rhythms. Ødger finished the movement and lowered his hands with a sigh.

"Thank you. That was a true pleasure."

"You play well. I will ask my father to give you regular access here, if you like."

He swiveled and stared at her. "You cannot be serious."

"Why not? You have a gift, and they won't be using this chapel much over the summer. Or will you be heading home some distance?"

He chuckled. "Depends what you mean by home. But no, I live in Decorah now with Magistrate Karlsson. My family—what I have here in America—is in Green Creek. Forsberg House."

"Ah, I see. Well, I'll speak to my father."

"Thank you, again." Ødger dipped his head. "I will be working here on campus on the construction this summer, but perhaps I can slip in here some evenings."

"Then perhaps I will see you again sometime." Miss Amundson extended a slender hand. "Good day, Mr. Gunderson."

He gripped her fingertips lightly. "Good day, Miss Amundson."

Ødger headed out into the warm sunshine of the June midday, his steps still lighter than they had been after finishing his last exam. An organ to play on occasion! What a luxury—no, a gift. And one unlooked for at that. Often the best kind.

He walked through the tree-lined streets of Decorah more slowly than usual, savoring the rare lack of pressure on his afternoon. No classes to study for, nor exams to cram for. He wouldn't start on the construction crew again until after the weekend.

He stopped at the mercantile to pick up a few groceries Magistrate Karlsson had asked him to collect and wended his way through the center of town, finally reaching the magistrate's home. The shaded, broad-porched house stood tucked just enough back from the road to feel private, while still accessible to clients, as the building served as both home and office for the magistrate and Absalom.

Ødger rested his hand on the gate a moment. So much had happened this past year—it made him fairly dizzy to think of it. Maya losing her husband last March, then his decision to accompany her to America instead. Her horrible illness aboard ship, leading him often to fear he'd lose her too, then the bewildering arrival in America, with its sights, sounds, language, and customs all so new. The news that Maya carried a child, explaining her illness, and seeing her slowly start to climb out of the pit of anger and grief. The blur of trying to get them settled in America—establishing a bank account, finding a job, seeking to enroll at Luther College, all while worrying over his sister—especially after she lost the baby late last summer.

Yet the Lord truly had brought beauty for ashes, as Maya's joy each time he saw her with Eben and Torvald showed plainly. His throat tightened. And he was finally beginning to feel he belonged here too.

Spying a familiar figure sitting on the porch, Ødger smiled and swung the gate open. All their paths here had been greatly eased by the man reclining there with his prosthetic leg stretched out before him, his face both keen and kind between silvered sideburns.

"God dag, young Gunderson. Have you bested those exams, then?"

Ødger chuckled and climbed the steps, shifting the brown paper parcels in his arms. "That remains to be seen, Magistrate. But I've finished them, at least."

"Ah. Then what's done is done, and you are to be congratulated." Magistrate Karlsson shifted his brass-headed cane out of Ødger's path. "Set those in the kitchen for Mrs. Skivens, if you would, then come out and enjoy the shade here with me."

"Takk, I will." Surely he'd earned a few minutes repose, at least. Ødger ducked inside and deposited the packages in the kitchen, then headed back out, taking the chair the magistrate indicated. "No cases demanding your attention today, sir?"

The magistrate lifted a hand. "I saw two clients this morning, but Absalom is out on the remaining case for the afternoon. He barely stopped for a bite of luncheon out here with me. Speaking of which, have you eaten?"

Ødger hadn't even thought of it, between the exams and the organ playing, but now his stomach rumbled in answer before he could open his mouth.

The magistrate chuckled and pushed a plate that still contained two sandwiches toward him on the small wicker table they kept on the porch. "Eat, son. Don't let it go to waste."

Dipping his head in gratitude both to the Lord and the magistrate, Ødger took one and bit into the savory filling of roast beef and cheese. "Mange takk."

"So." The magistrate tapped his fingers on the arms of his wicker chair and eyed Ødger. "What comes next for you, with the seminary? You have one more year, or just another class or two?"

Ødger swallowed a mouthful. "Both, in a way." He explained what Professor Amundson had said. "I didn't realize I would be sent away from Decorah to finish my training."

"Nor I." The older man nodded slowly. "Yet I do see the wisdom in it. How can you be released into ministry if you've never experienced it? Though we'd hate to lose you around here, dear boy."

The fatherly note in the magistrate's voice warmed Ødger's chest. Living here this past year in Absalom's old room, he'd come to feel like family indeed. And he knew it eased Absalom's mind knowing his father wasn't alone. "And I would dearly miss you all."

The magistrate's gray eyes peered keenly. "Any special young woman around here you might find yourself missing also?"

"I, ah." A morsel of bread and roast beef seemed to stick in Ødger's throat, and he coughed. "I'm—not sure how to answer that, sir."

"I see." The magistrate chuckled. "Well, that's all the answer I need, then. For now."

Ødger focused on his sandwich, resisting the persistent heating of his neck and ears. For the graceful image of Helen Stenerson *would* keep floating through his mind.

That Sunday, Ødger headed early to Green Creek Lutheran Church, as was his habit, to help set up for the Sunday service, which he'd begun doing for Pastor Larsen last fall. He attended services here rather than in Decorah, so he could worship with his family.

The faintly musty quiet of the small brick church welcomed him as he stepped inside, the building still cool from the night. He breathed in the scent of hymnals, faded flowers, and communion wine, walking up the aisle between the pews. He set the communion bread and cup which he'd brought on the white tablecloth beneath the cross at the front, then checked between the rows of pews, adjusting the Bibles in the racks, picking up a dropped prayer book here and a stray scrap of paper there. At the front, Ødger dusted off the pulpit and checked the list of hymns Rev. Larsen had given him, then left it on the piano for Miss Stenerson, who typically played for services. She should be arriving before long, to run through the hymns before service—at least she often did.

He hadn't made the decision to attend services here on account of *that*—hadn't even realized he'd see the schoolteacher more when Rev. Larsen first asked him. But the possibility of seeing her early certainly added an extra brightness to Sunday mornings now.

With everything in order, Ødger sat down on the little seat behind the pulpit to look over today's Scriptures, which he would read as lector today—a position he now held more and more often. It felt good to be involved in this church family, to feel a part. And, he hoped, to be able to minister to the congregation here, even if in small ways.

The side door creaked open after a bit, admitting Rev. Larsen's shuffling feet.

"Ah, Ødger, good morning." The elderly man fumbled a bit to put his hat on the hook by the door. "Thank you for setting up once again. You are a blessing."

"Glad to help, pastor." Ødger rose and helped the minister into his clerical robe. "Anything else you need?"

"I see you have the communion bread ready." Rev. Larsen squinted through his spectacles at the table. "The wine also?"

"Ja. Shall I help you up on the platform?"

"Takk, but no. I can manage." He had to lift his foot several times before he managed the first step and tottered a bit on the second.

Ødger squeezed his hands together to keep from leaping to steady the older man. He didn't want to intrude on the minister's independence, but . . .

Rev. Larsen made it to the platform, though, leaning heavily on the communion rail as he made his way behind the lectern, then sank into his seat with a sigh. "There we are." He folded his hands and smiled tranquilly, then cast a glance at the piano. "No Miss Stenerson yet?"

"No." Ødger gazed down the aisle, frowning slightly. Usually she came about the same time as the pastor, if not a few minutes before. "Surely she'll be here soon, though." He'd always known Helen to be prompt to a fault—what could have delayed her today?

Six

Helen stared at the letter in her hands.

It had come in the Saturday afternoon post yesterday, but she'd been helping Amalia out in the garden along with Ruthie, Thomi, and Hank when Absalom brought the mail back from an errand to town. With her hands and skirt smudged with dirt, Helen had asked him to set it on the entry table and forgotten to collect it till heading up to bed. Weary after the unaccustomed manual labor in the garden all afternoon, she hadn't opened the letter from Aunt Ophelia till this morning, after she'd dressed early for church.

Now she wished she hadn't delayed.

Her great-aunt wrote her regularly if not frequently, with kind inquiries about Helen's students and teaching as well as updates on her own social and charitable doings in Cincinnati. But this . . . this letter was different.

I would like to see you, my dear, and soon. It has been nearly two years, and I know you are building your own life there in Green Creek—and I rejoice in it. Yet I have had a bad spell or two of late—trifling, I believe, and no matter what the doctor says, I, for the most part, still feel fit as a fiddle. But I know age comes upon the best of us, and there are a few things I should like to say to you while we still have time . . .

The ink there trailed a bit, as if her aunt had paused, unsure what to write next. Then, in stronger letters, as if she'd dipped her pen again—

. . . about your mother.

Her mother? Helen lifted her head and stared at her window, at the morning sunshine beaming through the white curtains trimmed with blue. Aunt Ophelia rarely spoke of Helen's mother, her own niece—rarely had even when Helen first came to live with her, after her mother had, well, gone away. First to the asylum, then to her final resting place.

Helen hadn't minded, mostly—had indeed been grateful not to speak of the woman who held her early affection and memories, yet tainted so many of those memories with her outbursts, her wild swings of mood, her violent grief over . . . Helen didn't know what. Still, so much of her young childhood felt muddled, shrouded in mist. She both ached and feared to have some of it cleared away.

And why would Aunt Ophelia wait so long to tell her . . . whatever it was? Helen usually visited her in the summers, at least every year or two. She'd gone the first summer she lived at the boardinghouse, in August before school started, while Amalia was in a haze of summer canning and Absalom preparing for his legal exams. Last year she had stayed in Iowa, busy with the summer classes she'd begun for the first time. She had thought perhaps to go this year, but hadn't made plans yet, still figuring out what this summer's classes would look like.

But now this.

Helen smoothed the elegantly written page of thick letter paper and read it again, but no new clues to the mystery appeared.

She would go, of course. Likely would have anyway, but now certainly, with such a summons from her aunt. She would just need to cut the summer classes a bit shorter this year, leave time for the visit in August before the fall term started up again. Or . . . Helen scanned the lines again.

I would like to see you . . . and soon.

Something pressed in her chest, urgent. Perhaps she should go before starting summer classes instead. In June . . . this very month. Perhaps she should not wait, not even another week.

A tap at her door made Helen jump, and she folded the letter once more and pressed it in her lap. "Come in."

Ruthie poked her head in, braids freshly tight and blue Sunday dress pressed. "Tante Malia wanted me to check on you. She says it's 'most half past eight."

"It is?" Helen checked the small fob watch she wore pinned to her bodice. "Oh heavens." She stood so fast she nearly lost her balance. "Thank you, Ruthie. I lost track of time."

"Breakfast is ready." Ruthie disappeared, her footsteps tripping lightly down the stairs.

Helen snatched up her Sunday boots and sat down again to button them, fumbling with the buttonhook, the skirt of her pin-striped navy Sunday poplin getting in her way. What was the matter with her? She should have been out the door on her way to church by now. She liked to walk alone on Sundays, arriving early to play through the week's chosen hymns well before service. A private time of worship between her and the Lord, as it were, and time to settle her heart and allay any nerves before the congregation began to arrive.

Well, so much for that today. She'd do well to even have time to glance through the hymns before having to play them for service, at this point.

The last recalcitrant button finally fastened, Helen shook out her skirt, pinned on her cameo, and, catching up her pocketbook and modest Sunday straw hat, hurried out of her room and down the boardinghouse stairs.

In the kitchen, Amalia glanced over her shoulder from dishing up ham and eggs in the kitchen for the boarders. "Are you all right?"

"Yes, just lost track of time." Helen would have to tell her about the letter later.

Ruthie emerged through the swinging door of the dining room. "Can I take those plates?"

"Ja, thank you, den lille." Amalia relinquished the plates and turned to flip another batch of pancakes on the stove. She swiped her hand across her forehead, the kitchen already steaming with warmth ahead of what promised to be a hot day. "Let me serve you a plate, I know you need to go."

Helen glanced at the clock and bit her lip. "I'll just roll a pancake or two with jam and take them to eat as I walk. I'm not very hungry anyway."

Five minutes later, she hurried along the lane toward Green Creek, nibbling her pancake, still warm and moist with melted butter. Birdsong rose around her, a morning hymn of praise, as sunlight filtered through summer foliage, dappling her face and skirt. The knots in her middle unwound a bit, and she sang along with the birds after she finished her pancake, music lifting her heart and ironing the troubles from her mind as it had since she was a little girl.

> "Fairest Lord Jesus! Ruler of all nature!"

She passed fields growing green in the golden light and crossed Green Creek itself, accompanying her with its contented burble.

> "Fair are the meadows, fairer still the woodlands,
> Robed in the blooming garb of spring;

Jesus is fairer! Jesus is purer!
Who makes the woeful heart to sing . . ."

She arrived at Church Street slightly out of breath, yet with a lighter heart. But it sank again to see a few people already heading toward the church or visiting on its steps. How could she have let herself be this late? She quickened her steps along the lane, through the churchyard, up the steps. Nearly in the door . . .

"Ah, Miss Stenerson." The slightly nasal voice of Vera Flinch, mother of two of her students, snagged Helen just before she made it into the church door.

Pasting a smile on her face, Helen turned, her fingers tightening on her pocketbook. "Mrs. Flinch. Good morning."

"I'm so glad to catch you here this early." The woman smiled blandly, as if Helen usually came to church late, rather than typically arriving an hour before everyone else. "I've been meaning to speak to you about the school program."

Helen's middle knotted, but she kept her smile in place. "Both Bertram and Archie did quite well."

"Oh yes, I thought so too. And it was all very nice, of course. But my Bertram, he's been saying how you always favor that little Italian girl in class. He says that's why she won the geography bee."

Helen forced herself to mentally count to five before she responded. "I'm sorry Bertram feels that way. I assure you, I always endeavor to treat my students equally. Unfortunately, that evening Bertram didn't know the answer to the question, and Thomasina did. So that decided the matter."

"But the question was about Italy!" the woman burst out. "Of course that girl had an advantage."

"Thomasina has not lived in Italy since she was a toddler, Mrs. Flinch." Helen kept her voice level with an effort. "And she answered plenty of questions about other countries correctly also—as did your son. Bertram had the same access to the information on the exports of Italy as Thomasina did, from our geography book and class discussions of current events." She glanced at the door, rapidly crowding with congregants. "And now I really must—"

"Well, I do think education in this town has gone downhill ever since Forsberg House started filling up the school with orphans and immigrants." Mrs. Flinch's mouth pinched as if she'd eaten a sour pickle. "I've half a mind—"

"Please pardon me, Miss Stenerson." A steady, accented voice cut in. "But Reverend Larsen is asking for you."

Helen looked from Mrs. Flinch's sour expression into Ødger's bearded face, with eyes that had never seemed kinder or more blue. He held out his hand to her from the church doorway with a polite but insistent expression.

Helen drew a breath. "Excuse me, Mrs. Flinch."

The woman muttered something under her breath, but Helen gratefully ignored it.

Ahead of her, Ødger held open a path through the congregants streaming inside, and she slipped through the door.

"Thank you." She hurried after him down the side aisle toward the front, keeping her voice low. "I'm so sorry I'm late. I lost track of time, and then Mrs. Flinch fairly accosted me at the door—"

"Please, do not worry." He paused between the front pew and where she would step up to the piano, shielding her from view of most of the congregation. "But are you all right?" His eyes examined her face, a pucker of concern between them. "It isn't like you to—what did you say? Lose track of time."

"No." She clenched and unclenched her fingers, hoping she could relax enough to play. "I suppose not. I got a letter—but never mind that now. I do apologize. Is the list of hymns on the piano?"

"Ja, I made sure. And I believe they are all hymns you've played before, quite familiar." He smiled at her, his eyes crinkling. "I imagine you could play them in your sleep." With a slight bow, he stepped aside for her to climb the step up to the piano.

She let out a breath, giving him a slight smile in return, then seated herself on the bench and closed her eyes a moment as Ødger moved to answer a gesture from Rev. Larsen. First Aunt Ophelia's letter, then running late, next Mrs. Flinch—what else could this day hold? She opened her eyes and tried to concentrate on the list she found on the music rack, as Ødger had said. True to his word, the hymns were familiar, ones she'd played since girlhood, if not quite in her sleep. Her lips twitched, the knot in her middle easing at the memory of the twinkle in his eyes. She rested her fingers on the familiar coolness of the keys and played a few soft chords, segueing into a prelude based on "'Tis So Sweet to Trust in Jesus," the opening hymn for today.

Sweet indeed—she knew that. So why so often did she find it hard to simply trust?

Ødger wished he could talk to Helen.

After a generous Sunday dinner, they had all gathered on the Forsberg House front porch, a broad, shaded wraparound deck that welcomed any cooling breeze the afternoon had to offer. As was custom by now, the magistrate had come for dinner after his morning attendance at First Lutheran in Decorah, and Ødger had ridden over with Maya and Eben after the service in Green Creek.

The little girls played a string game on the porch steps, while Hank wrestled a stick with his black hound, Dog, on the grassy yard below. Meanwhile, Helen spoke in low tones to Amalia on the porch swing, both women's faces serious.

Had it something to do with why she'd been late this morning? Ødger longed to ask Helen about the letter she'd mentioned, learn whether she had family in some sort of trouble, or something else. He knew next to nothing about her family, he now realized—nor much more about Helen, at least not her life before she came to Green Creek as schoolteacher. The thought niggled uncomfortably in his gut. Shouldn't he know something of a woman whom he held more and more serious thoughts of courting? But then, that was why he wanted to get to know her better.

Ødger pushed up from where he'd been sitting on the top step above the little girls, passed the Rykavyk brothers playing checkers by the railing, then excused himself between Absalom and his father, visiting in chairs near the front door. He stepped inside to grab his guitar case, tucked just inside the boardinghouse entryway, then headed back onto the breezy porch.

JJ snorted slightly and lifted his head from where he'd been dozing in a rocking chair. Always felt strange to see JJ sitting still on the Sabbath, with his gnarled hands never idle the rest of the week.

"Bringin' us a bit of music, eh, son?"

Ødger smiled and perched on a chair next to the older man. Something about JJ reminded him of Onkel Kristoff, though in other ways the men were nothing alike. The gentle wisdom, though, and understanding of other people, old or young—that they shared. "What would you like to hear?" He plucked at the strings, tuning his instrument.

"Hmm." JJ rubbed a hand over his gray beard, thick and full beneath his near-bald head. "Always was partial to 'Rock of Ages.'"

Ødger plucked out the melody, which he knew from the Norwegian version but had heard more often since coming to America.

JJ closed his eyes and rocked in time with the music, humming along. He sighed long at the end. "That was mighty nice, son."

Ødger watched as Helen rose from the porch swing and headed inside. He'd hoped she would stay and enjoy the music, but she must have other matters to attend to. He segued into a familiar Norwegian hymn, "Velt alle dine veie." After picking out a verse or two, he softly sang the words to his own accompaniment.

Maya, sitting near in the other rocking chair with a sleeping Torvald in her arms, sang with him, their voices blending as they had Sunday evenings back home. He smiled at his sister, and she smiled back. The light in her eyes lifted his heart, thinking of the darkness she'd carried so long last year.

"That's right purty," JJ said after a bit, creaking his rocker.

"What do those words mean?" Eben, sprawled on a stool near his wife with his long legs akimbo, leaned forward. "I couldn't catch 'em all." Though he knew some Norwegian from his mother, he wasn't fluent.

Ødger plucked the strings absently, translating the lyrics in his mind. "It is about, well, giving all our ways over to the Lord, all our sorrows and burdens. And He, who commands the clouds and air and wind, will also direct our paths."

"I like that." JJ nodded. "And He surely does."

"That He does." Eben exchanged a gentle look with Maya, then reached to cradle Torvald's chubby foot with one hand. At nearly ten months old, the baby now filled much of his adopted mother's lap, arms spreadeagled and blond hair mussed. A living reminder of how the Lord could bring beauty from sorrow, as was Eben and Maya's marriage.

So then, Ødger could trust Him with Helen and his feelings for her too, couldn't he? Ødger sighed a bit and smiled at himself, strumming a few chords. Trust music to preach him a sermon when he wasn't looking for it.

"Hey." Hank bounded up to the steps. "Can Dog and me go an' see if we can find some wild strawberries?"

Thomi jerked her head up. "Us too?"

"I suppose so." Amalia smiled from the swing where Absalom had now joined her. "But take the girls with you."

"Come on, then, you two. See if you can keep up."

Ruthie and Thomi hopped up from the steps and took off after the loping boy and dog.

By the time the children returned with a pailful of wild strawberries, Helen emerged from the boardinghouse to share the treat.

Her face looked more rested, somehow—not exactly more composed, she nearly always was that, but at peace.

The only time he'd ever seen her ruffled, in fact, was that morning before church, whether more from Mrs. Flinch or her mysterious letter, he couldn't tell.

After eating his share of the sun-warmed, sharply sweet berries, Ødger returned to playing, wandering from one tune to another till he landed on "Sweet Hour of Prayer," one of his favorites he'd learned since coming to America.

As he played, he became aware of someone drawing near, a full dark blue striped skirt stopping by his feet. Then, leaning against one of the porch pillars nearby, Helen softly began to sing.

> "Sweet hour of prayer! sweet hour of prayer!
> That calls me from a world of care,
> And bids me at my Father's throne
> Make all my wants and wishes known . . ."

His chest warming with pleasure, Ødger glanced up at her as he played, grateful she wasn't looking at him. Helen gazed out across the front yard toward the lane, the orchard, the creek, her blue eyes soft and thoughtful. One graceful hand wrapped around the pillar while her voice rose clear as a meadowlark's, though she sang softly.

On the second verse, Ødger joined his voice with hers.

> "And since he bids me seek his face,
> Believe his word, and trust his grace,
> I'll cast on him my every care,
> And wait for thee, sweet hour of prayer!"

They sang through the third verse, then Ødger resorted to playing and humming through the fourth, since he didn't know it well yet.

Helen drew a long breath as the final plucked notes faded away. "Thank you. That was lovely."

"Ja, it was, thanks to you." Ødger quirked a brow at her.

Her cheeks faintly pinking, Helen leaned against the railing. "Music always has seemed to me the language of the soul. I've been wanting to add music classes in school—more than just the few songs we do now for the end-of-year program, I mean."

"Have you?" Ødger set his guitar back in its case. The light was turning golden toward evening, and Amalia and the girls headed in to prepare the simple supper, Hank and JJ to the barn for chores. Maya and Eben were preparing to go home, and while Magistrate Karlsson still chatted with Absalom on the porch, Ødger would need to drive the older man back to Decorah soon.

He pushed the thought away and focused on Helen. "What do you have in mind?"

"I'm still figuring that out. A bit of theory, a bit of music history, along with more intentional choral work for those interested."

"You have musical training. More than just playing piano." It wasn't a question, yet her obvious knowledge and skill prompted more questions in his mind. The more he knew of this woman, the more he wanted to know.

"I do. My aunt made sure I studied voice and theory as well as piano and organ. Even Italian to learn opera—not that I would ask that of my students just yet." She smiled and tapped her fingers together. "I even wondered about trying out a small music class this summer—along with my classes in English for those seeking to improve their language skills, reading and writing, of course."

"Which gave great help to me last summer." He smiled up at her as he snapped the clasps on his guitar case shut. "I am hoping to attend again this year, if I can manage it with the construction schedule."

"And we'd love to have you." A line pinched between her blond brows. "I just . . . have to figure out how to make it all work."

"To add the music?"

"No . . . well, yes. That too. But this letter I got yesterday, the reason I was late this morning . . ." She sighed. "I need to visit my great-aunt, in Ohio. Sooner rather than later."

"Is she ill?" Ødger straightened.

"Perhaps. Her letter was rather vague. I had thought to visit her in August, in the break between summer classes and the start of the fall term. But now . . . something tells me I should go before the classes begin. I've decided to leave next week. Yet I hate to think of pushing classes too late into haying season, much less toward harvest." She rubbed her forehead. "Forgive me. I shouldn't be bothering you with all this."

"Please. You could not be a bother."

She met his gaze with a hint of startlement in her eyes.

Ødger's neck burned. "What I mean is, we are friends, ja? At least I hope so, after this last year. And friends are always glad to listen when friends are worried, or troubled. And to help if they can." He set his guitar case upright and rested his hands on the rounded end of the neck. "And if there is anything to help I could do, I wish you to tell me. With the music classes, perhaps, or something of else."

Her lips twitched. "Something else."

Ødger grinned and shrugged. "You see? I still need the classes."

She laughed. "You are doing very well. But thank you. Your words mean a great deal, Mr. Gunderson."

"Please." He lifted the guitar case in one hand. "Can you not call me Ødger by now?"

Her cheeks pinked again in the late afternoon light, and she nodded, an uncommon shyness in her eyes. "Very well, Ødger. And you may call me Helen, if—if you wish."

She bid him good evening and hurried inside then, seeming a bit flustered, and Ødger gazed after her, hope rising in his chest like a bird with strong, beating wings.

What had she been thinking?

Upstairs, Helen sank into the chair before her vanity mirror and covered her face with her hands.

Giving Ødger Gunderson permission to use her given name? She huffed a sigh at herself. The last thing she needed was to give that man ideas. She couldn't let him care for her the way she was beginning to suspect he did. Couldn't let herself . . . no. Her teaching contract explicitly forbid her from marrying during the term of her contract or even keeping company with a man. Strictures she'd not minded till now, indeed had welcomed, after . . . James.

"I can't believe you wouldn't have told me this. You truly expect me to marry you? Now?"

Helen shook off the piercing memory and took her hands from her face. Enough of that. She must focus on the next steps, what needed to be done. She'd penned her letter to Aunt Ophelia this afternoon when she slipped away from the gathering on the porch for a bit, promising to come by train the very next week, and that decision had lifted half the burden from her shoulders.

But now, what to take? She wouldn't need much, to only stay a week or so. Her satchel should suffice, not the large trunk she'd lived out of when boarding round with different families early in her teaching career.

She flinched at the thought of the last home where she'd boarded, before she came to Forsberg House. That family had two teenage boys, plus an older son no longer in school. A son who took a none-too-welcome interest in Helen herself. After he'd cornered her out by their barn one evening on her way home and nearly stolen a kiss—she refused to think what more he might have done after, if she hadn't stomped on his foot and shoved him away—she'd lost no time in finding other lodging. Amalia's reopening of the boardinghouse right about then had been a true answer to prayer. She was thankful that family had since moved on farther west, so she didn't have to encounter any unpleasantness in town.

At least, from that direction. This morning's confrontation—for so it had felt—with Mrs. Flinch burned in her mind. Why did this ugliness keep resurfacing? Not often, true, and not from most people in Green Creek. But every now and then, especially from the Flinch family, this narrow-mindedness and prejudice toward anyone not quite like them . . . she couldn't understand it. And it kept circling back to poke at those here, in Forsberg House, this place that had become so dear to her, thanks to the people in it.

Helen sighed and crossed to her trunk in the corner, lowering herself to her knees.

She would start sorting through what to pack, just a bit. She had already told Amalia she planned to leave on Tuesday on the early train, so that left tomorrow to prepare more fully. But it would clear her mind to get matters at least a bit in order. Two skirts and waists ought to do, plus her traveling dress for Sundays. Nightgown, slippers, hairbrush, Bible. Her needs were simple, had become so with living so many places the last few years. Perhaps she would take one of the books from the two shelves she'd filled in the boardinghouse parlor over the last few years, to have something to read for a treat when Aunt Ophelia rested. Maybe *Sense and Sensibility*—she hadn't read that one in a while. She'd always related to Elinor Dashwood, with her need to remain steady for her tumultuous family and hide her emotions, however strong.

Setting aside an extra petticoat—her contract also stipulated she wear at least two at all times—her hands stilled on the carved wooden jewelry box she'd shown the little girls. Helen hesitated, then opened the lid. She needn't take anything but the brooch she always wore, yet something compelled her to finger the garnet necklace, the tiny gold bracelet. Relics of a mother, a history, that always seemed swathed in mist she couldn't quite blink from her mind's eye.

Would that mist be at last blown aside, at least in part, through this visit? And if so, would that clarity bring relief? Or greater dismay?

SEVEN

Helen sat at the piano, her nine-year-old fingers tripping lightly up and down the keys, scale after scale. A . . . B . . . C major . . . D. All the way through the major scales, then on to the minors with their awkward fingering and greater integration of the narrow, somber black keys. Yet sometimes, the pensive melodies of the minors suited her better than the cheerful majors.

Like today.

Maybe Aunt Ophelia thought Helen didn't notice anything unusual was going on, but she did. She always noticed more than grown-ups thought. She had with her mother—even if she didn't understand things, she noticed them. She'd known something was different two years ago, even before her mother told her she was sending her away on the train, by herself, to go live with Aunt Ophelia. Helen had been frightened of the snorting black locomotive, then of Aunt Ophelia's great brick house with its stern-faced butler and housekeeper and myriads of rooms and Aunt Ophelia herself, tall and stately in rustling black taffeta gowns and the eyepiece that she so often peered through back then. Frightened, at least, till she'd gotten to know her and found that Aunt Ophelia—and even the formidable butler and housekeeper—actually were quite kind to little girls, and she soon felt safer in that huge house than she ever had before.

But she hadn't shown how scared she was at first—not to Mother, and not to Aunt Ophelia. She'd seen what happened when people let their feelings out. It was scarier than anything else.

And today, something was different again. A telegram had come early this morning, and Aunt Ophelia had left the breakfast table quite suddenly, leaving Helen to finish her buttered eggs, smoked fish, and marmalade toast all alone. Then she'd barely seen her aunt all morning, Aunt Ophelia was so busy talking in a low voice to Mrs. Hoskins, the housekeeper, then shut up in her room writing letters—at least, that's what it looked like when Helen caught a glimpse through the door. She'd peeked when Maisie, the maid, went in to tend to Aunt Ophelia's fire.

Now Helen was still listening hard as she could manage, over the notes of the F minor scale, to the murmur of Aunt Ophelia's voice from the next room. She was in the adjoining parlor, speaking to a gentleman in a dark suit who had rung the bell a quarter of an hour ago. Aunt Ophelia had ordered Helen into the music room to practice her exercises then. But though she played softly as she could, Helen could barely make out a word.

Sighing, she finished her scales and moved on to other exercises. She'd played through the first four pages of Bach's Notebook for Anna Magdalena *when Aunt Ophelia suddenly called her from the doorway.*

"Helen, darling."

Helen turned, hitting a discordant note on the piano. Aunt Ophelia never called her "darling." "Dear" fairly often, or "child" on occasion, usually when she was exasperated. But "darling" . . . that had only happened once before, when Aunt Ophelia found Helen sobbing in the closet the day after she'd been sent here, back when she was only seven.

She had let her feelings out then, just a little bit. But only because she'd thought no one would hear.

"Helen," Aunt Ophelia said again. She stepped close to the piano

and laid her hand gently on Helen's head, softly stroking the blond ringlets that Aunt Ophelia insisted Miss Allan, her governess, roll in rags every night before Helen went to bed. "I must speak with you, my dear."

Helen sat straight on the piano bench and folded her hands in her lap.

"Your mother . . ." Aunt Ophelia hesitated and twisted her hands together. "Come, sit with me over here." She drew Helen over to the red velvet settee that stood beneath the window in the music room, at an easy distance for enjoying the music played on the grand piano and small reed organ that held places of honor.

Helen sat beside her aunt. The velvet seat felt hard beneath her. She wished her aunt would just say—whatever it was.

Even if she had a feeling she already knew.

"Your mother," Aunt Ophelia began again. "Well, there was a telegram from the asylum—that is, the hospital where she's been staying, this morning."

Helen curled her fingers till the nails pricked her palms. She stared at her aunt, wanting to ask what the telegram said, but no words would come.

"I'm so sorry, my dear." Aunt Ophelia laid her cool, veined hand over both of Helen's smaller ones. "Your mother—you know she's been ill a very long time. She has now departed this life. She is at peace."

Helen's heart stopped beating for a second, then continued on, but with a low, aching throb. Even if she'd been expecting it, she still felt as if someone had punched her in the chest. She knew what "departed" meant . . . she'd heard Aunt Ophelia use the term before, about one of her friends or their old minister. It didn't mean going on a holiday—it meant Mother had died, like Aunt Ophelia's husband, or the little bird she'd found lying stiff and cold in the rose garden last week. It meant her mother's body was cold and still, and her spirit had gone to be with God and the angels.

Even if she didn't fully understand it all, Helen knew that.

She worked her mouth, finding it a little hard to talk, since her tongue felt thick and dry. "Why?"

"She's been . . . sick, you know, for a long time." Aunt Ophelia squeezed Helen's hands, but she didn't look at her, not quite. "At least she's not suffering anymore. She's gone to her eternal rest." Under her breath, Aunt Ophelia murmured, as if she didn't want Helen to hear, "At least I pray so."

Helen nodded. Her throat felt too tight to say anything else, like she wanted to cry—only she couldn't, quite. She followed her aunt upstairs, then, where Aunt Ophelia told Miss Allan to put Helen's black dress on, and that she needn't do any more lessons before teatime. Helen did all she was told, but everything seemed a bit blurry, like she was in a dream.

But she did notice Aunt Ophelia hadn't really answered her question.

The brakes screeched as the locomotive lurched its passengers forward in their seats. Helen jerked out of her half-waking doze, out of the world of memory—or had it been a dream? One based strongly in memory, if so.

"Cincinnati, Ohio," drawled out the conductor, strolling down the narrow aisle of the train. "Last call for Cincinnati."

Helen straightened her hat and gathered the skirt of her wine-colored traveling dress to sidle out of her seat, reaching into the overhead compartment for her carpetbag. A gift from Aunt Ophelia when she set off for Iowa on her first teaching assignment, the sedate floral patterns on its capacious sides had now faded a bit, but the leather hinges and handles still held sturdy as ever. Her aunt never bought cheap.

She made her way down the narrow aisle between the seats. Aunt Ophelia would have insisted she travel first class, but on a teacher's salary, Helen felt it best to be prudent. Generous as her aunt always was, she didn't want to depend on a borrowed purse too much. Stepping out onto the train platform, Helen blinked at the crowds of people milling on the platform, cab drivers calling out, horses swerving through the street, well-dressed men and women hurrying along. Such a contrast to the quiet streets of Green Creek, or even Decorah. Only two years since she'd been back, but still, the bustle took her by surprise.

Old familiarity came to her rescue, however, and Helen hailed a cab with a practiced wave of her gloved hand, soon rolling along through the streets of Cincinnati in a hansom. She leaned back against the upholstered seat and drew a long breath, folding her hands on her lap and gazing out the window as busy boulevards turned to the genteel, tree-lined streets she'd grown up on—at least from seven years of age. Before that, it was thin shacks that froze in winter and baked in summer, holes in her shoes, beans to eat . . . if that. Her mother's raging tears . . .

Helen closed her mind on all that, at least for now. First, seeing Aunt Ophelia, learning what was going on with her health. *Lord, would you bless and guide this visit, I pray.*

The road rose more steeply as they neared the hilly area of Mount Adams where Aunt Ophelia and her husband had built their home once he made his fortune in steamboat building. Almost before she was ready, the hansom driver whoaed his horse in front of the familiar brick house with its large white columns, French windows in front, and black railings.

The driver handed Helen out of the cab, fetched her bag, and accepted her payment with a little bow. The cab rattled away, and she stood looking up at the house—so familiar, yet so strange, somehow.

Giving herself a little shake, she mounted the steps to the modest side entrance, which always seemed friendly despite the white columns on either side of the door. She'd just raised her hand to the bell when the door opened.

Helen felt a smile bloom unbidden on her face. "Mr. Faraday."

"Saw you comin' up the walk, Miss Helen, I did." The elderly butler's face sagged in more lines now, his hair whiter and sparser, but that same twinkle brightened his blue Irish eyes, the same warmth in his husky voice.

How could she ever have thought him stern and frightening? "It's so good to see you."

"And you, miss, and you. Here, let me take that for ye, if you please." He reached for her carpetbag, though she bit her lip to see how its weight threw him off balance for an instant.

Recovering himself, he straightened his shoulders beneath his crisp black coat and stepped aside. "Do come in now, lass."

"Is that our Helen?" A quavery voice that somehow still held strength echoed through the entryway, and Mrs. Hoskins bustled into view. "Goodness, child, it seems an age since you've been here."

"It does." Helen embraced the housekeeper gently, finding her frame smaller and frailer too than she remembered. Had everyone here aged so much in only two years? True, Mr. Faraday and Mrs. Hoskins had been gray-haired even when she first arrived here as a child, nearly seventeen years ago. They must be in their late seventies now. She should be grateful they were still here at all. Maids and other servants came and went, but she couldn't imagine this place without its two dear anchors.

"How are you, dearie?" Mrs. Hoskins stepped back and held Helen's shoulders to look at her, never mind that she stood a good six inches shorter than Helen did. "You're still teaching school?"

"Yes. Classes for adults too, now, at least in the summertime." Helen smiled. "But I came here before that starts up." She drew a breath. "Where is my aunt?" The house somehow felt too quiet, despite the warm welcome. Always on previous visits, her aunt would have swept in by now, commanding every room she entered.

"She's in the parlor, dearie. She has a bit of a nap after dinner now, you know."

"Humph." Mr. Faraday shifted the carpetbag from one hand to the other. "Aye, and after breakfast, supper, and tea too, often as not."

"Hush. You'll be worrying the child." Mrs. Hoskins frowned at him from beneath her small white cap.

"Should I go to my room first, then, so as not to disturb her?" Helen cast a glance toward the half-open parlor door.

"No, she insisted we send you in to her the moment you arrived. Mr. Faraday will take your bag upstairs. You go right in and greet your aunt, then you can freshen up and have a bit of a rest."

"Thank you." Helen gave them both a smile, then crossed the parquet floor of the entryway toward the parlor, softly pushing open the door.

Her aunt sat in an armchair near the parlor window in a posture Helen had never seen her in before—shoulders slumped, head drooping forward.

Helen hurried to her side, her chest pinching with alarm, till a snuffling snore gave her pause. She slowed and drew a long breath, her heart rate easing from its sudden gallop. Aunt Ophelia was only asleep—but how strange to find her in such an unladylike pose in the middle of the day. Helen hesitated, then sat down on a chair with curved walnut back and arms and upholstered cushion, just across from her aunt. Should she wake her? She hated to . . . yet Mrs. Hoskins said she wished to see Helen immediately.

After a moment, Aunt Ophelia gave a slight snort and cough, then lifted her head, blinking and ending Helen's quandary. Her gaze fell on Helen unfocused for a moment, then cleared. She smiled, her dark brown eyes lighting, and held out a quavery hand. "So. You have come, my dear."

Helen rose and took her aunt's hand, so much colder and more papery and starkly veined than she remembered. Bending, she pressed a kiss to Aunt Ophelia's wrinkled cheek. "It's so good to see you, Aunt."

"And you. You are good to take time from your busy life to see your old auntie. Sit down."

Helen sat, guilt pinching that she hadn't come last year. Did Aunt Ophelia mean to reference that? "I wanted to come right away, before my summer classes start." Oh dear, did that sound like she was squeezing the trip in, a dutiful inconvenience before returning to her regular life? "And because you wished it, of course. I planned to visit this summer regardless." Why was she rambling like this? Helen smiled into her aunt's eyes, steadying herself. "I have missed you dearly. But what is this about your health?"

Her aunt coughed slightly and reached for her handkerchief, dabbing at her mouth. "Time enough for that later. You should go upstairs and freshen up, have a bit of a rest. Send Winifred in to see to me, would you?"

"Winifred?"

"That's right, you wouldn't have met her." Aunt Ophelia gave her handkerchief a vague wave in the air. "My lady's maid since last summer. Mrs. Hoskins can fetch her for me."

Helen gave her aunt another kiss, then headed back into the entryway, where Mrs. Hoskins hovered. Passing the request along to the housekeeper, she turned toward the staircase, then hesitated and glanced back.

"Is she really ill, Mrs. Hoskins?" Something cold closed around her throat.

The housekeeper sighed and glanced toward the parlor door, then back at Helen, pressing her thin lips together. "It's not for me to say, dearie. She'll tell you in time, I trust. Mr. Faraday has put your things in your room."

Her feet heavy, Helen climbed the curving staircase, trailing her hand on the familiar dark wood banister, her buttoned boots silent on the carpeted steps.

When she reached her room, Helen paused in the doorway. Before her spread the same room she'd slept in for eleven years before she left for college to study to be a teacher. Here she'd cried at first at night, under the covers where no one could hear—here she'd begun to feel at home. Here she'd studied, worked, and played. Her old dollhouse, an elaborate three-story Victorian that now reminded her of Forsberg House, still sat on the small, child-sized table in the corner, along with several of her old dolls. Her lips tipping in a smile, Helen set her pocketbook and gloves down on the bureau and crossed the faded rose carpeting to lift her favorite doll, Elizabeth Rose. She ran her finger gently over the worn bisque cheek, the faded dimity dress. "Hello, there, Lizzie dear," she whispered.

Hugging the doll to her chest, she turned, scanning the room—the lace curtains, the high bed with rosebud counterpane and white ruffled canopy. A sudden wave of combined nostalgia and weariness washed over her. Helen laid the doll gently down, stepped to the washbasin to splash her face and hands, then removed the soot-dusted jacket and skirt of her traveling dress, laying them on a chair to be taken later for laundering. She then unbuttoned her travel-stained shirtwaist and indulged in a sponge bath at the washbasin, clad only in her corset, chemise, and petticoats. Feeling cooler and fresher, she opened her carpetbag and shook out a fresh blouse and simple but elegant dark gray skirt, then sat in the rocking chair she'd spent many a girlhood hour reading or dreaming in, looking out her high window at the treetops, the receding roofs of other Mount Adams houses marching down the hill, and far below, the Ohio River.

Home again—at least, this had long been home, the most secure she'd ever known. But now, beyond time with her beloved aunt . . . what purpose did this visit hold?

When the tea bell rang some time later, Helen descended the stairs, feeling more rested, even if she had only closed her eyes for a few minutes. A maid told her Aunt Ophelia hadn't come in yet, so Helen wandered into the music room. The reed organ still stood against one wall, and Helen ran her hand down its polished oak siding, then stepped to the piano. Here had been her main forte, though she played both instruments. She sat down on the piano bench, lifted the lid, and gently touched the black and ivory keys.

"I can't remember the last time anyone has played that." Her aunt spoke from the doorway, then made her way to Helen's side, leaning heavily on her cane.

"'Fingers high.' Miss Allan always told me that. 'Let them skip across the keys, not slouch.'" Helen smiled and lightly played an arpeggio, remembering. Here on this bench she'd first begun to feel a belonging at Aunt Ophelia's . . . here she'd felt happy, for the first time in longer than she could remember. Her governess had been an accomplished music teacher, and learning to ply her fingers on the instrument, to create beautiful, wistful melodies, had been a way Helen could release the feelings inside without words.

"You must play for me this evening." Aunt Ophelia rested her hand on Helen's shoulder, her touch seeming steadier than it had earlier. "But first, tea."

They had tea in the parlor, by the open window, a cooling breeze from the river easing the humid Ohio air.

Helen nibbled a biscuit with jam and cream, savoring the hint of lemon in her tea. "We don't have afternoon tea at Forsberg House."

"An old English habit from my mother, I suppose." Aunt Ophelia sipped her own tea. "Though some of the other ladies in Mount Adams keep the custom as well. But I've never been able to get through the afternoon without a cuppa."

Helen fingered a cucumber sandwich. "After traveling a day and a half by train, everything tastes wonderful."

"So tell me about this boardinghouse." Aunt Ophelia's bright eyes fixed on Helen's face, though she didn't use her lorgnette. "I presume it's a respectable place?"

"Certainly." Helen had only just moved into Forsberg House the last time she'd visited. "It's run by Amalia Karlsson—that's her married name. She came from Norway just over two years ago with her parents, but they died of cholera on the journey. She ended up becoming guardian to a little girl whose parents also perished, and that child—Ruthie—inherited this boardinghouse."

"Such tragedy so many immigrants endure," Aunt Ophelia murmured, dabbing her lips with her napkin. "So this Amalia took on not only a child but a business."

"She did. And very well too. She's taken in several other orphans also, along with paying boarders. It still makes me marvel to think of all she's accomplished at times."

"And so have you, my dear. Tell me about these summer classes of yours."

"I began them last summer as a way to help some of my more struggling students with reading and writing, but also to help adults who have immigrated and are trying to learn English. They proved a success last year, and this year I'd like to add music or even art, if I can."

"And any promising young men in these classes?" Aunt Ophelia's eyes took on a glint. "Or at this very respectable boardinghouse?"

Warmth started at the back of Helen's neck and spread up to her ears and cheeks. "You know I'm not allowed to marry or keep company while I'm teaching, Aunt."

"Humph." Aunt Ophelia helped herself to another biscuit and spread it liberally with jam. "They can't expect you to teach the rest of your life. And how are you supposed to find a husband that way? Surely most schoolteachers eventually marry."

"I suppose." Helen drew a breath, batting Ødger's bearded face and dazzling smile from her mind. "But I've enough to keep me busy just now. And the school board is quite strict. I had to get permission from the chairman even to travel on this visit."

"Even when school is not in session?" Aunt Ophelia's brows rose quite as stately as ever.

Helen nodded.

"Well. All very proper, I'm sure."

As her aunt subsided into sipping her tea, Helen let out a breath, her face cooling. "But I must know about you, Aunt. What is this malady you wrote of? What does the doctor say?"

Aunt Ophelia was a long time setting down her cup. At last she folded her hands and lifted a set face toward Helen. "All in good time, my dear. But first, I wish to speak to you of your mother."

Eight

"Would you care for some coffee and cookies, gentlemen?"

Hammer in hand and nails in his mouth, Ødger paused in setting a doorframe on one of the new dormitory buildings and glanced over his shoulder to find the source of the feminine voice.

Lena Amundson stood a few feet away, a coffeepot in one hand and plate in the other, smiling—at all the workers, but she cast a direct glance at him.

"Really?" Eivor Rykavyk, working on a window frame nearby, lowered his level and stared down at the young woman. "For us?"

"Certainly." She stepped forward, holding out the plate. "Freshly baked."

A whiff of cinnamon and ginger made Ødger's mouth water. More men lowered their tools and gathered closer, some climbing down from the roof.

"To what do we owe this honor, miss?" Leif Benson, who had served as Eben Miller's foreman on the threshing crew alongside Ødger last year, grabbed a cookie, engulfing it in one bite.

"My father is a professor here, as some of you know." Miss Amundson deftly balanced the plate of cookies on a sawhorse nearby and produced a stack of tin cups from a basket over her arm. She began filling each with coffee and passing them out. "I work for him part-time as a secretary of sorts and saw you gentlemen laboring out here in the heat. It seemed you could use some refreshment."

Ødger and Eivor exchanged glances. Was that really all there was to it? Ødger shrugged and grinned at his friend. He wouldn't pass up mid-morning coffee and cookies to break up a hot day's work, that was certain.

"What's all this? Why aren't you men working?" Mr. Bowman, the construction overseer, barreled over, a frown on his ruddy face, though many of the men, Ødger included, towered over him.

"Getting right back to it, sir." Leif quickstepped back to the dormitory, swinging his hammer in his hand.

"Please, sir." Miss Amundson tipped her head with a smile, adjusting her basket on her arm. "It's my fault. I simply thought these hardworking men could use a bit of a drink and a treat."

"Treat?" Mr. Bowman's brows drew even further together.

"Oh, forgive me. I should have offered to you first of all." Quick as a sparrow, Miss Amundson caught up the plate of cookies and offered it to the supervisor.

He glanced between her and Ødger and Leif, then took a cookie, sniffing at it suspiciously.

"Coffee?" She held up the pot.

"Uh. I suppose." Mr. Bowman blinked hard.

Ødger bit the inside of his cheek to keep from chuckling. This slender woman seemed quite a force of nature to have nonplussed the site superintendent.

The older man accepted the cup of coffee and sipped it silently.

Miss Amundson waited a moment, watching him. "I thought I might bring something out most mornings to the crew, at least when I'm working on campus. But if it's too much of an intrusion . . ." She left the words trailing in the air.

"Humph. Well." Mr. Bowman finished his cup and handed it

back to the young woman. "I suppose, as long as it doesn't disrupt work for long, you won't do much harm. But if I see things falling behind around here . . ." He cast a glare at Ødger and Eivor. "Well, I'll have no choice but to put a stop to it."

"Thank you, sir. The men are fortunate to have such a generous superintendent." Miss Amundson made a slight curtsy.

Eivor shook his head and chuckled as the overseer walked away. "I've never seen Mr. Bowman at such a loss." He handed the cup back to the young woman. "Much obliged to you, miss." He headed back to his work.

Ødger helped her collect the rest of the cups, which some men had left sitting around on the sawhorses or stacks of lumber. "So, you are a woman of many talents. Organ playing, cookie baking. Supervisor disarming."

She laughed. "But not embroidery or quilting, much to my mother's chagrin. I prefer a ledger—which my father appreciates, but she does not."

"You did not tell me the other day that you worked for your father."

"Didn't I? I suppose I was focused on the music. Or we both were." She smiled up at him as he handed her the last cup. "Thank you, Mr. Gunderson—or should I say, mange takk?"

"So you speak Norwegian?" He remembered her "Velkomst" when they'd first met.

"No, I'm afraid that must add to my list of non-accomplishments." She sighed and lifted the coffeepot. "But in this area, one picks up a word or two, intentional or not." She smiled at him and turned to go. "Good day to you, Mr. Gunderson."

"And to you." Ødger tipped his hat, then picked up his hammer and returned to his work, whistling "Sweet Hour of Prayer." Nice how a cup of coffee and a few cookies could bolster one's spirits for the rest of the day.

The sun beat hot on his head and shoulders by the time the men broke for dinner, and Ødger found a shady spot under a cluster of nearby trees to eat the sandwich he'd packed that morning. The magistrate had offered for Mrs. Skivens to pack his lunches, but Ødger wouldn't hear of putting the aging housekeeper to that extra trouble. He could stick slabs of ham and cheese between two pieces of bread as well as anyone.

"So." Eivor Rykavyk sat down next to him, unwrapping his own sandwich—doubtless packed by Amalia that morning for both him and his brother, Asgar. "You are a man of many trades also. Clergy student during the year, construction worker like us in the summer."

Ødger shrugged. "We all do what we must, do we not?"

Eivor nodded, his mouth full. He brushed a crumb out of his brown mustache. "That Miss Amundson has a pretty face. You know her?"

"Not really." Ødger swallowed a bite. "I met her at the end of term, she was playing the organ in the chapel."

"For a service?"

"Nei, just to play. No one else was there. Her father is one of my professors. She learned I play the organ and offered to let me try it."

"Ah." Eivor quirked a brow. "So you are quite acquainted with the lady."

Ødger stared at him. "We have met once before today."

"Whatever you say."

Ødger returned to his sandwich, somehow not quite liking his friend's tone. His thoughts drifted to Helen. She would be back in Ohio by now, from what she'd said. How was she? Was her aunt's illness severe? And why did she never speak of parents, only her aunt? Another thing he'd never thought to ask, but now wanted to.

By the end of the day, the muscles in his back and shoulders burned, unused to this intensive labor after months of study. Of course, he'd helped out at the boardinghouse farm on the weekends this spring, but nothing constant like this since threshing last

September. He packed his tools in the leather toolbelt he'd brought from Norway, then reached one hand to massage the screaming knots in his neck, wincing at the sting of sunburn. And that also came of spending months indoors buried in books.

Serves you right for getting soft. He pushed what his far might say from his mind and concentrated on putting one aching foot in front of the other, heading back down the road toward the center of town.

He hummed a hymn to help set his weary pace, then began practicing the English words of JJ's favorite aloud, his voice blending low with the evening birdsong and golden sunlight slanting low through the trees sheltering the rows of houses.

"Rock of ages, cleft for me,
Let me hide myself in Thee!"

He flexed his aching fists with a wry grin at the irony of the second verse's words, even as their truth poured balm over his spirit.

"Not the labors of my hands
Can fulfil Thy law's demands;
Could my zeal no respite know,
Could my tears forever flow,—
All for sin could not atone:
Thou must save, and Thou alone."

At the turnoff to the main road into Decorah, he paused, then headed the other direction instead, toward Green Creek. He'd just remembered he'd told Rev. Larsen he'd stop by after work this evening, to discuss any ways he might help out this week. While his official apprenticeship at a church wouldn't begin till next term, he enjoyed assisting the elderly pastor. Not to mention that whenever he got a taste of dipping into ministry himself, the joy that filled his heart made all the long months of study feel well worth it.

He enjoyed the two-mile walk to Green Creek, his weary muscles loosening, then turned off at the small, peaked-roof manse tucked next to the church like a calf nestled near its mother. Wending his way past rosebushes on a quaint path of stepping stones, he reached the door and knocked firmly, having learned from experience that Rev. Larsen had begun to lose his hearing. After knocking a second time and a third, still no one came.

Ødger chewed his lip and glanced around. Should he try the church? Yet Rev. Larsen had distinctly asked him to stop by his home. He hesitated a moment longer, then tried the door. It opened with a welcoming squeak, and Ødger peered inside.

"Hello? Reverend Larsen?" His nose twitched at a sharp, pungent odor. Smoke? His chest tightening, Ødger stepped inside. "Pastor! Are you here?" Following the smell, he hurried through the small, neat parlor to the kitchen, where he found a pot of stew on the hottest part of the stove, billowing smoke and the smell of burnt meat. Ødger snatched a nearby towel and moved the pot to the front corner farthest from the firebox, then opened a window to let out the smoke—as well as let in cooling air, for the little kitchen had turned into an oven. He turned down the damper on the stove.

"Pastor Larsen?" Ødger searched through the four rooms of the manse, feeling an intruder, yet his gut clenched at the thought of finding the elderly man collapsed somewhere, without anyone nearby to hear his calls. Rev. Larsen's wife had passed on to glory several years before, and the pastor seemed to manage quite well as a widower—until today.

At last he opened the narrow door at the end of the hall and exhaled to see Rev. Larsen kneeling in the small back garden, patting soil around marigolds.

The elderly minister looked up at the slap of the back door and smiled, resting dirt-smudged hands on his knees. "Ødger, there you are. Thank you for stopping by."

"Of course, Pastor." Ødger trod the neatly narrow path between the beds of flowers and vegetables and offered his hand to the older man, who leaned on his arm heavily to haul himself to his feet. "Forgive me for entering your house, but I smelled smoke."

"Smoke?" Rev. Larsen's eyes pinched behind his spectacles.

"Ja. A pot of stew was burning, I believe."

"Oh, did I forget that?" Rev. Larsen shook his head, brushing the dirt from his hands as he made his way—rather unsteadily, Ødger thought—to the back steps, then leaned on the handrail to climb them.

Ødger followed him, finding the pastor scraping the top portion of the stew into a bowl.

"You must think me a doddering old fool to leave this pot like this, but I assure you, I'm usually much more careful. I didn't mean to do more than take a peek at my garden, but I'd forgotten those marigold and zinnia starts came in from Nygards'. And I thought I'd just get them into the ground. I do love those bright flowers, perhaps because my wife always did, rest her soul." Rev. Larsen peered into the burned pot. "I might be able to scrape out enough for the two of us. Would you care to join me for supper?"

"Mange takk, but I think the magistrate expects me and will wonder if I do not come. But I wanted to ask how I can help you this week, Pastor."

"Ah yes." Rev. Larsen raised a finger and pushed his spectacles up his nose, then shuffled over to the table, where a jumble of papers joined a half-empty coffee cup and a well-worn Bible. He sifted through the papers, then found some sort of list set to the side and peered at it. "I wanted to ask you if you would accompany me on a sick call this evening."

"Tonight?" Ødger tried to keep his voice neutral. He loved the idea of making calls with the pastor, but tonight—his muscles ached for his soft bed at the magistrate's home. He'd have to take the buggy to come all the way back here again tonight.

"Yes. The Trotter family, their son is suffering greatly just now. I promised I would come by again later this evening to pray with them, and I'd appreciate your presence as well."

Ødger tasted shame. What sort of divinity student was he to hesitate at ministering to the suffering? "Of course, Pastor. I can come back. What time?"

"Round about seven or a bit after should be fine. And thank you, son." He reached over to pat Ødger's hand with a twinkle in his eye. "You saved my supper."

The sun still shone, albeit lowering and gold, when Ødger emerged from the magistrate's home after supper, restored by Mrs. Skivens's roasted chicken with new greens and mashed potatoes. He took the horse and buggy and arrived back at the manse just as Rev. Larsen stepped out of the manse gate, the older minister now wearing his simple black cassock and collar rather than the shirtsleeves and trousers he'd worn in the garden.

Ødger had donned his dark gray Sunday suit, though a bit worn by now and a different style than he saw American young men wearing. After tying the horse to the hitching post, he fell into step beside Rev. Larsen. "Where do the Trotters live?"

"Only just around the corner."

"What ails their son?" Ødger slowed his long strides to match the elderly minister's, though Rev. Larsen stepped along quite briskly now, despite his cane.

"Ah." The older man shook his head. "That . . . I'm afraid only the Lord knows."

Ødger rubbed his bearded cheek. *Lord, what am I heading into here? Please guide us, and make us a blessing.*

The Trotter home was set well back from the road, a pleasant white boarded house with fresh green trim and a fenced flower garden. Rev. Larsen mounted the steps without a falter this time and tapped at the door.

Mrs. Trotter, a tall woman with a large auburn pompadour, met them at the door. She glanced from Rev. Larsen to Ødger.

"Ødger Gunderson. He is studying for his ordination and is assisting me." Rev. Larsen smiled gently at the woman, then beckoned to Ødger.

"Thank you for coming." She opened the screen door and stepped back.

"How is he?"

"No better."

Ødger followed Rev. Larsen down a hallway to the family parlor, where several little girls played on the large braided rug in the fading light. At a word from Mrs. Trotter, the children scampered from the room, and she stepped to the side of a boy, perhaps fifteen or sixteen, who sat by the parlor window, staring out at the back garden with his head leaning on his hand.

"Phillip. The pastor's here."

Silence. Mrs. Trotter hesitated, then laid her hand on his shoulder.

He jerked his arm up, throwing her hand aside. "I told you to leave me alone."

"Don't talk to your mother that way." Across the room, a burly man, doubtless Mr. Trotter, half-rose from an armchair. Ødger didn't remember seeing the man in church.

"Silas, please." Mrs. Trotter held up her hand, her face twisting.

"I told you I don't want to see anyone." Phillip spoke to the window, his voice falling flat now.

"He's just here to pray, son. To try to help you." Her voice caught.

Silence.

Wringing her hands, she turned to Rev. Larsen.

"It's all right, Mrs. Trotter. Would you and your husband like to stay, or step out for a breath of air?"

Muttering, Mr. Trotter pushed himself to his feet and stalked out of the room. Ødger caught something about "if the boy would just pull himself together."

With a half-sob, Mrs. Trotter followed him.

Standing in the middle of the room, Rev. Larsen folded his hands atop his cane, then drew an unhurried breath in—and out.

"My old legs are a bit weary after that walk. Mind if I sit with you, young Phillip?" Rev. Larsen stepped to the rocking chair just across from the boy, a small round table between them topped with a doily and an etched-glass lamp.

The boy said nothing, still staring out the window.

The minister sat, nodding to Ødger to take a nearby chair. Ødger eased down into it.

"Ah." Rev. Larsen sat back, creaking his rocking chair, blinking behind his spectacles. "Nothing like the peace of a summer evening." He glanced at the boy's blank face across from him. "Except when that peace can't seem to reach our hearts, eh, Phillip?"

The young man made an impatient gesture with his arm. Ødger caught a glimpse of something on his wrist—a bit of stray thread from his shirt? Or a fresh scar?

"We're not going to preach at you, young man—not my friend, Mr. Gunderson, nor I. I'm sure you've had more than enough of that. I'm just going to read you something from another young man who felt like giving up." Withdrawing a small black Bible from his pocket, Rev. Larsen opened it to a marked place and began to read.

> "How long wilt thou forget me, O Lord? for ever? how long wilt thou hide thy face from me?

> How long shall I take counsel in my soul, having sorrow in my heart daily? how long shall mine enemy be exalted over me?
>
> Consider and hear me, O Lord my God: lighten mine eyes, lest I sleep the sleep of death;
>
> Lest mine enemy say, I have prevailed against him; and those that trouble me rejoice when I am moved.
>
> But I have trusted in thy mercy; my heart shall rejoice in thy salvation.
>
> I will sing unto the Lord, because he hath dealt bountifully with me."

Rev. Larsen closed the book and glanced at Ødger. "Would you pray for us, Mr. Gunderson?"

Ødger nodded, his throat tight. His heart ached for this young man and his raw pain, and he thought of his tante Anne and her years of mental suffering. He bowed his head, gripping one hand inside the other. *Lord, give me words.* "Father in heaven . . . we come to you now, with thy beloved child Phillip." He drew a breath. "You alone know what he needs, O Lord. You know what weighs his heart, his mind. Open up to him the knowledge of thy love, even amid his pain. Let him know thy presence, even now." He waited, sensing a subtle shift in the room. "In the name of Jesus we ask it, Amen."

Phillip didn't look at them as they bid him good-bye and left. Did his face seem smoother, though, less fraught with tense lines? More peaceful? Ødger wasn't sure, and his heart weighed with the knowledge of his own insufficiency. How was one to minister to those who suffered so—not in body, but in mind? *Lord, show me the way.*

"Thank you for coming." Mrs. Trotter gripped their hands at the door.

"Always." Rev. Larsen patted hers. "Has the doctor been back to see him again?"

She sighed. "Last week. He says it's all in his head now, there's little more he can do, besides dosing him with laudanum when he gets his bad spells." She glanced at Ødger. "Phillip has always had these . . . moods, from childhood. But this March, he lost a friend in a skating accident, and Phillip broke his leg. Since then, he's been worse than ever. He . . ." She pressed her fist to her mouth. "He tried to harm himself again, yesterday."

"Your husband told me, when he came by today and said you wanted me to come."

She huffed a sigh, tears tracking down her face. "That's the other thing. I barely could get Silas to even agree to ask you to stop by. He is so angry with Phillip, thinks he just needs to buck up and be a man, as he says."

"I think we know this runs deeper than that." Rev. Larsen leaned on his cane. "You'll let me know if you want me to contact the hospital in Independence?"

She nodded, pressing her lips together. "I pray God we never come to that."

"And I pray with you. Every day." He set his hat on his head. "Call me again as you have need, day or night."

Ødger walked Rev. Larsen back to the manse, silent, his shoulders weighted now with more than the day's labor. And to think he'd balked at first in driving back to visit this family tonight . . . how his own meager inconvenience paled.

Rev. Larsen paused after unlocking his door. "Perhaps I should have prepared you better, son. But at times in ministry, nothing will prepare you except seeing. Being there."

Ødger cleared his throat, trying to find words for what had been pressing on him ever since his prayer at the Trotters'. "I—I had an aunt who was mentally troubled. I never saw her much, but my uncle, her husband—he is why I entered the ministry. He went through . . . so much. So, of course, did she."

Rev. Larsen gazed into the summer dusk, lines about his eyes.

"Perhaps someday we will learn how to better help such sufferers. I pray so." He glanced at Ødger, and his gaze softened. "Perhaps you may even be part of that."

"Do you ever feel . . . inadequate for the ministry, Pastor?"

"Every day, son. Every day." The minister gave him a slight smile. "But perhaps that is the point."

Nine

"I wonder how much you know."

Helen gripped the delicate porcelain handle of her teacup, meeting her aunt's gaze. "Know about what?"

"Your mother's story." Aunt Ophelia took another sip of her own tea, then set the cup down with a slight clink.

"Her story—you mean from childhood?" She tried to gather the fragments of knowledge from her memory, like scattered scraps of yellowed newspaper. Once she moved to live here in Ohio, her mother was rarely, if ever, mentioned. "She was your sister's daughter, correct?"

"Yes, my youngest sister's only child." Her aunt gazed out the window, her dark hair that used to be only threaded with gray now almost fully silver, and sighed. Her chin trembled slightly. "My sister died young . . . consumption, the doctors said. Adelaide, your mother, was only fifteen then. She was always . . . sensitive. She took her mother's death hard, starting having these 'spells,' they called them. She'd take to her bed for weeks, wouldn't get up, or she'd weep for hours. Then other times she'd be bright and cheerful—almost too much so, laughing, singing, dancing about, till something would happen and she'd fall into despondency again. Her father didn't know what to do with her. He was lost without his wife, my sister.

He tried different doctors, castigating or coddling his daughter by turns. One physician suggested a change in environment, so he sent her away to finishing school. She got in trouble there—sneaking out after hours, keeping company with young men—and not always the most desirable young men." Aunt Ophelia's voice hoarsened and she paused for another sip of tea. Her veined hand shook. "How much of this is familiar to you?"

Helen used her fork to gather crumbs on her plate. Half her tea cake remained, but her appetite had fled. "Not much, really. Except she used to talk about her escapades at school sometimes. When she was in one of her happy moods."

"Yes." Aunt Ophelia sighed. "That sounds like her. The life of the party, she was—when she wasn't in her phases of melancholia. Manic-depressive psychosis, they finally called it. But that wasn't until she was . . . committed, later on."

"How did she end up in Iowa? Is that where the school was?"

"No, it was here in Ohio, though farther west. But when she was seventeen, her father received word that she'd run away with one of those young men. It was two years before he could find further news of her. He even hired a private detective. He eventually heard that she'd had a child, and that cad—he never was her husband—had abandoned her."

The tea cake turned to a rock in Helen's stomach. "So he—that was my father, then. So I am a . . ." She couldn't say the ugly word. The back of her throat burned. She'd never known much of anything about the man who had fathered her, though her mother kept a picture she occasionally brought out to either kiss or cry over. She'd never dared to ask much.

"None of the family ever thought of you that way." Her aunt's voice firmed. "None of this was ever your fault. You were fatherless, that was all."

"Do you know if he is still alive?" Helen forced the question out. Not that she wanted to find him.

"He isn't. He worked on the steamboats, something with the boilers. Best we could discover, he died in an explosion a year or two after we learned where you and your mother were."

"Did my grandfather try to reach out to us?"

"You don't remember?" Aunt Ophelia cast her a quick glance, then shook her head. "No, of course, you were too little. But he did come, once he finally learned Adelaide's location—took the train to Iowa, where she was working part-time as a laundress."

"Yes." That had been her mother's work of choice, at least when she could work. Quite a comedown for a privileged young woman . . . taking in laundry for boardinghouses, single men, large families. The stench of lye and soiled clothes permeated Helen's early memories.

"Your grandfather found you, and your mother. You were only about two at the time. He said she came to the door and let him see you. But she wouldn't let him in, and she refused to come home with him."

"Why?" Helen's throat closed. "Wouldn't that have been so much better, for her?" *And for me?*

"I don't know, my dear." Aunt Ophelia met her gaze, her eyes dark and wet. "They hadn't understood each other for many years, by that time. Too much time and pain had passed, I suppose. And she . . . she wasn't well, not ever, as you know. Only God knows what was going on in her mind, but she insisted she was making a life for herself and her child without him. And she bade him leave and never come back. He tried to at least take you, but she caught you up in her arms and slammed the door in his face."

Pressure built in Helen's chest. She glanced down and took a sip of tea, willing her nerves to calm.

"I'm sure this must be difficult for you to hear, my dear." Aunt Ophelia reached across the table to touch Helen's hand as she set down her teacup.

Helen withdrew her hand and folded it with the other in her lap. "Please go on."

"You know much of the next few years. She scraped along somehow, and we heard little until you were seven years old. Apparently her episodes had gotten so bad by then that some women from the local church, who had met your mother through her laundry services, became concerned for your well-being. They spoke to the local doctor and minister, who tried to contact your grandfather, but he had passed away the year before. So their letter eventually reached me—this was shortly after your uncle died also. I arranged for your mother to be taken to the Iowa Hospital for the Insane in Independence—it wasn't as far a journey for her, and it's a respected establishment. I was afraid she'd refuse, again, but I suppose even she could see how bad things were getting—or it was divine intervention. I certainly thought so at the time, when you came to me."

"I remember that." Helen offered a tremulous smile.

"Did she explain anything to you then?"

Helen drew a slow breath. "She said I was going for a visit to see her aunt. That she would see me soon. But I knew—I knew something was different. She'd been crying for days, hadn't been able to shop or cook." Her stomach pinched at the memory. "Then she became very bright and determined, bathed me, packed my bags. And when she sent me off in the hansom to the train station, I saw another carriage pull up. It seemed—different, somehow. The sides were all closed in." Helen repressed a shudder. "Later, I realized it must have come to take her to the asylum."

"You have had far more to bear than any child should have, so young. And I'm sorry to bring up these troubling memories." Aunt Ophelia reached for a dark green–covered book lying to the side. "But in the last month or two, I've been having Faraday bring down some old trunks and boxes from the attic. It seems the time in my life to be sure all my affairs are in order, you might say. Among them, I began going through some of your mother's old things that the asylum sent here after she passed on. And I found this diary of hers, kept from her girlhood through much of your childhood. I'd never looked in it before—I hesitated to encroach on her privacy, even still, and I confess I somewhat feared what I'd find there. But when I began to read . . . well, I felt you should read it too."

Helen took the little book and ran faintly numb fingers over the cover. Her mother had held this diary, touched this green cloth cover, written in these pages. What would she find within them?

Aunt Ophelia pushed her chair out a bit and stood, leaning on her silver-headed cane. "I'm sure you will wish to discuss what you read once you begin. For now, though, I must lie down a short while."

Helen stood, shaking out her skirt, and stepped close to support her aunt's elbow. "Shall I help you to your room?"

"No, here on the chaise longue will be fine. Just a half hour or so, dear. Forgive me."

Helen saw her aunt settled, her eyes quickly closing, then stepped out of the parlor.

Mrs. Hoskins met her in the hall. "Does your aunt need anything, dear? Or do you?"

"She says she needs to rest a bit, so I think I'll head up to my room." Helen hesitated, wanting to tell Mrs. Hoskins about the diary she cradled in her arms, but instead, something else came to her lips. "Thank you, Mrs. Hoskins, for always being so kind to me."

"Goodness, dearie." The elderly woman laid her hand on Helen's arm and gave a quick squeeze. "You've been nothing but a blessing ever since you walked through that door as a wee girl. Even for having such a rough go of it in life, you always had the sweetest spirit. Though I always thought you kept things inside a great deal, I did."

A sudden choking filled Helen's throat, and she could only press Mrs. Hoskins's hand and then flee upstairs more quickly than her deportment classes at college would ever have condoned.

Back in her little rosebud room, she stepped to the window, her breath coming hot and fast. She pushed open the window, the evening air now cooler on her face. Helen closed her eyes, letting the breeze tease tendrils of hair away from her hot cheeks.

It wasn't that her aunt had shared anything so very new about her mother—though she had about her father. More details, yes, and some clarifications. But hearing the words brought it all back, so vividly Helen could see her mother's tear-streaked face and red eyes, smell the sooty shack where they'd spent most of her early years, the lye stench of the laundry bubbling over the fire. Feel the pinch of cold and hunger in her small stomach and limbs. The searing shame when she made it to school, how the other children whispered and pointed at her ragged clothes.

Coming to live with Aunt Ophelia had been like Cinderella moving to the palace, she'd thought at the time. From rags to riches. Her mouth quirked. Perhaps that was overly dramatic, but certainly from cold and hunger to thick carpets and roast beef, ruffled dresses, and penmanship and music lessons. She had missed her mother, at first, of course—yet the relief of being free of her tumultuous moods had cut sharp through the homesickness. And at last, she had begun to relax . . . to thrive . . . to heal.

But today . . . the past seemed tripping on the heels of the present today.

Helen pressed her fingertips to her eyes, then sat down in the small rocking chair and ran her hands over the cover of the little book. Did she dare open it? What secrets, perhaps better left so, might it hold? And yet . . . she drew a breath and opened the book at random to one of the early entries.

July 7, 1868

We are really going to run away. I almost fear to write the words, though no one reads this diary except me. I don't even let Alf, though he teases to see it most awfully. But he has it all planned, Alf does, for him and me—we're to run off west together and be happy. Oh, I feel as if I'm living in a fairy tale! No more dull books or harsh teachers or disappointed papas. We'll be free, and we'll have our love and each other. When I'm with Alf I'm so happy I can scarcely breathe. That will be more than enough.

Helen swallowed. How young and happy her mother sounded! Obviously in one of her "good" spells. But such a girl . . . almost a child. Something in her chest softened, warmed toward this Adelaide who had been. She turned a few more pages.

July 29, 1868

I don't know what is wrong with Alf now. He seems angry all the time, mostly at me. When I try to talk to him and cheer him up, he snarls and tells me to shut my mouth. That hurts me, deep inside. He keeps saying he's going to get a job and find us a better place to stay than this ratty old hotel, but then he doesn't—though he leaves for hours at a time, looking for work he says, but then comes home smelling of liquor. I'm so miserable sometimes I huddle under the quilts and cry long into the night. I cry for my mother—why did she have to die and leave me? I never would have left home if she hadn't. She loved me, as Papa doesn't. I thought Alf loved me, but maybe no one does. He hates it when I cry—sometimes he hits me to make me stop, but I don't.

Helen's chest tightened. So this had been her father. Her eyes hot and burning, she almost closed the book, but instead turned further and kept reading.

September 19, 1868

I am going to have a baby! I can't believe it, but the woman at the hotel here—I've started learning to do laundry for the hotel so we can keep staying here till Alf finds work—she tells me I'm right. I want to sing all the time, except when I'm sick in the mornings. I haven't told Alf yet, but when I do I know he'll smile that beautiful grin of his, and everything will be all right.

Everything has to be all right.

Helen ran a trembling finger over the faintly penned words. She smiled a little at her mother's delight in carrying her, though the ache in her chest grew stronger. So, such were her beginnings—humble, even shameful. But at least she knew she had been wanted.

Still, she couldn't take any more of this just now. Drawing a breath, Helen set the diary aside and picked up the novel she'd brought and left on the small table alongside her Bible. She'd just read a bit of *Sense and Sensibility* to settle her nerves while Aunt Ophelia rested. Stories always had helped carry her away from the turmoil of real life, even as a little girl.

Helen cracked the cover of the beloved book and began to read.

> *The family of Dashwood had long been settled in Sussex. Their estate was large, and their residence was at Norland Park, in the centre of their property, where, for many generations, they had lived in so respectable a manner as to engage the general good opinion of their surrounding acquaintance . . .*

The tension in her middle relaxed, her mind quieted by the familiar words as the story drew her in. She'd first read this book as a girl, then many times since.

> *Elinor, this eldest daughter, whose advice was so effectual, possessed a strength of understanding, and coolness of judgment, which qualified her, though only nineteen, to be the counsellor of her mother. She had an excellent heart;—her disposition was affectionate, and her feelings were strong; but she knew how to govern them: it was a knowledge which her mother had yet to learn; and which one of her sisters had resolved never to be taught.*

Helen skimmed quickly through the early pages that chronicled the family's history to get to the unfolding of the story as the fatherless sisters were cast on the mercy of a weak half brother and his mercenary wife. Then the brother of that wife entered the drama, a kind, amiable young man who wanted to be a clergyman. Edward Ferrars, who captured the quiet heart of sensible Elinor.

Helen smiled and sighed. Once she'd dreamed of finding her own Edward, but James's rejection of her had effectually quenched that dream. And understandably so . . . yet the memory still carried the familiar stab to her heart, even if its sting had lessened over the years.

Ødger came unbidden to her mind, another young aspirant to the clergy. Noble and truehearted as Edward Ferrars, as best she could tell. And sometimes, she did think . . . her fingers tightening on the pages, she acknowledged it again to herself . . . that he showed a more than passing interest in her.

But it didn't matter. As with Edward, there were doubtless other circumstances than she knew of for Ødger, perhaps even other attachments. And even if not, if he truly knew her—knew her family history and background—surely Ødger would lose interest as quickly as had James. Any respectable man could not be blamed for doing so. Especially with what she was learning now.

Helen blew out a breath and adjusted the satin ribbon to mark her page. She should go check on Aunt Ophelia before supper. She made use of the upstairs water closet—a luxury installed a few years ago, and one she never took for granted on her visits here—and then came back to open her window wider, hoping to catch a cooling breeze as the sun lowered toward evening.

She saw she'd left the diary open on the table and bent to close it. Catching sight again of the date on the last entry she'd read, she paused.

September 1868. That couldn't be right. Helen had been born in October of 1867, nearly a year earlier. At least, so she'd always thought.

She stood frozen a moment, her fingers perched on the page,

then shook herself and closed the little book. There must be some mistake—perhaps her mother, in her confusion of mind, had put the wrong date.

But for every entry that year?

Helen headed downstairs, her heart thudding oddly with each carpeted step.

Ten

"There's nothing like a garden in June."

Amalia tipped her head back and drew a long breath of the summer air, the sun smiling warm on her forehead and cheeks despite her sunbonnet.

"Ja." Maya paused in picking early peas to grab Torvald's hand back from grabbing up the winding green vine by the roots. "And we certainly can grow more sooner and faster here than in Norge."

Ruthie and Thomi came hopping over the rows of vegetables toward them.

"Careful, you don't want to risk trodding on a plant."

"We are." Ruthie halted and grinned at the basket at Maya's feet. "The peas are ready?"

"Ja, some of them." Amalia smiled back. "I think we can pick some lettuce leaves too. Will you girls help me?"

While Maya cleaned Torvald's hands and feet at the outdoor pump, Amalia knelt back between the lettuce rows with the girls.

"See, we gently pluck off the outer leaves, then the plant can keep growing." Amalia demonstrated, adding the tender green fronds to the basket atop the pea pods.

"I remember." Ruthie pushed back her swinging blond braids

and gathered leaves from another lettuce plant. "Can we eat some right now with sugar?"

"Sugar on lettuce?" Thomi frowned, her fingers pausing while tearing a leaf. After growing up in Chicago till last summer, much of country life still surprised her.

"Ja, it's good." Ruthie nodded hard. "We'll show you."

"That's enough for now, we want to leave plenty to grow." Amalia stood and led the way back to the pump. Maya had taken Torvald inside, but the girls and Amalia took turns pumping and rinsing the lettuce under the gushing cold water, shrieking with laughter as the coolness splashed their hot, dusty faces and hands.

Smiling, they all trooped inside, and Amalia brought the crock of sugar from the pantry. She sprinkled a bit on a fresh, damp lettuce leaf for each girl.

Thomi's dark eyes widened at her first bite. "It's good."

"Told you." Ruthie crammed a tender leaf into her mouth.

Amalia handed a sprinkled frond to Maya, who sat at the kitchen table nursing a sleepy Torvald, then closed her eyes as she bit into her own lettuce leaf. Sweet and slightly bitter, fresh and juicy . . . the taste of late June in the garden.

"When will Miss Stenerson be back?"

Amalia opened her eyes at Thomi's question, faintly surprised she was the one to ask it rather than school-loving Ruthie. "I believe by this weekend, next week at the latest. Why?"

Thomi shrugged. "Just wondered. I want to practice my reading more this summer."

"Good for you."

"The other girls my age are going into the fourth grade." Thomi frowned and crunched the rest of her leaf. "I want to catch up."

"I'm sure Miss Stenerson will be glad to help you." Amalia placed the rest of the washed lettuce in a bowl on the countertop and glanced at Maya, who sat cradling Torvald with one arm and shelling peas with the other hand. "Will you and Ødger be joining the classes again too?"

"I want to." Maya shifted Torvald's weight a bit, then reached for another pea pod. "I still struggle with my English, far more than my brother. But I'm not sure what to do with Torvald. He won't sit through a class like that."

"Couldn't Mrs. Miller keep him those evenings?"

"I suppose so." Maya flicked the peas from the pod into a bowl and tossed the shell aside, then caressed Torvald's damp blond hair. The baby gave a sleepy grunt and snuggled closer. "I just haven't left him much so far, except for the night of our wedding. But he loves his bestemor. I'm sure he'd be all right for a couple of hours."

Amalia watched her cousin kiss the baby's forehead, a sweet ache tugging in her chest. In just a few months, she'd have her own little one to hold, God willing. Who would he or she be? Boy or girl? With her blond hair, or Absalom's brown curls? Her heart fluttered as the baby kicked beneath her ribs, and she drew a long breath, rubbing her growing belly.

"What's for dinner, Tante Malia?" Ruthie leaned her head against Amalia's arm.

Amalia hugged her and pressed a kiss to the part between Ruthie's braids, still warm from the sun. "Most of the boarders won't be here for dinner today, just Mr. Dahl—they're all out on the railroad or working on the construction at Luther College. There's a leftover meat pie in the well house, would you girls run and get it for me? Then we'll cook the peas and make a salad."

"Yum! Come on, Thomi." Ruthie dashed for the door, Thomasina on her heels.

"Can you stay for dinner?" Amalia crossed to the table and helped Maya shell the last of the peas, then dumped them into a small pot. She stirred up the stove and added just enough kindling to the coals left from breakfast to cook the peas, not wanting to overheat the kitchen today.

"I'd love to, if that's all right." Maya gently shifted the now-sleeping Torvald and rebuttoned her bodice. "May I lay him on a blanket on the parlor rug?"

"Ja, of course." Amalia smiled. More time with her cousin, what a gift. Since Maya and Eben married, she hadn't seen Maya nearly as much—all right and as it should be. But her heart skipped to think of sharing a lunch together. She had just covered the peas and pushed them to the center of the stove when Maya came back in.

"What can I do?"

"There's a loaf of sourdough in the pantry if you want to slice it. I should have told the girls to bring the butter from the well house—hopefully they'll remember." Amalia tore lettuce leaves into a bowl, then thinly sliced a few radishes she'd pulled from the garden also, another quick-growing vegetable.

"Have you found a boarder for my old room yet? I keep meaning to ask."

"No one permanent, but we've used it for a traveler or two. I'm hoping we might find someone new this summer. A friend of Declan and Finley's has been staying in Ødger's old room for some months now, though he's away with them right now on the railroad." She glanced at her cousin. "So, how have you been, really? You and Eben, I mean."

A faint pink blossomed in Maya's cheeks as she cut the bread. "Over a month married now—it's hard to believe. Sometimes I wake up and still feel the ache of Einar's space empty beside me. And then I look over, and it's Eben there, his broad shoulders, the warmth of his body beside me. And his snore."

They both giggled, then Maya sighed. "He is so good to me, Amalia. I don't deserve him . . . but I'm so grateful. He's so patient, so gentle, works so hard. And he loves Torvald so much."

"And you," Amalia put in gently. With a fork, she mixed sugar, vinegar, and mustard with a bit of salt and pepper for salad dressing.

"Ja. I know. And I love him too." Maya stacked the sourdough slices on a white stoneware plate with a blue design. "It's not as if he's replaced Einar, exactly—they are so different from each other. But he has helped fill up those lonely, empty places in my heart. Him and God." She smiled as the little girls clattered back into the kitchen.

"Here's the meat pie." Thomi presented it like a grand crown for royalty.

"And I thought you might want the butter." Ruthie held out the crock, damp with condensation from the cool well house.

"Indeed we will, mange takk, den lille." Amalia sent Maya a wink. "You girls set the table, and Ruthie, would you ring the bell so Mr. Dahl knows it's time for dinner?"

The girls ran off, and Amalia cut the meat pie, setting the cold slices onto plates. "I do wonder how Mr. Dahl spends his days, cooped up in his room most of the time. Writing, I know, but doesn't one need inspiration out in the world to do much writing? Absalom did learn he publishes regular articles in some magazine back East. He says he's working on a novel also."

"I suppose we each have our own gifts. By the way, Eben and I want to have all of you over for supper sometime soon," Maya said. "Our first gathering in our own home."

"That would be lovely. Just let us know when."

"Maybe the weekend after this, once Miss Stenerson gets back? I'd like her to be there."

"Do you still think there might be something between her and your brother?"

Maya lifted her hands with an exaggerated sigh. "I still see looks between them at times, but Ødger goes quiet when I try to ask him about it."

"I'd say that's suspicious. Maybe they are hesitant because of her teaching."

"Do you know what's happening with her aunt?"

"Just that she isn't well, and Helen felt an urgency to go see her." Not for the first time, Amalia sensed a nudge that more lay behind the sudden visit than Helen had said, but she hesitated to pry into the teacher's life. Friend though she'd become these last two years, she still really knew so little about Helen. "Perhaps we'll learn more when she comes back."

"Perhaps so. And maybe you and I should put our heads together on some matchmaking."

Amalia shook her head. "You always did try to get me into trouble."

Ruthie had an idea.

While sluicing down the boardinghouse front porch on Friday afternoon with a bucket of soapy water, Ruthie's thoughts marched in time with the push and pull of her mop. Tante Amalia and Thomi were cleaning the kitchen, giving her plenty of time to think.

Thomi's birthday was coming up in mid-July, only a few weeks away. Shouldn't they do something about that? It was just over a year ago that Amos had brought Thomi to Forsberg House, when she'd been kicked off the train for stowing away. At first they'd thought she was a boy, with her dirty breeches and hair stuffed into that newsboy cap. But it hadn't taken long before they figured out Tommy was actually Thomasina.

Near the beginning, she and Thomi hadn't gotten along so well. But now Thomi felt like a sister—if a sister she still got mad at sometimes. But real sisters would be like that too, wouldn't they? That's what Cousin Maya had told her.

At any rate, Ruthie figured Mr. JJ was the best one to start with, for sharing her idea. And probably the best one to make it happen too. They'd have to come up with something pretty quick, but Mr. JJ would be up to that. She just knew he would.

Ruthie finished scrubbing down the porch and pushed back loosened strands of hair with a wet wrist. She had the cooler job, out here on the porch and getting wet. She'd talk to Mr. JJ before Tante Amalia and Thomi finished the kitchen cleaning. She'd go down the outside entrance to the cellar, not the stairs through the narrow door in the kitchen.

Ruthie rounded the north side of the boardinghouse and hauled open one of the two slanted doors that led to the cellar. They kept canned goods down here in winter, and Mr. JJ would stoke the furnace. But in summer, it made a good place for him to work. Or for Ruthie to talk to him.

Down in the dark coolness of the cellar, she found Mr. JJ making a new dasher for Tante Amalia's butter churn—the old one had broken—in a patch of light that came through the grate high above him, near the coal chute. He looked up when she came down the stairs.

"Well, hello there, little lady." Mr. JJ's grin matched Ruthie's—they were both missing a couple of teeth. "What can I do for you?"

Ruthie perched on the stool where she often sat to watch him work. "I need your help."

"Well, at your service as always, Miss Ruthie. What's the problem?"

"It's not so much a problem." Ruthie leaned her elbows on her knees, chin on her hands. "But I want to do something for Thomi's birthday."

"And when's that?"

"In July. We didn't do anything last year—she had just come then, and she didn't even tell us it was her birthday. But when mine came in November, she told me hers was in July. July thirteenth."

"I see." JJ cupped a piece of sandpaper in his hand and ran it up and down the center dowel of the dasher, up and down. It made a soft rasping sound, smoothing the wood. "And why is this so important to you, Miss Ruthie?"

"Because . . ." Ruthie squirmed a bit on the stool. "Because people haven't always been nice to Thomi. I haven't always been nice."

Mr. JJ glanced at her. "I've never seen you treat her badly, little lady."

"Well, sometimes I felt it inside."

He nodded slowly and set the dasher upright on the floor to check its balance on the base, the round part that would churn up and down in the cream to make butter.

"I want her to feel special. Because she is special, even if she doesn't always feel like it. Don't you think?"

"You're right about that. The good Lord makes each of us unique and gifted in our own way."

"Exactly." Ruthie sat up straight. Her chest felt lighter. "That's what I want Thomi to feel. So what can we do?"

JJ set his sandpaper aside and rubbed his gray beard. "Well, s'pose I could make a batch of ice cream for everybody. The weather is sure to be hot enough for it."

"But we've done that before. I mean, I love ice cream. But I want this to be something *different* and special for Thomi." Ruthie's mouth watered thinking of the fresh peach ice cream JJ had made last summer. "Although, I suppose we could have ice cream *also*."

"So what did you have in mind?"

Ruthie ran her tongue over the spot where a tooth had fallen out earlier that week. "Tante Amalia had a special supper for me on my last birthday, with a cake. And I got presents. But my friend Lisa Miller, she said they play games at her house on their birthdays. Maybe we could do some of all of that."

"Have you talked to your tante Amalia about this?"

"Not yet. She's so busy. And nobody's as good at helping think things out as you are, Mr. JJ."

He chuckled and tested the new dasher inside the churn, then took it out and began trimming the edge just a bit more with his knife. "Well then. What do you think we've thought out here?"

Ruthie tried pushing her tongue through the gap between her teeth. It didn't fit. "I think," she said slowly, unrolling the ideas in her mind like a spool of ribbon. "I think we should surprise Thomi, after supper on her birthday. I'll talk to Tante Malia about it, but I don't think Thomi would want everyone paying attention to her at the big boardinghouse table like at my birthday. Thomi's not shy, exactly—but about some things she is."

"Very thoughtful of you, young lady. So what's my part in all this?"

"You could make the ice cream, and help Hank set up the games and presents and things in the parlor while we're doing the dishes." A bubble of excitement rose in Ruthie's chest. "Then we can take Thomi into the parlor, and all our friends will be in there. We can shout 'Surprise,' and then play games and have dessert." Holding her breath, she looked at Mr. JJ. "What do you think?"

He slid the dasher into the churn, now smooth as the cream it would hold. "Sounds like a right fine plan to me."

"And will you help me and Hank make presents?"

"I'll help however I can." He cocked his head. "But jest now, I do believe I hear your tante calling you."

And so she was, her voice faint from upstairs.

Ruthie hopped off the stool and kissed JJ's whiskery cheek. "Thank you, Mr. JJ."

"You're most welcome, Miss Ruthie."

"And remember, don't say anything about it around Thomi."

"Mum's the word."

Ruthie emerged from the cellar stairs into the kitchen to find Tante Amalia standing by the stove, her crown of braids mussed, a frown on her face red from the heat.

"Where have you been, Ruthie? Our work is not finished."

"Down in the cellar." Ruthie glanced at Thomi, who stood wiping down the table. Was Thomi upset with her too? Her stomach twisted. That certainly wasn't what she wanted. "I needed to ask Mr. JJ something."

"Did you finish the porch?"

"Ja, and I scrubbed it good too."

Tante Amalia sighed and swiped the back of her hand across her sweaty forehead. "All right. You girls take out the buckets of dirty water to the garden now, we don't want any wasted. I'll start fixing supper. But this time come right back, you hear?"

"Yes, ma'am."

Ruthie and Thomi filed out of the kitchen, where they each hefted a wooden bucket of dirty, soapy water, then hauled them out the back door, tipping sideways to balance the weight.

"I'm sorry I made Tante Malia cross." Ruthie shifted her grip on her handle. "I didn't mean to."

Thomi glanced at her, then shrugged and gave a half grin. "It's all right. I think she's just grumpy because of the heat."

Reaching the garden, Ruthie tipped her bucket over at the edge of the rows of bush beans, Thomi doing the same in the strawberry patch. "Next time I'll clean in the hot kitchen, and you can do the porch. It's nicer."

"Turnabout is fair play." Thomi sat back on her heels. "Here comes Magpie."

Ruthie's black-and-white cat picked her way between the garden rows toward them, meowing, the tip of her tail waving above the plants.

"There's my girl." Ruthie stroked her hand over Magpie's smooth black head, then scooped her up for a hug, laying her cheek against the cat's ears. "Did you catch any gophers today?"

"She must be catching a lot." Thomi reached over to scratch the back of Magpie's neck. "Look how fat she's getting."

Ruthie smoothed her hand down Magpie's round side. "Oh! I wonder if she's going to have kittens again."

"Like last year, before I came?" The kittens had been old enough to gambol about by the time Thomi had arrived at the boardinghouse last summer.

"Ja. She got round like this before she had them."

"So the kittens are . . . in there?" Thomi's eyes widened. She stroked Magpie's belly gingerly. The cat arched her head against Ruthie's chin and purred.

"Ja, just like when a cow has a calf." Ruthie cocked her head. "I wonder where the kittens come from. Guess I'll have to ask Tante Amalia."

"Better wait till she's in a better mood, though."

Ruthie giggled. "Ja."

Eleven

"You still haven't told me, Aunt Ophelia."

Helen took her last bite of veal fillet and mushrooms, meeting her aunt's gaze across the polished walnut dining table. Despite it being only the two of them, her aunt insisted supper be served in the dining room each evening, though she acquiesced to the small table in the parlor for other meals.

Aunt Ophelia eyed her and coughed slightly into her white linen napkin. "Told you what?"

"Your health." Helen's fingers tightened on her own napkin in her lap. "It's clear you're not well, and you've told me that much yourself, by letter. But what exactly have the doctors said?" The savory meal settled hard in her stomach.

Aunt Ophelia sat silent a moment, clearing the last bites from her plate with her fork, every movement formed with polished propriety, even if her hand trembled a little. At last she laid down her fork and rang the small bell by her plate.

Mr. Faraday appeared in the door and bowed. "Ma'am?"

"Thank you, Faraday. We have finished."

Helen rose to help her aunt from her chair while two maids slipped into the dining room and began clearing the dishes.

"To the parlor, Aunt?" Helen asked once the elderly woman leaned firmly on her arm, the other gripping her cane.

"The music room, I believe. I should like to hear you play."

But they needed to talk. Helen swallowed the objection and led her aunt toward the music room, lowering her gently to an armchair near the piano.

"Aunt, I really should like to—"

"Play for me first." Aunt Ophelia drew a knitted blanket over her knees despite the warm summer breeze floating through the window. "Please."

Helen straightened her spine and sat down at the piano. At first she played a series of broken chords and awkward scales, her fingers mirroring her unsettlement. Then the music, flawed though it was, began to seep into her muscles and mind, and her hands relaxed, her fingers flowing over the keys like the ripples of the creek at home. She segued into a Mozart Fantasia in D minor, the pensive melody rocking and soothing her like a child. Memories poked up in her mind like stubborn blades of grass . . . all the times she had played for Aunt Ophelia's guests as a girl, entertaining after teas, after luncheons, after suppers. Always playing the dutiful niece, the accomplished young lady. She loved to play, and she knew it pleased her aunt.

Helen played a series of chords, transitioning into the hymn she and Ødger had sung together on the boardinghouse front porch, "Sweet Hour of Prayer." How long ago that Sunday afternoon seemed now, with so many long-ago memories surfacing.

At sixteen, when she had finished the education the local grammar school could offer, Aunt Ophelia had sent her to finishing school, then offered the further training of a women's college. Helen had gladly accepted, at first hoping for the vocation of music teacher. Only when she'd visited a school in a poorer region of the city and seen the educational state of the children there—and the valiant work of enlightening young minds, which the teacher had bravely striven for despite that—had her dream been planted to teach all subjects, at an ordinary school in some small town.

And then she'd seen an advertisement for a schoolteacher in a small town in Iowa, and some thread had tugged at her heart. Because her earliest years had been there? No doubt—yet now she knew her mother, Adelaide, had landed in Iowa only through tragic happenstance. Still, her heart drew her back there.

The last note sounded, and Helen lowered her hands and rested them in her lap.

"That was beautiful, my dear. I've always loved that hymn." Aunt Ophelia's voice came gently through the falling twilight.

Helen turned on the piano bench, smoothing her dark wine-colored skirt over her knees. "How are you feeling this evening?"

"Better, I think. Just tired." Aunt Ophelia used the tip of her cane to indicate the chair across from her. "Come, sit with me."

Helen sat, folding her hands in her lap, her palms dampening. "Will you tell me now, what exactly is wrong?" She firmed her voice. She'd tried and been denied enough times in the past days, her aunt continually diverting her attention, whether with carriage drives, shopping trips—she'd sent her maid with Helen to purchase an entire new autumn wardrobe, over Helen's protests—social visits from the Ladies Aid, or with discussions of Helen's plans for new music and art classes for the fall. In between, she had read more snatches of her mother's diary—which often raised more questions than it answered.

Aunt Ophelia sighed and folded a lace handkerchief between her palms. "I know, my dear. I know I have kept putting you off. Perhaps because . . . I do not wish to dwell on it myself." She met Helen's eyes suddenly, directly, with her brown ones, still dark and clear despite a faint cloudiness in one iris. "I have consumption, just as my sister did. The doctors say it is only a matter of time."

However much she might have suspected, Helen's heart still

caught for an instant, then resumed beating with a dull and painful throb. She swallowed and reached for her aunt's hand. "How long?"

"Who knows? Only the Almighty. They say it could be weeks—or months. Even years." She coughed, that dry, deep cough Helen had heard many times over this visit, even echoing through the hallways at night when she tried to sleep.

"So that is why you asked me to come."

"Well, you were overdue for a visit to your old auntie." A glint came back into Aunt Ophelia's eyes. "But nothing like an ominous word from a physician to get relatives on a train right smart." She gave Helen's hand a quick squeeze.

Helen smiled and shook her head, her eyes pricking. "I was planning to come this summer anyway."

"So you say. But yes . . . when I got the news, I couldn't stop thinking. About all I hadn't told you . . . all I hadn't said." Her gaze rested on Helen, gentle yet pained. "Have you read much of your mother's diary?"

"Some." Helen's middle tightened, and she withdrew her hand. "I read a few scattered entries, then started back at the beginning and have been reading straight through. I—I can't read too much at a time, though." At times, her mother's effusive happiness on the page brought bittersweet tears to her eyes . . . at others, her dark despair weighed Helen's heart with a palpable oppression.

"Yes." Aunt Ophelia glanced toward the twilit window. "I can imagine."

"I've reached the part where she speaks of—of carrying me." Helen's ears warmed. She'd never discussed such topics with her aunt, but she had to ask. "I can't quite make sense of something, though. She writes of—being in the family way—in the fall of 1868, and of expecting her little one in the spring. But I always thought—we always celebrated my birthday in October. And I thought that I was born in 1867. Could she have been confused on the dates? On what year it was? Was that part of her condition?"

The lines on Aunt Ophelia's face appeared to deepen. She sighed heavily and folded her wrinkled hands in her lap, where they quivered slightly.

"Aunt?"

Aunt Ophelia sat silent so long Helen almost wondered if she were falling asleep. When she finally spoke, her words came slowly, thickly, as if from a long ways off. "We always wondered a bit that you were already two years old when your grandfather found you, when your mother had only been gone two years herself."

Helen's scalp prickled. "What? I—what are you saying?"

"We assumed she must have already been with child when she ran off, and that perhaps you were born prematurely. But when I read those entries in her diary this spring . . . I saw the discrepancies. Just as you did."

Helen stared at her aunt's drawn face. Her pulse thudded erratically in her ears.

"I tried to put it out of my mind, explain it away. But I couldn't. So in May, I wrote to the hospital where your mother had been in Independence, and asked if they had any mention of your birth in her medical records, or could find one. Just to put it to rest, in my own mind. They looked into the matter and wrote back with what they discovered. Apparently, after that good-for-nothing abandoned her while she was with child, Adelaide ended up at the Benedict Home for Women, run by the Salvation Army. There was record of her giving birth—but to a stillborn child. In the spring of 1869."

"Stillborn?" The word came choked.

"Yes."

Helen gripped the seat of the chaise longue. The parlor spun dizzily around her. "But . . . what—what does that mean?"

"I don't know." Her aunt's voice trembled. "I didn't want to tell you this, my dear—I knew it would distress you. But when I discovered what I did these last months, between my health and this revelation about your mother—well, I didn't know if I could in good conscience keep it from you, either. Especially her diary, that seemed rightfully yours. I thought perhaps you might not notice the discrepancy with the dates, but I should have known better. You always were our smart girl."

Helen drew a constricted breath. "So . . . if Adelaide's baby was stillborn." Her stiff lips could hardly form the words. "Then—who am I?"

Aunt Ophelia's dark brown eyes met Helen's, full of tears. "You are my dear, dear niece, and nothing can change that." Her voice faltered. "But beyond that—I am truly not sure."

Helen barely slept that night, the warm summer air dampening her hair and cheeks on her pillow . . . when they weren't dampened with tears. What was she to do with this revelation? How to even begin to wrap her mind around it? She—wasn't her mother's child? How could that be? Where had she come from? How had she ended up with Adelaide?

When the parlor clock bonged three, she sat up from another restless doze and pressed her fingertips to her eyes. A slightly cooler breeze shifted the gauzy curtains, and Helen got up and went to her window, breathing in the fragrant summer night air.

"Lord," she whispered into the night. "I knew I never quite fit in anywhere . . . but at least I thought I knew where I came from. Who my family was. But now . . . truly, who am I?" Her throat clogged and she pressed her fingertips to the cool windowsill.

You are mine.

Quick and sure as Aunt Ophelia's response had been, the words came, pressed deep into her heart there in the darkness. She closed her eyes, hot tears slipping down her cheeks. Yet the tight coil that had strangled her chest since last evening's conversation released as an unseen embrace wrapped her, like a soft blanket draped around her shoulders by a loving hand.

Helen lay back down on her bed and slept.

"I need to go home." She found her aunt in her room the next morning, writing letters at her desk in a white lace morning cap.

Aunt Ophelia looked up, her eyes pained. "Must you, so soon?"

"I've been here a full two weeks, Aunt . . ." Helen halted and nibbled her lip. "May I still call you that?"

"You are my family and always will be." Aunt Ophelia sat up straight and thumped her cane on the carpet with a soft thud. "Don't you get any ideas other than that. Have you never heard of adoption? I became your legal guardian not long after your mother was committed, years before she passed away. No one can say any more than that."

Helen released a breath and crossed the room to her aunt and knelt beside her, laying her hand gently on the older woman's frail arm. "Thank you."

Aunt Ophelia coughed, the dry, rattling sound clenching Helen's middle. She nodded at her water glass, and Helen helped her sip once the spasm passed.

"I have one more thing to give you." Her aunt lifted a small box of carved maple out of the recesses of her desk and handed it to Helen. "These are a few personal things of your mother's—the hospital sent them after she passed on, and I've saved them for you. The box is locked, so I have never pried—but they should be yours." She pressed a tiny, tarnished brass key into Helen's palm, closing her fingers over it with a pat. "How I wish I could keep you here with me, my dear." Her aunt met her gaze, but her eyes showed understanding. "But you don't belong here anymore. Do you?"

"I—" Despite the assurance she'd found in the night, Helen's throat squeezed again as she clenched the tiny key. "I don't know where I belong, really. Especially now. How am I to move forward, with so much unknown?"

"You live your life, my dear." Her aunt's voice, though raspy, came stronger now. She pressed Helen's fingers with surprising strength. "Whatever your origins—God's hand has been on your life. You wouldn't be here otherwise." She drew a quavering breath. "The question is, What would He have you do with it now?"

Helen bowed her head, blinking hard.

Her aunt's hand rested on her hair, gentle. "For now, I think you are right. You must go, to this new home you have made for yourself in Green Creek. But know you always have a home here as well—no matter what."

TWELVE

"I think I may have found a place for your field training in ministry this coming year."

"Really, sir?" Ødger stepped into Professor Amundson's office, his heart rate picking up a bit. "Where?"

"Independence, Iowa." The professor smoothed his silver goatee and indicated the chair across from his desk for Ødger, sitting down himself in a capacious armchair. He leaned forward and handed Ødger a letter. "Reverend Bakke of Immanuel Lutheran Church says they'd be very pleased to have you."

"How wonderful." Ødger studied the letter, still slower at making out the English words. He anticipated rejoining Helen's classes this summer for that reason as well as others. "Where is Independence?" He shaped the unfamiliar syllables carefully.

"Something around sixty miles south of here. Not next door, but not the other side of the country, either—or the ocean." His mouth tipped. "It's a thriving community, growing, as is much of Iowa. The Lutheran church has been there since 1861, though not in their own building till ten years later. There are other churches too, of course, the Wapsipinicon Mill, several schools. Even the Iowa Hospital for the Insane."

Ødger looked up. "Really. For those with, how do you say it—illnesses of the mind?"

"Precisely, yes." The professor cocked his head. "Have you a particular interest in that subject?"

"A bit, actually." Ødger clasped his hands between his knees. "I had an aunt, back in Norway, who suffered much. And recently, I accompanied Reverend Larsen on a call, to a family with a troubled son. I keep thinking about him."

"Ah, well, that shows a true pastor's heart." Professor Amundson shook his head. "It is no easy field, mental illness—and no easy answers. But if your interest lies that direction, I believe they have chaplains at the asylum there. I could ask Reverend Bakke to introduce you."

"Thank you, ja. I would be glad to learn more."

"So." The older man folded his hands on his desk and leaned forward. "Shall I respond that you would like to spend this next year in Independence?"

"Ja, I think so. That is . . ." Ødger hesitated. Was he being too hasty? "Perhaps I should think and pray it over a bit more. Where would I board? I will have some saved up from working construction here this summer, but still . . . I must think these things through."

"Certainly. But Reverend Bakke will help with that. He mentions a family who often lets young seminarians board with them, or there is a rooming house in town. You may not be paid anything." He cracked a smile. "But they won't allow you to go hungry either."

Ødger smiled back. "It sounds an ideal situation. I should just like to pray about it, and talk it over with my sister." He thought of Helen, but he had no claim on her as yet, no reason to discuss his future with her. Much though, as he realized more and more, he might want to do so. "May I give you my answer by next week?"

"I suppose so, considering it is Friday. But I wouldn't linger over it any longer than that. Plenty of other eager young divinity students to snatch up an opportunity like this. I offered it to you first because I see much promise in you, young Gunderson." The professor quirked a brow. "And it's not terribly far from home, seeing as you have family here."

"And I thank you." Ødger dipped his head. "I deeply appreciate this, and I will not take long."

The oppressive humidity of late afternoon hit him like a heavy blanket when he stepped out of the cool darkness of the college building. The foreman had let them off work a bit early today, since they'd started at dawn this morning to try to beat some of the heat, so he'd had time to stop in to see Professor Amundson before he left. Lena Amundson had brought cool lemonade and cookies out again this afternoon—a habit she seemed to keep at least once a week, usually twice, for the refreshment of the workmen. She'd told Ødger her father wanted to speak with him.

Leif and Eivor continued to tease Ødger about Lena now and then, but he didn't see anything in her, not really. She was kind and pretty, but she wasn't Helen Stenerson.

His steps slowed as he walked the tree-lined lane, and from more than the muggy heat and weariness from laboring all day in it. When would Helen be back in Green Creek? It seemed far longer than two weeks that she'd been gone. She would return soon, surely. Unless her aunt's condition were worse than she'd known . . . if so, would she even come back for the start of the school year?

Do not worry about tomorrow. Ødger blew out a breath and pulled off his hat, wiping the back of his wrist across his forehead and grimacing at the streak of grimy brick dust. Working all day laying brick for one of the new buildings would do that. He needed a good wash, even before Saturday's usual bathtime.

He stopped at the post office, a small errand he did daily for the magistrate, then finally reached the broad-porched home where they lived, sheltered under the spreading branches of mature trees.

Opening the front door, he stepped to the half-open door of the magistrate's private office and tapped.

"Come in."

"Letter for you, sir." Ødger poked his head in and held out the envelope.

"Ah, thank you." The magistrate looked up from a stack of legal papers and nodded to his desk. "Just place it on the stack there, I'm a bit behind on tending to my mail."

But Ødger held on to the envelope, running his thumb over the smudged postmark. "It's from Italy."

Magistrate Karlsson's bushy gray brows rose. "Italy? I'll take it now, then."

"You think it could be from Thomasina's family?"

"One can hope."

Ødger watched as the magistrate slit the battered envelope with a silver letter opener, his own chest tightening. They'd all become invested in the little girl's story, her search for belonging. And it had been over six months since Amalia wrote, through the magistrate, to the child's grandparents' last known address in Italy.

The magistrate withdrew the sheet of paper and examined it. "It's in Italian."

"Ah." Not surprising, but Ødger's insides deflated. "I don't suppose you speak that, sir?"

"Afraid not. I wonder who might." He tapped his fingers on his desk. "I should have thought of this possibility before."

"You can't predict every turn of events." Sometimes Ødger felt the older man took too much responsibility on his shoulders—for the town, for the family, for everyone. Suddenly something pricked in his mind. "I remember Miss Stenerson mentioning she studied Italian, since she trained to sing some opera. Perhaps we might ask her."

The magistrate's brows rose again. "Excellent. That's something, at least." He pushed back his chair and rose, leaning heavily on his cane. His leg always bothered him most when he'd been sitting for some time. "Absalom left early to pick Miss Stenerson up from the train this afternoon. Suppose we drive the letter out to them now?"

"Really? That is, he did?" Ødger's tongue seemed to trip over itself, his mind spinning. He'd had no idea Helen was coming home today, much less that he might have a chance to see her. "You don't wish to wait until Sunday?" That was their usual day to visit.

"That little girl has been waiting long enough." The magistrate's steely gray eyes twinkled. "And patience has never been my strong point, I'm afraid."

Ødger stared at him a moment, then grinned. "Let me wash up, and I'll hitch the buggy, sir."

They rode in companionable silence down the road toward Green Creek, then through the small town, so much quieter than Decorah, turning down the lane toward Forsberg House as the late afternoon sun gilded fields where farmers would soon begin haying.

Ødger held the reins easy in his hands, letting the gentle rock of the buggy ease his weary limbs and sore muscles, the bay gelding knowing his way over the familiar path.

When they pulled up in front of the three-story boardinghouse, Absalom's buggy already sat outside the barn. Hank waved at them while unhitching the black mare, Maybelle.

Had Absalom just arrived with Helen, then? Ødger jumped down and looped the reins to the hitching post, trying to steady the sudden tremor in his hands. What was the matter with him? He'd seen the teacher nearly every week for over a year now—every day when they both lived at the boardinghouse after he and Maya first arrived. But somehow, with her being gone over a fortnight, his feelings had shifted, deepened. Or had her absence just made him that much more aware of them?

At a grunt from the magistrate, Ødger hurried to the other

side of the buggy, where the older man was attempting to clamber down.

"Sorry, sir." Ødger reached to steady Magistrate Karlsson's arm while he lowered his cane and prosthetic leg, following with his good leg in a final heave.

"Mange takk, son." The older man patted Ødger's arm, then let go and leaned on his cane. "Blasted thing's been acting up more lately."

"Have you spoken to Dr. Armitage?"

The magistrate waved his hand in the air and stumped toward the boardinghouse. "He's got plenty on his hands without bothering over me. I'm all right."

Absalom opened the door before they reached it, grinning. "Thought I saw a familiar buggy out there. Come to join the welcome party?" Chatter and laughter came from within.

"Perhaps." His father smiled and gripped his son's shoulder in greeting. "But we won't intrude for long." He withdrew the letter from inside his jacket pocket. "A letter came from Italy."

"About Thomi?" Absalom's face sobered.

"I assume so. I haven't been able to read it."

Absalom stepped back inside the entryway. "Please come in, both of you. I'll tell Amalia, she and the girls are in the kitchen."

"We'll wait in the parlor, don't want to be in your way." The magistrate headed toward the open parlor door, cane tapping.

Ødger hung back, glancing toward the voices emitting from the kitchen. Was Helen in there? Or had she, more likely, headed upstairs to rest and unpack?

Magistrate Karlsson paused at the parlor doorway and looked back, waiting. Ødger cast one more glance up the empty staircase and followed.

"Ah." The magistrate eased himself into an armchair and leaned back, stretching his bad leg out before him. "I always find this a pleasant room. Amalia has done wonders with this place."

"So I understand." Ødger glanced about. Amalia had to start from scratch when she and Ruthie arrived, since Zelda Berg had sold most of the original furniture. Now the red velvet chaise and various chairs, though simple and some secondhand, were comfortable and neatly maintained, the walnut side tables polished and set with cut-glass lamps. A few good pictures hung on the walls, along with Ruthie's first embroidered sampler. A cooling breeze wafted through the open windows, and on shelves beneath the largest one spread the collection of books Helen had begun—the "boardinghouse library," they called it.

"There's a letter about Thomi?" Amalia appeared in the doorway, still wiping damp hands on her apron.

"Yes, my dear." The magistrate held out the envelope as she sat down beside him.

Amalia opened it with trembling hands, withdrew the sheet of paper. She glanced it over and frowned.

"Yes, I'm afraid it's in Italian."

"So we can't read it?"

"I cannot. Does Thomasina speak any?"

Amalia shook her head, glancing down at the written lines again. "I don't think so, not anymore. She was tiny when they left. She certainly can't read it."

"Your cousin wondered about Miss Stenerson." The magistrate nodded toward Ødger.

Ødger cleared his throat. "I believe she mentioned studying Italian once, in her schooling days. I'm not sure how much she knows."

"Well, it's certainly worth asking. Sounds like more than any of us can do with it. Helen is upstairs, but I'll ask her when she comes down." She carefully refolded the letter and slid it into the envelope. "Will you stay for supper?"

Ødger glanced at the older man, a bubble of hope rising in his chest.

But the magistrate shook his head. "We won't trouble you with extra mouths to feed unannounced. We'll just leave the letter with you, and we can talk more on Sunday." He pushed to his feet.

Swallowing his disappointment, Ødger stood also and nodded to Amalia as she rose. "Did Miss Stenerson have a good trip?" Mentally he shook his head at himself. One would think he was a lovesick schoolboy.

"I believe so." Amalia led the way out into the entryway. "She hasn't said much yet."

"Suppose you ask her yourself."

At the familiar voice, Ødger looked up to see Helen descending the last steps of the stairs. His breath caught in his chest. Though tired lines etched her forehead, her eyes smiled blue as ever, her blond hair swept up into its usual soft, neat bun on top of her head. A few curls now framed her forehead—a new style she'd learned back East?

Ødger tried to speak a greeting, but it croaked in his throat. Ears burning, he cleared it. Heaven help him, he was a goner—to borrow Leif Benson's wording. "Velkommen tilbake," he managed at last. "Welcome back."

Helen smiled at him. "Mange takk. It is good to be back. How are you, Ødger?"

When had he turned into a bumbling fool? "Well, thank you. How did your journey?"

"It was . . . enlightening." A shadow seemed to cross her face, and she passed her hand over her forehead as if to brush it away.

"You said your aunt seems stable for now?" Amalia asked.

"Yes, though I'm afraid the doctors say she has consumption." Helen sighed, fingering the carved end of the banister. "It's hard to know how long she has."

"I'm so sorry." Ødger met her eyes, hoping she could see how much she meant it.

"As are we all." Amalia took a step closer to her friend. "Will you need to go back again before the school year begins?"

"For now, she insists I continue on with life as usual. But I'll be in communication with her housekeeper, Mrs. Hoskins, as well as my aunt. In case things take an unexpected turn." Helen drew a breath and came down the final step. "For now, I'm ready to dive back into starting my summer classes." Her gaze sought Ødger's, something he couldn't quite read in her blue eyes. "You are still interested?"

"Ja, of course." He clasped his hands behind him and smiled, hoping his enthusiasm didn't come out too strong.

"Oh, Helen, we want to ask you." Amalia clasped the letter in both her hands. "Do you read Italian?"

"A little." The teacher raised her brows. "Why?"

"We've had a letter from Thomasina's family—at least, we think so. Someone in Italy, anyway. Ødger thought he remembered you knew some."

Helen glanced at Ødger, then held out her hand for the letter. She scanned the lines, her forehead pinched.

"Can you read it?" Amalia twisted her hands in her apron.

"It's been so long, and I mostly used it for reading opera librettos. But I can make out some of it." Helen lifted her head. "Where is Thomi?"

"In the kitchen. Shall I get her?"

"No—I don't think so. Not right now." Helen folded the letter. "May I take this up to my room? I have an old Italian grammar book in my trunk, I think. I'd like to take time to properly translate it as much as I can. I don't want to misconstrue the meaning—this is too important."

"Right, my dear. You are very wise." Magistrate Karlsson nodded to Ødger. "Shall we?"

"You're sure you won't stay?" Amalia asked.

Ødger glanced back at Helen, saw the weariness around her eyes. And knew the magistrate was right. "Nei, but takk. Helen needs rest, and you all have enough to handle tonight. We will look forward to seeing you all Sunday."

Helen smiled and tipped her head. "Perhaps we can discuss the classes some more then. I hope to start next week and would value your input on the music."

"Till Sunday, then." Ødger gave her a slight bow and fairly floated out the door after Magistrate Karlsson.

"So, it's Miss Stenerson, is it?" The magistrate chuckled and settled back against the seat as Ødger turned the horse out of the Forsberg House lane.

Ødger's hands tightened so suddenly on the reins that the gelding tossed his head with a snort of protest. "Beg pardon, sir?"

"I've been trying to make out which young woman you've had your eye on. Call me a meddling old man, but I like to keep my finger on what matters to those in this town—particularly those I care about." He patted Ødger's trouser-clad knee.

Ødger scratched his cheek, resisting the heat rising under his beard. "Am I that obvious?"

"Tonight? Yes." Magistrate Karlsson chuckled again. "I hadn't discerned it in previous interactions with Miss Stenerson, however, so you've been curbing yourself well enough."

Ødger sighed and leaned his head back. "I didn't know she was coming back today—then seeing her again after all this time . . ."

"Ah yes, a fortnight is an age to a man in love." The magistrate sighed, then pushed his spectacles up his prominent nose. "Well, you couldn't do better, lad. She's a fine young woman, a gifted teacher, respected by all in the community."

"Most, at least." Ødger thought of Mrs. Flinch. "At least those worthy of her." Was he—worthy of her, that is? His chest tightened.

"She'd make a fine minister's wife. Though you are aware, of course, that she cannot marry or even keep official company with a man while under her teaching contract."

His heart thudded. "What—why?"

"It's a common enough regulation. Of course, that doesn't keep female teachers from marrying. They simply have to stop teaching when they do."

Ødger turned onto the main road through Green Creek, the summer evening sunlight still gleaming golden through the trees. He shifted his jaw. Helen couldn't keep teaching if she married him? Had that been the rule in Norway as well? He'd no idea, having never had reason to care, though he remembered learning from both men and women teachers as a child.

"Of course, we're forgetting the most important question of all."

Ødger swallowed. "Yes, sir?"

The magistrate bumped Ødger in the ribs with his elbow. "Why, what the young lady thinks of you."

THIRTEEN

A pleasure, to work in Italian again.

Sitting at her desk in her room on Sunday afternoon, Helen dipped her pen and wrote out the next phrase, carefully translating from the smudged and blurred lines of the letter. So many miles these words had traveled to get here . . . across train tracks in Europe, over the Atlantic Ocean, then more railroads here in America. Through salty wind and heavy rain, by the look of the envelope and edges of the paper. Yet it had come, here to Forsberg House in Green Creek, Iowa.

To young Thomasina Benetti. But how would she receive it?

Helen's throat tightened as she penned the nearly final line. She wasn't sure what Thomi's hopes were, for hearing from her family . . . yet she sensed this letter might hold some disappointment for the little girl.

And that ached her heart, tender from her own recent revelations.

Helen finished her translation, imperfect though it felt, and set her pen in its stand, leaving the newly copied letter open to dry while she folded the original and tucked it inside its stained and spotted envelope. Gratitude for her girlhood Italian lessons swept over her . . . another blessing from Aunt Ophelia, and part of her music studies at finishing school and college.

Helen steepled her fingers against her lips and glanced about her room. The air pressed stuffily, despite the open window, though today's cloud cover had lowered the temperature a bit. She'd stayed home from the town Independence Day celebrations yesterday to rest and unpack, more weary from this trip's discoveries than from the travel itself. Though she found herself trying not to think too hard about what Aunt Ophelia had told her, the questions kept cropping up, whether waking or sleeping.

Who were her parents—really? How had she ended up in Adelaide's care? Did she have other family—somewhere? How could she possibly find out?

She should look in that box of her mother's, at some point. Perhaps it might hold some clue. But she hadn't managed to find the mental energy or motivation—not yet.

Helen sighed and swiped a finger under the fringe of curls Winifred had insisted on cutting over her forehead while at Aunt Ophelia's. Bangs, she said they were called—all the fashion these days, but Helen couldn't see much use for them other than increasing perspiration, at least in midsummer.

She lifted the letter and waved it lightly in the air to ensure the ink had fully dried. Everyone else had doubtless gathered on the porch right now per their Sunday afternoon custom after dinner, and with her withdrawal from company yesterday, she should go and be sociable for a while. And perhaps find a chance to speak privately with Thomasina.

Stepping out into the hallway, Helen headed for the stairway, then stepped back as Thomasina herself came pelting up the stairs. The little girl halted near the top, seeing Helen.

"Oh. Hello, Miz Stenerson."

"Hello, Thomi. Where are you off to in such a hurry?"

"I was going to get my marbles. Hank says his are better'n mine, but I've got a fine one from Mr. Nygard at the mercantile, and another'n that a boy at the children's home gave me."

Helen smiled. Thomi never let anyone get ahead of her, including boys, or at least didn't take it sitting down. "Might I speak with you a moment first?" It wouldn't be often the two of them could be alone like this.

Thomi eyed Helen, then shrugged. "Sure."

Heading back down the hallway toward her room, Helen beckoned.

Thomi followed into Helen's bedroom and plunked onto the bed, bouncing slightly on the blue-and-white quilt. She hadn't been in here since that day Helen let the girls look through her trunk . . . and they found her baby bracelet. A sudden catch at her heart froze Helen's limbs a moment. That bracelet—the etched "Primrose." Had that been a clue all along, that her origins held a different story than she'd always thought?

Helen drew a breath and gave her head a shake to clear the sudden fog. She'd have to deal with that later. Forcing a smile at Thomi, Helen fetched the original letter from her desk, then sat down on the bed beside the little girl, both letters between her hands.

"What're those?" Thomi's bouncing stilled.

"A letter, Thomi. For you, from Italy."

She felt rather than heard the child's slight intake of breath. Rather than reaching for the letter, Thomi folded her hands tight in her lap. "Why do you have it? I thought Tante Amalia wrote to them."

Something warmed in Helen to hear Thomi use that familiar moniker for Amalia. "She did—well, through Magistrate Karlsson, since he has so many connections, and an official name. But the response was written in Italian, see?" Helen pulled out the original battered page and handed it to Thomi. "Can you read Italian?"

The little girl took the page gingerly between her fingers and studied the lines. She gave her dark, curly head a quick shake.

"We didn't think so." Helen kept her voice gentle, level. "But I can—at least some. I studied Italian in school."

Thomi jerked her head up. "Why?"

"Because I studied music, and much great music is written in Italian. And I always enjoyed it—it's such a beautiful language."

"I only remember a little bit, from what my papa used to talk." Thomi shoved the letter back at Helen, crumpling one corner a bit. "What's it say?"

"I wrote out a translation the best I could, here." Helen held out the fresh, crisp sheet of paper. "Would you like to read it yourself, or have me read it to you?"

Thomi folded her arms across her pinafore. "You."

Lord, give her grace to hear this. Helen smoothed the sheet out and began.

"Dear Magistrate Karlsson and Mrs. Absalom Karlsson,

Thank you for your letter regarding our granddaughter, Thomasina Benetti. We were grateful to have news, as we had heard nothing from our son and his family for nearly six years, when he wrote that his wife had died."

Helen glanced at Thomi. So she had her mother until she was about four—but Thomi had never mentioned her. The little girl just tucked her hands between her knees, her brown eyes boring into the letter as if she yearned to see beyond to those who had sent it.

"We were distressed to hear that Thomasina had been left at an orphanage, but we thank God she has now found a home with good people who care for her. Our hearts are heavy to know that our son has left his daughter and not returned, but we pray to God that he may find his fortune and come back for her. We regret to say we do not have the health or funds to either come to or send for our granddaughter, nor do we have any other relatives able or willing to come to America at this point." Helen gentled those last words as much as she could, then touched Thomi's arm. "They included a special note for you here at the bottom, dear one. *'Thomasina, be a good girl and always remember to say your prayers. May God*

watch over and keep you always, nostra gioia.'" Helen glanced at Thomi. "Do you know what that means?"

Thomi nodded, blinking hard. A tear glimmered, caught in her dark lashes. "Umm . . . joy?"

"Yes. They call you their joy." Helen hesitated, then slipped her arm around the little girl's slender shoulders. Thomi tensed, but she didn't pull away. Questions clamored on Helen's tongue, but she bit them back. Thomi didn't need that . . . not now. They sat together in silence a moment, a bird trilling from outside Helen's open window. At last Helen felt a faint release in Thomi. The muscles of her shoulders and back relaxed, and she leaned ever so slightly against Helen.

"Do you remember your grandparents?" Helen asked softly.

Thomi sat silent a moment longer. "A little bit. I remember picking grapes with my nonna, and eating bread dipped in olive oil. I remember my nonno beating olives down from a tree. I remember saying good-bye, and my mamma crying." She picked at a loose thread on her pinafore pocket.

"How old were you then, do you know?"

"Three. Times got too hard for farmers, my papa said. Because of the government." Thomi drew in a breath, then let it out in a long, shuddering sigh.

Helen gave her a slight squeeze. "I'm glad you can remember your grandparents. I never knew mine at all."

"Why not?" Thomi rubbed her nose and sniffed, pulling away from Helen to sit back a bit.

"Well . . . it's complicated." Helen sighed. "But my mother died when I was young also, and my aunt raised me."

Thomi eyed her. "Well, you seemed to turn out pretty good."

A laugh burbled up from Helen's chest. "Thank you."

"I just wish I would get a letter from my papa." Thomi's voice quivered.

Helen's chest ached at the rare vulnerability. "I know. And we will keep praying for that. But in the meantime . . . we love you here, Thomi. Tante Amalia, Onkel Absalom. Ruthie, Hank. Me. One thing I'm learning is . . . wherever people love us, we can be home."

Thomi nodded, but something closed back over the openness in her eyes.

Enough moralizing, schoolmarm. Helen stood and smoothed out her skirt. "Would you like to keep both letters?"

Thomi nodded and took the envelope and the translated sheet, holding them against her chest.

"Why don't you put them in a safe place in your room, then let's head down where it's cooler. Besides, isn't Hank still waiting to see your superior marbles?"

With a slight grin, Thomi dashed out the door, her feet pattering down the hallway toward her room.

Helen followed, closing her door behind her, then fingered her cameo as she headed down the stairs. Forsberg House truly had become a sheltering place for orphans, of all ages and backgrounds. Yet would Thomi ever truly let herself feel at home here?

"So we don't know much more than before," Amalia said a short while later, sitting on the porch swing beside Helen. She gazed thoughtfully at Thomi, now shooting marbles with Hank in the dirt near the bottom of the porch steps. Ruthie watched from a few steps above, stroking Magpie, while Dog flapped his tail in the dust near Hank.

"Well, we know her grandparents are alive, and that Thomi will be staying here for now. At least that's a bit more stability." Absalom reached for a bunch of cherries from the bowl Amalia had set on the porch railing for everyone to share.

"I did learn a bit more from Thomi herself just now," Helen said. "She told me she remembers her grandparents, and Italy, at least a little. And that her father said they left because the government was making things too hard for the farmers."

"I've read about that a bit, the economic downturn of 1887." Absalom nodded. "Started a huge wave of Italian immigrants coming to America."

"And not always welcomed as they should be, I fear." Magistrate Karlsson shook his head. "But such has been the case for each new group who reaches America's shores, I'm afraid—the Irish, the Chinese. I hope someday we will learn we are all God's children and need one another."

"Did you read about those awful lynchings of Sicilians in New Orleans this March?" Absalom lowered his voice, but Amalia still shook her head at him.

"Shh. The children."

He tipped his head and said nothing more.

"I just hope that ugliness doesn't keep coming against Thomi, or the boardinghouse." Amalia turned toward Helen, her hand tracing her rounding belly. The baby was growing more and more obvious as the summer progressed. "Has there been any more trouble with the Flinches, Helen?"

"Not except for that confrontation with Mrs. Flinch at church several weeks ago. But then, I haven't been around much, and school is out."

Amalia nodded, pushing her feet gently on the porch floorboards to sway the swing. "I wonder if there's some way for the boardinghouse to do something to bring the community together."

Absalom leaned against the porch railing. "You mean, go on the offense rather than the defense?"

"Something like that."

"What do you have in mind?" At the strum of a guitar, Helen glanced over to where Ødger sat on the other side of the porch, tuning his instrument and chatting with Erik, who sat nearby. Something tugged in her middle, drawing her toward the seminary student and his music.

"I don't know. A gathering at harvesttime perhaps? A charity bazaar? Something for people to focus on that does good for the town, and helps us see we're all not that different after all." She sighed.

"You mustn't push yourself too hard, especially this year." Absalom nudged his glasses up his nose. "You shoulder too much as it is."

"Your husband is right, you know." Glad he was being protective, Helen patted Amalia's arm, then stood. "Here, I'll let him sit with you for a while."

"Well, perhaps we'll just think and pray about it for now. But I don't want to just let this undercurrent of gossip and prejudice keep simmering."

"You cheated!" At the shout from the steps, Helen stepped toward the marble game, which Ruthie had now also joined. Thomi sat glaring at Hank, arms crossed.

"Did not." Hank tossed his head, his hair growing shaggy again.

"Then how do you win every time?"

Hank shrugged. "Not my fault if I'm good."

Thomi's face reddened.

Helen bit her lip, watching them. Last summer, Ruthie had often been the one left out, Thomi and Hank finding an easy bond, perhaps due to their rough upbringings. Now Thomi and Hank seemed to be clashing more of late. But as in the classroom, she wouldn't interfere unless necessary. These growing young people needed to learn to sort things through on their own.

"But I saw you," Ruthie piped up. "You touched that last one with your thumb."

"Did not." Hank scowled at her.

"See?" Thomasina flung out her arms. "Cheater!"

Hank sighed and dragged his hands over his face. "Why do I even try to play with you girls?"

Ruthie sat up on her knees. "How about a rematch, then? If we can't agree?"

Helen hid a smile. Bless Ruthie, ever the peacemaker.

"Fine." Thomasina regathered the marbles into the circle drawn in the dirt. "But we'll be watching you, Hank."

Chuckling to herself, Helen crossed the porch to where Ødger sat picking out the tune of an unfamiliar hymn. She looped her hand around the porch pillar next to the steps. "I don't believe I know that tune."

Ødger glanced up and smiled at her, the look in his eyes making her heart stutter. "It was new to me also. It is called, 'Just as I Am.' Reverend Larsen wanted to use it in last week's service, so since I have been playing the piano for church while you were gone, I learned it. And I like it."

He continued plucking, but began softly to sing.

"Just as I am, without one plea,
But that Thy Blood was shed for me,
And that thou bidst me come to Thee,
O Lamb of God, I come, I come!"

Helen leaned against the porch pillar, sudden tears pricking her eyes, though she hardly knew why. Not seeming to notice, Ødger played on, his rich baritone voice gaining strength as he sang.

"Just as I am, though tossed about
With many a conflict, many a doubt,
Fightings and fears within, without,
O Lamb of God, I come, I come!"

Many a conflict, many a doubt . . . that was her heart just now. Helen swiped a finger under her eyes as Ødger finished playing, humming through another verse. "That's beautiful. I'm surprised I've never heard it before."

"Written by a woman poet, apparently, and one who struggled

with chronic illness. Charlotte Elliott." Ødger strummed a cadence of chords.

"Thank you for filling in to play the piano for me while I was gone." Helen drew a steadying breath. "I hope that wasn't too much trouble."

"Music is never trouble to me." He cast her a gentle grin. "I think you understand that?"

She smiled back. "Indeed." The pull of his blue-gray eyes grew too strong, and she glanced away, her heart hammering. Erik had moved away, leaving the two of them apart from the others. "So. You and Maya are ready to join the summer classes, if I start this Tuesday?"

"Ja." Ødger nodded to where his sister rocked and visited with Amalia, Torvald playing with wooden blocks at her feet while Erik helped him stack them. "At least, I am, and I will do my best to drag my sister along with me." He met Helen's gaze again. "You still wish to add music this summer?"

"I'm still trying to figure that out." Helen tapped her fingers on the railing. "I don't want to take away time from the reading and writing, since I know people need that. I wondered about adding an extra class on Saturday evenings, perhaps alternating music and art, for those who want to come. What do you think?"

Ødger stopped playing and stroked his bearded chin. "Ja, that could work. Perhaps some simple musical instruction, then learning some group songs?"

"That sounds ideal." Helen's fingers tingled at the thought. "You would be willing to help?"

"Ja, of course, with the music." He flexed his fingers and chuckled. "I'm afraid I will be no good at the art."

"I have another expert for that." Helen turned her head and called down the steps. "Hank!"

"Yes'm?" Hank looked up from scrambling after an errant marble.

"Would you be willing to assist me with a drawing class, perhaps every other Saturday evening? As part of the summer classes."

Hank tipped his head to the side, scrunching his nose. "For kids or grown-ups?"

"Whoever wants to learn."

He chewed his lip a moment, then shrugged. "Sure. Whatever you want."

Thank you, Father. How far they had come since last summer, when Hank hotly resisted any attempt to get him inside the schoolhouse at all. Helen turned back to Ødger with lifted brows.

He balanced his guitar on his knees and grinned at her. "So we have a plan."

Helen smiled back, her heart lighter than since she'd gotten the letter from Aunt Ophelia.

She could scarcely wait for Tuesday evening.

Fourteen

"So how was your trip?"

Seated across from Helen at Eben and Maya's new puncheon dining table the next Saturday evening, Ødger studied her face, awaiting her answer to his question. He'd tried to hide his delight when Maya indicated this seat for him at the supper table. Did his sister suspect his intentions?

"It was . . ." Helen wiped her fingers on her napkin and gave her head a slight shake. "I hardly know how to answer that."

A bit of a strange reply. But Ødger gave her time, taking another bite of Mrs. Miller's fried chicken and savoring the crispy skin and succulent meat. Everyone had contributed to this meal—the chicken from Mrs. Miller, bread from the boardinghouse, and Maya provided new potatoes and peas from the garden, along with dessert.

"Did you enjoy your time with your aunt, or is she too ill?" Perhaps a more specific question would help, a tactic he'd noticed Rev. Larsen employ in visits to congregants.

"We had some pleasant times together. She even took me to the Cincinnati Music Hall one evening." A smile touched Helen's lips. "I thought it would be too much for her, but she insisted."

"Ah! What did you hear?"

"Just a concert, but it was lovely. It had been so long since I heard live orchestral music."

"My father took me to hear the philharmonic in Bergen once when I was a boy. Edvard Grieg was artistic director then." Ødger drew a long breath, remembering. "I will never forget it."

Helen's eyes widened. "Grieg? He is quite a composer. What a treat that must have been."

"Ja." Ødger smiled at her. "Who are your favorite composers?"

"Bach, always."

"But he is mine." Ødger set his fork down and leaned forward. "There is none like him, I feel—his artistic mastery and understanding of each instrument, but also—how do you say it? The heart behind his music, it throbs through. I can truly feel that he dedicated each piece to the glory of God."

"I never thought of it quite like that, but you're right." Helen tipped her head. "At times when I was growing up, it seemed only playing Bach could calm my soul. Though I love Mozart too, and I've played plenty of Chopin and Schumann."

"So you grew up playing piano, then? At your aunt's home?"

"Yes, she has a grand one. A small organ also, though I always played piano more."

"It is a pity the boardinghouse has no piano." Ødger passed the bread to Amalia on his other side. "Then you could play more often than at church."

"That's true, that would be a nice addition to our parlor," Amalia put in. "But I don't know where we'd get the funds for a piano right now."

"That's all right. Though I do miss it at times, I'm grateful to still have a chance to play at all." Helen smiled up a thanks as Maya refilled her water glass. "And I have little time to play for recreation during the year, with teaching."

"Have you ever seen the organ at Luther College? They have a fine one. Someone let me have the privilege of playing it once earlier this summer." Somehow saying *who* had let him stuck on Ødger's tongue. Not that there would be anything awkward about mentioning Lena Amundson—would there?

"I haven't. I should love to hear you play sometime, though." Pink tinged Helen's cheeks, as if she feared being too forward.

Beneath the table, Ødger clenched his hands on his thighs to quench the urge to reach across the table and brush back the golden curls that fell gently over her forehead. *Get ahold of yourself, Gunderson.*

"Always did like to hear a good pipe organ myself. Want some butter?" On the other side of Ødger, JJ passed the butter dish, then spread his portion liberally on his cornbread. "Can't play a lick on any instrument, though. Nor much good at singin'. Not like you talented young folks."

"I've heard you carry a tune very nicely, JJ." Helen smiled across the table at the older man. "And as for me, I couldn't carve something out of wood if my life depended on it. We all have different gifts."

"That's sure and certain, and the Almighty knows what he's about. But I surely do enjoy appreciatin' others' gifts too. And learnin' more of my own—why, now that young Ruthie and Hank taught me my letters last summer, I kin make out more an' more words all the time. Read myself an article in the newspaper just t'other day, though it took me a good while."

"That's wonderful, JJ." Helen fairly beamed. "Do let me know if there's ever any way I can help."

"Well now." JJ wrinkled his brow. "I've always wanted to read those books you have in the parlor, Miss Helen, with the gold letters on the covers. But I don't rightly know if any of them'd be fittin' for me as yet. If you might take a look at them with me some evenin', I'd be much obliged."

"Of course. And, JJ, I don't know why I haven't thought of this before—but you'd be welcome in my summer classes, if you ever want to join. We only started this week."

"Ja." Ødger turned toward the older man. "Miss Stenerson is a fine teacher. I would not have made nearly the progress in English I have without her classes, last summer and this."

"I don't doubt it." JJ tugged at his gray beard. "Jest figured an old codger like me didn't have much business in a schoolroom."

"We have students of all ages, from older children through farmers and up to a grandmother who came with her family from Norway last year." Helen spread her hands. "You'd fit right in."

JJ gave a nod. "I'll think on it."

Maya stepped up behind Ødger's chair, a squirming Torvald on her hip. "Someone would like some time with his onkel."

"Ah, would you, young man?" Ødger pushed his chair back from the table, having already cleared his plate. "Come to your onkel Ødger."

Maya swooped the baby toward him, and Ødger caught him under the arms and nuzzled his chubby neck with his beard, making Torvald chortle.

"Mange takk." Maya sighed and rolled her shoulders. "He's teething and wants to be constantly held—a bit difficult when giving a supper party."

"Everything is lovely, Maya." Helen smiled up at her. "You must let us help with the dishes after."

Maya waved her hand. "We've been wanting to have you all over since we got married. This is a joy. And no talk of dishes yet—we still have dessert." With a mouthed "takk" at Ødger, she stepped away toward the kitchen.

Torvald reached after her with a whimper. "Moh?"

"She'll be back, you young rascal." Ødger turned the baby around to stand on his lap, facing him. "So. Where are those teeth? Show me those teeth." He tickled under the baby's drooly chin, earning a toothy grin. Torvald giggled and bounced on Ødger's lap, clapping his hands. "Ouch." Ødger winced as the small feet pummeled his thigh muscles. "He's got strong legs."

"Is he walking yet?" Helen asked. "I don't know how much I've missed being gone."

"Not yet, but soon, Maya thinks. He walks holding on to furniture." The baby grunted and twisted beneath Ødger's hands, squirming to get down. "And I think he heard me." Ødger chuckled and stood. "All right, young sir, let's go for a walk. Please to excuse us."

"Of course. You are a good uncle."

Something in Helen's voice caught Ødger's ear, and he turned, baby in his arms, to catch a look in her eyes he'd never seen before. She glanced away almost as soon as their eyes met, but it was there. Was it the baby? Was she thinking of her own someday? Or . . .?

His heart suddenly thumping at the hopes and images that sprang to his own mind, Ødger set Torvald down just outside the circle of chairs around the table and let the almost-toddler walk his way along them, holding on from one chair back to another. They circled behind Amalia, the magistrate at the foot of the table, Absalom next to his father, then Helen, Ruthie and Thomi, Erik, and Eben and Mr. Miller sharing the host's place at the head. Ødger was frankly surprised they'd all managed to fit at one table. Next came Mrs. Miller, Hank, JJ, and back to his own spot. Ødger sat back down and hauled Torvald up into his lap.

"Have a nice walk?" Helen spoke to the baby, not to him.

Torvald reached for Ødger's spoon and stuck it in his drooly mouth.

"Guess that is his now."

Helen laughed, and Ødger's chuckle mingled with hers, warming and easing the air between them.

"Dessert," Maya announced as she and Mrs. Miller carried in plates of raspberry pie, met by cheers from the children and groans from the adults. But despite claiming they couldn't eat any more, the men and women nevertheless settled in with their slices of pie.

Ødger alternated feeding himself and Torvald bites of the ruby-filled pastry till the baby's head drooped forward in sleep.

"You are good with children," Helen said softly.

"Grew up with a houseful of little brothers and sisters." Ødger shifted Torvald into the crook of his arm, the baby's head heavy against his chest. "How about you?" He hadn't heard Helen mention any family other than her aunt.

"No, I was an only child. I spent much time alone, with my books or my music." Something shifted in her face, but then she smiled. "Perhaps that's why I was drawn to teaching. I spend my days surrounded by children who are never still, and then I can appreciate the quiet of my room once more."

"You manage your classroom well, from what I see." Ødger chuckled. "Though you should be glad you did not have me as a student when I was a boy."

Helen arched a brow at him and lifted a forkful of pie. "I hope you're not questioning my authority as a teacher, young sir."

"I would not think of it." He put on his most innocent expression.

She laughed, her blue eyes sparkling. "I can see you must have been a troublemaker."

Ødger rolled his eyes. "You need only ask my sister and my cousin. I think I got in trouble more than the rest of the family put together."

"So from class clown to the ministry." Helen tipped her head. "Why?"

"Ah, well, that is a big question." Ødger shifted the baby's weight a bit, Torvald's head growing sweaty against his shirtsleeve despite the breeze through the open doors of Eben and Maya's hilltop home. "I think I always wanted adventure, to do something . . . important. But I could not seem to find what that might be. Then, when I was a teen, a missionary to the Zulu people in southern Africa spoke at our church in Bergen. He told of mighty works of God and the faith of the people there. For the first time, I felt my eyes were opened, that God did not belong only to stone churches and long-ago stories, but was truly alive and at work in our world today." He shrugged and gave a half grin. "I wanted to be part of that. So from then on, I studied toward becoming a minister."

"And you attended seminary in Norway?"

"Ja, the School of Mission and Theology in Stavanger. When we first came to Iowa, I did not realize Luther College no longer has a full seminary. But since they do train students in preparation for the ministry, and I had already attended two years in Norway, we have made it work."

Maya approached the table. "Mange takk for holding him."

"Always glad to." Ødger stood to transfer Torvald, heavy and warm with sleep, into his mother's arms. The baby yawned and twisted his head against Maya's shoulder, settling again without opening his eyes. Around them the magistrate, Absalom, and Amalia stood, the children having already been excused to play outside in the cooling evening light.

Helen pushed back her chair also. "This has been so lovely, Maya. Thanks to you and Eben for having us all over."

"It has been a pleasure." Maya stood swaying, slumbering baby in her arms, in the unconscious rhythm of mothers the world over. "Takk for coming."

Helen began clearing the dishes, helping Amalia.

"Nei, you needn't do that," Maya protested.

Amalia gave her cousin a look. "Are we going to listen to that sort of nonsense, Helen?"

Helen smiled, stacking saucers. "Certainly not."

"Mrs. Miller is already starting the dishes in the kitchen. You go lay Torvald down while the men visit, and we will have that kitchen cleaned up in no time."

Ødger joined the men on the shaded front porch, its boards still newly sanded and smelling of sawdust, as Eben had added it only last month.

"Fine work." Ødger ran his hand along the railing and nodded to Eben. "You should have had us all come help you put it up, though."

"Erik helped me a couple days, my brother too." Eben patted a post with a loving hand. "Didn't take long, nothin' like the whole house that everyone helped us with last fall. Now that was a right neighborly comin' together. 'Sides, I know you've been mighty busy with the construction at the college. How's that goin'?"

Eben seemed to have gotten more talkative since he got married. What changes might matrimony work in *him*, if he managed to take that step? Batting away the thought, Ødger nodded. "It's coming along well. We're continuing to do finishing work on the main building, then also building dormitories, even with heat and indoor plumbing."

Eben shook his head. "Progress sure keeps a'comin'. You'll have to tell me more about those newfangled features sometime."

"Be glad to." Ødger smiled to see Ruthie and Thomi playing with a new batch of kittens from the Miller barn. On the other side of the porch, the magistrate and Absalom visited with Mr. Miller. "So, how do you find married life?"

A gentle grin spread over Eben's face. "Maya and me, we'd a long road to walk gettin' this far—you know that better'n most. Now seems we're settlin' into each other, so to speak. Findin' our way easy like. Not that we don't come upon a rock or two in the path now and then, you might say. But seems with patience and listenin' to each other—and the Lord—we find our way to movin' forward again." His face sobered, and he glanced at Ødger. "I don't take it lightly, your sister trustin' me after all she's been through. I give you my word I'll do my best to make the rest of her days as lovin' and peaceable as I can, God helpin' me."

Ødger patted Eben's broad shoulder. "I know you will, my friend. She is truly blessed to have you for a husband." He noted the patient lines on Eben's face, his heart squeezing with gratitude. This man had taken on no small challenge, wooing and wedding his sister after her dark season of grief—losing her husband and then her child, albeit being gifted another. Would Ødger have had the faith and grace for such a step, almost-clergyman though he was? But God gave each his or her own path to walk, with challenges and gifts uniquely suited. He should know that by now.

Question was, What was his?

Ødger clapped Eben's shoulder once more, then released his grip. "You know we are always here for you, should you have any need, my friend."

Eben grinned. "And the same goes for you. Speakin' of, do you still want to join the threshin' team again next month?"

"Ah." Ødger ran a hand down the side of his beard. "Forgive me, I have meant to talk to you about that. I did want to, but now it seems I will be sent to a town called Independence." He had given Professor Amundson his answer, though the thought of leaving still sent a hitch into his chest. But how could he say no to such an opportunity?

"Independence in Iowa?"

"Is there more than one?"

Eben chuckled. "At least one in Kansas and another in Missouri, far as I know. Maybe more."

Ødger shook his head and laughed too. "You Americans do like your independence. But I am sorry the preparations will likely keep me from the threshing team."

"Not to worry." Eben nodded at Amalia's brother, who had just come out on the porch. "Erik here said he'd like to join this year, so he can fill your place."

"Mange takk, cousin." Ødger met Erik's eyes, glad when his cousin looked back straight into his own. Perhaps the shadow of prison shame was finally lifting from this young man he'd grown up with like a brother.

Erik nodded. "I look forward to seeing how that steam engine works."

Amalia and Absalom emerged next through the screen door, followed by Helen, Maya, and Mr. and Mrs. Miller.

"Ruthie, Thomi, Hank. Time to go." Amalia embraced Maya. "Mange takk for having us. This was lovely."

"We must do it again. Soon, before the baby." Maya came and stood next to Eben on the porch. He looped his arm around her, and she leaned her head against his chest as the family began making their way across the farmyard toward the fence that marked the line between the Miller farm and the Forsberg House property.

Ødger lingered back a bit, waiting while Helen thanked the Millers and bid them good-night. She arched a brow as she came down the steps toward him at last.

"You didn't have to wait for me."

"I wanted to." He swallowed. "That is, if you do not mind?"

She tipped her head in acknowledgment, a faint flush on her cheeks—or was that just from the rosy glow of the sunset?

Ødger glanced away to give her a moment as they fell into step side by side, gazing at the western clouds blushing fiery pink and orange as the sun dipped lower. They had stayed longer than he'd realized—it must be near half past eight. Amalia would be hurrying the children toward bed.

"Did you enjoy the evening?" Helen asked, her footsteps softly crunching on the grassy dirt near the edge of the pasture.

"Ja." He turned toward her and smiled. Had she any idea how the sunset light gilded her hair, turning the blond to gold? "And you?"

"Yes, it was lovely." Helen glanced back at Eben and Maya's house on the gentle rise at the north end of the Miller property, the main Miller farmhouse a little ways below them. "I'm so glad for Eben and Maya. They went through so much . . . but you know that better than anyone."

"Ja." Ødger's throat tightened, thinking of the valley of shadow his sister had walked through last year. "To see her happy, at peace—it fills my heart with joy."

"I can only imagine." Her words, so sincere, also came tinged with something else.

Ødger turned to study her face as she gazed off into the distance at the sunset—or something else, only she could see? "What about you? Do you see yourself teaching forever?"

She drew a breath and glanced at him, as if pulled from some far-off memory. "Why do you ask?"

"I—" He swallowed, heat suddenly rushing up the back of his neck. "You are my friend. And I care about you. As a friend." Was he making any sense? He drew a long breath. "Sometimes, I confess I have a wish that I to be more than a friend, to you." He winced at the clumsiness of his English words. "Forgive me, I do not wish to offend."

"Ødger." Helen stilled beside him. "I—I understand, what you are saying, I think."

He dared to look at her, finding her face flushed, her eyes not quite meeting his.

"And I am grateful. You are a truly good man, one any woman might . . ." She paused, her breath catching. "But you don't know who I really am. In truth, *I* don't know who I really am."

"I know you are a teacher who loves to teach—and loves her students." He took a step closer to her, wishing he dared reach for her hands, clasped so tightly at her waist just now. "I know you have a voice like a songbird and a heart that loves to give and serve others. I know there is something in your family, in your past, that gives you pain."

She breathed a laugh, looking down. Her throat muscles trembled beneath her high lace collar. "I don't see how you know so much."

"I see you. I see you help Amalia, though as a boarder you have no obligation to. I see you care for each student as an individual, going—how do you say?—above and beyond what is required. How you take extra time to reach Hank, and Thomi. How little Ruthie adores you. How you stand up to prejudiced people like Mrs. Flinch."

She glanced up, meeting his eyes for an instant, her lashes damp. "You do see a great deal."

"You are right, I do not know you well. But I should like to." Ødger drew a breath, his heart pounding hard. "Would you allow me—to get to know you better?"

"Ødger." She shook her head, clasping her elbows and taking a step back. "What you are asking—I cannot keep company with a man. Not under my teaching contract. And I certainly cannot . . ."

"Marry. Ja, I know, not yet. But could we not get to know one another more—as friends?" He spread his hands, trying for a grin. "It is not like we never see each other as it is, after all."

A sudden laugh bubbled from her, a clear, trickling sound like the music of the creek. "That is true."

"I only hope we might keep getting to know one another, as friends, but perhaps with a bit more . . . intention. And when your contract is up for the year, then . . ." He shrugged. "We will see. How you feel. And how God is leading us." Though he kept his voice calm, his heart seemed about to hammer right through his chest.

"I—I suppose there lies a certain . . . wisdom in that." Her eyes darted away, then met his again, a vulnerability in them that caught his breath. "But—did I not hear you telling Eben you will be leaving soon?"

Ødger felt as if he'd been flying and then suddenly plummeted to earth. "Well, ja. Yes, there is that." The window must have been open, near where he and Eben had been speaking. Of course it had. "But I would not be leaving till the first of September. And even then, it is not so very far away, still in Iowa. And . . . we could write letters."

A smile touched her lips. "I suppose that would not be against my contract." She lifted her chin. "Where will you be going?"

"Independence, Iowa. I am to assist the minister at Immanuel Lutheran Church there." Though sixty miles seemed an awfully long distance away, a flicker of excitement still sparked. They began walking again, side by side, Helen and him, her skirt swaying so near his steps. "They often have young seminarians stay for a while to help, and there are many ministry opportunities. Even a hospital for those mentally ill."

Helen halted. "An asylum?"

"Ja. I visited a family with Reverend Larsen recently, where the son is ill somehow in his mind—I am not sure what is wrong, but it made me want to learn more. I am hopeful I might somehow find a way to minister at this hospital. I hear they have chaplains."

"Is it . . . the Iowa Hospital for the Insane?"

At the altered tone of Helen's voice, Ødger looked at her. In the falling twilight, she had gone quite pale. Her eyes bored past him, staring at the shadowed fields.

His chest squeezed, though he didn't know why. "Ja, I believe that is the name. Why?"

"I—I'm sorry. I cannot—I cannot do this now. I must go." With a fluttering gesture of her hands, Helen strode away from him, nearly running, despite her long skirt. She hurried across the boarding-house yard, up the steps, and disappeared inside Forsberg House.

Ødger stared after her, his heart thudding dully. Dear Lord, what had he done?

Fifteen

"I need to let out this dress again."

Amalia shifted the bodice of her already-expanded blue calico work dress with a grimace one morning in mid-July.

"He's growing big in there." Absalom stepped aside from fastening his collar at the oval mirror on their dresser to kiss her cheek and lay his hand on her mounding belly. The child kicked, making his hand bounce, and they both chuckled.

"Or she." Amalia laid her hands over his, cradling their child between them. "I'm starting to feel big as a cow with calf."

"Never that. And you've got at least two months to go." Absalom kissed her nose. "What do you have before you today?"

"Harvesting in the garden, and then we need to start canning. The cherry tree is overflowing, and so are the bean plants. Oh! And Thomi's birthday is today. You know Ruthie wanted to make this evening special for her. I still need to find a way to bake a little cake so that Thomi doesn't notice."

"And I'll try to make sure to be back early tonight. But I have a client meeting with my father at eight, so I'd best be on my way."

"Can you stay for breakfast?"

"I'll take something with me."

Disappointment nipped faintly, but at least he'd make an effort to be there tonight. They'd had to learn to give and bend with each other, adjusting to a marriage with both carrying such busy schedules. Amalia leaned against her husband a moment, laying her cheek on the shoulder of his brown suit jacket. "I love you."

"And I you."

Soon she bustled about the kitchen, sliding a tray of sourdough biscuits into the oven and frying stacks of sliced ham, grateful the day hadn't heated up too much yet.

Ruthie and Thomi burst in through the back door from feeding the chickens.

"Tante Malia! That broody hen's chicks hatched." Ruthie carried the basket of eggs into the pantry.

"Really? That's wonderful. How many?"

"Eight little puffballs." Thomi leaned her elbows on the counter next to Amalia. "I never saw brand-new baby animals till I lived here."

"You'll see more when Honey and Kaprifol have their calves. And Magpie has her kittens." Ruthie pulled open a side drawer to set the table. "Tante Malia, where do the babies come from?"

Amalia nearly dropped the hot pan of browned biscuits she was withdrawing from the oven. Setting it carefully atop the stove, she set aside the dishtowel she'd used to shield her hands from the heat. "What do you mean, den lille?"

"Like Magpie—I know the kittens are in her belly, but how do they get there?"

Amalia blew out a breath, sweat already gathering along her hairline with the building heat from the oven. *Lord, help*. "Well, God puts them there."

"And He puts the baby chicks inside the eggs?"

"Well, He makes them grow there."

"What about the eggs we eat?" Thomi spoke up, a frown beneath her dark curls parted and tugged into braids. "Would they grow into baby chicks?"

"Only in, ah, certain circumstances. Like when a mama hen sits on them." Amalia glanced at the clock on the kitchen wall. This was entirely too early in the morning for such conversations—though she probably should talk to the girls about the coming baby before too long. "Thomi, would you please help Ruthie set the table in the dining room? The boarders will be down soon."

The little girls disappeared through the swinging door into the dining room, and Amalia shook her head and surveyed the kitchen, trying to collect her thoughts. Biscuits done, ham nearly so. She needed to fry the eggs and serve the oatmeal that had cooked through the night. The little girls could take the butter and jam to the table. Amalia cracked eggs into the still-hot ham drippings and watched them bubble and sizzle, grateful the aroma no longer made her stomach roil.

"So what about people babies?" Thomi pushed through the dining room door again, followed by Ruthie.

"What about them?"

"Where do they come from?"

Amalia glanced over her shoulder, facing twin pairs of wide eyes, brown and blue. She swallowed.

"A lady at the children's home told me storks brought babies."

Ruthie scrunched up her nose. "We don't have storks here. So how did baby Torvald come, then?"

Land sakes, was it Thomi's birthday getting them so curious?

Heavy boots sounded down the stairs, and Amos, tall and black-bearded, stepped into the kitchen. "Want me to take the coffeepot in, Missus Amalia?"

"Ja, thank you." Amalia drew a breath and smiled at the girls. "We will have to talk about this more later, ja?" Her own mor, wonderful though she was, had never said much of womanly matters, though maybe it would have been different if she had lived to see her daughter married and about to become a mother. A sharp pang of missing her caught Amalia's breath, and she leaned her hands on the counter a moment despite the bustle around her, bowing her head. *Oh, Mor . . . I wish you were here. To help me through this season, to meet your grandchild.*

"You all right, lillesøster?"

At the clang of milk pails—and the name only one person called her—Amalia looked up to see Erik, one brimming pail in each hand, his head cocked and brow furrowed at her.

"Ja, sorry." She sniffed and reached to flip the eggs, already bubbling crisp around the edges, onto plates before they got overdone. "Just was missing Mor all of a sudden. Funny how it sneaks up on me sometimes."

"Not funny." Erik carried the milk pails into the pantry to strain them, then came back and touched her shoulder. "Happens to me too, you know."

"Really?" She looked up at him, into those smoke-blue eyes she still struggled to read, ever since he came back after their years apart.

He nodded, then lifted two hot plates of ham and eggs. "Want me to take these in?"

"Please. Mange takk." Something easing in her heart at even this brief exchange, Amalia followed with the basket of biscuits, finding the dining table already crowded with boarders, Amos making the rounds with the coffeepot while Ruthie and Thomi placed the butter and jam, then trailed her back into the kitchen for more plates, as well as bowls of porridge. Thankfully they all kept too busy for the next hour for the girls to think of any more questions.

Once the breakfast rush was past, Helen came in to help with the stacks of dishes while Ruthie and Thomi cleared the table.

"You really don't have to do this, you know." Amalia poured hot water on the skillet to soak it and added lye soap.

"So you've told me—what, dozens of times by now?" Helen smiled. "And as I've told you, I know, and I want to. At least when school is out of session."

"How are your summer classes going?" Amalia swiped a soapy dishrag around another plate, dunked it in the rinse water, then handed it to Helen, an easy rhythm between them by now despite her obligatory protests. Or maybe she didn't need to protest anymore, simply accept the help of a friend?

"Well enough."

Was that an altered tone in Helen's voice? Amalia glanced at her friend, who wiped her towel around the plate over and over before finally blinking and turning away to set it in the cupboard.

"Is Ødger helping you add music, as you'd talked about?"

"I—I think I may wait on that for this year."

Amalia paused, holding a dripping dish in the air. "Really? I thought you were looking forward to that."

"Yes, but—I'm already having Hank offer drawing lessons. I don't want to add too many new things at once."

"And two feels like too many new things?"

"I have a good deal demanding my attention just now." Helen set the next plate in the cupboard with a sharp clatter. "Between my aunt's health and getting a late start on the summer classes and planning the upcoming school year, I think I might be excused for delaying music lessons."

"Of course. I didn't mean to imply otherwise."

For a few moments, only the swish of sudsy water and clink of dishes sounded between them.

At last Helen sighed. "I'm sorry. I didn't mean to snap at you."

"It's all right." Amalia swished the forks and spoons through the rinse water. "But—are you all right?"

Helen pressed her lips together. "I will be. That is . . . I don't know."

"You know you can always talk to me . . . as a friend."

"Thank you. I'll let you know." She gave a tight smile. "So, how can I help with the surprise tonight?"

Amalia glanced over her shoulder to make sure Thomi wasn't

around. Still, she lowered her voice. "JJ will make the ice cream, and Ruthie and I have put together a few little gifts. Hank says he has some games planned—I don't know what, which makes me a bit nervous. I do hope it all goes well, Ruthie has her heart so set on it."

"Thomasina has had a rough go of it in life, that's certain—at least till she came here. I hope she does feel special tonight. But what can I do?"

"Perhaps help to distract her and keep her from the parlor, then bring her in when it's time? That's the part I feel most unsure on. But you always seem to know how to manage things."

"Not as often as you might think. But I'll do my best for Thomi."

They finished the rest of the dishes in mostly silence. What had been troubling Helen ever since her visit back East?

And had it anything to do with Ødger?

Ruthie's insides were jumping up and down.

The surprise for Thomi had to work. It just had to.

She could hardly eat her supper, though Thomi munched creamed chicken and peas calmly beside her at the dining table. Thomi had been rather quiet today—did she suspect something? Or did she feel bad because no one said anything about her birthday? Ruthie kept catching Mr. JJ's eye, then looking away as fast as she could before she burst out giggling. One time Mr. Amos, who had been let in on the secret, winked at her, and Ruthie had to pretend to cough into her napkin.

She made herself chew a bite of sourdough roll and swung her legs beneath the table. When would the boarders ever be finished eating?

As last the scraping of forks against plates turned to the scraping back of chairs, and Ruthie hopped up to clear the dishes so fast she nearly knocked her own chair over.

"Steady there, young lady." Mr. Amos caught the back of her chair before it hit the floor. "Haste makes waste, they always say."

Her stomach skipping even more, Ruthie helped Tante Malia clear the table faster than greased lightning, as Mr. JJ would say. JJ himself had disappeared—to get the ice cream? He'd cranked it in the cellar this afternoon, where it now sat staying cold. But oh, suppose it got too cold from the salt around it and was too rock hard to eat? Or suppose it got too warm and melted?

Ruthie blew out a breath as she'd often seen Tante Malia do. Organizing birthday celebrations was an awful lot of worry. She and Thomi wiped the dishes as Tante Amalia washed them, but not with their usual chatter. Ruthie wouldn't let herself talk lest she say something about the surprise—or the little cake hidden in the pantry—and Thomi didn't talk for, well, Ruthie didn't know the reason.

Ruthie was still wiping her last dish when Thomi hung her damp towel on the edge of the sink to dry and headed toward the door—the door that led into the hall, and then the entryway, and beyond that—the parlor.

"Wait!" Ruthie fairly screeched, clutching her dish towel between her hands.

Thomi turned back, frowning. "What?"

"I—I mean—where are you going?"

Thomi stared at her as if Ruthie had sprouted wings like a chicken. "To the parlor. I want to find a new book." Thomi had been working hard on her reading, trying to move up a class by the time school started.

"No! I mean—don't you need our help more, Tante Malia?" Ruthie turned to her tante, pleading with her eyes.

Tante Amalia opened her mouth, but just then, a voice spoke from the doorway.

"Ah, Thomasina, there you are. I was looking for you."

Thomi stared now at Miss Stenerson. "Why?"

"I have a few new books I brought back from Ohio that I haven't shown you yet. Would you like to come up to my room and take a look?"

Thomi glanced between Miss Stenerson and Ruthie, her forehead still pinched, but then she shrugged. "Sure."

As their footsteps tapped up the stairs, Ruthie's arms sagged, nearly dropping the dish towel. "Whew. I thought everything was about to get spoiled."

"Surprises are complicated, aren't they?" Tante Amalia dried her hands and smoothed Ruthie's braids. "So, what's next?"

It gave Ruthie a funny feeling in her stomach to have her tante looking at her like that, as if she were in charge. She took a deep breath. "Let's check on Hank and Mr. JJ."

They found Hank in the parlor, clearing all chairs to the sides of the room to leave the rug open in the middle.

"Whatcha doing?" Ruthie asked.

"Making room for the games. Where's Thomi?"

"Miss Stenerson has got her upstairs." At a muffled knock, Ruthie flew to answer the door, finding a grinning Ned and Lisa, the Millers's grandchildren, on the doorstep, along with Mr. Eben and Cousin Maya holding baby Torvald.

"You came." Ruthie pulled Lisa into a hug.

"Where's Thomi?" Ned peered around the girls.

"Shh!" Ruthie pulled them into the parlor. "She could be down any minute. Now you two hide."

"Hide?"

"They don't need to hide, Ruthie." Hank took on that I'm-older-and-I-know-better-than-you tone that Ruthie found particularly exasperating. "She won't see 'em till she comes in the door."

"Fine, then." Ruthie sighed. "Just stay out of sight. Tante Malia, have you seen Mr. JJ?" Her voice was getting tired from saying everything in a loud whisper.

"Here I be." Mr. JJ paused in the doorway, lugging the bucket of ice cream. "Now, where shall I put this here treat?"

"In the dining room." Ruthie clapped her hands to her cheeks. "I forgot to get the bowls and spoons!"

"I'll get them with you. And the cake." Tante Amalia laid a gentle hand on Ruthie's shoulder. "And shall I tell everyone who wants to be part of the surprise to come in here?"

"Ja." Ruthie hurried after Tante Malia, grabbed handfuls of spoons and set them on the sideboard in the dining room, then dashed back across the entryway to the parlor again. Amos and Onkel Absalom filed in, the room filling up now, warm and noisy.

Ruthie peered out the door, her heart thumping hard. Were they coming? Would Miss Stenerson guess the right time to bring Thomi down? She held her breath, listening. Behind her sounded whispering, then a giggle from Lisa. Ruthie waved her hand behind her. "Shh!"

There—voices on the second floor, then footsteps on the stairs. Ruthie ducked back into the parlor, holding her finger to her lips. Tante Amalia and Cousin Maya shushed everyone.

Ruthie held the door half closed, hardly breathing, her heart thudding so hard she hoped Thomi wouldn't hear it.

"Where do you want the books?" Thomi was asking.

"Just in the parlor with the others," Miss Stenerson answered. "I've been meaning to bring them down to the bookshelves for everyone to enjoy."

Miss Stenerson was wonderful, bringing Thomi just right without sounding suspicious a bit.

Thomi stepped in through the doorway, then froze.

Everyone jumped out from their places, shouting "Surprise!" and "Happy Birthday!"

Ruthie caught Thomi's arm and dragged her farther in. "It's a birthday surprise for you. For your tenth birthday." She hugged Thomi's stiff shoulders. "Don't you like it?"

Thomi stared around the room, her dark eyes round. Everyone stood beaming at her—Tante Malia and Onkel Absalom, Cousin

Maya and Mr. Eben with Torvald bouncing and crowing, Mr. Amos and Mr. JJ, Hank and Lisa and Ned. Miss Stenerson stood by the door, smiling and looking on.

But Thomi didn't say a word. She just looked at everyone, her face gone quite pale. Then suddenly, she dumped the pile of books in her arms on a chair and fled out the door.

Ruthie felt her arms grow cold. Her face tingled. She glanced at the room full of grown-ups, who were all looking at each other, then out the empty doorway where Thomi had disappeared. And she did the only thing she could think to do.

She ran right after her.

Ruthie found Thomi where she'd thought she would, in the barn up the hayloft. Thomi had run here before, when she and Ruthie had a quarrel or after the Flinch boys teased her at school. Up in the loft that smelled sweetly of hay and animals, Thomi would curl on a golden pile and sulk or pound things out. Ruthie had taken refuge here a time or two also.

But why did Thomi need the hayloft now? They were only giving her a birthday party.

"Thomi?" Ruthie whispered, climbing over a prickly, sweet-smelling pile of hay. "What's wrong? Don't you like it?"

Thomi turned a reddened face to Ruthie, and she saw she'd been crying. Thomi—crying? Ruthie tried to think if she'd ever seen that before. She sat down beside her and hugged her knees up to her chest.

"I only wanted to make you feel special, to give you a happy birthday." Her throat clamped tight till it hurt. "I'm sorry it made you cry."

Thomi shook her head hard, dark curls springing loose from her braids. "You didn't—I mean, it's not your fault. It just—was all so much. So many people, and—I didn't expect . . ." She pressed her thin lips together. "I never had anything like that for my birthday before."

"Didn't your parents do something for your birthday?" Ruthie leaned her head back against the hay. She didn't remember much about her birthdays in Norway, but she thought she remembered her mor making her a little cake.

"I think my mamma did." Thomi rubbed her nose. "Maybe something special to eat. But after she died, and at the children's home—nobody even knew when it was." She slanted a glance at Ruthie. "I didn't think *you* even knew."

"You told us last fall, remember? When it was my birthday."

"And you remembered all this time?" Thomi's face softened. "We didn't have all this fuss for your birthday."

"I know. But I wanted yours to be special. Because . . ." A lump stuck in Ruthie's throat, and she shifted away from Thomi. "Never mind. I'm sorry I ruined it all."

"No." Thomi reached for Ruthie's hand and squeezed it, crackling the hay between them. "*I* ruined it. You were just trying to be nice—like a sister."

Ruthie stared at Thomi. "You think I'm like your sister?"

Thomi wrinkled her nose. "You can sure be bothersome as one, for starters."

Ruthie giggled. "Do you want to at least have some ice cream? We don't have to play the games."

"There's ice cream?" Thomi scrambled to her feet. "Why didn't you say so in the first place?"

When they got back to the boardinghouse, Tante Amalia had already started serving the ice cream—"So it wouldn't melt," she said, giving Ruthie a special smile when she saw her and Thomi together. With everyone milling around the dining room instead of crowding the parlor, things felt easier, and Thomi was soon laughing over her bowl of ice cream and cake while talking with Lisa and Ned. Then, when their bowls were empty, Hank showed them how to play blindman's bluff. How everyone shrieked with laughter when Thomi caught Mr. JJ and couldn't figure out who he was, till she felt his bald head!

When Tante Amalia tucked Ruthie and Thomi into bed an hour past their usual bedtime, Tante Malia handed Thomi a little box.

"At ten years old, we thought you were a young lady ready for this," she said as Thomi pulled out a little silver locket.

Thomi fumbled with the clasp. "What do I put in it?"

"That's up to you. Sometimes people put a lock of hair, or a photograph of someone special. You have that tiny photograph of your papa—I thought you might like to have that put in."

Thomi nodded, then suddenly hugged Tante Amalia tight. "Thank you."

After Tante Malia put the light out, Ruthie turned onto her side and closed her eyes. She was almost asleep when Thomi whispered, "Thank you, Ruthie. I had a good time."

Ruthie smiled and pillowed her cheek on her hand. *Mange takk, God. Thomi liked her birthday surprise after all.*

But she didn't think she'd try to plan another surprise for a good long while. She was all worn out.

Sixteen

Lord in heaven, what did I do wrong?

Ødger tried to focus on what Rev. Larsen was saying about tonight's prayer meeting, but all he could think of was the stricken look in Helen's eyes after that supper at the Millers's.

Here he'd entertained thoughts of taking Helen to prayer meeting some Wednesday evening—surely he could drive her without breaching her contract, if someone else came along. But now she'd barely looked at him at last night's class, only called on him once to answer a question when no one else had raised their hand. He'd hardly been able to focus on the lesson, jumbling his English verb tenses more than he had in months.

"How does that sound to you for this evening, then?"

Ødger blinked and rubbed his forehead. He sat on a front pew, Rev. Larsen next to him thumbing through a prayer book. "Sorry, could you repeat that, please?"

"Are you all right, son?" The elderly minister pushed his spectacles up his nose and eyed Ødger with a kind but too keen gaze.

"Just my mind wandering a bit." He shook his head. "Forgive me."

"Not to worry. I merely asked if you could open the prayer meeting tonight with these two hymns, then invite the requests. I will read the psalm and close in prayer at the end."

Ødger nodded automatically. "Ja, I can do that." Certainly he felt in need of prayer himself today. He took the prayer book from the pastor and rubbed his thumb over the worn cover.

"Thank you. I will go home for a bit of supper, then, before the meeting. I trust you will do the same." Rev. Larsen pushed stiffly to his feet, leaning on his cane, and turned down the aisle, then paused and looked back. "Is there anything I can be praying for you, dear Ødger?"

He looked up, the question hitting him hard in the chest. "I—mange takk." His throat worked suddenly. "Ja, I need . . . wisdom. Guidance, from the Lord."

"I thought perhaps." The elderly man nodded, then laid a hand on Ødger's shoulder, his grip surprisingly firm. "You are at one of those crossroads in life, are you not? I remember that age well. Do not fear, my son. He knows His plans for us when we do not."

Ødger nodded, swallowed, blinked hard. "Ja. Takk." As the reverend's cane tapped away down the aisle, he leaned his head in his hands and sat there till silence filled the church and eased the pounding in his temples. *Lord* . . . he hardly knew how to pray. But Rev. Larsen was praying for him. That thought eased the tension in his chest with a curl of comfort.

Despite the reverend's suggestion, Ødger had little appetite tonight to go all the way back home to Decorah for supper. Instead, he swept the interior of the church and set all the prayer books neatly in the pew backs, then sat down at the piano to run through the hymns Rev. Larsen had indicated. Ødger played a few scales to warm up his fingers, stiff and calloused from construction work, then segued into "He Leadeth Me." He played through the melody a time or two, as this wasn't one he played often, then began reading the words in the hymnal as well, softly singing under his breath as his hands began to memorize the chord progressions.

"He leadeth me: O blessed thought!
O words with heavenly comfort fraught!
Whate'er I do, where'er I be,
still 'tis God's hand that leadeth me."

Ødger's throat tightened, cutting off the words while his hands kept maneuvering the keys. *Lord, that is what I want . . . what I need. You brought me to this land . . . I do believe that. But what is the path you have for me? I thought it was Helen . . . I hoped it was Helen. But has that just been my plan, not yours? Or is it my fault that she pulls away like this?* He cleared his throat, fighting the burning in his eyes as his fingers began the melody again.

"Lord! I would clasp thy hand in mine,
Nor ever murmur nor repine;
Content whatever lot I see,
Since 'tis my God that leadeth me."

His voice strengthened as he reached the refrain once more.

He leadeth me! he leadeth me!
By his own hand he leadeth me;
His faithful follower I would be,
For by his hand he leadeth me."

The Lord had led him to this land, with his sister—he truly believed that. He had directed his steps to Luther College, to the magistrate's home, to assisting Rev. Larsen. Maybe even to Helen.

His heart lifted at the thought. Perhaps he just needed to talk to her.

Ødger drove Maya, Helen, and Hank to class the next evening, stopping at the boardinghouse along the way as had become his habit. He and his sister both tried to engage Helen in conversation during the wagon ride, but she answered in monosyllables. At last Ødger gave up and talked to Hank about haying instead. Perhaps Helen would speak more freely after class—and if he could approach her alone. Surely whatever had come between them was merely a misunderstanding, easily cleared up. Or had nothing to do with him at all.

"So you are learning to drive the mowing machine this year?" Ødger turned down the main street of Green Creek toward the school.

"Yep." Hank shifted onto his knees in the wagon bed. "Eben taught me how, and Erik's been helpin' me. But he says I'm doin' so good I might be able to manage on my own pretty soon. 'Course, we take turns, and whoever's not drivin' walks through the field ahead, warnin' us about rocks an' stuff." His voice rang high with excitement.

"That is good." Ødger smiled back over his shoulder at Hank. Oh to be a boy again, with the simpler joys and hopes of life. Not that Hank's life had been easy, or simple. He glanced at Helen, sitting on the seat beside him, seemingly as far over to the edge of her side as she could scoot without danger of falling off, and the heaviness pressed in his chest again. But soon—soon he would talk to her, and perhaps all would come right. *Please, Lord.*

They arrived at the school only a few minutes early, and Ødger helped light the kerosene lamps, bringing a warm gleam to the dimness of the schoolroom. Other wagons rumbled into the schoolyard, bearing adults and older children, mostly, though a few mothers brought their little ones, having no one to keep them at home. Maya had barely begun to get used to leaving Torvald with her mother-in-law, and she hugged her arms against herself often, as if missing her baby to hold.

Tonight in class, Ødger found himself grouped with the more advanced students—Hank, Inga Jorstad who still helped at the boardinghouse one or two afternoons a week, and a young American farmer who had missed much of his schooling. Helen set them to work on parsing the first few stanzas of a poem, "Paul Revere's Ride," by Henry Wadsworth Longfellow.

"For those of you new to American history, this will introduce you to one of our most beloved founding stories." Helen spoke in her bright, formal schoolmarm voice. She did not look at Ødger. "Those familiar with the story can share it with the others, but I also want you to note the rhyme scheme and meter and mark it out as best you can. Help one another, and enjoy Longfellow's delightful cadence." She smiled and moved on to a group of students still struggling with English grammar, including Maya.

"So who was Paul Revere?" Ødger leaned forward and clasped his hands on the too-small desk, his legs cramped beneath its childish size.

Hank shrugged. "Some feller back around the Declaration of Independence, I think. I dunno."

"You don't know?" The young farmer slapped his knee. "I ain't had much schoolin', but my pa used to talk about old Paul Revere. Back when we was fightin' the British, for our independence, as you say, Revere was the one who gave the alarm afore the first battle. He galloped all through Lexington and Concord, hollerin' out, 'the Redcoats are comin'!' Sounded the alarm right fine, he did."

Despite the history not being his own, Ødger felt a thrill run along his arms. And he was American too now, after all—this country's history would become his. "Then what happened?"

Quiet young Inga leaned forward, examining the poem before them by lamplight. "Maybe it says here."

Together they took turns reading the stanzas—the first eight, as Helen had directed. Ødger recalled Hank's stirring recitation at the end of the year as the boy read tonight, putting unconscious drama and expression into the lines. He examined Hank's youthful profile, his shock of hair falling over his eyes as he read. Someday, that boy might be a poet himself, or an orator—or a soldier. He shook off that last thought. Please God, there would be no more wars in their lifetime, at least not close by.

They had finished marking the rhyme scheme and begun on the meter by the time Helen called the class together to finish with a series of joint grammatical exercises, then dismissed them as darkness fell. Most families had to rise early for farm chores, after all. Men, women, and children rose from the cramped desks and bid each other good-night, friendly chatter and laughter rising like warming steam from a coffeepot.

Ødger waited, hanging back while Helen spoke with various students, dispensing encouragement and advice like a physician gave out pills and powders. At last only one immigrant couple remained in the room, Maya and Hank having headed out to the wagon, and the husband and wife seemed absorbed in a Norwegian conversation of their own in the back row.

Breathing a prayer, Ødger squared his shoulders and walked up to Helen's desk, his insides as knotted as when he got called before the teacher years ago as a refractory youth. But this was Helen—his friend, for more than a year now. And he merely wanted to talk to her.

"May I help you?" She didn't look up from the papers she was marking—they had all turned in written accounts of a favorite summer memory this evening, assigned on Tuesday.

Ødger flinched at the polite distance in her voice, his courage failing. "I, ah. I wanted to ask. Do you still wish for me to help you with the music class? On Saturdays." After all, two weeks of classes had passed now, yet she'd made no further mention of the plans they'd discussed.

"I—I think not." Helen ran a finger along her hairline and made another mark on a paper. "I think I may have been too ambitious, to try to add that this summer."

His heart thudded painfully. "Perhaps this fall, then?"

"We will see." She glanced up, but only met his eyes for the briefest instant. "You have your assignment?"

Swallowing hard, he handed his paper over.

"Thank you." She bent her head again, dividing the papers into two stacks. The flickering light from the kerosene lamp on her desk gilded the edges of her hair with gold.

Ødger clenched his hands at his sides, willing her to look up, to actually talk with him, as she used to—willing himself to be braver, to ask her what had gone wrong. "Helen?"

She did look up then, and for an instant, the shield seemed to drop from her eyes, here in the dim room. "Yes?"

"Have I done something to offend?"

Her face softened. With the barest shake of her head, she opened her mouth—then her expression shifted, the polite schoolmarm guard sliding back over her face as she looked over his shoulder. "Yes, Mr. and Mrs. Kristoffson? Did you have a question?"

Swallowing hard, Ødger stepped aside for the immigrant couple to speak with the teacher. "We'll wait for you outside," he murmured. With one last glance over his shoulder, he turned and headed between the rows of school desks and out into the cicada chorus of the summer night.

"So when do you leave for Independence?" Asgar Rykavyk asked the next day as they laid a new brick walkway under a blazing sun.

"Beginning of September, I think." Ødger hefted another load of bricks, their rough edges scraping his fingers.

Asgar paused in spreading mortar and cocked a brow. "You don't sound too happy about it."

Ødger said nothing, but his grip slipped as he bent to set the next brick in place. It slammed onto his toes, sending frissons of twanging pain up to his knee.

Clamping his teeth on a Norwegian phrase hardly befitting an almost-minister, Ødger bent to grip his ankle with his hand, clenching his jaw.

"You all right?"

"Ja," Ødger ground out, releasing a breath as the throbbing eased. He grabbed the recalcitrant brick and set it into place before the mortar hardened.

"Good." Asgar nodded beyond Ødger's shoulder. "Your lady friend approaches."

Ødger swung his head around, his heartbeat jumping into a gallop. Helen—here? Had she come to continue their conversation from last night? But his gaze landed on the young woman in hat and visiting gown coming down the shaded lane toward them, and his heart settled back into a dull thud.

Not Helen. Lena Amundson.

She smiled at them from beneath her flower-trimmed leghorn hat and held out the tray she carried.

"What do you have for us today, Miss Amundson?" Eivor called from where he knelt working with Leif a short ways away.

"Cherry fritters and iced lemonade." She smiled at all of them, her gaze lingering on Ødger. "I thought those might cool you off a bit in this heat."

Despite himself, Ødger's mouth watered, his lips parched. A drink of lemonade sounded like pure heaven, but he sat back on his heels, unmoving.

Asgar glanced at Ødger with quirked brow as if suggesting he ought to do something, then rose himself. "Let me give you a hand with that pitcher, miss."

"Thank you." Her smile stiffened a bit, but with one last glance at Ødger, she let Asgar take the pitcher, then set down her tray of glasses and fritters on a nearby low wall. With the drinks filled, she passed them around to the men, who all paused in their work to accept the frosty glasses.

Miss Amundson came to Ødger last. By design? "Here you are, Mr. Gunderson."

"Thank you." Ødger took the lemonade in great gulps, his thirst overcoming any reluctance.

"You all must be fairly parboiled out here." Miss Amundson fanned herself with her handkerchief. "I wish you didn't have to work so in this heat."

"The college must get done." Ødger lowered his empty glass with a sigh. "But the lemonade does help. Mange takk."

"Velbekommen." She gave him a smile as sweet as the lemonade. "Will you help me pass out the fritters?" With a tip of her head, she invited him to follow her into the shade.

Ødger followed. He wouldn't be rude, anyway. Together, they passed the fritters around to all the men on the crew.

"I trust you will not have to labor with your hands beyond this summer, at least." Miss Amundson handed him the last two fritters, the dark red cherry juice gleaming through the pastry.

Ødger frowned. "Why not?"

"My father told me about your upcoming field training in Independence. He thinks they may well even offer you a position afterward."

Did he? And he had spoken to his daughter about it, but not to Ødger. More, why was he discussing Ødger's life with Lena to begin with? He took a bite of fritter, but the sweet pastry soured in his mouth now.

Perhaps he was being foolish. Perhaps Asgar and Eivor had been right all along, that Miss Amundson was, how did they put it—"setting her cap" for him. Perhaps he had merely been willfully blind to it, with having eyes only for Helen.

And now . . . he glanced at Lena, looking up at him with that dimpled smile, her honey-brown hair curled and done up stylishly under her hat. What did he have against her, after all? He should be honored to have the daughter of a professor take even this much interest in him. Certainly Luther College held no shortage of seminary-bound young gentlemen, many with better prospects than an immigrant laborer like himself. Yet she seemed to show special favor to him.

And it wasn't like they'd nothing in common—a love of music, for one thing. And surely a bent for ministry, since she showed such interest in his path toward that. As a professor's daughter with a gift for the organ, she'd doubtless make an ideal pastor's wife.

Ødger tried to smile back at her, but the fritter settled in his gut like one of the bricks at their feet.

Lord, if this is your plan for me, why does it feel so wrong?

Seventeen

Helen cradled the small wooden box between her hands. Dare she open it?

Sitting on her upstairs window seat, her window open to the night air, she rubbed her thumbs over the carved lid, the etched flowers and vines. Someone had taken care in crafting this little box, and clearly her mother valued it. What treasures—or secrets—did it hold?

The flame of the lamp on her desk flickered a bit, a breeze from her open window bringing a hint of coolness to the muggy night. The boardinghouse lay asleep, only the chirp of the crickets and rustle of the breeze in the trees sounding through the window.

But Helen hadn't been able to sleep. Not with Ødger's hurt blue-gray eyes gazing back every time she tried to close hers. Her fingers tightened on the box. *Lord, what came over me to flee from him like that? Like a fool. What must he think of me?*

And here he had been asking to court her—or as close as he could come with the strictures of her job. A sweet, warm ache spread through her chest. And she wanted him to . . . oh, how she wanted him to. She knew that now, as she hadn't before . . . before she'd ruined her chances of that ever happening, by running away like a frightened rabbit. And she'd been running ever since, avoiding Ødger at church, in class. He'd tried to speak to her last

Thursday, she knew it—and perhaps they might have cleared the air a bit, had she not needed to talk to the Kristoffsons. But what would she have said? What could she have said, when she still held so many unanswered questions herself?

Hence the box on her lap.

She nibbled her lip a moment, then set the box on her desk and inserted the tarnished brass key into the lock. It stuck a bit, then shifted, clicked. The lid likewise needed a bit of encouragement, a fingernail slid into the crack, before it yielded to open with a faint squeak.

Inside it resembled a simple jewelry box, with an inlaid tray and a larger space beneath. Helen scooted the box closer to the lamp, the better to see inside.

The locket, lying on the top tray, caught her eye first—a tiny silver heart on a thread-like chain. A child's locket, perhaps. Helen lifted it, her fingers fumbling at the minuscule clasp. Within lay two photographs, one of a man, one of a woman, so tiny she had to peer close to make out their features. But she didn't recognize either one. The woman certainly was not Adelaide, having lighter hair. Who were they? Could they possibly be her birth parents? If so—how had Adelaide come to have them? To have—Helen? Had the locket been her own, as a child? It was small enough.

Still too many questions, with no answers.

She lifted off the tray and peered into the bottom compartment. A folded scrap of newspaper lay atop something cloth.

Helen unfolded the newspaper clipping. A single article by the look of it, from a Winneshiek County newspaper. She smoothed out the headline, from June 1869, and read.

TRAGIC ACCIDENT LEAVES COUPLE SERIOUSLY INJURED, CHILD MISSING

A tragic carriage accident occurred in Winneshiek County last Friday evening. A lightning storm being thought to have spooked the horses, they bolted and dragged the carriage off the road and down the banks of the Upper Iowa River. Due to the late hour and location, the disastrous scene was not discovered until the next morning. The horses had broken free and run off, leaving the driver dead along with the husband of the family traveling inside, Prof. Johan Paul Harstad. His wife, Mrs. Christiana Harstad, was found unconscious from a serious head injury and was taken to the hospital for treatment, but is not expected to live. The couple's daughter, aged twenty months, was not found within the carriage and is unhappily presumed to have been washed downriver. Notices have been posted to the police in surrounding counties in hopes of the child's discovery, however dim.

Helen's ears tingled. Twenty months . . . that would have been her age in June of 1869, if her birthday were indeed in October, as she'd always been told. Was this her story, then? Her . . . family? Had Adelaide somehow found her as an orphaned toddler and taken her in?

Or kidnapped her. She shivered at the ugly word. Had her mother—Adelaide—been as disturbed as that?

She looked again inside the locket, at the man's sober, kindly mustached face, the woman's gentle eyes. Did Helen resemble them at all? Perhaps . . . she couldn't tell. "Johan and Christiana Harstad." She tried the names out in a whisper, foreign on her tongue, then clicked the locket closed, clutching it warm in her palm a moment, then laying it back on the tray.

Lord . . . I don't know what to think. How to take all this in . . . or even make sense of it. Please, help me.

One more item lay in this box, the cloth at the bottom. Helen drew a breath and gently lifted it out. It unfolded in her hands—a small white garment. A tiny chemise made for an infant, or perhaps a toddler.

Perhaps a missing little girl, aged twenty months?

White cotton, carefully trimmed with dainty lace. A snatch of pink caught Helen's eye and she peered inside the small neckline to find a name stitched in faded pink floss.

Primrose. The same as on her baby bracelet.

For some reason the tears came then, swift and hot, blurring the lamp's dancing flame before her eyes. Helen pressed the little frock to her face, weeping into it, the dry, musty scent of old muslin filling her nose.

All the tangled tapestry of her early life seemed to be unraveling, then reweaving to form a wholly different pattern—yet still unrecognizable.

Helen rose early the next morning before church after a fitful night, her eyes heavy but dry at last.

Where she had come from . . . that still needed much untangling. She little knew if she'd ever discover the full truth there. But who she was . . . she knew something of that, at least. As the Lord had reminded her that night when she needed it so desperately, she was His. He knew all the murky depths of her parentage and history, even if she never unearthed it in this lifetime. And she was the Green Creek schoolteacher. Adopted niece to Aunt Ophelia, bless her. A boarder at Forsberg House and, she believed, a friend to many in this town.

And today, the church pianist, who must not be late.

She washed her face and dressed in the cool morning dimness, then crept downstairs, fetching herself some bread and cheese from the pantry and setting off just as she heard stirring from Absalom and Amalia's room.

She didn't want to speak to anyone this morning, not yet, though she waved at JJ heading for the barn as the first glints of sunrise peeked over the eastern horizon.

This morning, she wanted to just be quiet with the Lord, walking slowly down the rutted road, meadowlarks singing hard from the tall grasses lining her path, other birds twittering from the trees or flitting over her head. She didn't sing with them today as she usually did, just let their melodies flow over her and balm her soul.

She reached the church early and let herself in, grateful Rev. Larsen left it unlocked. Inhaling the familiar scents of old hymnals, dried flowers, and communion wine, she felt her shoulders relax. Helen set down her Bible and pocketbook, seated herself on the worn seat of the piano bench, and caressed the yellowed keys of the church piano like an old friend. While she'd like to see the church obtain an organ someday, she loved this piano. Her fingers moved silently over the keys a moment, then began to play, finding music when her voice yet could not, her mind filling in the unsung words of the beloved hymns.

Abide with me: fast falls the eventide . . .

How firm a foundation, ye saints of the Lord . . .

Be still my soul; the Lord is on thy side . . .

Her voice finally emerged on the second verse of that hymn, coming shaky at first, then gaining strength.

"Be still, my soul; thy God doth undertake
To guide the future as He has the past
Thy hope, thy confidence let nothing shake;
All now mysterious shall be bright at last.

Be still, my soul; the waves and winds still know
His voice who ruled them while He dwelt below."

"I've always loved that one."

Helen started, striking a discordant note on the piano, and twisted on the bench.

Ødger stood near the front of the aisle, a mingle of amusement and hesitation on his face. He lifted a hand. "Forgive me. I do not mean to bother you." He took another tentative step forward and rested his hand on the back of the front pew. "I see I'm not the only one who sometimes seeks solace here early, before everyone else descends."

"I'm sorry." Helen rose hastily, closing the piano lid over the keys. "I didn't intend to intrude on your private time."

"No, please. You know this church is for all of us." He spread his hands, his eyes so sincere, so pleading, Helen's knees weakened. "Please—do not go."

Helen gripped her pocketbook and her courage with it. She must say something, they couldn't go on like this. "Ødger—I know things haven't been—right, between us lately. And it's my fault."

His jaw shifted, and he glanced away, no longer meeting her eyes. One hand went to his jacket pocket, then out.

Helen's chest pinched. She'd hurt him even more than she'd known.

"Please, forgive me." She stepped down from the low platform at the front of the church, bringing them onto the same level, at least.

"I thought perhaps I must ask you to forgive me." He glanced at her, then away again. "But I know not what for."

"No—it was nothing you did." Except to be wonderful, but she couldn't say that. "I merely . . ." She drew a shaky breath. How to even begin to explain? "I have some—areas of my own life I am trying to sort out. I have nothing against you, truly, nothing at all. I merely need—some time. I have no right to ask, but I hope you might give me that—as a friend?"

A long moment, then Ødger met her eyes, straight on this time. Their blue depths still reminded her of a troubled, stormy sky, but he nodded. "Ja. Of course."

How she ached to tell him of all the swarming tangle that filled her mind, her heart. He would know then, truly, that this wasn't about him—and perhaps might even help her to sort it all out. But she couldn't ask that of him, had no right. Not now, perhaps not ever.

The side door creaked open, and Rev. Larsen shuffled in. He glanced up at the two of them and beamed his kindly smile. "And here I thought I was getting to church early today."

Ødger smiled back, though it seemed a bit forced. "Seems we all had the same thought."

Helen dipped her head and slipped back to the piano to run through the hymns for today while Ødger and the pastor began discussing the order of service, her heart eased from at least broaching the subject with Ødger.

If only a little.

Eighteen

"Tante Malia! Kaprifol dropped her calf last night."

Ruthie burst into the kitchen where Amalia stood stirring oatmeal at the stove for breakfast.

"Ja? Finally, I thought she'd have it a week or two ago. Is all well?"

"Ja, Mr. JJ says mother and baby look good. It's a little bull calf, red and white." Ruthie spun about the table with the basket of eggs.

"That's wonderful news." Amalia set down her wooden spoon. "Put the eggs in the pantry, please, before they get broken." She began slicing a rasher of bacon.

Ruthie returned from the pantry and leaned against the counter, one boot toe tapping on the floorboards. "Tante Malia?"

"Hmm?"

"Can we have a baby sometime?"

Amalia paused her knife and glanced at Ruthie. "What do you mean, den lille?"

"We always have baby animals, and Maya has baby Torvald. It would be fun to have a baby at our house too."

Amalia drew a breath and laid the slices of bacon in the hot skillet to sizzle. Was she ready to have this conversation now? She glanced out the window at the barnyard and garden painted with early morning light. JJ and Hank wouldn't be in from chores for a few minutes, anyway. She rinsed her hands at the sink pump and dried them, then reached for Ruthie's hand.

"Come sit with me a moment."

Ruthie followed her to the kitchen table and plopped into a chair, leaning one elbow on the table.

"Remember how you and Thomi asked a while back where people babies come from?"

"Ja." Ruthie twisted her braid. "Thomi said the storks, but Dr. Armitage brought Torvald, not a stork." Her eyes brightened. "Could we ask the doctor to get us a baby?"

Amalia swallowed a laugh. "Nei, den lille. That isn't usually how it works." *Lord, give me the words.* "You know that baby chicks come from eggs, and baby calves grow inside their mothers' bellies."

"And baby kittens too."

"Ja, that's how it works with many animals. And it's . . . rather similar with people, actually."

Ruthie stared a moment, then her eyes widened. "Really?"

"Ja." Amalia hesitated, then laid her hand on her swollen abdomen. She was getting so large, she rather wondered the little girls hadn't mentioned it on their own. "In fact, you might have noticed my belly has been getting a lot bigger lately."

Ruthie sat up straight so fast her chair rocked. "You—you mean—you have a—a baby? In there?"

"Ja." A smile stretched Amalia's cheeks as Ruthie's mouth formed a perfect O. "You will have a little brother or sister sometime soon, God willing."

Ruthie's beaming face near to outshone the sun. "Can I tell Thomi?"

"I suppose so. Would you like to?"

"Ja!" Ruthie dashed off outside to where Thomi must still be watching the new calf, the door banging behind her.

Amalia pushed to her feet to check the bacon, still smiling.

Doubtless her mor would have been scandalized that she'd just told a little girl where babies came from, but what good did it do to hide the facts of life? Whatever society thought. And the joy on Ruthie's face . . . flipping each sizzling slice with a fork, she ran her hand over the mounding place that cradled her child, feeling the drum of little feet beneath her ribs. "Min lille . . . we are so very glad you are on your way."

Less than two months to go now. Sometimes the flying weeks made it feel hard to catch her breath—as did the lessening room for her lungs. Now that the little girls knew, she could set them to helping her hem diapers and sew other baby things. Thomi had been learning to use the sewing machine quite handily lately. Perhaps Ruthie might like to embroider a bib.

Yet more changes to come for them all. *Lord, help us to be ready.*

July melted away and August came in blazing, with days of harvesting in the garden under the beating sun followed by more days steaming in the kitchen, canning as the stove attempted to outdo the sun in heat.

"I think it's hotter in the kitchen than the garden at midday," Ruthie said, her little face pink and damp as she clamped lids on the jars.

"Ja, you are not wrong." Amalia felt her face getting stewed along with the plums she stirred on the stove. She wiped her upper lip with the corner of her apron. Had the heat always gotten to her so, or was it being in the family way? Maya had suffered in the heat last summer when she'd been carrying. She wished her cousin were here today, but she was canning with Mrs. Miller. "Why don't you go see if Thomi has that next bushel of beans almost full. We can sit out on the back porch to snap them once I get the rest of these jars filled—that will be a bit cooler."

Ruthie ran off, always glad for an excuse to go outside. Amalia stirred the plums once more, then dipped the steaming preserves into a dozen clean, waiting jars. She clamped the rest of the lids down, then pushed the empty stewpot to the cooler part of the stove. She'd let the fire die down and wash it later. Blowing out a breath, she wet a towel at the sink pump and dabbed her face and neck, then filled a cup and took a long drink. Mrs. Miller had told her it was important to get plenty of water for the baby.

Small footsteps and a thump on the porch told of the girls' arrival. The screen door squeaked open and Ruthie's head poked through. "We brought the beans, a whole bushel."

"Mange takk. I'll be out in a minute."

The door banged shut again, the girls' chatter muffling.

With a sigh and a smile, Amalia dabbed the back of her neck again, then fetched the large blue enamelware pot to hold the snapped beans, ready for canning tomorrow. They would fill jars with the fresh snapped beans, add salt and cover with hot water, then process in a water bath for winter. She headed out onto the porch just as the girls dragged an old chair over for her.

"Ah, this is better." Setting down the empty pot beside the basket, Amalia sank into the chair and fanned her face, blowing a breath up to loosen the strands of hair sweat-stuck to her forehead. The muggy air still pressed on them, but the porch's shade and hint of a breeze helped. At this time of day, they got more shade here on the back porch, facing north, than around front.

"Better than the garden too." Thomi pushed back her brown gingham sunbonnet, her dark curls damp against her tanned forehead.

"Why don't you girls go get a drink from the pump? I'll start the beans." Amalia leaned forward and gathered a pile of the fresh, crisp string beans into her lap. "Oh, and bring back a bowl for the ends, will you?"

The girls flew off, blond and brown braids flying.

Amalia sighed and shook her head. Where did they get that energy, even in this heat?

They came skipping back a few moments later, faces and hair now plastered wet.

"Did you put your heads under the pump?"

The girls glanced at each other guiltily and nodded.

Amalia chuckled. "My brother and I used to do that back home too in the summer—not that it got nearly so hot as here."

"Chicago was hotter." Thomi knelt down by the bushel basket and began snapping beans, her fingers grown nimble and quick.

"Hotter than here?" Ruthie's blue eyes widened as she grabbed a handful of beans also.

Thomi nodded. "Felt like it, anyway. The buildings pressed in on you, and the heat rose off the streets like steam. So much dust and flies and garbage—it stank to high heaven." She shook her head. "Inside was even worse. I lived on the top floor of the children's home, and it was like an oven."

Amalia glanced at Thomi, but she didn't seem upset, just stating facts as they were. Ruthie listened, her little face pinched. "That sounds awful."

Thomi shrugged and reached for more beans. "I'm glad I'm here now."

The words crept into Amalia's heart, as Ruthie cast her a small smile. They'd never heard Thomi actually say that before.

"When is the baby coming?" Thomi asked. Since Ruthie had shared the news, the girls could talk of little else.

"Sometime around mid to late September, I think. After you start school."

"Will it be a boy or a girl?" Ruthie snapped two more beans, then bit the end of one.

"Only God knows right now."

"I hope it's a boy." Thomi grabbed another handful. "Boys are more fun."

Ruthie frowned at Thomi. "I hope it's a girl. We already have enough boys with Hank and Torvald."

"We already have enough girls too. Two of each."

Ruthie wrinkled her nose and threw a bean at her.

They snapped beans all afternoon till Amalia's back ached and even the breeze seemed to fade away under the heat's pressure. Ruthie and Thomi's chatter faded, their fingers slowing as they neared the bottom of the bushel basket. Flies buzzed and cicadas hummed a scratchy chorus.

"C'mon, Ruthie. We'll never finish if you keep daydreaming like that." Thomasina's tone scraped sharper than the insects.

Ruthie scratched a mosquito bite on her arm and frowned, digging back into the basket. "I've snapped more beans than you anyway."

"Have not."

"Have so."

Amalia slapped at a fly. "Don't pick at each other, girls. You've both worked hard, and we're almost finished."

"Seems like we do nothing but work hard," Thomi mumbled.

"What was that?" Amalia's spine tightened, her own voice sharpening

"Ja, I thought you were *so glad* to be here." Ruthie's eyes narrowed, and she snapped two beans at once.

Thomi glared at Ruthie and snatched the last three beans from the basket just as Ruthie reached for them.

"Ow!" Ruthie clamped one hand over the other. "You scratched me."

"Serves you right."

"Girls!" Amalia slapped her hands on the arms of the rocker. Both girls swiveled their heads to look at her. Ruthie's lower lip stuck out a bit. Thomi's dark eyes still smoldered.

Amalia sighed and rubbed her sweaty forehead. Her back was aching dreadfully. "Listen. I know we've all been working hard lately. But that's summer on a farm—and one that's also running a boardinghouse. Believe me, I'd like nothing more than to lie down right now, preferably somewhere with a cool breeze."

Golden and dark brown heads lowered.

"But this is life. We have to work together, or what needs to get done won't get done. And I appreciate you girls' help, more than you know. Just look at this bushel of beans—I couldn't have snapped all these on my own this afternoon."

"But then we have to can them, and then there's more to pick. It never ends." Thomi threw the last beans into the pot with a groan.

"I wish we could go play in the creek." Ruthie scratched her arm again and glanced over her shoulder toward the green smudge of trees that marked the stream to the north.

Amalia glanced up at the sun. "I'm afraid we haven't time today. It must be past three o'clock."

"But you say that every time." Ruthie tipped her head and met Amalia's eyes. "We can't just work *all* the time."

Amalia opened her mouth, then closed it. Were the little girls right? Had she gotten so consumed with all that had to be done lately for this life of theirs that she'd forgotten—to actually live it?

Worse, had she put that on these children too?

"Look." Ruthie stood and pointed. "Here comes Cousin Maya."

Sure enough, Maya came striding across the yard from the Miller property line with Torvald in her arms.

"God dag." With a sigh, Maya climbed the steps and set her squirming son down to toddle. He'd begun to walk on his own last week and now lurched toward Amalia with a drooly grin.

"How are you today, big boy?" Amalia caught him under the arms just as he started to totter and lifted him onto her diminishing lap. Leaning her cheek against his sweet-smelling hair, she let out a long breath, the tension melting from her shoulders.

"He was getting awfully fretful in that hot kitchen, so since Mother Miller and I just finished canning for today, I thought I'd bring him over for a visit." Maya pushed back her sunbonnet and blew out a breath. "Feels a bit cooler over here, but not much."

"We've been on the fretful side over here too." Amalia eyed

the girls. "Thomi and Ruthie have been trying to convince me we should go to the creek for a while."

Maya's gray-blue eyes brightened. "What a wonderful idea. May we come?"

"Of course, if we—" Amalia chuckled as Ruthie and Thomi sprang to their feet in unison. "I didn't actually say yes yet."

"But why not?" Maya fanned herself with her hand. "You work hard enough every day, twice as much lately."

Amalia rolled her eyes. "I see you're all conspiring against me." She pushed to her feet. "Very well, then. We'll go, but only for a short while. Girls, lug the beans into the kitchen, then see if Miss Stenerson wants to go. She's in the parlor doing lesson plans." Between the summer classes and the fall term starting in a few weeks, Helen had been buried in books and papers.

Stepping into the kitchen, Amalia glanced at the clock. Her heart sank. "It's later than I thought." She glanced at the girls who had just reappeared in the doorway. "I don't think I'd better go after all. You all can go ahead, but I've got to get supper started for the boarders."

"Nonsense." Helen appeared in the doorway, her eyes brighter than Amalia had seen for some time. "You need a break more than any of us."

"But—"

"Just leave a cold supper and a note. They'll be fine."

Amalia stared at her friend. "A cold supper? And a—note?"

"Ja." Maya stepped next to Helen, Torvald on her hip. "Why not?"

"But . . ." Amalia glanced from her friend and cousin to the waiting stove, already grown cold from the canning fire earlier. She'd been going to fire it up again to make biscuits, though she dreaded the increased heat once again.

"What do you have in the larder?" Maya stepped toward the pantry.

"Well. I suppose that ham could be served cold. And there's plenty of bread."

Helen poked her head behind them. "Just add pickles and butter and some of those preserves you've been making."

"And cheese!" Ruthie piped up from behind the women. "Mr. Amos likes cheese."

Amalia stared at them all. "You are serious."

"Of course we are." Maya reached for a loaf of sourdough. "Come on."

With a shake of her head, Amalia followed with the ham. Together, they laid out the bread, butter, cheese, and ham on the sideboard in the dining room, covering the food with dishcloths to keep off any flies. The little girls added the crocks of pickles and preserves while Helen packed some of the food in a basket to take along with them.

Amalia breathed a laugh as she penned a note—*Gone to the creek. Please help yourselves to supper*—and set it in the middle of the table against the earthenware crock of daisies, pressing a hand to her lower back. "I can't believe I'm doing this."

"It's about time you had a bit of fun." Maya took her hand and tugged her through the kitchen and out the back door. "Come on."

The little girls ran ahead of them, barefoot and shrieking with glee. Maya bounced Torvald on her hip, singing a Norwegian folk song. Helen followed in her blue-trimmed straw hat, carrying the basket.

Crossing through the garden, Amalia glanced at the hayfield to the west, where far off she could see the dots of the men working on the mowing machine. Guilt pinched her middle again.

"Come on." Helen looped her arm through Amalia's. "Maybe they'll join us later."

Releasing a breath with the last of her resistance, Amalia trod the path toward the creek with her friend. "I feel like a guilty schoolgirl." Her lips twitched. "But it's fun."

"Playing hooky, we call it." Helen squeezed her arm. "And if anyone ever deserved an evening off, it's you." She lifted her head at a splashing and squealing ahead of them. "I think the girls found the creek."

Amalia chuckled. "I think they did."

Soon the burble of running water filled their ears. They picked their way down the creekbank, holding on to the branches of the slender trees that shaded the water. Maya came more slowly, holding Torvald's hand as he toddled his way along, stopping every few steps to pick up and examine each interesting rock, leaf, and beetle.

"Tante Malia!" Ruthie grinned up at her, ankle-deep in the creek, her gingham dress sopping to the knees. "It feels so good."

"Ja, I imagine." Amalia drew a long breath of the cooler air. "Even out of the water, it's nicer here."

"Told you." Tugging up her bloomers, Ruthie splashed through the water to where Thomi dug with a stick in the other bank. "Whatcha doing?"

"Digging for worms. We could go fishing, like Hank taught us."

"But we don't have poles."

"We could make 'em out of branches."

"But we don't have hooks."

"Oh." Thomi shrugged and tossed her stick aside. "Then let's look for frogs." The girls scrambled up the other side of the bank, braids and skirts dripping, and disappeared into the reeds.

Amalia and Helen looked at each other and burst out laughing.

"Oh, we needed this." Amalia sank onto a flat rock and set Helen's basket on the moss beside her. "Mange takk for making me come."

"Aren't you going in the water?" Bending over, Maya held tight to Torvald's tugging hand, struggling to untie her boot laces with the other.

"You are?"

"I won't get any peace unless I let him splash."

Amalia reached for the toddler and swung him onto her lap, tickling his tummy when he squirmed till he dissolved into giggles. "You are a water baby, aren't you?"

"There, takk." Maya kicked off her shoes and tugged off her stockings, setting them all neatly on a flat rock. "Come now, den lille." She took Torvald's chubby hands and let him walk down the muddy bank. He stuck one fat bare foot into the water, then pulled it back and tipped his head up to stare at his mor. Maya chuckled. "Is it cold?"

Torvald giggled, showing a toothy grin, then stepped in with both feet. Maya followed him, wetting her skirt hem. She glanced back at Amalia and Helen, eyes dancing. "You ladies are missing out."

Amalia looked at Helen, who sat on a fallen log looking composed and proper as ever in her white blouse, dark blue cotton skirt, and straw hat. "You aren't going to go in, are you?"

Helen arched a brow. "Are you?"

A giggle began somewhere in Amalia's chest. "I'm thinking about it."

"I will if you will."

Giggling outright now, Amalia began tugging at her bootlaces. "After all, it's just us girls."

Helen unbuttoned her boots, setting them carefully aside on the log. She offered her hand as they began making their way down to the creek, and Amalia took it, grateful for the extra security in her condition. The last thing she wanted to do was slip and fall. But they made it safely to the water, and the first touch of rushing coolness on her bare feet made Amalia draw in her breath, then let it out. "Ahh." Pure comfort pulsed from her soles to her head.

"What luxury." Helen held up her skirt, wading to her ankles. "I don't think I've ever set foot in a creek before."

"Really?" Maya held Torvald under his arms, the baby shrieking with glee as he danced his toes in the water. "We used to all the time as children. There was a stream near our farm. Amalia, remember when Ødger and Erik found that grass snake on the bank?"

"Ja." Amalia shivered but laughed.

Helen gave a half smile. "I envy you two, growing up with cousins and siblings. I was altogether too much alone as a child, I suppose. And once I moved to live with my aunt, I spent much of my time studying or practicing music. Though she did have a garden I loved to spend time in, but—no creeks."

They waded and splashed and took turns dancing Torvald's feet in the water or leading him through the pebbly shallows. When the sun slanted lower through the trees and Ruthie and Thomi splashed back up the creek, Helen pulled out the basket. They sat on the bank and feasted on ham and cheese and cold bread and butter.

"What a good idea to bring these." Amalia bit into one of the fresh peaches from the orchard that Maya had tucked in. "They are just starting to ripen, not enough yet for canning."

"Peaches always taste like summer to me." Maya fed a bite to Torvald, the golden juice running down his chin.

"Can we do this every day, Tante Malia?" Ruthie leaned against her side, munching a piece of cheese.

Amalia kissed the blond head leaning on her shoulder, smelling of sunshine and creek water. "Not every day, I'm afraid. But I'm certainly glad you suggested it today."

"Thomi and I found that old hut Mr. JJ used to live in, down the creek a ways. Remember, where I went when I was lost that time?"

Amalia's arm tightened around the little girl. "I certainly do." As if she'd ever forget it.

"Do you think we could make it into a playhouse or something? It's just sitting there."

"That's an interesting idea. Better ask Mr. JJ about it."

A barking sounded through the trees, and Dog came crashing through the brush, followed by Hank.

"What're you all doin'?" The boy stared from the basket to the multiple muddy, bare feet sticking out on the bank.

"Playing in the creek and having a picnic." Ruthie spread her arms as if it were obvious. Dog splashed into the water, barking and spraying droplets everywhere.

"Here. Have some." Thomi nudged the food basket closer to Hank with a bare foot.

Amalia tucked her feet under her. "Didn't you see my note?"

"JJ an' Erik found it, they told the boarders to go ahead an' eat. Absalom and Eben're comin' behind me, Eben came over wonderin' what happened to Maya."

Amalia and Maya exchanged guilty grins. What would their husbands think of their escapade? They began gathering the remaining fragments of food into the basket, but soon the crunch of leaves and snap of twigs came down the bank.

"There you are." Absalom ducked under a branch to join them, grinning. "Gone to the creek, huh?"

Amalia looked up at him, crinkling her nose. "Were the boarders upset?"

"Surprised, a little, but not upset. Once they saw the food, they were perfectly content." He settled onto the bank next to her with a sigh. "I see why you came. This is nice."

"Ja." Amalia reached for his hand. "I never planned to just run off—but Ruthie and Thomi wanted to go to the creek, it was so hot, and they've been working so hard—and then Maya and Helen convinced me, and, well . . ."

Absalom leaned over and kissed her nose. "I'm glad they did."

Eben appeared next, his big boots crashing through the brush.

Torvald looked up and grinned, holding up his arms. "Fa!"

"Hey, my little man." Eben swung his adopted son up into his arms, bending a little to avoid hitting the overarching branches with his head. "So. Here's where y'all ran off to." His gentle grin scanned the group and rested on Maya.

Maya smiled and shrugged. "It was so hot."

"Sure was. Seems like you had a right fine idea." Still holding Torvald, Eben kicked off his dusty boots, then waded into the water right in his stockings. The little girls squealed with laughter. Torvald drummed on Eben's chest with his fists, then lurched toward the water again.

"He thinks he's a fish. Or a turtle."

Barefooted, Hank jumped into the creek with Dog for a game of chase and tag, and the little girls joined in, shrieking and splashing.

Absalom chuckled, watching them and cradling Amalia's hand in his, his thumb rubbing gently over her knuckles. "Seems like this was long overdue."

"We've all been working so hard. Maybe a bit too hard." Amalia reached over to take a stray twig out of her husband's dark curls. "Certainly including you."

"Well, I know what to do next time I'm overwhelmed with clients and cases." He glanced at her, his eyes twinkling behind his spectacles.

"What?"

"I'll just say I'm 'gone to the creek.'"

Nineteen

Nearly the first day of school.

Helen laid down her new fountain pen, a gift from Aunt Ophelia before she'd left Ohio after this visit, with a sigh. Despite beginning to plan out this year's lesson plans for the various grades some weeks ago, she'd never felt so lacking in inspiration at the start of a new school year.

Her mother's diary lay on a corner of her desk, its dark green cover familiar to her hands by now. She'd continued to read an entry or so a day, sometimes more, though at times she had to force herself to. Lately the entries came shadowed with a palpable darkness, sometimes incoherent lines of grief and despair. Jotted sketches of her mother's life when Alf abandoned her, the hotel evicted her, and she wandered the streets, pregnant and alone, till someone from the Benedict Home for Women took her in.

No one loves me . . . no one cares. Will my baby even love me? All I can see around me is darkness . . .

Helen drew a breath and glanced out the second-story window of her room at the boardinghouse, a cool breeze wafting the blue-and-white curtains and blowing the fog from her own mind. Despite this sunny morning, the very end of August always held a tinge of change in the air—the temperatures lowering, especially at night, darkness falling sooner. She had ended her summer classes last week, in deference to those diving into harvest season. So she hadn't seen Ødger since, except briefly in church on Sunday—and he had come later than usual, arriving only with Rev. Larsen. He hadn't even come to the boardinghouse for Sunday dinner, since he was so busy getting ready to leave for Independence.

Her chest squeezed at that thought. Soon he would be gone, sixty miles away, and she still hadn't really told him why she'd reacted the way she did to that news. Why couldn't she have simply smiled politely and said yes, she'd be happy to exchange letters with him? Never mind that he was headed to minister in the very town where her mother had been committed to an insane asylum, or that he even hoped to minister to its inmates. Like the good and godly man he was.

And yet . . . how could she risk his heart, with so much of her own life still to sort through? The thought of the lingering hurt and hesitant hope she'd last seen in his eyes made her swallow.

Helen shut her desk drawer with a sharp tap. She owed him an explanation before he left. At least something. Their friendship—that word he kept mentioning—at least demanded that. Surely she could find a way . . . on Sunday, if he weren't too busy, or perhaps she could make it over to the magistrate's home in Decorah some evening after he finished one of his last days of work at the college. Though that would mean asking JJ to drive her, which could require a bit of explaining.

Helen pushed her chair back and stood. Thinking of JJ, she should see if he might drive her to the mercantile this morning. The day wasn't too hot yet, not even noon, and she'd ordered some supplies from Nygards' for the school. Might as well see if they'd come in yet, if he weren't too busy.

She found JJ in the orchard among the apple trees.

"Any ripe yet?" she asked, ducking under a laden branch.

"Not quite yet. But these here trees'll be the first, just give 'em a coupla weeks. I'm just checkin' on 'em, makin' sure we don't have any pests gettin' to the fruit."

"Have you found any?"

"Few signs of coddlin' moth, but don't look too bad." He tipped back his hat and gazed up at the leafy canopy, then eyed Helen. "But you didn't come out here to talk apples, I'll wager, Miss Helen. What kin I do for you?"

She smiled. "You wouldn't happen to be going to town today, would you?"

"Sure can, if you're needin' to make a trip. Missus Amalia's got a list for me for Nygards', though she said 'twasn't urgent."

"If it wouldn't be too much trouble, that's just where I'd like to go. I have an order of supplies coming in for school."

"Sure thing. Just let me check these last two trees, and I'll have the wagon hitched up in a jiffy."

Soon they rumbled along the road toward Green Creek, the wagon wheels and horses' hooves stirring up dust that made Helen's nose itch.

"Sure could use rain." JJ squinted at the horizon. "Been a right dry summer. See some clouds over there to the west, though."

Helen shaded her eyes to peer at the darkening mass on the horizon. "Think it'll reach us here?"

"I pray so. Would give the garden a nice drenchin' we've been needin'. Miss Ruthie and Thomi been waterin' it with buckets this week, got so dry."

"They are good workers, those two."

"That they are." JJ chuckled. "Though they find plenty o' time for mischief too. Lately they been pesterin' me to turn my old shack into some sort o' playhouse for 'em, till they got distracted with Magpie's new batch o' kittens last week."

"What do you think of their idea?" Helen glanced at him.

"Not sure Missus Amalia wants 'em playin' that far from the main house on the regular." JJ scratched his gray beard. "Still, I acknowledge it's a shame for it to jest stand there unused, 'cept for the critters that take shelter there. Eben and I been talkin' about some ideas for fixin' it up. Even got some notions about creatin' a pond back there."

Helen smiled. "Well, the two of you make a fine pair of builders, that's certain."

When they reached Nygards' Mercantile, JJ hitched the team to the rail and helped Helen down. Stepping inside the store, she breathed in the cool dimness, scented with leather, pickles, molasses, and dry goods.

"Well, hello there, JJ. Miss Stenerson." Mr. Nygard beamed at them from behind the counter. "What can I do for you?"

"Good afternoon, Mr. Nygard." Helen stepped toward him. "I wondered if my order has come in?"

"I seem to recollect some parcels bein' delivered. Let me check in the back." Mr. Nygard aimed a glance at JJ. "If you got a list for the boardinghouse, leave it there on the counter, and I'll get to it when I come back."

JJ nodded and pulled the paper from his pocket. "Much obliged."

A few moments later, Mr. Nygard emerged from the storeroom with two brown paper packages in his arms. "Here you are, miss. Want to check and see if all's as should be?"

"Thank you." As the storekeeper moved to fill Amalia's list, Helen untied the string and peeled back the rustling paper, a prickle of excitement running up her arms. A dozen new slates and three dozen slate pencils appeared neatly stacked in one package—while in theory students should bring their own, she always tried to have plenty for new students or those who couldn't afford them. The familiar chalky scent made her smile. Perhaps she was more ready for school to start than she'd thought. She unwrapped the other package, revealing a rolled world map, a new set of Baldwin's Readers to supplement her McGuffey's, a new volume of American history, and at the bottom, a copy of *The Supreme Song Book*.

Helen ran her fingers over the tan cover, a sudden knot in her throat. She'd intended to use this book as the basis for her new music classes. Would she follow through with her plans to add them this fall—still? Certainly not with Ødger's help, not at this point. She'd already failed at adding music this summer.

"Ain't those a fine-lookin' set." JJ approached. "Help you carry 'em to the wagon, Miss Helen? Nygard's about got the rest of our order ready."

Helen nodded. "Thank you." She rewrapped the parcels, staying silent as together they loaded the wagon, then climbed in to head back down the road.

Once more, thoughts of Ødger filled her mind. Singing with him on the porch, laughing with him at that supper at the Millers'. Their easy camaraderie—and perhaps, a budding of something more. And now, it seemed it all would so quickly be merely a memory.

What would she tell him, if she had a chance? *My mother went insane and was committed to that asylum you mentioned, and I'm terrified that any man who pursues me will think I'll end up there as well. So, Godspeed.* She flinched. No, not that.

Just at the turnoff toward Forsberg House, JJ slapped his knee. "I plumb forgot. I been needin' to pick up some wood from the lumberyard in Decorah, for those new wheelbarrows Amalia wants. But it's clear over past the college. I kin drop you off back at the boardin'house afore I head all the way out there."

"There's no need. I don't mind going with you." A thought buzzed through her mind, and Helen's pulse picked up. Could she—should she? She shouldn't disturb him at his work, but it might still be the hour for the laborers' lunch break. "Actually." She cleared her throat. "Could you possibly drop me at the college on your way? And pick me up when you return?"

JJ eyed her, raising his scraggly gray brows. "Sure could, Miss Helen. But might I ask what you plan on doin' there?"

"I . . ." Helen swallowed, heat rising in her cheeks. "I thought I might walk about a bit, on the campus, I haven't been there. And Ødger is working there, you know. I might . . . say hello."

"Ah, so he is." JJ nodded as if a schoolmarm wanting to visit a young single man were the most natural thing in the world. "A right fine idea."

Helen wasn't at all sure she agreed when JJ rumbled off in the wagon, promising to return within the hour and leaving her under the arching shade of one of the many trees on the college campus. Drawing a long breath, she adjusted her hat and walked down one of the quiet, tree-lined paths across the campus. The green lawns and sun-dappled shade quieted her heart and mind despite herself, and she tipped back her head at the familiar trill of a robin, trying to spot the songbird. This was a lovely place. Why had she never come to walk here before?

She half-laughed at the thought. As if she hadn't enough to keep her busy between teaching eight grades, helping at the boardinghouse, adding summer classes, visiting Aunt Ophelia. . . . Her steps slowed at the thought of her aunt. How was her health? She hadn't received a letter in nearly a fortnight. Helen should write again this week, and to Mrs. Hoskins as well, to receive a more accurate report.

She followed the path—and the distant sound of hammering—till the large brick main building of the college rose up before her. She paused to take it in, the tall central tower and three tiers of Gothic-esque windows. Hard to believe it had burned only two years ago, now rebuilt quite in its former glory, though work on the interior and additional buildings still continued.

Her pulse speeding up once more, Helen approached the expansive building, then looked around for the source of the hammering sound. Seeing a smaller building—perhaps a dormitory?—off to the side and obviously under stages of construction, she drew near.

A broad-shouldered young man turned to pick up a board, stared at her, then snatched off his hat. "Why, Miss Stenerson."

"Good day, Mr. Rykavyk." Helen smiled to see the boarder's familiar face.

"Good day to you." He gripped his hat between his hands. "I didn't expect to see you. Is all well at the boardinghouse?"

"Yes, perfectly well. No cause for alarm." She hesitated, then pressed forward, resisting the warming of her ears. "Is Mr. Gunderson around, by any chance?"

"Ja, I mean, yes, ma'am." Asgar Rykavyk thumbed over his shoulder. "Believe he's right around the corner."

"Thank you." Straightening her spine, Helen strode around the corner. After all, she was doing nothing improper, here in broad daylight, with plenty of people around. She merely wished to speak to a friend, to explain why she had pulled away. And if he were working, she'd merely say hello, and at least it would be something. At least she would see him—

She stopped short, nearly stumbling on a stray brick. There stood Ødger, certain enough. But not working, though he held a hammer in his hand—talking, not with another member of the crew, but a young woman. A lovely young woman, with curly hair and a becomingly flowered hat, who stood handing a tin cup to Ødger and laughing. At something he'd said?

Helen stood still a moment, her heart beating, her breath hitching painfully in her chest. Then she spun around to go, her eyes smarting, hardly seeing where she stepped on the uneven ground.

"Miss Stenerson?"

At the call behind her, that familiar, richly accented voice, she halted, squeezing her eyes shut an instant. Then made herself turn, and smile. "Mr. Gunderson."

Ødger half-ran to catch up with her, staring as if she'd materialized from thin air. "What brings you here? Is all well?"

"Yes, all is well." Why on earth had she come? "I merely—" She drew a breath, trying to steady her voice. "JJ and I came to town on some errands, and he dropped me here to walk awhile." Nothing could bring her to add *and see you*. She glanced about the serene grounds. "Such a lovely campus you have here."

"Have you never been?"

"No, not really. I've driven past, of course."

"Ja, of course." Ødger shifted his hat in his hands, then glanced behind him at the young woman approaching. "Oh. May I introduce Miss Lena Amundson, daughter of one of my professors. Miss Amundson, Miss Helen Stenerson. She teaches the school in Green Creek."

"How charming." Miss Amundson flicked a smile from Ødger to Helen and extended a graceful hand. "How do you do?"

"How do you do?" Helen briefly grasped the other woman's hand, hoping her smile stayed genuine. "Do you attend the college also, Miss Amundson?"

"Oh dear, no." She gave a light laugh. "Surely you know only men are admitted?"

Of course that would be the case, for a college focused on preparation for theological training. Helen's ears burned. "Forgive me. I attended a college for women in Ohio, so I wasn't certain."

"Ah." Miss Amundson arched a brow. "How fascinating. I'm afraid my own advanced studies have been mostly limited to music, as Mr. Gunderson knows." She cast him another smile.

A weight leadened in Helen's stomach, but she kept her own smile stubbornly in place. "So you share an interest in music?"

"Indeed. I've shown Mr. Gunderson the organ we have here at the college—it's one of the finest in the state, I've been told."

"It is indeed a very fine instrument." Ødger nodded, clasping his hands behind his back. The breeze teased his unhatted hair. "Miss Stenerson also plays the organ, though she prefers piano. She often plays for our services in Green Creek."

"Ah." Miss Amundson's delicate brows rose beneath her stylish fringe—which she wore much better than Helen did. "How lovely. Of course, I've never attended there—we always go to First Lutheran in Decorah."

Suddenly the little Green Creek church seemed quite provincial. Helen swallowed and stepped back. "Well, it was a pleasure to meet you, Miss Amundson." Or at least, quite enlightening. "And to see you, Mr. Gunderson. I'm afraid I must be going, but I wish you both a good day." With the utmost self-control, she moderated her steps as she turned and headed back up the path toward the road where JJ would fetch her, keeping her feet from running as fast as she could flee.

JJ didn't press her to speak on the ride home, though she felt his grandfatherly gaze and the pucker between his brows, however hard she didn't look at him. The gray clouds he'd noted had blanketed the sun by the time they reached Forsberg House, the first drops of needed rain making dark blotches on the brown paper packages from Nygards' as he pulled into the yard. Hank and Amalia came out to help them unload as the raindrops splatted down faster and faster.

"I'll take the horses into the barn," Hank hollered above the first clap of thunder.

Amalia laughed as she and Helen tumbled the final packages onto the kitchen table. "What a gift, summer rain." The downpour drummed now on the porch roof like a battalion of marching soldiers. "Thank you for going to town with JJ."

"Actually, I asked him to take me." Helen unpinned her wet hat, trying to ignore the choking lump in her throat. "If you don't need me anymore—?"

"No, I'm fine, but are you all right?"

But Helen had scooped her own parcels into her arms, fleeing up the stairs.

In her room, she clicked the door shut behind her and set her hat to dry on the windowsill with trembling fingers. The sharp, sweet scent of rain rushed in through her open window with a cooling breeze, but her eyes still burned. She lowered the books onto her desk, crumpling aside the wet paper, then pressed a trembling fist to her lips.

Be strong, Helen. Don't let mere emotions get the better of you. But she didn't have an instrument to play here to release the storm inside. She pressed her fingertips to her eyes, trying to quell the first sob. Still it burst through, so raw it frightened her. Then another, and another, choking, gasping. She crumpled onto her bed, as she hadn't since she was a little girl first arrived at Aunt Ophelia's, and wept.

Both storms, outside and within, had blown out much of their fury by the time a faint tapping came at her door. Helen sat up, wiped the backs of her fingers across her eyes, and pushed at her hair, doubtless hopelessly mussed by her lack of restraint. Shaking her head at herself, she sniffled a long breath and went to the door.

Opening it just a crack, she saw Amalia's face, a pinch between her friend's light brows.

"Helen? Are you all right?"

Helen opened her mouth, then shut it. She didn't feel capable of pretending anymore—at least not just now, not to this friend closer than any she'd had in her life. As if her reddened eyes and swollen nose wouldn't give her away anyway. With a slight shake of her head, she stepped back to let Amalia in, then shut the door again behind her.

"I'm sorry." Helen pressed her lips together, trying to hide their trembling.

"Dear one." Amalia cupped her elbows, her own eyes sheening. "You have nothing to be sorry for. You are always so strong, but something's been troubling you for some time, I think. Won't you let me in and tell me what it is?"

Helen squeezed her eyes shut against the stubbornly brimming tears. Tell her—could she tell her everything? Of her mother, who wasn't actually her mother, and her aunt, and her childhood, and this new, mysterious family she hadn't known of, and all the unknowns and questions that had swirled up in new and dreadful shape this summer?

But all that choked from her lips was "Ødger."

"Oh, my dear friend." Amalia's arms came around her, held Helen as gently as if she were Ruthie as she sobbed, again so hard it frightened her, into Amalia's shoulder. "I wondered."

Helen pulled back, sniffling, tear-blinded. "Wondered? How could you—I mean, how did you know?"

"Maya has suspected something between you and her brother for some time. She told me—we've always shared so much, you know." Amalia dug out a handkerchief from her apron pocket and held it out to Helen. "So I've been watching too. It's not hard to see some feeling between you two."

Helen dabbed at her eyes. "You truly think he—cares—for me?"

"Ja, I do—we both did." Amalia cocked her head. "But something has felt different, the last few weeks, with you, and even with him. Did something happen?"

"Yes—and no. I don't know." Helen sank onto the side of the bed, all the strength gone out of her legs. Amalia sat down beside her, the bedstead creaking. "If it did, it's all my fault." She told her what Ødger had said after the supper at the Millers', and how she had responded—or not.

"We talked a little before church a couple of weeks ago, which helped—but things still haven't felt right. So then today, when JJ needed to go to Decorah, I asked him to leave me at the college a little while. I thought perhaps I could explain—or at least make clear that I value his friendship, if nothing more." The tears flooded again. "But he was—he was with . . . another woman."

"What?" Amalia's blue eyes snapped.

"Oh, nothing improper. She was bringing refreshments to the

workers, I believe—a professor's daughter, he said. But she—I could tell she had eyes for Ødger. At least, I think so. And it seemed everything she said shot as a little arrow straight at me."

"Maybe you just imagined it."

"Perhaps. I don't know." Helen splayed her fingers over her face. "All I'm sure of is I've made a complete fool of myself in everything related to . . . him."

Amalia breathed a laugh. "I don't think it's quite as bad as all that. And if I know my cousin, he isn't so easily swayed as you may seem to think. I'd be very much surprised if he didn't still carry a strong interest in you, dear friend. But . . . " Amalia hesitated. "I still don't understand. What made you distance yourself from Ødger to begin with? Is it that he's going away for the year? There are such things as writing letters, you know."

"It wasn't that—not just that." Helen lowered her hands and sighed. How much shame must she drag herself through today? Yet already the weight in her heart had lightened, to not have to bear it all alone. "I've told you my mother was ill, that that's why Aunt Ophelia raised me."

"Ja." Amalia searched Helen's face.

"What I didn't tell you—what I suppose I was ashamed to tell you—is her illness wasn't what you might think. She was committed to the Iowa Hospital for the Insane. In Independence, where Ødger is to go."

Amalia's eyes cleared. "So when he told you he was going there . . ."

"Not just that. He brought up the asylum itself, said he hoped to minister there. I . . ." Helen's chest clenched again, her fingers twisting together of their own accord. "I told you I was to be married, once."

"Ja, of course. You loaned me your beautiful wedding dress." Amalia's brow pinched again, doubtless trying to connect all these tangled threads. "I always wanted to ask you the story, but I didn't want to pry."

"I told you I'd tell you one day." Helen managed a smile. "My fiancé, James . . . he jilted me when he learned my mother had been ill in her mind, that she was committed to the asylum. I should have told him sooner, but it never came up till we were engaged—Aunt Ophelia raised me in the best society, and I suppose he assumed my parents were dead. But when he found out . . ." Her lips tightened. "He didn't want to risk that sort of disease being passed on to, well. Our possible children. Or the chance that I might even develop it later in life."

"Oh, Helen." Amalia covered Helen's hand with her own. "Surely you don't think Ødger would treat you so."

Helen let out a long breath. "No, I suppose not. But how could I ask anyone, really, to connect to such a tangled heritage as mine? You don't even know the half of it yet. I learned this summer she probably wasn't even my real mother." She chuckled slightly at her friend's widened eyes. "I know—I have a lot to explain. But with Ødger, I suppose it seemed safer . . . to just pull away. Stay with my teaching, where I'm not supposed to marry anyway."

Amalia sat quiet a moment. "Safer, perhaps. For now." Her fingers tightened on Helen's. "But think carefully, friend, before you throw this possibility of the love of a good man away. I know I felt tempted to pull back too, once, from Absalom . . . but I'm so glad I didn't."

Helen leaned her head on her friend's shoulder. All her strength seemed drained right out her toes. "All my life it seems I've been trying to find my place, to prove myself as—I don't know, enough. Worthy, somehow, despite my supposed accomplishments. I still can't believe such a good man as Ødger, and a minister besides . . . that he would truly want me."

"I wish you could see yourself as we do." Amalia gently stroked her hair. "The impact you've had on all of us . . . think of Hank, and Ruthie. And Thomi . . . none of them would be where they are without your influence, your diligent tutelage, you believing in them and not giving up on them." She lowered her hand and gave Helen's one more squeeze. "Perhaps someday, you will see we feel the same about you. Or at least see yourself as your heavenly Father does."

Helen sighed and sniffed again. "Perhaps you're right. But in the meantime, what am I to do about Ødger?"

"I think, despite everything, you had the right idea today." Amalia patted her hand and rose. "You need to talk to him."

TWENTY

"So this shall be your last Sunday with us?"

Ødger looked up from unfolding the white cloth for the communion table at the front of the church. Rev. Larsen, settling his stole as he sat behind the pulpit, peered over his spectacles at him.

"Ja, it is." Ødger spread the cloth over the table, the fine fabric catching on his work-roughened hands. Friday had been his last day on the construction crew. His departure had been pushed back a week, but now it was settled. "I leave for Independence on the day after tomorrow."

"I thought so. The eighth of September." The reverend shook his head. "We shall dearly miss you, my boy. I certainly shall."

Not for the first time, guilt pinched Ødger's chest. Would the elderly pastor manage all right without him? "I have asked young Hank from Forsberg House to come early to help you prepare the church on Sunday mornings. And Professor Amundson hopes to have another student scheduled to help you with visitations. By the end of this week or at least next."

Rev. Larsen waved a hand whose knuckles swelled with arthritis. "Oh, don't you worry about me. I got on fine before you came, and the Lord and I will make our way together after. But you've become more than an assistant, these past months—more an associate, a true friend." He laid his hands on his cassock-clad knees and nodded. "Any congregation will be blessed to have you."

"Mange takk. I have learned so much from working with you, Reverend. Yet at the same time, I feel I have hardly begun."

Rev. Larsen chuckled. "As it should be." He waved a gnarled finger. "If you thought you knew everything, now, then I would be worried."

Ødger chuckled too. "What else can I do?"

"I think we're about ready." At a creak from the front door, Rev. Larsen peered over the top of the pulpit with a nod. "Here comes our faithful accompanist."

Ødger swung his head around, his heart thumping.

Sure enough, Helen Stenerson came down the aisle, in her quiet, dove-gray Sunday dress, though the fashionable bustle showed it had come back with her from Cincinnati. She nodded at the pastor. "Good morning, Reverend."

"Good morning to you, Miss Stenerson. A lovely day, is it not?"

"Indeed." Her eyes flicked to Ødger's face. "Good morning, Mr. Gunderson."

So they were back to that formality? He'd thought, after what she said before church a few weeks ago, that they were making progress. Though when she'd stopped at the college . . . he still didn't know what to make of that. Ødger's chest tightened, but he dipped his head. "Good morning."

Helen turned to the piano, laying her light shawl atop it.

"Ødger." Rev. Larsen settled back with his Bible. "Would you show Miss Stenerson the hymns we discussed for this morning's service?"

"Ja, of course." Lifting the hymnal they'd perused together this morning , he crossed the slightly elevated wooden platform at the front of the church, where the pulpit, communion table, and piano all sat, his footsteps creaking on the floorboards.

Helen sat down on the piano bench and opened the lid over the keys, not looking at him.

Ødger cleared his throat and set the hymnal on the music rack. "We thought to begin with 'It is Well with My Soul.'"

Helen stilled a moment, then opened the hymnbook, turning the pages to that hymn. "I love that one."

Something released in Ødger's chest. "Ja. I do too." The story behind the hymn's writing never failed to move him. "Did you know Spafford's wife was Norwegian?"

"I did." Helen's fingers moved lightly over the keyboard, reviewing the melody, then stopped, and she laid her hands in her lap. "Ødger—I want to apologize for interrupting you at the college the other day."

Ødger glanced behind him, where Rev. Larsen sat absorbed in the Scriptures. "There is no need—"

"Please." She turned on the bench to meet his eyes.

He closed his mouth.

She twisted her fingers together in her lap. "As I said, JJ and I were doing errands, and I asked him to drop me by the college. I hadn't walked around the campus before, true, but mostly . . . I wanted to see you."

Ødger sucked a silent breath.

"I wanted . . . to apologize, again. And explain." Her eyes sheened, looking into his. "I know I have distanced myself, from our friendship, after that evening at the Millers'—goodness, over a month ago now."

He clasped his hands behind his back. "You already apologized for that. You owe me no explanation, Miss Stenerson."

"Helen." She gave a small, trembling smile.

He dipped his head, grateful. "Helen. But I fear it is I who should apologize. The way I spoke to you that evening at Maya and Eben's—I presumed things that I had no right to." He kept his voice low, though he doubted Rev. Larsen heard. At least his presence kept them from any impropriety, though.

"No—no. You were a perfect gentleman. As you always are." Her voice thinned. "It was nothing you did, or said—at least, nothing for which to blame yourself. Merely . . ." She sighed and rubbed her forehead. "Your new position in Independence."

He frowned, then nodded. "I see. Because I was leaving."

"No, not just that. It's—" Helen glanced down the aisle, where a few early arrivers had begun to trickle into the church. "I can't tell you all now. But that hospital you mentioned. The asylum." She closed her eyes, then opened them again. "My mother was committed there. When I was a child."

He stared at her, sudden light pouring into the dark fog that had come between them. "I see."

"What I mean to say is, it truly was nothing you did. Merely my own memories that came up to haunt me." She sighed and glanced at the filling pews again. "I have no good excuse, but—I'm sorry."

"You have nothing to be sorry for. Not really. But takk for telling me." He gave her a smile, heartened to see an answering one tip her lips. "And now I had best let you practice before the church fills."

She breathed a laugh. "I suppose you are right."

Ødger headed back across the platform to the pulpit, where Rev. Larsen had asked him to give the invocation today. The minister, in his tucked-away seat, looked up with a smile, a twinkle behind his spectacles.

Ødger's neck heated suddenly. Just how much did this mild-mannered man hear? Or suspect? Well, no matter. Ødger laid his hands on the pulpit top and drew a long breath, his chest lighter than in some time. He still had so many questions—even more than before. Helen's mother had been in a mental institution? What a shadow that must have cast over her childhood. His heart ached for her.

And yet—she had not been angry with him. She had reached

out to him, to mend what had come between them, even coming to his place of work to try and explain. She cared enough for that. Though the sudden memory of her face when she saw Lena Amundson burned in his memory. Had she thought there was something between them? And—did that matter to her? A sudden leap in his chest told him what that might mean. And yet . . .

Ødger turned away from the gathering, murmuring congregation to light the candles at the altar, a twist in his gut. Yet now—he was going away.

Lord, help me. I want to do your will. Inhaling through his nose, he blew out his match, then turned to focus on the people entering, one pew at a time. He saw Erik, followed by Amalia and Absalom chatting with Maya and Eben, Ruthie and Thomi and Hank trailing behind into their row. Magistrate Karlsson came down the aisle, cane tapping, bestowing a smile or a kind word on all he passed—he visited here once in a while to attend with his family and better know the Green Creek community, though his home congregation was in Decorah. The Trotter family slipped into a back pew, even—Ødger's eyes stung—their troubled son, Phillip. The boy kept his head lowered, but he was there. *Father, please bring healing to this precious young man and his family.* Other faces, most so familiar now—the Nygards, the rest of the Miller clan, the Flinches.

He glanced behind him at Rev. Larsen, who gave him a nod, then faced the rows of beloved faces once more, clearing the lump from his throat. "In the name of the Father and of the Son and of the Holy Spirit."

"Amen," the congregation responded.

Helen sounded the opening chords of the hymn, and Ødger joined in the swelling chorus.

> "When peace like a river attendeth my way,
> when sorrows like sea billows roll;

whatever my lot, thou hast taught me to say,
'It is well, it is well with my soul.'"

He glanced at Maya, singing with all her heart beside her husband, Torvald resting his little head on her shoulder. His throat tightened . . . how fitting these words for his sister, last year especially, when ocean waves took her first husband. Yet seeing the peace on her unlined face now, he knew the words rang true for her heart.

"It is well
with my soul;
it is well, it is well with my soul . . ."

Ødger bowed his head, leaning his hands on the wooden pulpit, letting the words wash over him. *Lord, whatever you have for me, I want to trust you. I want it to be well with my soul. So why this turmoil within me? Is it not your will I go to Independence? I thought it was. And Helen . . . what am I to do about Helen?*

A rustling silence raised his head. The hymn had ended, the congregation settling. Ødger stepped aside for Rev. Larsen to take his place for the confession.

With his usual shuffling steps, the minister made his way to lean on the wooden pulpit, looking out over the congregation with a smile. He didn't even need to look at the book of service, knowing the words by heart.

"Almighty God, to whom all hearts are open, all desires known, and from whom no secrets are hid: Cleanse the thoughts of our hearts by the inspiration of your Holy Spirit, that we may perfectly love you and worthily magnify your holy name, through Jesus Christ our Lord."

"Amen."

Rev. Larsen continued through the responsive confession and

absolution, then Ødger stood to announce the next hymn. After Helen sounded the final chords of the "Amen" on the piano, she slipped to her seat, and Ødger took the pulpit again. He would read the Scripture, then Rev. Larsen would give the sermon, as had become their pattern these last months. Someday, he would preach his own first sermon, but he didn't feel quite ready for that yet.

"Our text this morning comes from Luke 10, verses 35 through 37." The parable of the Good Samaritan, always one of his favorites. Ødger cleared his throat and began. "'And, behold, a certain lawyer stood up, and tempted him, saying, Master, what shall I do to inherit eternal life? He said unto him, What is written in the law? how readest thou? And he answering said, Thou shalt love the Lord thy God with all thy heart, and with all thy soul, and with all thy strength, and with all thy mind; and thy neighbour as thyself . . .'"

He finished the passage, then crossed the platform to sit backward on the piano bench, as he typically did during the message—near at hand if needed, yet not crowding the minister.

Rev. Larsen stood and laid his hands on the papery pages of the Bible. "Good morning, friends. Our text today addresses the great question . . . the great question of . . ." Blinking hard, he stared at the Bible before him.

Ødger frowned, leaning forward.

The minister lifted a trembling hand. "Forgive me. Our text today . . . our Lord tells us . . ." His words slurred. His face slackening, he leaned forward, resting his forehead on the Bible, then crumpled to the floor behind the pulpit.

Ødger leaped to his feet, rushing to the minister's side. Gasps and exclamations erupted from the congregation.

"Reverend Larsen!" Supporting the elderly man's head and shoulders, Ødger tried to ease him into a more comfortable position. "Sir, can you hear me?"

Other hands appeared beside his—Absalom, Eben. Together they stretched Rev. Larsen out to lie on the platform.

"Is he breathing?"

Absalom bent his ear to Rev. Larsen's still face, then lifted his head. "Yes, but he's unconscious."

"Someone go for the doctor," Magistrate Karlsson's steady voice boomed out.

"I will." Eben sprang up and sprinted down the aisle toward the door. A child wailed.

Helen knelt beside them. "Here." She held out the pillow from the piano bench.

"Takk." His hands shaking, Ødger lifted the minister's head a bit for her to slip the cushion under. "He's been weakening, I knew, but I didn't realize—"

"You couldn't have. None of us did." She laid her hand on his arm, just a slight squeeze, then released before anyone would have seen.

Ødger nodded, his throat too tight for words. *Lord, help this good man. Please.*

It seemed hours before the doctor arrived from Decorah. Ødger had dismissed the congregation, asking for their prayers. Only Absalom, Eben, and the magistrate stayed with him and the minister. And Helen, quiet and off to the side.

Dr. David Armitage knelt on the platform and opened his black bag with his usual taciturn focus. "How long since he collapsed?"

"I'm not sure." Ødger shook his head, trying to clear it. "An hour?"

Helen checked the chatelaine watch pinned to her bodice. "Three-quarters of one."

Once more, he knew a stab of relief at her presence. "Thank you."

"And his symptoms before the collapse? Any pain, clutching of his chest?"

"Not that I saw. He seemed confused, then collapsed."

"Any slurring of the speech?"

Ødger nodded. "Ja. Right before."

The doctor looked into Rev. Larsen's unresponsive eyes, felt his pulse. "I see few signs of a heart attack. My guess would be a fit of apoplexy, sometimes called a stroke."

A stroke? The word settled heavy in Ødger's gut. "What causes that?"

"A blockage in the brain, often. Sometimes a hemorrhage."

"What can be done?" Absalom asked.

"Not much, I'm afraid. The most we can do is make him comfortable and let him rest. If he regains consciousness, he may have impairment of at least one side of his body. I can then begin treatment to try and help him regain some of his faculties, but . . ." The doctor shook his head, his black-bearded face sober. "At his advanced age, I can promise little. Is there someone who might be able to stay with him in his home, care for him? At least for a few days?"

Eben and Absalom glanced at each other.

Eben gave a firm nod. "We'll figure somethin' out."

But those men had families and worked from sunup to sundown.

"I will stay." Ødger reached for the minister's limp hand and gripped it.

Independence would simply have to wait.

Twenty-One

The first day of school, and Amalia could hardly wait for everyone to get out of the boardinghouse.

With breakfast over, the Rykavyk brothers, along with railroad workers Declan and Finley, shouldered their rucksacks for a day's labor and stomped out to the porch amid good-natured banter, taking their lunches packed last night by Amalia. Meanwhile, Ruthie, Hank, and Thomi darted around in a last-minute scramble for their books, slates, and stray shoes.

"I can't find my slate pencil!" A cry from Ruthie. "Oh, a kitten was playing with it under the sofa." At four weeks old, Magpie's kittens had begun to venture beyond their basket and scamper about underfoot.

"Where's my other boot?" Thomi demanded.

"Right there, silly." Hank took the tone of an older, wiser, and much beleaguered older brother. "Where you put it last night."

Amalia lined up four filled dinner pails on the kitchen table and blew out a breath, pressing a hand to her aching lower back. She hadn't slept well, kept awake by the irregular tightenings Mrs. Miller called false labor contractions. She'd been having them for weeks, and their motherly neighbor assured her that was perfectly normal, but the cramps were definitely coming more frequently as her time drew nearer.

"Hank, girls," she called, stepping to the kitchen doorway. "Your dinners."

The children stampeded into the kitchen and snatched up their pails just as Helen hurried down the stairs in her white shirtwaist and dark skirt, teacher's satchel in hand.

"You look ready for a new year." Amalia smiled as she handed her friend the last dinner pail, then put a hand to her belly at another tightening.

Helen, despite her hurry, paused with a frown. "You all right?"

Amalia let out a breath. "I will be, once these wild ones have cleared out." She smiled. "Really, I'm fine. I've got a couple of weeks still yet, at least. I just could use a bit of rest, and quiet."

"If you're sure." Helen gave her another long glance. "Want me to tell JJ to stick close to the house? I don't think he's headed out to the fields quite yet."

"No need." Amalia kissed each of the little girls, and even tugged Hank in for a quick hug. "You all have a good first day, now, and mind Miss Stenerson."

"We will," they chorused, then flew out the door to where Hank had the wagon hitched and ready since before breakfast.

Amalia stepped out to the porch to wave them off, inhaling the scent of cooling September air, the hint of apples and turning leaves. Her shoulders relaxed, and she turned back to the gentle silence of the boardinghouse. Quiet at last—this was what she'd needed. Even the piles of breakfast dishes didn't daunt her, since she'd no lack of time to do them now. How she loved each person who contributed to the bustle and noise of Forsberg House, but sometimes, it came as a breath of fresh air to be alone. Amos was away on the railroad this week, and even Mr. Dahl had taken a trip—writing research, he said.

She washed, wiped, and put away the dishes, pausing occasionally to notice the intermittent clenching of her abdomen. The cramping didn't hurt, exactly—but it did seem stronger than she'd remembered. *Just your body practicing, getting itself in shape,* she repeated Mrs. Miller's reassuring words to herself. *Nothing to worry over. When it's time—you'll know.*

With the last pots and pans wiped clean and dry, Amalia hung the damp dishtowel and waddled her way to the parlor. Walking normally had seemed harder the last couple of days, the baby was growing so big. She eased herself into the rocking chair, rocking luxuriously a few moments, then tried to reach for her sewing basket set on the floor nearby. She stretched and strained over her mounding belly, then laughing at herself, lowered herself to the floor and hefted the basket up onto the table where she could reach it easily from the rocking chair. She wanted to hem a few of the remaining baby garments so they would be ready. Thanks to Mrs. Miller's contributions, Maya's hand-me-downs from Torvald, and her own sewing all summer, she now had a pretty good stock.

She had just pushed herself to her hands and knees, preparing to stand, when a sudden gush of liquid made her gasp.

For a moment she knelt frozen there on the floor, feeling the fluid soak her skirts and begin to puddle beneath her. Then a contraction seized her belly, grinding deeper and with more purpose than any she'd ever known.

"Ohhh." She glanced around at the empty parlor, the emptiness of the boardinghouse beyond, her chest tightening too. "Oh, no—oh, no, no, no."

She knew now—just as Mrs. Miller had said she would. It was time. But she hadn't known soon enough. And now she was all alone.

Once the contraction passed, Amalia dragged herself to her feet, dripping her sodden skirts along the parlor floor as she hobbled to the front door and flung it open, then lurched out onto the porch.

"JJ!" she hollered toward the barn, so loud her voice cracked. "JJ?" She leaned against a porch post, gripping the railing.

No answer. She glanced toward the oat field, her chest caving as she glimpsed the mowing machine far in the distance already. JJ was beginning the harvest here on his own, a bit at a time, to be ready for the threshers when they returned.

Another contraction began, clenching her lower back, reaching iron fingers around her belly. Amalia groaned, gripping the railing till her fingernails dug into the wood. Was it supposed to feel this hard, this fast, so soon? Or had she been in labor since last night, and just foolishly not realized it? Oh, why hadn't she listened to Helen?

"Mrs. Miller," she whispered as the cramping passed. She must get over to their neighbors' property. Mrs. Miller would know what to do. *Please, Lord, let her be home. Please—help me.*

She made her way down the steps, then across the yard, past the chicken coop, stopping to lean against it for another contraction. The fence marking the property line seemed a mile away, but at last she grasped the solid rough gate of it, panting.

"Mrs. Miller . . ." Her first weak attempt at a call made her shake her head and clear her throat. No one would hear a whisper from here. "Mrs. Miller!" She scanned the gray farmhouse, the barn, the garden—there. A familiar figure in a sunbonnet bent between the rows. *Oh, God, thank you.*

"Mrs. Miller!" Amalia yelled again, managing a few more steps toward the garden. The figure shifted, straightened, shaded her face with a hand. Then dropped her basket and came hurrying toward Amalia.

Mange takk, Lord. Oh, tusen takk. Amalia backstepped a bit to lean against the fence.

"Amalia, are you all right?" The older woman took in Amalia's face and soaked skirt in one glance. "Oh, my dear. It's time, isn't it?"

"Ja." Sudden tears sprang to Amalia's eyes, blurring her vision. "And everyone is gone—I didn't realize, I'd had cramping all night, but I didn't realize till my water broke, and—" She broke off with a moan, grabbing for Mrs. Miller's arm.

"That's it, just breathe right through it. Deep breaths now." Mrs. Miller's hand moved in soothing circles on Amalia's lower back. "Good. Now," when the contraction passed, "let's get you back to the boardinghouse, and we'll send JJ for Dr. Armitage right away."

"He's way out in the fields—I couldn't reach him."

"Then I'll send Abram to fetch JJ, he's still in the house, finishing up his breakfast. He doesn't get out in the fields as much these days, you know, since his operation—leaves that more for the hired help, and I'm glad of it." Mr. Miller had at first resisted the doctor's recommendation of surgery for an abdominal mass last spring, but at last his wife and Eben had convinced him to take that step. "But he'll be more than up to this task—happy to be useful, mind you."

Amalia let out a long breath and leaned into her friend's shoulder. "I'm so glad you're here."

Before she hardly knew what had happened, Mrs. Miller had summoned her husband and dispatched him for JJ, gotten Amalia into the boardinghouse, changed her dress for a muslin nightgown, and even cleaned up the mess in the parlor.

"Should I get in bed?" Amalia asked, leaning on the bedpost.

"Goodness, no, not yet. We'll walk awhile first. Best thing for moving a labor along and will keep you and baby more comfortable too." Mrs. Miller cocked her head at the murmur of voices just outside. "That'll be Abram and JJ now. I'll pop out and tell Abram not to waste any time fetching the doctor, this baby seems to be in some hurry."

"And Absalom?" Amalia whispered, her chest clenching for wanting him.

"Of course. I'll tell him to stop in at the magistrate's straight after." Mrs. Miller squeezed her shoulder and stepped out.

Once the men had gone, they took advantage of the empty boardinghouse to walk freely, from the bedroom to the parlor to the kitchen, even through the dining room and back. The chime of the parlor clock marked the morning away—ten o'clock . . . half past ten . . . eleven.

Amalia let her breath out in a whoosh as the pressure eased after another contraction. "How much longer, do you think?"

"First babies often take their sweet time." Mrs. Miller helped her resume their pace once more, Amalia leaning on her arm. "I labored a day and a half before my Lawrence was born. Eben, bless him, only took four hours, like the bundle of good nature he's always been. You seem to be making right rapid progress for a first-time mama."

"You've done this so many times." Amalia puffed at another contraction. "And—I know it—only will get—harder."

Mrs. Miller put firm pressure on Amalia's hips as she leaned over a chair, breathing hard. "But it's worth it the moment you hold that baby in your arms. I can promise you that."

Amalia only nodded, drawing a deep breath as the pain passed. She caught Mrs. Miller glancing at the kitchen clock once as they made their rounds. Past noon now—what was taking so long? Perhaps the doctor was on another call—he kept so busy between serving both Green Creek and Decorah, he'd been talking of hiring on an assistant physician.

Please, Lord. Help them to get here soon. Though she knew Mrs. Miller had delivered a number of babies and would doubtless manage just fine, she couldn't help but remember Maya's own struggled labor, barely a year before.

As they passed the bedroom again an hour or so later, Amalia groaned and reached for the doorjamb as the bone-deep cramping spread through her once more. Her limbs began trembling, shaking, a deep pressure building in her lower back. Her legs gave way, nearly sinking her to the floor.

"There, dearie. I've got you." Mrs. Miller supported her from behind. "I think it may be time for you to lie down now." She helped

Amalia to the bed, where she'd already drawn back the coverlet and spread extra linens over the sheets.

Amalia sank into the pillows Mrs. Miller had propped up. "That feels good." She looked up at the older woman and tried to smile. "Do you think they'll get here in time?"

As if in response, another contraction jerked her forward off the pillows. She grunted, grabbing at Mrs. Miller's hands, her body pushing of its own accord.

Mrs. Miller chuckled. "Whether they do or not, this baby is ready." She helped Amalia lean back, bracing her with pillows, propping up her knees.

Amalia started to shake again. "I'm a little s-scared."

"I know." Mrs. Miller laid her hand on Amalia's belly, looking into her eyes. "But you can do this. I'm right here with you, and the Lord is too."

"Ja." Amalia let out a slightly easier breath. "Mange takk."

"Now." Mrs. Miller smiled and sat back as Amalia tightened with another contraction. "Let's get this baby born. Go ahead and push whenever you feel like it, dear."

Amalia arched forward, pushing, her groan deep and guttural.

"That's it. You're going to meet this little one in no time."

She'd only pushed a handful of times when they heard footsteps and voices outside in the entryway.

Amalia lay back, panting, and met Mrs. Miller's smiling eyes.

"Sounds like the doctor just made it." The older woman turned her head to the door, which they'd left ajar. "In here," she called.

Dr. Armitage hurried in, black bag in hand and shucking off his coat. "Sorry I couldn't get here sooner. On another call."

"Not a problem." Mrs. Miller moved from by Amalia's feet to her side, gripping her sweaty hands. "She's been doing just fine. I think we're almost there."

"Hot water?" The doctor rolled up his sleeves.

"In that basin."

As the doctor washed up, Amalia groaned and clutched Mrs. Miller's hands. "It's coming."

Dr. Armitage bent over her. "Good, I see the head. Push, Mrs. Karlsson, hard."

She pushed, her groan rising to a scream.

"That's it. Now, easy, easy."

Amalia cried out at the fiery pain, strangling Mrs. Miller's hands.

"One more time, Amalia. You're almost there."

She pushed with all her strength. And then—the most precious, sweet cry rent the air.

Amalia collapsed back onto the pillow, gasping, staring in awe at the squirming, wailing, beautifully pink infant the doctor held up for her to see.

"You have a little girl." Dr. Armitage grinned, transforming his usually sober bearded face. "Congratulations."

Amalia laughed through her tears. After the doctor cut the cord, Mrs. Miller wrapped the baby in a blanket and laid the tiny, warm bundle in her arms.

Amalia cradled her daughter with shaking hands. "Oh, my baby. Oh, God, thank you. Thank you." She pressed her lips to the tiny, warm, wet little head, then looked up at Mrs. Miller, who bent over her beaming, her own eyes full. "Is Absalom here?"

"His buggy pulled in right after mine," the doctor said.

"I'll go tell him." Mrs. Miller hurried from the room.

A moment later Absalom tiptoed in, his eyes wide behind his spectacles, curly hair wild as if he'd driven like the wind to get here.

Amalia's eyes pricked with fresh tears at the sight of him, and she reached out her hand. "Come meet your daughter."

He made a sound between a laugh and a sob as he knelt beside the bed and pressed Amalia's hand between both of his. "I shouldn't have left you today."

"I had no idea myself. But here she is."

"She's so beautiful." Tentative, Absalom traced the rosy curve of their daughter's petal-soft cheek with his finger, then pressed Amalia's hand to his lips. "Just like you."

"What shall you name her?" Mrs. Miller adjusted Amalia's pillows.

"We never did decide on names." Amalia chuckled and sighed.

Absalom studied the baby's face, her alert, searching eyes. "What about Sarah Marie?"

"Sarah for your mother . . . Marie for mine." Amalia smiled at her daughter, then her husband. "I like it."

A sudden commotion at the front door heralded the school contingent had arrived, so Absalom hurried out to tell them the news while Mrs. Miller and the doctor helped Amalia with the afterbirth and getting the baby to nurse. Mrs. Miller slipped a fresh nightgown over Amalia's head and removed the soiled sheets, then laid little Sarah Marie, now bathed and swaddled in a soft yellow blanket, back into her arms.

"Can you bring in the little girls? And Hank?" Amalia sank back into the pillows, cradling her daughter.

"Are you sure you're up to that?" Absalom hovered near.

Amalia smiled up at him. "Actually, I feel surprisingly well."

A moment later, Ruthie and Thomi crept in, their eyes wide, while Hank hung back by the door. Helen peeped in too, smiling.

"Come." Amalia shifted the bundle higher in her arms. "Meet your little sister."

Ruthie crept to the bed and peered at the baby's face, eyes alight. "She's so tiny. And pink, like a rosebud." She beamed. "Can I hold her?"

"Ja, soon. Let the others see."

Thomi came over next, peering down at the baby. "She looks about like most babies I've seen. 'Cept smaller than most."

Amalia chuckled. "Well, she was just born."

Ruthie gave Thomi a look. "I think she's the most beautiful baby in the world."

"What's her name?" Hank finally stepped closer, peering over the girls' shoulders.

"Sarah Marie."

Hank stared down at the baby. Little Sarah Marie squirmed, then opened her rosebud mouth in a yowl. The boy started back slightly, then grinned. "She can use her voice, anyhow. Guess she'll fit in here just fine."

They all laughed, then the doctor and Mrs. Miller shooed everyone out. "Mother and baby need their rest."

A gentle fog of weariness creeping over her, Amalia dozed off as the afternoon light waned and supper dishes clinked from the kitchen, little Sarah Marie nestled in her arms.

A day full of the unexpected, that was certain. And ending in overflowing joy.

Now, to learn to manage the boardinghouse with a baby in tow.

Twenty-Two

Three long days.

Ødger laid his hand over Rev. Larsen's thin, veined one once again, checked that the older man was still breathing, then leaned forward in the chair beside the bed, resting his hands between his knees. Three days the pastor had lain unconscious since his collapse at church, Tuesday afternoon now stretching with no change. Would he ever wake again, this side of eternity?

Father God . . . please restore this dear man. Or, if it's his time, gently take him home.

Ødger rubbed his eyes, bleary from lack of sleep, though he slept in snatches on the sofa in the next room, waking often to check on his charge. The reverend's daughter, who lived in Green Creek, had been by to stay with him each afternoon while Ødger did his best to tend to church business, but she was helping her own daughter, who had several small children and was on bedrest carrying another—she couldn't bear the burden of her father's care.

Ødger could, at least for now. He'd sent a message to Professor Amundson on Monday, asking him to give his regrets to Immanuel Lutheran in Independence, explaining that he would need to postpone his field training there. For today—this hour, this week, however long it took—this was his field.

He made himself get up and head into the kitchen, where he brewed a cup of coffee, the strong, rich scent relaxing his senses and sending a rumbling through his stomach. The women of the church had been dropping by, often several times a day, to fill the reverend's larder, never mind that their pastor couldn't partake of it yet. Ødger opened the pantry and took out a cold chicken from Mrs. Trotter and dark rye bread seasoned with caraway seed from Mrs. Miller. He made himself a sandwich, adding to the plate a hunk of molasses gingerbread from, of all people, Mrs. Flinch. The usually snippy woman had handed it over with an odd catch in her voice, saying she hoped the good reverend felt better soon.

Perhaps there was hope for her yet.

Ødger settled back in his chair by the bed, plate on his lap, and bowed his head for a silent grace. *I Jesu navn, går vi til bords* . . . The familiar words were a balm to his weary mind. A gentle breeze wafted the curtains at the open window. Despite his grief over Rev. Larsen, the gaping uncertainty of what was to come . . . the Lord was here. And He knew. For now, that was enough.

He had dozed off in the chair some time later when awakened by a tapping at the back door. Groggy, he stumbled through the narrow hallway and kitchen to find his sister standing on the back porch, Torvald in one arm and a basket in the other.

"Maya." His face relaxed into a smile.

"God dag." She smiled back, though her gray-blue eyes held concern. "How is the reverend?"

"No change, yet." He took her basket and held open the screen door for her to step into the kitchen. "How did you get here?"

"JJ brought me. He's picking up something in town for Absalom, since he doesn't want to leave home just now." Maya beamed. "I wanted to tell you the news myself. Amalia had her baby yesterday."

"What?" Ødger felt his eyes widen, then he grinned. "How wonderful. Is all well?"

"Ja, mother and baby girl both very well. Little Sarah Marie.

Absalom is struggling to get Amalia to rest, she says she feels fine and wants to be up and about already."

Ødger shook his head. "Those stubborn Norwegian women. Please give them my congratulations."

"I will. I can hardly wait to tell Eben."

"When do the threshers get back?"

"Next week, at least I hope so. Four weeks seems long—though not as long as last year."

They both quieted, thinking of last year, when Maya lost her baby—and gained Torvald—all while he and Eben were gone on the threshing crew. It was shortly after they returned that Eben and Maya begun their gentle courtship. Ødger would be forever grateful for Eben's patient, unselfish loving of his sister.

Ødger touched her elbow. "Would you like to see the reverend?"

Maya nodded, shifting Torvald on her hip. "If that's all right."

"On-kuh," Torvald said, lunging toward Ødger.

"Come here, young fellow." Ødger set the basket on the kitchen table and caught the one-year-old under the arms. He lifted Torvald high, earning a squeal. "Did you just try to say onkel?"

"I think so. He's been saying more words—Mor, Far, chicken."

"Chicken?" Ødger raised his brows, settling his nephew on his shoulders.

"Well, it sounds like 'kih-kih,' but he says it whenever he sees a chicken out in the yard. He loves to follow them around." She glanced at the hallway. "I hope we aren't disturbing the reverend."

Ødger shook his head. "If only you would. What better sound to wake him than a child's laughter?"

Holding Torvald's chubby hands tight to steady him on his high perch, Ødger led the way down the dim hallway to the small bedroom where their pastor lay.

Maya stilled when she saw him, her eyes filling. Slowly, she approached the bed and laid her hand on Rev. Larsen's arm, so thin and vulnerable, clad in his nightshirt. She stood silent a moment, head bowed. Ødger stayed near the door, swaying gently to keep Torvald content. The toddler thumped him on the head and giggled.

At last she drew a breath and took a step back from the bed. "Such a good man. What a blessing he has been to this community."

"Ja, indeed. And I pray he will continue to be."

She sniffed and swiped under one eye, then turned to Ødger. "What will you do now?"

"Stay here—for now. I'm needed."

"Does the doctor say how long he might stay unconscious?"

"He says we should know something within a few days. Either he awakens, or . . . he doesn't. But there's only so long he can last without food or drink."

Maya nodded. "We will keep praying."

"As shall I." Ødger inhaled through his nose. "If he does recover, I thought to ask Professor Amundson if I might do my field training right here in Green Creek. Since Reverend Larsen probably won't be able to perform his duties for some time, regardless."

Maya quirked her brows. "Wouldn't that be a bit of a trial by fire? To take on all his pastoral duties at once?"

Ødger shrugged. "It's just a thought. Dr. Armitage will be by in a short while to check on him, we'll see what he says."

"Good. I'm glad I got here before the doctor, though, or he would have told you about the baby and spoiled my surprise." She cocked her head at him. "I suppose in some ways, you'd rather stay in Green Creek anyway."

"Of course." Ødger swung his nephew down from his shoulders, settled him in the crook of his arm, and tickled his belly. "I would miss my family dearly, going sixty miles away."

"And no one else in particular?"

Warmth crept up Ødger's neck to his ears, but he kept his focus on Torvald's beaming face as he tried to grab his onkel's nose. "Like who?"

Maya let out an exaggerated sigh. "Honestly, min bror. Do you think I don't know about you and Miss Stenerson?"

A boulder seemed to lodge itself in Ødger's throat—no, a volcanic rock, given the heat that flushed his neck and face. When at last he managed to look his sister in the eyes, they gleamed with suppressed mirth.

He let out a breath in a long whoosh. "How long have you known?"

"Let me see now." She tapped her finger on her chin, aggravating him like she used to as a little girl. "Since the hayrides last summer?"

His jaw dropped. "What?"

"Did you even know at that time?"

"I . . ." He sat down in the chair by the bed, dandling Torvald, his knees too weak to stand any longer. "I remember noticing her then. Feeling a . . . a lightness and gladness that I hadn't, in so long. Not since . . ." He glanced at his sister, thinking of the tragedy that had dogged them last spring. "But I didn't start thinking seriously till your wedding."

"Ah." She tipped her head, eyes gentling. "I suppose weddings often put such thoughts into our minds."

"Ja." He cleared his throat. "As did her singing."

"I remember it was lovely—though to me, much of that day is a happy blur, except for Eben's face. So have you spoken to her?"

Ødger shifted in his seat, bouncing Torvald on his knee as the baby started to fuss. If only the noise would rouse the reverend, but he slept still as ever. "I have—sort of."

"Sort of?"

He rubbed his bearded cheek. What was this, a sisterly interrogation? "After that supper at your house, I walked back with her. We talked, and I told her I was interested to pursue—beyond friendship. She was hesitant at first, about her teaching contract and such, but then she seemed receptive. Until I mentioned going to Independence."

"I suppose that makes sense, with you going away."

"That's what I thought at first—but the change was so sudden, I didn't know what to think. And she wouldn't talk to me about it, at least not at first. Got all withdrawn and cold."

"I noticed." Maya nodded slowly. "I've wondered what was going on . . . but I didn't want to pry."

"Until today?" He raised his brows.

She smirked at him. "It's not like I get you alone very often. And what are sisters for?"

He groaned. Torvald grabbed at his beard. "We've talked a bit now. Some on Sunday, just before the service and, well, all that happened there. She's helped me—understand a bit more, though her reasons have to do with her family . . . I probably shouldn't share without her permission."

"Well, I'm very glad you are talking again. And I hope you'll keep it up." Maya reached for Torvald. "But unless I'm mistaken, that's the doctor's buggy pulling up outside."

Ødger walked them to the kitchen to fetch Maya's basket, once she emptied it of the sweet Norwegian bolle buns she had brought, then to the front door.

Dr. Armitage was just approaching down the narrow walkway. He nodded to Maya. "Mrs. Miller. I was just out near your place, at Forsberg House."

"Ah, how did you find the new mother and baby?"

"Doing quite well." He eyed the toddler in her arms. "And he looks to be growing into a sturdy boy."

"Ja. We are ever grateful for him." Maya smoothed her adopted son's white-blond curls. Dr. Armitage had been the one to bring Torvald to her last August, as a red-faced newborn when his immigrant mother died in childbirth, a day after Maya lost her own baby.

A spasm of emotion passed over the doctor's usually stoic, black-bearded face. "I'm glad. And how is your father-in-law?"

"He's almost fully recovered from the surgery. Though still a bit weak sometimes."

"Good." He looked to Ødger. "How is the reverend?"

"No change." Lifting a farewell hand to Maya, Ødger held the door open for the doctor.

In the bedroom, Dr. Armitage bent over the pastor's still form, taking his pulse, lifting his eyelids, listening to his breathing. "Has there been any movement or reaction at all?"

"Not that I've seen." Ødger swallowed. "Unless while I was asleep."

"I doubt it. We'd see some indication now." He sighed and clasped his black bag closed. "I hate to say it, but each day he doesn't waken lessens the chance he ever will."

Chest squeezing, Ødger slipped his hands into his pockets. "Is there any more I can do for him? Should I try and get him to drink?"

"Not if he's still unconscious. He could choke."

Flinching, Ødger nodded.

"Send for me if there's a change. Feel free to talk to him, read to him, as you like—we believe patients can sometimes hear us, even in a coma. I'll try to get back again sometime tomorrow, but I'm very pressed with cases right now. I've advertised for an assistant, someone to help me carry the load, or perhaps take over calls in Green Creek so I can focus on Decorah."

"That sounds like a good idea, sir." He'd wondered how the doctor managed tending to two communities at once. "Thank you for coming."

He showed the man out, wondering not for the first time what went on in the doctor's head. Dr. Armitage had married Absalom's former fiancée and always seemed oddly cold and distant for a physician—even proud, at times—yet he'd seen enough to know the man cared deeply for his patients. Amalia and Absalom maintained that he'd saved Maya's life last summer, not to mention brought her Torvald. And now, he'd delivered Amalia's healthy baby—a joy for them all.

The door clicked shut. *Lord, please provide whatever help the doctor needs. Lighten his load, and bless him and his family.*

Ødger headed back to Rev. Larsen's bedside. Only the faintest rise and fall of the bedclothes bespoke that the man still lived.

Sitting down in his habitual chair, Ødger reached for the Bible on the nightstand. *Read to him*, the doctor had said. He should have thought of that himself sooner, though he'd prayed aloud over the reverend a number of times.

Paging through the well-loved old book, Ødger opened to Psalms and began to read where his eyes fell on the twenty-fifth.

> "Unto thee, O Lord, do I lift up my soul.
>
> O my God, I trust in thee: let me not be ashamed, let not mine enemies triumph over me.
>
> Yea, let none that wait on thee be ashamed: let them be ashamed which transgress without cause.
>
> Shew me thy ways, O Lord; teach me thy paths. Lead me in thy truth, and teach me: for thou art the God of my salvation; on thee do I wait all the day.
>
> Remember, O Lord, thy tender mercies and thy lovingkindnesses; for they have been ever of old . . ."

Ødger glanced at Rev. Larsen. Had his face grown even more peaceful? His own shoulders relaxing, Ødger kept reading the beloved words.

> "What man is he that feareth the Lord? him shall he teach in the way that he shall choose.
>
> His soul shall dwell at ease; and his seed shall inherit the earth."

He paused, his throat tightening unexpectedly as the words suddenly seemed as much for him as Rev. Larsen. "Lord . . . please teach me the way I should choose. I keep thinking I see your path clear before me, and then it takes such a turn I hardly know which way is up. And Helen . . . Father, I can't get her off my mind. Thank you for her talking with me more, but it still feels like we've barely begun to truly know one another, each other's stories. And now here I am confined to the manse for only you know how long."

So write her a letter.

Ødger caught his breath at the thought, impressed so sudden and clear, yet gently on his mind. Of course. He chuckled under his breath. Why hadn't he thought of that before? He'd always been better at expressing his ideas in writing, anyway—it was what made him a good student, though if he had time to prepare beforehand, he could communicate well before a crowd also. That talent had won him more than one lead in a school play, and would be a mercy in his chosen career that entailed plenty of public speaking.

Thank you, Father. He finished reading the psalm, then found letter paper, pen, and ink in the reverend's desk in the corner of the room. He would replace the paper and ink later, though he knew Rev. Larsen would give it freely. But sudden urgency pressed in his chest, to get the thoughts that pulsed in his heart written out to the woman who had held it longer than he half-realized.

My dear Helen,

Forgive me if I take too much liberty in addressing you so, though you did give me leave to call you by your Christian name. I write first of all to thank you for the sentiments you expressed this Sunday morning before our dear pastor's grievous collapse. Your words may have been few, but you might be surprised how much they gladdened and lifted my heart. The weight of not knowing what I had done to displease you these recent weeks has burdened me greatly.

He swallowed, relief smarting his eyes once more, then dipped his pen. Nearby, the reverend slept on.

I, too, should apologize, for I fear I did a poor job expressing my feelings and intentions after that supper at my sister's in July. At times I find words easier with a pen and paper, so I beg your patience as I try to articulate them now. I realize that in all propriety, I should approach your father or some other guardian with my desire to court you—for that is indeed my hope. Yet I understand that, sadly, no such gentleman remains living. However, I would be grateful to write a letter expressing my hopes to your aunt, should you be willing for me to do so.

And that is what I most wish to know—whether you should wish that. If not, you have only to say so, and I shall never say another word about it, but remain solely your friend, and grateful to be. I fully realize I am merely a poor seminary student, and I have no illusions that an accomplished and—dare I say it—beautiful young woman such as yourself should necessarily find any attraction in the prospect of joining your life to mine.

If, however, I am not mistaken that some interested feeling does exist in your heart toward this humble cleric, then I am ready to devote my life to making yours as comfortable as possible, as we follow together the path our Lord might lay before us.

Thank you for your indulgence in allowing me to speak to you such by letter, since I cannot leave our dear pastor's bedside.

I remain, your faithful servant,
Ødger Gunderson

Blowing out a long breath, Ødger laid down the nearly dry pen, a tangible weight lifted from his chest. He glanced toward the bed from habit, then looked again, springing to his feet and hurrying to the bedside.

Perhaps he'd been mistaken—no—yes—Rev. Larsen's hand

twitched, moved. Shifted up from lying at his side to resting on his chest.

Ødger bent over him, his heart hammering. "Reverend, can you hear me? Sir?"

A tremor passed through the papery face, his forehead wrinkling, smoothing. The corners of his mouth twitched, his eyelids quivered, and then—first a sliver, then more—opened.

Ødger gave a laugh mingled with a sob and grasped the man's frail hand. "Velkommen tilbake, Reverend Larsen."

TWENTY-THREE

The end of the first week of school.

The September light slanted golden through the windows of the schoolhouse as Helen laid her books down at her desk Friday morning. She inhaled the familiar scent of slate pencils and aging wood, dry leaves and stove blacking. Before this week, she had swept and scrubbed the schoolroom top to bottom along with young Inga Jorstad, who had also helped several days at the boardinghouse this week and would soon enter the fifth reader in Helen's classroom, making rapid progress since her arrival from Norway about the same time Amalia and Ruthie came.

What an eventful first week it had been—chiefly with the newest arrival at Forsberg House. Helen smiled at the thought of how Ruthie, especially, ran instantly to find wee Sarah Marie as soon as she got home from school each day. She'd dubbed the infant "my baby sister" and would barely give Sarah Marie up to be nursed and changed.

Helen smiled, sighed, and ran her hands over the worn wood of her desk. Her fourth year of teaching here in Green Creek, and this classroom truly felt hers now. She couldn't imagine giving it up . . . and yet, when she thought of simply teaching other people's children for the rest of her days, that old emptiness tugged in her chest. The mental image of Amalia cradling her child, that new mother love blooming on her face and lighting her eyes, filled her with a sweetly gentle ache. Then, unexpectedly, the image changed to Ødger holding little Torvald, and her middle fluttered. Was he—could he be, part of God's path for her? How was she to know? Everything seemed upended yet again, now that he wasn't going to Independence—at least not yet—and instead watching over Rev. Larsen and trying to tend to the elderly minister's duties. Last she heard, the pastor had awakened, yet still not spoken since his collapse Sunday morning.

Lord. She bent her head and closed her eyes in the early morning quietness, her fingertips still pressing into the desk. *Be with Reverend Larsen, and Ødger. And thank you for Amalia's safe delivery and for carrying us all through this week. Please continue to bless this school and all who enter it this year. Let them know your love and encounter your beauty and truth in all we learn and study. Help me love each child and see each one through your eyes. And . . . guide my steps, and Ødger's. Show us what to do.* A meadowlark sang out the open window in the grassy field beyond the school, and Helen lifted her head. *In Christ's name, Amen.*

Almost before she knew it, the clock had ticked nearly to eight, and childish voices rang in the yard. Giggles, a boyish shout, a ball tossed perilously near the window. Stepping out into the cool September morning, Helen smiled out over the yard of capering children, then grasped the rope of the large brass bell that hung just above the door and pulled hard.

At the deep clang-clang, the children paused their play, grabbed dinner pails and books, and clattered onto the porch, a flurry of hobnailed boots and a few bare feet, chattering and laughing. Then lining up as she'd taught them the first day—she always had to establish good habits again each year—they filed into the classroom.

As the students settled into their seats, Helen waited at the front of the room, scanning the rows of little ones in the front, older ones whispering in the back, taking special note of those who had been new to her this week. Ada Gibbs, a little girl in the primer class who had no older siblings here and had melted into tears when her mother left that first morning. Nine-year-old Ingrid and Kristina Baard, twins who had just come from Norway and barely spoke a word of English. Still wearing their traditional woolen skirts and vests, they at least now smiled and chatted with Ruthie in Norwegian, having lost the stiff, lost look they'd had on the first day. Helen smiled to herself. Trust Ruthie to make newcomers feel at home. Then Jack O'Brien, an older boy with curly black hair and blue Irish eyes who had already made friends with Hank and showed a ready aptitude for both arithmetic and smart remarks. She'd have to keep an eye on those two.

Today, though, a child she hadn't seen earlier in the week, a little boy who looked about eight, sat in the second row. With a stiff collar and flaxen hair combed so smooth it shone, he kept his hands folded on his desk and examined everything and everyone around him with great interest.

Why hadn't he attended till now? Perhaps his family had just moved to town.

"All right, boys and girls." Helen rapped on her desk with her ruler. "School come to order."

Whispers and giggles hushed. Thirty expectant faces lifted toward hers—many familiar, even beloved. Ruthie and Thomasina and Hank, Ned and Lisa Miller, the Nygards and Flinches and Larsens. Others she hardly knew, yet by the end of the year their gifts and foibles, triumphs and naughtinesses would be near and dear to her.

She smiled over her new classroom. "Let us begin with prayer and our Scripture reading for the day."

After the opening exercises, Helen worked her way through roll, noting the new boy's name on her list.

"Reginald Schneider. And what grade are you in, Reginald?" she asked him.

"I'm Reginald Robert Schneider the Fourth, actually," the boy piped up, lifting his chin and staring down a couple of children who tittered. "But you all may call mc Reggie."

Helen bit the inside of her cheek to hide a smile. "Very well, Reggie. And your grade?"

"I'm s'posed to be going into third. But Mother says I'm smart enough to be in the fourth."

"Well, we'll see about that. Why don't you recite from the third reader today, and we'll see how you do."

"All right." Reggie shrugged. "But I'm pretty sure it'll be too easy."

"Sissy smart aleck," muttered Bertram Flinch from the next row.

Helen shot him a warning glance, and Bertram slid lower in his seat. "That will do. We will now move into our history lesson." After studying American history last year, she had decided this year to begin with the earliest civilizations and move through in a general overview of world history. The large map she'd paid for herself and hung on the back wall had garnered oohs and ahhs the first day.

After the history lesson, she set the older students to writing about what connections they saw between Bible stories and these ancient civilizations while the younger ones worked on their ABCs. Mathematics took up the rest of the morning.

At dinnertime, Helen had just settled at her desk with her sandwich and the apple Ruthie had brought her when shouts from outside brought her to her feet and hurrying to the door.

Out in the yard, Archie Flinch danced about, holding a small tin pail over his head. "Nah-nah, who's a sissy boy and can't reach it? Aren't so big with your fancy name now, are ya?"

Red-faced and with collar now askew, Reggie pounded at Archie's chest with small fists, but he indeed couldn't reach his lunch that the older boy swung above his head.

"Boys!" Setting her jaw, Helen hurried down the steps.

"Hey." Ahead of her, Hank grabbed the dinner pail as it swung through the air above Archie's head. "Quit it."

Archie snickered, still holding tight to the pail's handle. "Oh, says you, orphan boy?"

"Yeah." Hank met the boy's eyes. "Only cowards pick on those littler'n them."

"Huh." Archie scoffed, glancing about the schoolyard at the watching children. His brother, Bertram, looked down and scuffed his boot toe in the dirt. Slowly Archie's shoulders sagged. He glanced back at Hank's steady gaze, then away and released the dinner pail. "Whatever. You fellas are the cowards, don't know how to have any fun."

"Here you go." Hank handed the dinner pail to Reggie.

"Thank you." The smaller boy straightened his jacket and took the pail, then retreated under the maple tree to eat alone.

The children dispersed, Archie heading around the corner of the schoolhouse with his brother.

Helen cleared her throat. "Excuse me, Archie."

He froze, slowly turned around. "Yes'm?"

"You may finish your dinner hour in the schoolroom. Alone," she added as Bertram made to follow him.

Archie's shoulders slumped. "Yes, ma'am." He dragged his feet up the steps.

Before following him inside, Helen stopped by the steps where Hank stood watching some other boys shooting marbles.

"Hank." She touched his arm.

He lifted his head to look at her.

She met his eyes. "Thank you." Only a year ago, Hank had come to fists with Archie and also Bertram. Perhaps it helped that he'd now shot up in height over the bullies, but she also saw a new steadiness, a surety in who he was. She wouldn't say all that just now in front of the others, he'd hate it, but she hoped he read at least some of what she meant in her gaze.

He met her eyes steadily a moment, then gave a half grin. "Sure."

"Fifteen more minutes, children." Smiling to herself, Helen drew a deep breath and headed into the schoolroom to face Archie.

After poetry and penmanship that afternoon, Helen erased the copy work she'd written on the board and turned to the class. "To finish our first week, we are going to begin a new tradition for this year."

Students looked up from wiping their slates clean.

"You all seem to have enjoyed the songs we have learned for our end-of-the-year programs, so I thought—why save music only for the end of the year? From now on, we will end our class days with music at least on Fridays, perhaps more often if we can manage it. Music benefits us intellectually, physically, morally, and socially—and beyond all that, many of us simply enjoy it. I know I do." She stepped to the board. "While I do not expect you all to become advanced musicians, I would like to introduce the basics of reading music as well."

She sketched out a simple musical staff on the blackboard, then dotted notes on it. "This line of music represents the tune of a song most of you probably know—'Home, Sweet Home.'" She smiled at Ingrid and Kristina. "If not, do not worry, you will learn it soon. We will sing the first verse and the chorus as I point to each note. For now, simply notice how the melody follows the rise and fall of the notes." Her instructors at college would be horrified at her plebeian explanation of the musical staff, but this was a one-room school in rural Iowa, not a finishing academy. "Let us begin." Helen tapped her tuning fork, which most students knew from their practices for programs, and began the song.

"'Mid pleasures and palaces though we may roam,
Be it ever so humble there's no place like home!

A charm from the skies seems to hallow us there,
Which seek through the world, is ne'er met with elsewhere.

"Home! Home, sweet sweet Home!
There's no place like Home! There's no place like Home!"

They sang the song through three times, voices growing stronger with each repetition. Once a slight scuffle made her look sharply toward Thomasina and Bertram, but Bertram subsided with a reddened face, and Thomasina refocused toward the front, only a faint snapping in her dark eyes. Helen shook her head and continued on with the song. Those Flinch boys seemed as determined to try her patience as ever, but at least Hank and Thomi seemed to be doing their best to rise above their provocation. This week, at any rate.

Once she dismissed class, chatter erupted, desk lids slammed, boots stampeded down the aisle. Having long ago given up the ideal of students trooping out as orderly as she insisted they enter, Helen ignored the commotion and set to organizing the older students' written papers from the week. After a few moments, she looked up to see Reggie still sitting in his seat, hands folded, though other children shouted and played out in the schoolyard, including the boardinghouse contingent who would ride home in the wagon with Helen shortly, driven by Hank.

She laid down her pen. "I'm sorry, Reggie, I didn't realize you were still here. Is someone coming for you?"

"My mother said she would." His thin voice sounded less confident than earlier.

"Then I'm sure she will be here soon." Helen stood and walked nearer, sitting down in a desk across the aisle from Reggie. "Where do you live? You must be new in town."

"We live with my grandmother right now." Reggie fiddled with his starched cuff. "Though she doesn't like having us there."

Helen swallowed back her surprise. "I suppose it can be difficult to share space at times."

"She didn't like my father. But he's dead now, so we moved in with her. Mother says she didn't know what else to do." Reggie glanced up, a wavering in his hazel eyes.

Something twisted in Helen's chest. No wonder Reggie put on such bravado. "Well, I'm very glad you're here in my classroom, Reggie. And I trust soon you will make some friends." If he could drop the high-and-mighty act, that would work wonders to that end, but some lessons took time to learn.

At a tap on the half-open door, Reggie twisted in his seat, a smile breaking over his face like sun from behind clouds. "There you are, Mother."

Helen stood to greet a thin slip of a woman with mouse-colored hair pulled into a bun, wearing a simple but well-made black widow's dress. "Mrs. Schneider?"

"Yes." The woman came down the aisle, her movements quick and birdlike. Reggie hopped up out of his seat and threw his arms about her waist. Hugging him to her side with one arm, she extended the other hand to Helen. "I'm sorry to be late."

"Not at all." Helen took her hand. "I'm Miss Stenerson, Reggie's teacher."

"So he already lets you call him Reggie." A smile broke over the woman's face much like her son's had. "That's a good sign."

"I understand you're new in town."

"We are." Mrs. Schneider ran her hand over Reggie's flaxen hair, less smoothly combed now than it had been this morning. "We are staying with my mother for now, until . . . until we can find somewhere else."

An idea buzzed through Helen's head. "Would you be open to a boardinghouse?"

The woman's forehead pinched. "I suppose it would depend upon the boardinghouse."

"Forsberg House, just outside of Green Creek. I live there myself, have for over two years now. It's very respectable, clean and safe, but more than that, it's a home, a family. Amalia Karlsson runs it—her husband is the son of the magistrate in Decorah."

Mrs. Schneider's eyes lit. "Ah, Magistrate Karlsson. I've heard of him." She glanced down at her son. "Are there other children there?"

"Yes, three, all of whom also attend school here. Ruthie, Thomasina, and Hank."

"Hank? The boy who—" Reggie darted a glance at his mother and pressed his mouth shut.

Clearly he wasn't ready to mention the noontime incident. "Yes, Hank is one of our older boys, and becoming something of a leader, I think."

"How much does it cost?" Mrs. Schneider fingered the small brocade pocketbook that dangled from her arm. "We have some money my husband left us, but I've no source of income just now. Do you think the proprietress might let me work for part of our board? I can cook and clean and sew."

"Mother." Reggie twisted under her arm. "You can't hire out as a servant."

"Things are different now, Reggie." His mother steadied her voice against a faint tremble. "And you know Father always said I kept the neatest house in town."

"Actually, I think Mrs. Karlsson might indeed be open to some extra help. Especially now—she just had a baby this week." She'd been wondering just how her friend would manage, since Inga wouldn't be able to keep coming as often as she had this week—as the oldest of seven, her own family needed her help too. Maybe this could be God's provision for everyone. "If you'd like to stop by sometime soon, I can introduce you and the two of you can talk it all over. Perhaps tomorrow?"

"Thank you." Mrs. Schneider's eyes shone, whether with gratitude or tears, Helen wasn't quite sure. "I'm truly very grateful."

After bidding them good-bye, Helen gathered her books and papers from her desk, then headed out into the cooling September light where Hank and the girls waited with the wagon. She would have quite a report for Amalia this evening. Helen's mouth tipped. What would it be like to have Reginald Robert Schneider the Fourth under their roof?

Twenty-Four

"May I hold her again, Tante Malia?"

Amalia buttoned her bodice from nursing wee Sarah Marie and lifted the baby to her shoulder, gently patting her tiny, warm back till an enormous burp made Amalia smile and Ruthie giggle.

Thomi, lying on the parlor rug nearby reading a book this Saturday morning, shook her head. "That baby makes bigger noises than anybody that small should be able to."

"She makes just the right kind of noises, *I* think." Ruthie danced on her tiptoes. "Please?"

"All right, but sit on the sofa and scoot all the way back so you're stable."

Ruthie obeyed, spreading her skirt neatly and holding out her arms.

Amalia rose and lowered the baby into Ruthie's arms. The little girl supported Sarah's head as she'd been taught and cradled the baby carefully, gazing down at her with rapt eyes. Amalia smiled, watching them. Sarah Marie had instantly been claimed by Ruthie, who hovered within arm's length of the baby whenever she was home, or allowed. Thomi stayed a bit more cautious thus far, or perhaps she was so used to babies from living in the children's home that an infant didn't hold the wonder she did for Ruthie.

How had it been less than a full week since this tiny person entered their home? Already it felt hard to remember life without little Sarah. So much to be thankful for.

Helen stepped into the parlor doorway, smiling. "Isn't that a sweet scene." She glanced at Amalia. "I'm sorry to bother you, but Mrs. Schneider is here. The mother of my student whom I told you about?"

"Oh, of course." Amalia smoothed the front of her dark blue calico dress, checking to be sure she'd fastened all the buttons. "Please show her in."

"You're sure you're up to this?" Helen paused. "I'm surprised you're even on your feet."

"Compared to being heavy with child in the heat of summer, I feel wonderful." Amalia smiled at her friend. "I know, Absalom keeps wanting to send me back to bed too. But I promise I'm not pushing too hard. It feels good to be up and around. And between Inga's help and Mrs. Miller and Maya constantly bringing food over, I've barely been allowed to enter the kitchen so far. Still, I know they can't keep that up, so Mrs. Schneider may prove a godsend."

Helen nodded. "Very well. I'll show her in."

A moment later, a small, slender woman in black entered, a little boy in a navy blue sailor suit dragging his heels behind her.

"Mrs. Schneider?" Amalia held out her hand, and the woman shook it with a timid grip. "Amalia Karlsson. I am so glad to meet you."

"Hey, Reggie." Ruthie spoke up from the sofa, where she'd been softly crooning a Norwegian lullaby to Sarah. "Want to see my baby sister?"

Reggie slowly approached and peered down at the baby. "She sure doesn't have much hair."

"I've seen babies with hair like that plenty of times." Thomi sat up from the rug and glared at Reggie. "Her hair'll grow soon."

Amalia hid a smile. So Thomi was growing protective of little

Sarah too. "Please, do sit down." Mrs. Schneider settled on a chair, as did Amalia. "Miss Stenerson said you are looking for a place to live?"

"Yes. That is, we have one now—with my mother." Mrs. Schneider fingered the strings of her pocketbook and glanced at her son, who was leaning over the arm of the settee, studying the gilt titles of the book collection on the shelves under the window. "You see, my husband died a few months ago."

"I'm so sorry." Amalia waited a moment. "Where did you live before?"

"In Dubuque. But I grew up in Green Creek, where my mother still lives. I thought it would be good to be near family, and it is, but . . ." She gave a slight shrug of her slim shoulders. "I think all of us are finding the shared space more challenging than we expected."

"Well, we would love to have you join us here at Forsberg House, if you determine that would be a good fit for you and your son." Amalia smiled at the boy. "What was your name?"

"This is Reginald." His mother reached for her son, but the boy turned away. Mrs. Schneider sighed. "Please excuse Reggie. He's finding it—rather difficult to adjust to all the changes of late."

"Of course." Amalia followed a thought, unconventional as it might seem to discuss with a near stranger. "You know, many of us here at Forsberg House have lost family also. My brother and I lost our parents just over two years ago, on the journey from Norway to America. And Ruthie—her parents died on that same voyage, which brought the two of us together and to this boardinghouse."

"Really." Mrs. Schneider's eyes widened. "That sounds like quite a story."

"Ja, it is." If she only knew. "Thomasina here, and Hank, whom Reggie met at school, came here by their own adventures. And my cousin Maya, who lives on the neighboring farm, lost her husband just before she immigrated, though she remarried this spring. So you see, many of us have come from loss. But the Lord has brought us together into a true family here."

"That sounds . . . nice." Mrs. Schneider's hazel eyes sheened. "And we would still be close enough to visit my mother often, just with a bit more . . . space between us." She clenched her purse strings tighter. "My only concern is the money. As I told Miss Stenerson, my husband left us some—he was an accountant—but I have no monthly income."

"Miss Stenerson mentioned that. She said you might be willing to work for part of your board?"

Reginald made a soft sound with his lips and glanced back at them. Amalia blinked at the derision in his young eyes. What pain must this boy be hiding?

"Yes." Mrs. Schneider straightened her spine without looking at her son. "I'm not too proud to work. And I'm a good housekeeper. I can help with cooking, cleaning, sewing. I hired out our laundry back before—before Arthur died, but I'm willing to learn to help with that also."

"I don't deny I could do with more help just now." Amalia nodded at baby Sarah with a smile.

"Yes, congratulations." The young widow's eyes softened. "Such a beautiful baby."

"Thank you. She came a bit earlier than we anticipated, and while I have help from family right now, having another capable woman living here would be a true blessing." Sarah whimpered, and Amalia rose to lift her from Ruthie's arms. Propping the baby on her shoulder, she swayed back and forth. "Depending on how much you're able to help, I might be able to pay you a bit each week in addition to room and board. What do you think?"

Mrs. Schneider met Amalia's gaze straight on. "The blessing would be ours."

"Miss Stenerson, is this better?"

Helen turned from the letter in her hand to peer at Ruthie's slate held up in the parlor lamplight. Ruthie had been struggling to slow down enough for careful penmanship of late, so Helen had suggested she practice her letters at home in the evenings.

"Yes, that's looking much better." She smiled at the little girl. "Just be careful with the flourishes on your Fs and Ts. You want to make sure they look different enough from each other."

Ruthie sighed. "I like reading better than writing." She headed back to the hearthrug where Thomi lay on her stomach, reading a book, while Magpie's kittens scampered and tumbled about. Next to wee Sarah's cradle, Hank leaned against Dog as if the big black hound were a bolster, pencil flying on a sketch pad propped against his knees.

Helen smiled to see him drawing again. She should have him do another art lesson sometime in these next few weeks at school—he had such a gift. "What are you drawing, Hank?"

"Little Sarah." He held up his sketch pad for her to see.

Her heart warming that he would show his work to her so willingly—that hadn't always been the case—Helen took the pad and caught her breath. Though still rough, the baby's likeness already almost breathed on the page. Her round, fuzzy head, eyes wrinkled in sleep, pursed mouth and tiny clenched fists amid the blankets . . . Helen shook her head. "Hank. It's one of your best yet."

With a half grin and a shrug, Hank took the sketch pad back. "I dunno about that."

Helen glanced back at the folded sheet of paper in her hands. She should be going over lesson plans for next week, but she couldn't seem to stop reading over Ødger's letter, which Absalom had brought home this afternoon after a trip to the mercantile, sending her mind and heart into a whirl they'd yet to recover from.

She lowered her gaze once more to the letter, smoothing out the closely written page on the small table under the cut-glass shaded lamp. His penmanship was bold and looping, and the formality of his wording caught her off guard, yet swept her away with his words. No doubt he would be a powerful preacher.

My dear Helen . . .

Each time she read the salutation, a warmth flushed from her scalp to her toes. *Lord, I hardly know what to make of this.* So long, she'd convinced herself love and marriage, for her, were not to be. And yet, here lay Ødger's words, plain as his heart on the page.

I realize that in all propriety, I should approach your father or some other guardian with my desire to court you—for that is indeed my hope.

Her heart pounded just reading the words again.

I would be grateful to write a letter expressing my hopes to your aunt, should you be willing for me to do so.

Was she willing? Helen lifted her head to glance about the parlor, the others gathered about the fire on this cool September evening seeming somehow far away, in a separate realm from her and her letter. Maya and Eben had come over for supper, Maya now rocking a sleepy Torvald and chatting with Amalia on the other side of the table where Helen sat, while Amalia rocked Sarah's cradle with her foot. The low fire snapped, one window half open to let in the sleepy chirp of crickets. Eben and JJ bent their heads together over some project or idea while the Rykavyk brothers played a chess game. Absalom was deep in legal papers, but he looked up to interject now and then.

"So you're thinkin' to dam the creek?" JJ paused in carving a new wooden spoon to rub a hand over his balding head.

Eben nodded. "Hank and I been talkin' it over. Not the whole thing, we'd still let water through, but enough to make a nice little pond. Some beavers been makin' their own dam upstream a bit, gave us the idea."

"And in the winter, we can go ice skatin'," Hank put in, sitting up. Dog lifted his head and thumped his shaggy black tail on the floor till Hank fondled his ears.

"Well, seems a mighty fine notion." JJ shaved another curl off the spoon with his knife.

"Started with you and Ruthie talkin' about fixin' up your old shack," Eben said. "I thought, if we're goin' to the trouble of makin' that a place usable for folks, why not make it a real gatherin' place for Forsberg House? Folks can have a place to shelter and rest, change clothes after swimmin'. And in the winter, we could have real shindigs with ice-skating parties. Have a snug place for mothers and babies in the cabin, a stove with hot chocolate and whatnot. And outside, a bonfire, skating, singin' round the fire, all sorts of larks."

Ruthie clapped her hands together, heedless of the slate she still held. "Oh, I wish winter would come right now."

JJ chuckled. "We got a lot of work to do first, little lady."

"I've never been ice-skating." Thomi swung her stockinged feet in the air behind her, looking into the fire with her chin in her hand.

"It's fun. I remember skating with my mor and far."

Amalia paused in her knitting to glance keenly at Ruthie. "You remember that, den lille?"

Ruthie tipped her head and tugged on one of her blond braids. "A little. I remember them holding my hands."

"I'm glad you do." Sarah whimpered, and Amalia bent to lift the baby from her cradle, cuddling her close to her chest. "Absalom, remember I said I wished the boardinghouse could sponsor some sort of event to bring the community together? I wonder if it could be an ice-skating party to celebrate once this project is finished."

Absalom looked up from his papers and pushed his spectacles up his nose. "When do you think that might be, JJ and Eben?"

JJ tapped his fingers on the wooden spoon handle. "We've already started fixin' up the shack. It ain't a big place, so shouldn't take too long there. Mostly just needs a lot of loose boards fixed an' replaced, plus addin' a better stove an' some furniture."

"Once harvest is finished, I'll have time to work on the dam, with Hank's help." Eben rubbed his knees. "I see no reason 't'all we can't have it finished by the time the snow flies."

"Perhaps around Christmastime?" Amalia's eyes sparkled.

"You think you'd be up to that?" Absalom glanced at her and the baby.

"I think so. Sarah will be three months old by then. What do you think, Helen?"

"I like the idea. And I'd be glad to help however I can. I can certainly invite the families of my students and ask them to help with refreshments or whatever is needed."

"That would be wonderful." Amalia settled a shawl over herself and Sarah to nurse her. "How has your first week gone?"

"Quite well, overall. Only a few scuffles with the Flinch boys so far. And I had to stop Jack O'Brien from carving his initials on the outside of the schoolhouse yesterday." She lowered her voice. "So far he doesn't seem to be having a negative influence on Hank, but I'm keeping my eye on them. I don't think he's a bad boy, but he seems a bit too smart for his own good at times."

"Hopefully you can steer his mind in a better direction. As you have Hank."

Helen smiled but shook her head. "By the sheer grace of God."

"Amen to that." Amalia yawned a bit. "Goodness, is it only eight?"

"You should head to bed." Maya rose, shifting her dreaming son to her shoulder. "And we should go. When will your new boarders arrive?"

"Monday, I believe. I'm so grateful—it's been a while since we had a new long-term boarder, though I'm thankful for all the short-termers we get also. Ruthie, Thomi, time for bed. You too soon, Hank."

"Soon's I finish this drawing."

Alone in her room, Helen lit an oil lamp and set it on her desk, blowing out the match and setting it in a porcelain saucer she kept for that purpose. By the flickering flame in the glass shade, she sat down and drew out a sheet of cream-colored writing paper, then dipped her pen and sat a moment, nibbling her lip.

How did one respond to such a letter as this?

Dear Mr. Gunderson, she wrote in her best script across the top of the page. *Thank you kindly for your letter* . . . No, that didn't feel right. Too stiff and formal—one would think she didn't know the man at all. She pushed the sheet of paper aside and drew out another.

My dear Ødger . . . her pen lingered on his name till an ink blot splotched it. But dare she write with such intimacy yet, even if he had? Her heart yearned to, she suddenly knew that much . . . which in itself set her pulse to an irregular skitter. But . . .

She sat there long, pen idle in her hand. What exactly did she wish to say? She might give him permission to write to Aunt Ophelia . . . whom she needed to write to herself again. Mrs. Hoskins's last letter indicated her aunt continued to decline, if slowly. In fact, perhaps she should write to her aunt first, or at least include her own letter with Ødger's. But first, surely she owed Ødger more of her own story, at least what she knew of it herself. And how could she fit all those questions and uncertainties into a letter?

Distant bongs from the parlor below marked nine o'clock, and Helen stowed both mostly blank sheets away and shut her desk drawer with a firm tap. She would stop by the reverend's after school on Monday, to speak with Ødger in person and tell him—well, everything that she could. The man had certainly been patient enough all this time. If he still wanted to court her after all that . . . then perhaps they would find a way.

A sudden weight lifted, she blew out her lamp.

Monday morning, Helen told Hank she would make her own way home today, rather than riding with the boardinghouse contingent he drove as usual. He nodded and asked no questions. There would be enough flurry with Reginald and his mother moving in, after all. Once the schoolyard cleared, Helen tucked the papers she wanted to grade into her history book, put the book into her lunch basket, pinned her hat securely, and shut the schoolhouse door firmly behind her.

Heading down the familiar lane between the school and the church, her heart pattered hard as it had before her teacher examinations years ago. Breathing deeply of the warm early autumn air, she straightened her shoulders and turned off at the church down the little lane toward the manse. *Father, help me. Guide our conversation . . . show me what to say. And . . . show us both what to do. Guide us in thy will, please.*

She could hear voices inside the manse even before she knocked at the door, making her knees quail on the doorstep. Should she just turn back? Clearly the reverend had company.

Stop your shillyshallying. Helen lifted her gloved hand and rapped on the door.

Ødger opened it quicker than she expected, a welcoming smile on his bearded face, which froze when he saw her.

"Helen." His eyes widened. "Forgive me, I did not expect you."

"No, forgive me. I'm the one stopping by unannounced." She tightened her grip on her basket. How silly to think she could just drop in. "It sounds like the reverend has other company—I can go."

"No, no. Please do not." He opened the door wider, the earnestness in his eyes weakening her knees and resolve. His Norwegian accent thickened, as it seemed to when he was discomfited. "It is only, the reverend's daughter and her family visit him now. Her husband will come for them soon, I thought you were him. Please." He extended his arm. "Come in."

"If you're certain." Helen stepped into the small, cozy parlor. The murmur of voices and laughter of children came from down the hall, doubtless the pastor's bedroom. "Thank you. How is the reverend today?"

"He is weak still but improving. The doctor is much pleased with his progress, though he urges caution still. But he has begun to get his appetite back, though he still does not speak much, nor can he greatly use his right arm or leg."

"The poor man." Helen reached in her basket and pulled out a small brown paper parcel. "We made these ginger cookies at the boardinghouse, I hoped he might be able to enjoy some. And you too, of course."

"Mange takk." Ødger took them with a smile. "They sound like just the thing to tempt his appetite. And I can never say no to cookies."

She smiled back. Silence hung, save for the children's muted chatter.

At last Helen drew a breath. "I do not wish to disturb the reverend, not with his family here. I hope you will give him my regards. But I was actually hoping to . . . to speak with you. To . . . thank you for your letter." Her cheeks burned.

Hope sprang into his eyes, so raw it caught her in the chest. Ødger tipped his head toward the kitchen. "Please, come with me to put away the cookies. Then perhaps we might talk in the back garden?"

She nodded and followed. "Thank you."

Out in the reverend's little garden plot, shaded by birch trees and crisscrossed with quaint stone paths between patches of zinnias and cabbages, Helen's pulse settled, the tightness in her chest easing before she or Ødger spoke a word.

Drawing a long breath, she glanced up at the blue sky peeking through the still-leafy branches overhead. "What a lovely spot."

"Ja, the reverend loves his garden. I need to get to weeding it for him, since he won't be able to for some time." Ødger nudged a stray weed with his toe.

"I know he must be very grateful for your care for him in this time."

He shrugged and glanced at her. "It is where God has put me, for now."

She nodded and squeezed her hands together. "So . . . I read your letter." She'd already said that, but one had to start somewhere.

"Ja?" The word came more a breath from him.

"And—I thank you, Ødger." She swallowed. "Your words . . . I know you've spoken of your feelings, your intentions before. But you still caught me rather by surprise."

"I didn't intend—"

"Not in a bad way." She held out her hand. "I just . . . I suppose I still find it hard to believe a fine man like you would harbor such feelings. For me."

"I am the one presumptuous, I fear." Ødger glanced at her, then away, the back of his neck reddening. "I have little to offer you just now. No home of my own, no established ministry . . ."

"You have the heart of a good and godly man, Ødger Gunderson." Despite herself, Helen couldn't keep a slight tremble from her voice. "And I confess I am quite inclined to let you write to my aunt, as you suggested."

He swung his gaze to hers.

"But first." She drew a breath. "I must tell you more of my story."

He nodded, his face softening. "I have been wondering about that."

She glanced about the garden, noting a little stone bench beneath one birch tree. “Might we sit?”

“Of course.” He held out his hand for her to go first, then followed and sat beside her on the bench, leaving a respectable distance between them.

Helen folded her hands on her lap, focusing on the bright oranges and fuchsias of the zinnia bed. Nothing would make this story easy to tell, but tell it she must.

“I told you my mother was committed to the Iowa Hospital for the Insane, in Independence.”

“Ja.” His voice came gentle, without a hint of judgment.

“I was only seven, but I think even then, something in me understood why. She was always—unstable. I never knew from one day, or even one hour, to the next whether she would be happy, singing and kissing me and dancing me about the house, or sunk in deep despair, unable to get out of bed, work her job as a laundress, or even cook me meals. Sometimes she seemed to forget about me altogether.”

Ødger made a soft sound in his throat.

“I was sent to live with my aunt Ophelia then—my mother’s aunt. She gave me the best of everything, raised me in Cincinnati’s high society, such as it was. I showed a talent for music, so she gave me piano lessons, organ lessons, singing lessons. I went to finishing school, then a women’s college, from which I took my exams to be a teacher.”

A bird twittered in the low branches above them. The September afternoon light slanted golden over the garden.

“Thank you, for sharing this with me.” Ødger’s voice came low. “It helps me better understand.”

“I’m afraid I’m not finished.” Helen tried to smile. “When I went back to visit my aunt this summer, I learned some things I never suspected before. Most importantly, that my mother—was not my real mother.”

Ødger shifted on the bench beside her. "What?"

"It's a long and convoluted tale, but we found information indicating my real parents may have been killed in a carriage accident when I was very small. In this part of Iowa, of all places." Helen's throat constricted. "I've been reading my mother's diary, and also found among her things a newspaper article, and a baby gown. Added to medical records my aunt discovered, which show my mother gave birth to a stillborn child, shortly before she presented me to my grandfather as her own. Except I was already about two. The timing doesn't match up."

"Good heavens."

"Yes." What was he thinking? Helen clasped her hands tighter to still their trembling. "I'm still trying to—to work all this through in my own mind. It was still very fresh when you spoke as you did, after that supper at your sister's, and then mentioned that hospital in Independence—where she had been. That's why I reacted so."

"You have already apologized for that."

"I know. But there's more—I was engaged once, to another young man." She drew a breath. "And he broke it off when he found I had mental instability in my family. He feared I might go wrong in my mind, I suppose, or pass an inclination on to possible children." Her ears warmed. "At least that worry is alleviated, if indeed I am not my mother's biological daughter."

"He refused to marry you just for that?" Ødger's voice heated.

Helen glanced at him, warmed by the look in his eyes. "It was understandable."

"Not if he truly loved you." He shook his head, pressing one fist into his other hand.

Helen pressed her lips together, hardly daring to ponder what he meant by that.

"So." Ødger blew out a breath and rubbed his beard. "Your mother—the one who raised you—she no longer lives?"

"No. She died when I was nine." Helen drew an easier breath, now that so much was told. And Ødger was looking at her so . . . not like James had. Not with fear and tinges of disgust, but with compassion, understanding, and—more, more she couldn't wrap her mind around just yet. "I think in many ways, I tried to forget her as I grew up . . . but she's still a part of me, in some deep way. I'm still figuring out how to reckon with that. Reading her diary is helping." Which she'd slacked off on lately, with all that had been happening.

"And what of this other family, who may be your birth parents? Do you know anything about them?"

"Only what was in the article." She drew it out of her reticule, having tucked it in there on a whim this morning, just in case it would be helpful in telling her story. "Here. You are welcome to read it."

Ødger unfolded the fragile page and perused it closely, a pucker between his brows. After a moment he sat up straight. "Professor Johan Harstad. Your father—or this man who may have been your father—he was a professor?"

"I—I don't know. Does it say that?" Helen leaned closer to see, her sleeve brushing his shoulder. "I suppose I missed that 'Prof.' amid absorbing everything else."

"If they lived here in Iowa"—Odger tapped his finger on the page—"might he not have worked at Luther College?"

Helen stared at him, feeling suddenly the past was crashing rather unceremoniously into the present. "I—I don't know. You think it could be possible?"

Ødger pushed to his feet, his face animated. "The college has archives, records in the library that were saved from the fire. We could go there and look, see what we can find." He paused, glanced at her. "If you wish to, of course."

"I . . ." Helen pressed her hand to her mouth. "I hardly know what to think. When would we go? I have school . . ."

"On Saturday I must go to the campus to meet with one of my professors, to discuss my field training since I wish to stay here for now. He has agreed to meet me on the weekend, due to the circumstances. You could come with me, if you like."

Helen stared up at him, blinking hard. Could answers she'd thought impossible to learn truly be accessible, right at the college in Decorah? Moreover . . . her middle tightened. Did she really want to learn them?

Ødger's steady eyes met hers, earnest yet not insistent—only extending an invitation.

With a shaky breath, Helen stood. "Yes. I will go with you."

Twenty-Five

How different it felt to walk the college grounds with Ødger by her side.

Helen glanced up at him, striding next to her, his gaze preoccupied as he gazed about the grassy, tree-dotted landscape around them. He caught her glance and sent her a quick smile, making her knees weaken.

Goodness, she was falling fast all of a sudden.

At last the many-towered brick fortress of the main college building loomed before them, and this time, she followed Ødger right up the steps. Inside, she breathed in the dim coolness of high ceilings and paneled hallways, echoing with subdued male voices and redolent with the scent of books and academia. A sudden homesickness for her own college sent an unexpected stab through her chest. She had loved that world of books and study and bells and digging deep into the thoughts and wisdom, fumbles and follies of the past, seeking to sit at the masters' feet and learn how to do better for the present and future.

"The library is this way, in the south wing." Ødger turned a corner and down another hallway.

"Goodness." Helen felt slightly out of breath, or was it just anticipation of what was to come? "This place is a regular labyrinth."

"Sorry." Ødger slowed his pace and sent her a half grin. "It is, how do you say? The back of my hand by now."

She smiled. "I can see that."

"Usually these halls are full of students hurrying between classes. Today is different. Quieter." At last he stopped at a pair of dark-paneled double doors. "Here we are." He pulled one door open for Helen and stepped aside, tipping his head for her to precede him.

"Thank you." Helen stepped in and looked around, breathing in the hush and scent of books—so many books. Lining shelves from floor to ceiling, rows and rows of them. Something deep within her relaxed as if coming home.

"May I help you?" A short, round little man rose from behind a large wooden counter.

Ødger stepped over to him. "Ja, thank you, Mr. Bauer. This is Miss Stenerson, she teaches the school in Green Creek."

"Ah, a schoolteacher." The little man rubbed his hands together, his eyes bright behind his spectacles, though he kept his voice to a stage whisper. "How wonderful to have you visit our library—it is not often we receive the presence of a lady. Are you in search of something particular? We have an extensive collection on Norwegian history and literature, as well as a delicious music section. Indeed, it is my pride and joy."

Helen smiled, liking this fellow book lover. "They sound wonderful. I'm very fond of music. But we're in search of something a bit different today."

Ødger laid his hands on the counter. "Does not the library keep archives? Of teachers at the college, its history, things like that? Or even local newspapers?"

Mr. Bauer held up his index finger. "I have catalogs from the college from every year since they began printing them. Would that be of help?"

"Possibly." Ødger glanced at Helen. "What sort of information do they have?"

"Let me show you." The little man turned to shelves of slender beige books behind him and pulled one out, flipping through the first pages. "We have here the board of trustees, faculty, even a list of students. Then course of instruction, etcetera, etcetera. Not to mention"—he beamed and turned the last pages for them to see—"a list of all Luther College graduates going back to 1866, including their professions afterward. Nearly all clergymen, as you might expect."

"Do you have a catalog from . . ." Helen calculated dates in her mind. "Somewhere around 1869? Or perhaps a year before and after?"

"I'm afraid not. The college didn't begin putting out a catalog till 1872."

Helen's shoulders deflated. "I see."

"However." Mr. Bauer spun around and ran his hand over the catalogs, at last pulling one out. "That 1872 catalog did give a general history of the college from its founding in 1861. You're welcome to peruse it if you like."

"Thank you." Helen took the catalog and ran her thumb over the cover. *Katalog for det Norske Luther-College*, it read. *Decorah Iowa, 1861–1872.* "Is it all in Norwegian?"

Mr. Bauer nodded. "Afraid so, miss. They print them in English now, but not back then."

Helen turned the first few pages, coming to a list of names. She held it out to Ødger. "These names at the bottom, they would be faculty, correct?" He read Norwegian better than she, though she could speak it thanks to Aunt Ophelia, whose husband and father had both been Norwegian. She'd seen to it that Helen was educated in that language along with several others—a gift she'd blessed many times in her teaching among immigrant families.

"Ja, that's right." Ødger scanned the names and glanced up at her, his eyes sober. "But I don't see his name."

"No." Helen's throat tightened, but of course, it wouldn't be there. If the professor in the accident were her father, then he was killed about three years before this catalog was printed. She handed the slender booklet back to the librarian. "Thank you very much for your help, Mr. Bauer."

"It doesn't appear I've given you any." Frowning, the little man looked back and forth between her and Ødger. "Pardon my asking, but what exactly are you looking for?"

"We were seeking information on a Professor—Harstad?" Ødger glanced at Helen.

She nodded. "Trying to learn if he ever taught here."

"Harstad, Harstad." Mr. Bauer nibbled his mustache and drummed his fingers on the heavy wooden counter. "Doesn't ring a bell for me, but I've only worked here twelve years. You might ask some of the professors who've been around longer, like Koren or Amundson."

Ødger's spine jerked as if he'd been stung by a bee. "Amundson?"

"Ja, he's been here longer than almost anyone. Started as a young professor way back in '66, I think it was. He might have known your Professor Harstad, if he was here." Two young men approached the desk, and Mr. Bauer gave a slight bow and moved away to assist them. "Excuse me."

"You know Professor Amundson?" Helen whispered as she hurried after Ødger back toward the library's double doors.

"Ja. He is the professor I am to meet with this afternoon." Ødger held the door for her once more, his blue-gray eyes sparkling. "Come on."

Back through the maze of hallways and doors, a murmur of voices rising now in the halls as students who lived in the dormitories upstairs began to head down to the basement dining room for the midday meal. At last Ødger paused at another dark-paneled door and rapped on it.

"Come in." The voice came muffled from within.

The door opened with a click, and they stepped inside to find an elegantly dressed man with a silver goatee sitting behind an expansive wooden desk. A young woman sat directly across from him. The young woman Helen had seen with Ødger on campus before.

She turned her head, brown hair done up in stylish curls, and rose, her taffeta bustle rustling. "Why, Mr. Gunderson." She smiled at him, then glanced past him to Helen, her smile stiffening. "And—Miss Stenerson, was it?"

"Ja. God dag, Miss Amundson." Ødger gave a quick bow to her, then to her father. "Excuse me, Professor. Is this time all right for our meeting?"

Professor Amundson waved his hand. "Certainly. Lena popped in to have dinner with me today, but this shouldn't take long. Please, have a seat." He extended his hand toward the chairs drawn to the side. "Will you be staying, Miss Stenerson?"

Helen gripped her hands together. "I could wait out in the hall."

"No, please. Sit." Ødger pulled out a chair for her, just a bit to the side.

Lena, by contrast, drew her chair nearer to Ødger's and sat down again. "I've been meaning to speak to you again about that organ, Mr. Gunderson. You seemed to enjoy its tone so much—perhaps we might schedule another time for you to play."

"Takk, but I don't think so. I have much to deal with just now." He gave her a polite smile, then turned back to her father. "As you know, Professor, I have been caring for Reverend Larsen since his collapse. Now that he has begun to recover, I plan to take over his ministerial duties until he is able to resume them himself."

"If he is ever able." Professor Amundson twirled a fountain pen between his fingers. "With his age and delicate condition, the church may need to make some difficult decisions."

Ødger dipped his head. "Of course. But I feel I must stay for now. I cannot let down the community, much less the reverend."

"Very commendable of you. I just hate to see your own career set back. We—some of the other faculty members and I—could look into finding an interim pastor to come to Green Creek for a while. Then you could go on to Independence as planned. They have not filled your position yet."

Ødger hesitated, then glanced back at Helen. Something in his shoulders firmed, and he faced the professor once more. "Thank you, but no. I think I will stay in Green Creek for the foreseeable future."

Professor Amundson raised a brow but nodded. "Very well. I will speak with the board. Perhaps we can arrange for your work there in Green Creek to count as your field training."

"Mange takk, sir." Ødger leaned forward, clasping his hands. "There is one other matter we wished to ask you about."

"We?"

Ødger nodded toward Helen. "Miss Stenerson, that is."

With the professor's piercing gaze now directed toward her, Helen cleared her throat. "Forgive my intrusion, Professor Amundson. But I was wondering . . . did you ever happen to know a man named Johan Paul Harstad? I am trying to discern if he was ever a professor here."

"Johan Harstad?" Professor Amundson's silvery brows shot up till they nearly reached his thinning hairline. "Yes, I knew him well—at least, until the accident." He laid down his pen. "Such a terrible thing, him and his wife gone, just like that."

"So she did pass away too?" Helen knew a faint stab in her chest, though she'd known it likely the woman—her birth mother, maybe—hadn't lived.

"Yes, in the hospital a few days later." He frowned. "Why? What is your interest in the Harstads?"

Helen glanced from him to Lena Amundson, who was staring with unconcealed curiosity and a touch of—was it disdain? Her palms damp, Helen swallowed and focused back on the professor.

"I think—I wonder if they might have been my parents."

Twenty-six

"You don't mean—you're the little girl? Their daughter?"

Ødger swung his gaze to Helen. She had turned very pale. Would she faint? She'd never seemed the fainting type, but this . . . He scooted to the edge of his chair, ready to reach for her if need be.

Professor Amundson had gone pale too. "Dear God," he murmured. "You're the very image of her too. Of Christiana."

Helen pressed a hand to her mouth, her eyes filling with tears.

"Lena." The professor darted a glance at his daughter. "A glass of water for Miss Stenerson, please." With a look at Helen, Lena hurried out to do his bidding.

"I'm sorry." Helen drew a shaky breath, her hand still covering half her face. "I didn't—quite expect this, when we came today."

Ødger went to her then, knelt beside her chair and pressed his handkerchief into her free hand. She grasped it, accidentally clasping his fingers in the process. She moved her hand quickly, but the warmth from her touch spread down his arm and clear to his toes.

Still on one knee, he glanced back at his professor. "What can you tell us about the Harstads, Professor?"

"Well." Amundson passed a hand over his forehead, blinking. "Johan came on staff a few months after I did. We were good friends—he taught Latin, I taught theology and church fathers, as you know. He came out here newly married, his wife had a baby girl the year after they moved to Decorah. Fall of 1867, it would have been."

Ødger looked to Helen. She gave a faint nod at the date.

"I just can't believe . . ." Professor Amundson shook his head again, staring at Helen as Lena reentered, handing a tin cup of water to Helen. She took it with a murmured thanks and drank. "I never thought to hear those names again, certainly not from their daughter."

"I still don't know if I am." Helen's voice came thin. "I have no proof, really."

Amundson expelled a breath that was half laugh. "That's because you didn't know your mother. I don't know why I didn't see it when you first came in, you're so like her. But one doesn't expect a ghost to come walking through the door. How . . ." He leaned forward, steepling his fingers on the desk. "That is, what happened to you? The papers—well, the police thought you'd been swept away and drowned. Of course, no one ever found a body. And with your parents gone, there was no one really left to keep looking. What on earth happened? And why come forward now?"

"I didn't know before. That is, I didn't know anything, not till this summer." Straightening her spine, Helen twisted the handkerchief between her fingers. "I went to visit my aunt—the woman who raised me, in Cincinnati."

"Cincinnati," the professor murmured under his breath. "How did she come to find you?"

"She didn't. My mother—the woman I always knew as my mother, she gave me into my aunt's care when I was seven and she entered a mental hospital." Helen kept her voice remarkably even, only a slight tremor now and then. "It was years before my aunt discovered things that made her suspect I wasn't really her niece's child. I still don't know exactly what happened—my mother is gone, and I can only try to put the pieces together. But since she kept a newspaper article about the carriage accident, I can only suppose that she somehow found me, at the scene or wandering around, and took me as her own. She did live in Iowa at the time. We know she was unstable in her mind, and she had recently lost a baby. She must have thought I was . . . meant to be hers."

Professor Amundson nodded, slowly. "I have heard of such things. But what an extraordinary turn of events."

"I was wondering." Helen gripped the handkerchief. "Do you know what—her name was? Or my name . . . their daughter's."

"I've been trying to remember." He pressed fingertips to his forehead. "Some kind of flower comes to mind. Violet, perhaps, or Rose, but that doesn't seem quite right."

"Was it . . . Primrose?" The word whispered from her.

Ødger glanced at her and saw Helen's face was quite white.

The professor's face, by contrast, lit up. "Yes, that sounds right." He then gave a quick frown. "You have some connection with that name, I take it?"

Helen pressed trembling lips together and nodded.

"What about Johan and Christiana's parents? Other family?" Ødger asked.

The professor shook his head. "I believe their parents were back on the East Coast. May well have passed on by now. Wait." He sat up straight, snapping his fingers. "Johan's brother—your uncle. I don't know how I could have forgotten."

Helen's lips parted. Without seeming to realize she did so, she reached for Ødger's hand and gripped it. "I have—an uncle?"

"Knut Harstad. He lives in Independence, I think—at least, he did twenty years ago. Johan and Christiana used to go visit him, he was Johan's older brother. Always a bit odd, I believe, but they were close. I tried to check in on him, after it happened, but . . ." He sighed. "Life goes on, you know."

Helen's fingers tightened on his. Out of the corner of his eye,

Ødger saw Lena watching them, a sort of resignation on her face. *Good*. He stood, gently pulling Helen up to stand also.

"Thank you, Professor. We do not wish to keep you from your dinner any longer, but—might you have an address for this Mr. Knut Harstad?"

Everything was happening too fast.

Helen stared ahead of her, barely noticing the early hints of gold and russet in the trees arching over the lane as Ødger drove them away from the college. He had borrowed the magistrate's buggy and bay gelding for the day, and the wheels rattled gently along the gravel. Helen focused on the horse's black mane bobbing up and down before them, her mind awhirl with so much, she couldn't keep up with it.

Ødger cast her a glance, his brow furrowed. "I will take you back to the boardinghouse now."

"Don't you need to get back to the reverend?" Her voice sounded thin, even to her.

"His daughter said she could stay till after supper. We have time."

She nodded, not trusting herself to speak more. Around her the early fall colors, the houses they had begun to pass, the road, it all began to blur. She squeezed her eyes shut tight.

"Hey. Whoa, now." Ødger reined the horse under the spreading branches of an oak tree, the leaves just beginning to edge with russet, and stopped the buggy. He just sat a moment, the reins lax in his hands.

Helen shoulders shook with a smothered sob, then another. Why couldn't she stop? "I'm s-sorry."

"No need to be."

She covered her face with her hands, let the tears come, with little gasps between sobs. Only a few minutes, but the pressing ache in her chest washed away, replaced by a weariness that trickled through her body to her limbs. She pulled out Ødger's handkerchief again and wiped her eyes and nose. "I'm making good use of this." Her voice came stuffy.

He chuckled. "It's what it's for."

Helen sighed, folding the damp handkerchief between her fingers, blinking at the late afternoon sun filtering golden between the leaves. "Why are you doing all this for me?"

"All this what?"

She made a little gesture with her hands. "Taking me to your professor. Listening to my mixed-up story. Trying to help me contact this—uncle, if that's what he is. You already have more than enough on your shoulders."

He shrugged those broad shoulders. "I have not done much."

She gave him a look. "Ja, you have."

He chuckled at her use of Norwegian. "I do want to be a pastor, remember. Caring for the flock is what we are supposed to do, all day, every day. And you . . ." He hesitated, not quite looking at her. "As I think you know, I care for you deeply. In a special way. Any time I can have with you, any small help I can give . . . it is a privilege."

She nodded, blinking away a stray drop on her lashes. How her heart swelled toward him just now, but she hesitated to trust it. She was caught up in the emotion of the moment . . . so many emotions, frighteningly so. She mustn't let her judgment be clouded, say something she might later regret. For should a minister truly be tied to her, with such a fraught family story as she seemed to have?

She breathed deeply, in and out. Somewhere overhead a bird twittered.

"I've always been afraid to let my feelings out." The words slipped forth before she meant them to.

Ødger shifted to face her more on the wagon seat. "Because of your mother?"

"Her feelings were—so much. All over the place. Spilling over onto me, threatening to drown us both at times. It seemed safer just to keep them inside. But lately I've been having more trouble doing that."

Ødger tipped his head back. "Many of us struggle with emotions, I think. Yet troublesome as they can be, they can also be gifts. For how can we know and experience this world, in all its beauty and brokenness, wonder and heartache, without feeling it? Even our God rejoices and rages and weeps."

Helen stared at him. "You should be a poet. Or a songwriter."

"Or a preacher?" He wrinkled his nose.

She laughed, then sighed. "True. You are so good for me, Ødger. I don't deserve you."

"I feel the same about you."

She tipped her head, tracing his strong profile, his neatly trimmed beard, as he watched a squirrel scurry along a nearby rail fence. "I want to learn more of your story too. Your growing up in Norway. I know you told me a bit of why you wanted to get into ministry, but what was your family like?"

"Plenty of chaos and noise, with eight children. Three of us boys. Our mor was a saint, and Maya and the other girls kept up pretty well."

"And you're the oldest?"

He nodded. "I never quite lived up to my far's expectations for the eldest son. Into trouble too much as a boy, then wanting to spend time on music and study rather than learn his trade."

"Which was?"

"Farming and clock-making."

"Clock-making, how interesting."

"To him, but not to me." He gave a brief smile.

So Ødger had his own pains and insecurities. As all of them did. Helen drew a breath. "Thank you for letting me talk. But we should go. I'm really not supposed to be keeping company with a man at all, by my contract, unless he's my father or brother or uncle."

Ødger picked up the reins. "Well, it's a good thing I'm helping you find your uncle, then."

She laughed again, the sound wafting on the breeze. A falling leaf landed yellow on her lap.

"So." Ødger clucked to the gelding, and the buggy rolled forward again. "Will you write to him? Knut Harstad?"

"Yes. And send what evidence I have. I don't know if he'll be willing to see me . . . but I can't come this far and not see it through." Her voice came steadier now.

"And how does this affect"—he hesitated—"how you see those who raised you? Your mother, your aunt?"

"I think . . . I still have much to work out in my mind about my mother, Adelaide. But Aunt Ophelia, she gave me everything. She will always be my family." Helen sighed. "I'll write to her tomorrow."

"And . . ." Ødger cleared his throat. "Are you still willing for me to include a letter as well?"

Her heart thumped hard, for she knew what he meant. "If you like." She dared to look at him then, meeting his eyes.

The smile he sent her made her wish he could catch her in his arms and kiss her right now.

September's pleasant days chilled into October's golden ones, the trees ablaze in red and russet and ocher, the fields turning sere and brown, resting Amalia's eyes when she gazed over them while hanging laundry or churning butter on the back porch, usually wearing baby Sarah wrapped snug in a sling against her chest or back. After the corn harvest came gathering in the last of the garden. Ruthie, Hank, and Thomasina helped dig up the potatoes and onions, then rolled the big orange pumpkins and squashes down to the cellar after the first frost. Reggie at first disdained the thought of getting his hands dirty, but when Amalia caught him climbing a tree with Hank in the orchard in search of the best late apples, she knew he was beginning to find his footing at Forsberg House.

One afternoon the week before Thanksgiving, Helen came downstairs just before supper with two opened letters in her hands.

"We stopped at Nygards' after school, and these were waiting for me." She paused next to the counter where Amalia stood opening jars of canned green beans from the summer.

"Who are they from?" Sarah shifted and whimpered on Amalia's back, and Amalia jiggled her shoulders to lull her back to sleep. "Just let me get the rest of supper on, min lille, and I will feed you." Emma Schneider had already headed into the dining room to set the long table, bless her. Goodness, did Amalia appreciate having another set of womanly hands around the boardinghouse.

"One is from my aunt." Helen's mouth quirked with a look Amalia couldn't quite decipher. "The other—from my uncle."

"Your uncle?" Amalia twisted to stare at her. "You mean—the one you told us about? Johan Harstad's brother?"

"Ja, Knut Harstad." Helen glanced down at the penned sheets in her hand. "It's short, a bit cryptic. But he says he wants to meet me. He suggests the Saturday after Thanksgiving, at his home in Independence."

"That's quite a trip." Amalia dumped the green beans into a pot and pushed it to the hotter part of the stove. Canned beans could bring dangerous illness if they'd turned, so her mor had taught her to always boil them well.

"It is. I'd thought of asking Ødger to go with me, since he nearly went to live in Independence, but, well . . ." Helen's cheeks pinked. "The other letter concerns him."

"From your aunt?" Amalia lifted her brows. "And how so, might I ask?"

Helen blew out a breath. "Ødger included a letter with my last. Asking her blessing to court me."

Amalia's cheeks stretched with a grin. "And you saw fit to hide this information till now?"

"I didn't mean to hide it." Helen rubbed her forehead with a grimace. "I just didn't know how—or what to say. I keep being afraid to hope this really could happen. And you've been so busy with the baby . . ."

"Hush, dear one. I'm only teasing. But oh, I would be so happy for you. I take it her answer was favorable, by your rosy red face?"

Helen lowered her eyes and nodded. "She says he has her blessing. That if a young man has managed to meet my approval, he must be worthy." She drew a breath and pressed the hand that didn't hold the letters to her flushed cheeks as if trying to cool them. "So now—what am I to do?"

"What do you mean? Do you want Ødger to court you?"

Helen's eyes softened, not quite meeting Amalia's. "I—I do. I'll confess that, to you. But we can't begin anything official, not while I'm under my teaching contract. Perhaps once the school year ends . . ." Her cheeks had pinked with a rare flush. "If he still wants to . . . then I'll be more than willing."

Amalia smiled and squeezed her friend's hand. "Oh, I'm pretty sure he'll still want to. But you should tell him, and let him tell you himself. In the meantime . . ." She checked the roast in the oven, then loosened the sling over her back and swung her two-month-old daughter into her arms, sitting down on a kitchen chair to nurse her while the supper finished cooking. "Why can't Ødger go with you to Independence? Surely it's not that far of a trip by train. Just take someone else along with you as chaperone."

"Who would we take?"

"What about the magistrate? He'd enjoy the journey. And be a good character witness, should your uncle have any questions."

"That's a good idea." Helen's shoulders seemed to relax a bit. "Thank you."

"What are friends for?"

Twenty-Seven

So they were on their way.

The rock and sway of the railway carriage lulled Helen as she leaned toward the window with her mother's diary. Across from her, Magistrate Karlsson dozed, his head drooping forward over his cane. Ødger sat next to Helen, not too close, but his presence eased her as always. He sat comfortably in the train seat, one leg crossed over the other, a volume of Spurgeon's writings open on his lap.

And she had the diary. She'd hesitated to read it of late, knowing she drew near to the most tender places . . . the places where her mother might describe meeting, or finding, her, little Helen. Yet surely now was the time, if ever there was, here on her way to meet her supposed blood uncle.

Helen drew a breath, opened to the spot she'd marked with a green ribbon, and began to read.

April 19, 1869

My baby is gone.

I do not want to believe it—every night I beg God to make me wake up from this nightmare, or to send my little angel back to me. Or, if He is determined to keep her, to take me to be with her also. And every morning, I wake up and she is still gone. And I am still here.

Stillborn, they told me. They only let me see her once—my sweet, beautiful little angel.

I do not want to wake up.

A tear dripped off Helen's nose. She brushed it away. *Oh, Mama.* Her chest squeezed. She hadn't thought of her mother by that name in years. So much pain Adelaide had brought to her own life . . . yet so much pain had she herself borne. *I didn't know.* She turned the page.

May 16, 1869

I have to leave the Benedict Home. It is for mothers and babies, they say, and I am not a mother and do not have a baby. More women need the room, need the beds. The headmistress says perhaps I should go into an asylum, because sometimes I cry and cry and cannot stop. But I won't let anyone lock me up. I'm going to slip away, early some morning, and find myself a job somewhere, and a little house. I can take in laundry and maybe—maybe get a dog. Or a cat.

Then I won't be alone.

June 20, 1869

I found her . . . my little angel. Did God hear my prayers, and send her back to me? Sometimes I think so . . . and then my mind goes all blurry, and I remember my baby should still be a wee thing, and this child can already walk and speak a few words. Still, surely stranger things have happened. When I saw that carriage crashed down by the river, near where I have made my home in a little cottage—I felt sick inside. Then I heard her crying, and I knew—I knew.

She was calling for me.

August 8, 1869

Little Helen, I call her. I read in a book once that "Helen" means "ray of light." She is my ray of light, the delight of my heart. Such a fairy-like little thing, with her golden hair and bright eyes. At first she cried day and night, but now she is inquisitive, into everything, and tries to imitate the birds in their singing. Today I had enough from my laundry job to buy us raisins and make sweet buns, and she smiled bright enough to light up our dark little cabin.

My little angel sent from above, to take the place of the wee babe I lost. I knew that as soon as I saw her, crawling out from that wreckage down by the river. She was sent to save me . . . and I was sent to save her.

Helen closed the diary and drew a long breath. A great deal to wrap her mind around . . . to have been thought of as a replacement of sorts for her mother's stillborn child, even if she'd known that were likely, given Adelaide's mental state. At least her mother hadn't thought she was, well, kidnapping Helen—but more rescuing her.

Rescuing them both.

A muffled snort made her glance over at Ødger, then roll her lips to keep from laughing. His head lolled forward, a faint snore whiffling from his nose.

Poor man, he worked so hard—between filling in for Rev. Larsen, finishing his own studies, still working on the finishing construction at the college when he could squeeze in the time, and sometimes helping with farmwork for Eben and Maya or the boardinghouse. Small wonder the train had rocked him to sleep.

"Next stop, Independence," bellowed the conductor, striding with his rolling gait down the train aisleway.

Ødger jerked and lifted his head, blinking, then rubbed the back of his neck and smiled at Helen. "So. We are almost there."

"Yes." Helen folded her gloved hands in her lap atop the diary. "We are."

The magistrate hailed a cab once they disembarked, and they found Knut Harstad's home without any trouble, a small brick cottage on a side street. Helen insisted on paying the cab driver herself, against Magistrate Karlsson's protests, and then stared at the little house, her feet suddenly rooted to the ground.

Ødger and the magistrate waited, watching her. Seeming to understand.

"Shall we?" Ødger asked at last, holding out his arm.

Drawing a breath, Helen slipped her hand through it, the warmth of his arm through his coat somehow steadying and grounding her. She found she could step forward now, up the little flagstone walk to the cottage porch, though her heart pounded hard.

The magistrate tapped his cane on the door, then stepped aside and waited.

They seemed to stand there for several minutes, no one speaking. Then a faint shuffle came behind the door, a fumbling with the latch. And it creaked open with a complaining squeak, revealing a stooped, silver-haired man wearing a patched gray cardigan and trousers seemingly too big for him. He blinked at them warily.

Magistrate Karlsson doffed his hat. "Mr. Knut Harstad?"

The man jerked a nod. "That's me."

"I'm Magistrate Karlsson, from Decorah. This," he indicated with a sweep of his hat, "is my friend Ødger Gunderson, and Miss Helen Stenerson. I believe you have corresponded with her?"

Knut stared a moment, then something flickered over his face. He nodded and shuffled backward, opening the door wider. "Come in."

They stepped into the dim little cottage. It held a faintly musty smell, but the rooms stood neat and tidy. Heavily favoring his right leg, Knut led them into a small parlor and pushed back curtains to let in the wan early December sunshine.

"Have a seat," he said, easing himself onto a chair with a grunt. He patted his leg. "Sorry. Old bullet from the war—hip's never been the same."

"Ah." The magistrate set forward his own cane and prosthetic leg. "I can commiserate. Minié ball took my leg at Gettysburg."

A flicker lighted Knut's face again. "Antietam, for me."

Magistrate Karlsson shook his head. "May we never see such fields of suffering on this earth again."

"Amen to that. So." Knut leaned his hands on his knees and stared straight at Helen. "You're the one that wrote to me."

"Yes. Thank you for agreeing to meet with me, Mr. Harstad."

"Call me Knut. Everybody does." He examined her face, shaking his head. "So you claim to be little Primrose. Long-lost daughter of my brother and Christiana. Guess you do take after her, more than a mite."

Helen straightened her spine. "I know this must come as a shock to you."

"Did at first. Almost didn't write you back." Knut tapped his fingers on his knee, glancing away from Helen, then back again. "But then I thought, we don't get many chances for certain things in this life. Might as well try to see who might be the only family I got livin' in this world."

Helen's throat tightened. "I have—many questions. About my—my parents."

He nodded. "Shoot."

She drew a breath. "My father. He was a professor at Luther College, I know that. But—what was he like? And my—my mother?"

A softening came over Knut's face. "My brother was the best man I knew. My best friend too—one of the only real friends I ever had. He was a quiet feller, you know, but always looking after folks. Didn't let his big book learning ever make him feel better than others. He looked after me all his life, gave to the poor. Didn't only keep his faith for Sundays, if you know what I mean. Looked after your mother, and you." He shook his head. "Land, they set plenty of store by you when you were born. Thought the sun rose and set over your little blond head."

Helen's eyes stung. She blinked hard. "And my mother?"

"She was Swedish, Christiana Lindstrom—and had a voice like

a bird. He used to call her his Swedish Nightingale, after Jenny Lind, you know. She came down from Minnesota to teach, then fell in love when they met at the Lutheran church."

"She—was a teacher?" Helen's breath caught.

Her uncle nodded, then cocked his head. "Wait, you're a schoolmarm too, aren't you?"

"I am." Helen folded her hands together. "At the school in Green Creek. And—I love to sing."

"And she has a lovely voice too," Ødger put in, then reddened slightly when Helen glanced at him.

"Well." Knut shook his head. "You do take after her. I can see my brother around your eyes, though. So how did you—find out? About them, I mean. You said you grew up in Ohio."

"I did—from age seven. But my mother—the woman who raised me—she lived in Iowa at the time." As briefly as she could, Helen filled in the story, in more detail than the bare bones she'd sketched out in her letter. And of course, now she could add a bit more from her mother's diary.

"Well, I'll be." Knut shook his head again, rubbing his bristled chin. "Quite a tale. Sounds like something you'd read in a magazine. They looked for you for weeks, you know—after the accident. Christiana's parents even came down from Minnesota to search, but they eventually had to give up. No trace of you to be found. Now we know why."

"They aren't—living, anymore, are they?" Helen had to ask.

"No, they've been gone some ten years now. Afraid all you've got left is me." He met her eyes then, a glint of vulnerability in his gray ones. "Imagine I'm quite a disappointment in the long-lost family department."

"Not at all. I just—I can hardly believe I've found you." Helen drew a breath. "May—would you mind if I called you 'uncle'?"

He studied her a moment, then a smile slowly cracked through the lines of his face. "I think that'd be kind of nice."

"So. What did you think of your onkel?" Ødger asked on the train ride home, as they shared the supper Amalia had packed of bread, cheese, and orchard apples.

"I like him." Helen nibbled a piece of cheese. "He takes some warming up to, that's certain. And yet—I feel a sort of connection with him. A kinship, I suppose that would make sense. I don't know how often I'll see him, but I want to make the effort. Perhaps both of us will feel less alone in the world."

"I don't want you to ever feel alone in the world, Helen." Ødger's voice came low, his hand so near hers on the train seat by the basket between them.

Helen clenched her fingers at an urge to slide them right into his, glancing at the magistrate dozing again on the opposite seat. She pulled her hand away and drew a breath. Perhaps this was the moment she'd been waiting for. "That reminds me. I wanted to show you the letter I received from my aunt."

"Oh?" Ødger's tone came altered now, and he shifted on the seat. "Does it—that is—what does she say?"

Helen smiled, withdrew the letter from her reticule, and pressed it into his hand. "See for yourself."

The lines of Aunt Ophelia's letter drummed through her mind as she watched him read and reread them as she had since the letter arrived last week. With the bustle of Thanksgiving, she just hadn't found the right moment to tell Ødger till now.

My dear Helen,

I must confess myself both surprised and overjoyed to receive the letter from your Mr. Gunderson. You must know that your future has weighed heavily on my mind, especially as my own remains so uncertain and likely short. Knowing that you have gained the regard of a good man does wonders to set my mind at ease.

I know you worry that I won't approve due to Mr. Gunderson's lack of wealth and material prospects, but while I may be a rich old lady rather set in her ways, I do know that some things will always remain more important than money. The character you have described in your letter, not to mention the sentiments he himself expressed, show he has these traits in plenty. Moreover, I believe you have a good head on your shoulders and know your own mind, so if you approve of him, I give my blessing with my whole heart and, I hardly need add, my love.

Ødger lifted his head and met her gaze, the sun seeming to rise on his face despite the falling dusk outside. He cleared his throat. "So. When your teaching contract is up?"

Helen smiled back at him, her own lips trembling. "When my contract is up."

TWENTY-EIGHT

Ruthie could hardly believe it was finally time.

Her stomach jumped with excitement as she tied on her blue knitted cap and buttoned up her coat. Everyone would be arriving for the ice-skating party soon.

"Come on, Ruthie!" Thomi called from outside.

"I'm coming." Ruthie shoved her hands into the black-and-white mittens Tante Amalia had knitted for her and burst out onto the porch. Dusk was falling, the first stars starting to twinkle in the pinky-gray December sky, the last sunset glow still turning the blanketing snow rosy.

"Reggie and Hank already headed down to the creek. Let's catch up with them." Thomi set off running, her dark braids swinging beneath her red knitted cap with the white pompom, her boots chuffing up snow.

With a squeal, Ruthie took off after her, her breath making little puffs in the air.

"Ruthie, wait," Onkel Absalom called from the wagon he was loading for the party.

Ruthie skidded to a stop and looked back. Thomi was getting way ahead.

"Don't go on the ice till an adult says it's safe." Onkel Absalom met her eyes, his own brown ones serious behind his spectacles. "Understand?"

"Ja." She nodded hard. "We won't."

"Good." He winked at her then. "Go have fun, we'll see you soon." Tante Amalia was just coming out of the boardinghouse in her new dark red woolen dress, swathed in one of Onkel Absalom's overcoats buttoned over both her and baby Sarah.

Ruthie took off running down the snowy path again, grinning as the cold air slapped her face. A cuddly baby in the family, the ice-skating party tonight, Christmas in two weeks—she felt like her feet might sprout wings.

She slowed when she reached the creek, picking her way along the frozen bank between the bare sticks and branches of the sleeping trees and bushes. The creek lay silent, missing its summer babble. But up ahead, lanterns bobbed and sleigh bells jingled as people arrived for the party in the clearing where Mr. Eben, Onkel Erik, JJ, and Hank had worked all fall as they dammed the creek and fixed up the cabin.

Ruthie emerged from the tangle of wintry brush to where the pond spread out in a silvery sheet. She clasped her mittened hands together. It was so beautiful—and already wagons were arriving, and some sleighs. On the other side of the pond, she spied Thomi's red cap and Hank's gray one. She hurried around the edge of the ice, careful not to step on it yet, as Onkel Absalom had warned.

"There you are!" Lisa Miller, her best friend next to Thomi, rushed at Ruthie and hugged her. They held hands and jumped up and down, their boots crunching on the snow.

Over in front of the snug cabin that used to be JJ's shack, Hank and Ned were building a pile of dry sticks and branches. Inside, Miss Stenerson and Mrs. Schneider had lit lamps and now worked to fire up the new wood stove.

"What's that stuff for?" Wearing a fashionable double-breasted wool coat and tweed cap, Reggie stuck his hands in his knickers pockets and stared at the stack of brush.

"They're making a bonfire, of course." Thomi tossed her braid. "Come on, let's help."

"I don't want to get my clothes all dirty. My grandma just bought me this coat."

"Fine." Thomi shrugged. "Stay all neat and tidy all by yourself, then."

Ruthie glanced back over her shoulder at Reggie as she began gathering armfuls of dry twigs with Thomi and Lisa. Reggie dug his boot toe in the snow, staring out at the pond. Something twinged in Ruthie's chest. He looked awfully lonely—but it wasn't like they were leaving him out on purpose. Like she'd heard Mr. JJ say, every person had to make their own choices.

They built the bonfire up till it was almost as tall as Ruthie, laying the bigger logs and kindling where Eben showed them to. By that time, Onkel Absalom and Tante Amalia had arrived, along with all the Millers. Little Torvald was bundled in so many layers he waddled like a fat duckling. Mrs. Miller, Cousin Maya, and Tante Amalia carried big pots into the cabin to heat the hot chocolate and cider, while Ruthie and the other girls helped lay out the cookies and pastries brought by families from school, all spread on the red-and-white checked tablecloth. The table Mr. JJ had made filled much of the room, along with some chairs and a low cot to lay sleepy babies on. They'd had a quick early supper at the boardinghouse today.

All of a sudden, shouts from outside sent Ruthie, Thomi, and Lisa dashing out of the cabin, the women crowding after them.

Out on the frozen pond, Onkel Erik skated toward a small figure in the middle of the ice.

Ruthie's chest squeezed. It was Reggie. Had he not known to wait for a grown-up to check the ice? Was it safe? Would the ice crack and send Reggie down into the cold, murky depths? But

Onkel Erik reached Reggie, and the ice seemed to hold solid. He grabbed the boy's arm and skated back with him to the edge, his face grim.

Ruthie swallowed hard. She couldn't hear what Onkel Erik was saying to Reggie, but she could imagine. Why hadn't he known not to head out by himself? If the ice cracked and he fell through, he could slide under the solid surface and never be found. She ran up to Onkel Absalom, who stood near the edge of the pond. "Is the ice okay? Why did Reggie go out there?"

Onkel Absalom looked to Onkel Erik, who headed toward them now, still holding Reggie's arm.

Onkel Erik nodded, his eyes ice blue under his cream-colored knit hat. "Ja, it seems solid enough, thank God. But you can't tell by looking at it. I still want to skate all around myself and be sure." He gave Reggie's arm a little shake, then let him go. "Don't you ever do that again, not till someone who knows how has checked first."

"Fine, I won't." Reggie's face looked little and scared, only a hint of his usual defiance sparking his hazel eyes. He glanced at Ruthie, then lifted his chin and strode off toward his mother, who hugged him close, then bent toward him with a scolding face.

Ruthie released a breath, her shoulders relaxing. *Thank you, Jesus, that Reggie is all right. Please show us how to be friends with him. And help him want to be friends with us. Help us all have a fun and safe time.*

Behind her, Mr. JJ lit the bonfire, with a slight whoosh and crackle. Wagons hung with lanterns circled the pond now, lighting the falling twilight like large winter fireflies.

"Hey, Karlsson!" someone shouted. "Can we go on the ice?"

Onkel Absalom glanced at Onkel Erik, who had just finished skating all around the pond. He held up his hand and nodded. Onkel Absalom stepped up onto the buckboard of their wagon and looked out over the crowd, who quieted and turned toward him. He pushed up his spectacles and smiled from beneath his brown plaid woolen cap. "Welcome, everyone, to our first Forsberg House ice-skating party."

Cheers and claps sounded out.

"We hope this may become a tradition, a way of gathering our community together for warmth and fellowship, celebrating God's goodness to us throughout the year. Erik Gunderson has checked the ice and found it sound. If you would join me for a word of prayer, we can then begin the festivities." Onkel Absalom pulled off his cap and bowed his head. "Father in heaven, thank you for this beautiful place you have given us and the friends who surround us. Thank you that the ice is sound and our new young friend was safe just now. Bless and protect all who gather here and give us joy with each other and with you, we pray. In Jesus's name, Amen."

Amens and applause rang around the frozen pond.

"And now"—Onkel Absalom grinned and held out his hands—"let's skate!"

Ruthie giggled at the shouts and laughter. Boys and girls around her began tugging on their skates, while others just stepped onto the ice and began sliding in their boots. She ran to the cabin door. "Tante Malia! Where are my skates?"

"Should be in the back of the wagon, den lille." Tante Amalia smiled at her, her cheeks rosy and eyes shining in the warmth from the stove as she stirred the hot chocolate. She looked like a queen with her crown of golden braids and dark red dress. Baby Sarah cooed nearby on the cot.

Ruthie found her skates and sat by the pond's edge to strap them on, her mittened fingers fumbling with the buckles. Tante Amalia and Onkel Absalom had given them to her for her birthday in November.

"Need help?" Hank crouched beside her.

"I thought I could do it." Ruthie sighed and stuck her foot out.

"Here." Hank tugged off his mittens and tucked them under his arm, then did up her buckles quick as a wink.

"Won't your fingers freeze?"

"Nah." Hank shoved his mittens back on, then stood and held out his hand to Ruthie. "Want a hand up?"

Ruthie let him pull her to her feet, then balanced. Wobbling, she took the few steps to the ice's edge, then hesitated. "What if I don't remember how?" She'd been excited about this for months, but now her stomach squirmed with butterflies. Out on the ice Jack O'Brien fell hard on his back with a thud that made her flinch, though he got up laughing.

"You'll be fine. Come on." Hank kept tight hold of her hand and stepped out onto the ice, his steps sure in the old skates he'd borrowed from Onkel Absalom. His feet were almost as big now.

Ruthie took one step onto the ice, then another. Maybe she did remember how. Hazy memories darted through her mind—holding tight to Mor and Far's hands, whooshing along the canal near their home.

"Slide your feet side to side, like this." Hank demonstrated.

Swish, swoosh. Swish, swoosh. Ruthie's cheeks stretched in a grin. "I'm doing it!"

"Sure you are."

Swish, swoosh. Swish—whoops! One foot went one direction and one another. Ruthie shrieked, flailing at Hank's arms.

He caught her just before she hit the ice. "Easy there. Don't get overconfident."

She drew a long breath and got her legs steady under her again. "I'm all right."

They skated all around the edge of the pond, then found Thomi skating with Ned. The four of them joined hands and skated in a circle, laughing, their breath joining in cloudy puffs as the stars came out above them in a deep blue sky.

When she couldn't feel her fingers and toes anymore, Ruthie shed her skates and hurried into the cabin for hot chocolate, joined by Lisa and Thomi. Tante Amalia and Mrs. Schneider dipped up the rich, chocolatey liquid into cups, or ladled spice-scented apple cider for those who preferred it.

Ruthie breathed in the steam from her cup, the heat of the tin seeping through her mittens to thaw her numb hands. "Can't you skate, Tante Malia?"

"I'm afraid not this year, den lille." Her tante glanced at baby Sarah kicking on the bed. "Maybe next time."

Onkel Absalom poked his head in. "Actually, Erik and I had an idea about that."

"What do you mean?"

"Put your coat on, bundle the baby, and I'll show you."

Her forehead puckered, Tante Amalia glanced back at Mrs. Schneider, who smiled and nodded, ladle in her hand. "Go on. I can take care of this."

Tante Amalia bundled up herself and little Sarah and stepped outside, the baby's round face cuddled in a warm woolen cap. Ruthie and the other girls followed, sipping their steaming chocolate.

Onkel Absalom paused at the edge of the ice and swept out his arm dramatically. "There, my queen. Your chariot awaits."

Onkel Erik stood on the ice, grinning. He held onto the back of a sturdy wooden chair covered with woolen blankets.

Tante Amalia stared from her brother to Onkel Absalom. "Are you serious?"

"Of course. You can hold Sarah and both skate. Dr. Armitage said it should be perfectly safe."

A smile broke out over Tante Amalia's face like a sunbeam. She hugged Onkel Absalom's arm. "You're the dearest man alive."

Soon Tante Amalia and Sarah sat enthroned in the chair. With a woolen blanket tucked over them, Onkel Absalom spun them around in gentle circles as he skated behind them, his red scarf and Tante Amalia's laughter streaming out behind them.

Ruthie sipped her chocolate and beamed up at the rising yellow moon. This must be the happiest, most beautiful night she'd ever seen.

Helen smiled, watching Absalom twirl Amalia and her babe about on the ice. She cupped her hands around her cup of hot chocolate, breathing in the fragrant steam.

"Nice party, isn't it?" A woman stepped near, stopping at Helen's shoulder.

Helen glanced at her, schooling her surprise. "I'm glad to see you here, Mrs. Flinch."

"Wasn't sure about it at first, but I'm glad we came." Mrs. Flinch nodded at her sons playing crack the whip in a linked chain of children out on the ice, whooping with glee whenever Hank, as the leader, changed direction and sent the line flying.

"I think it's a wonderful way to bring the community together." Helen emphasized the last two words just slightly, though she didn't know if the other woman would take her meaning.

"Maybe so." Mrs. Flinch nodded, a slight pucker between her brows. "I must say, this is one of the nicest festivities I've ever been to. You know I used to think Amalia was plumb crazy, taking in all the strays and vagabonds she does here at Forsberg House, but maybe it's all right. That Hank is turning into a right smart boy, and even Thomasina seems a nice enough girl after all. Here, it just feels like—a big family."

Helen smiled, tucking away the comment to tell Amalia later. "I quite agree."

Mrs. Flinch moved on to greet Mrs. Nygard of the mercantile, and Ødger stepped to Helen's side in a dark gray wool overcoat and blue scarf.

"Enjoying the party?" He sipped from his own tin cup, rimming his golden mustache with chocolate foam.

"I am." Helen nodded at the busy pond. "So sweet of Absalom to include Amalia like that."

"Ja." Ødger smiled. "It does my heart good to see my cousin so happy. And my sister." He nodded at Maya and Eben, building a miniature snowman with Torvald near the cabin, the light of the bonfire dancing over the little family.

Surely he must yearn for his own family. No, she knew he did . . . and with whom. Helen traced his bearded profile in the light and shadow, the lines of it growing so familiar to her now. Even . . . beloved.

As if reading her thoughts, Ødger glanced at her with a crooked grin. "So. Aren't you going to skate?"

Helen laughed. "Oh dear, no. I'm afraid I'm not very good at it."

"What?" His eyes widened. "The accomplished Miss Stenerson has something she's not good at?"

She swatted at his coat sleeve. "Stop it."

He ducked aside and drained the last of his chocolate, wiping the foam from his lips. "In Norway, we learned to ski and skate almost as soon as we could walk. Come." He set aside his cup and held out his mittened hand. "I will show you."

"No—no really. I'm sure I should fall."

He held her gaze, still holding out his hand. "Trust me."

Helen held her breath a moment, looking into his eyes, then set her cup aside and took his hand.

Ødger led her out onto the ice, her gripping his arm probably harder than was proper, but what else was she to do when her feet seemed about to take leave of her at any second? She desperately wanted to flee back to solid ground—and yet, Ødger was there, his arm so firm and steady beneath her grip, his feet balanced on the slippery ice, keeping him somehow solid as a Norwegian mountain.

Slowly, slowly, she took a step, then another. She slipped and nearly fell, but he caught her. He kept them out of the path of the shrieking and sliding children, letting her find her rhythm, till her feet slid back and forth in tandem with his. Nothing fancy, but not falling, either.

"You see?" He smiled at her, his teeth white in the moonlight. "You can do it."

When they had skated around the edge of the whole pond, he gave her a little twirl under his arm, then caught both her hands again. And she smiled at him, her heart winging with her feet as the moon rose over the snow.

TWENTY-NINE

"Can we go out and play in the snow?"

Helen glanced up from where she sat by the parlor fire, trying to plan lessons for the new term this week after Christmas. Ruthie stood by the window, peering out at the snow drifts outside.

"I don't think your tante wants you out much today. It's too cold. But your onkel Absalom should be home soon from town." A snowstorm just before Christmas had canceled the church Christmas Eve program, but when the sun came out Christmas Day, the magistrate, Ødger, Maya and Eben had all made it through the snowy roads to the boardinghouse for a joyous family celebration.

Ruthie sighed and dragged herself away from the window. "I'm tired of being inside."

Sarah whimpered, kicking in her cradle. Ruthie knelt by the baby and rocked her, murmuring softly.

Helen smiled. "You're a good big sister."

Erik and Asgar Rykavyk played a game of checkers by the fire, the snow making them sit still and rest inside for once. Helen stared at her lesson plan sheet again. School would resume next week, but she struggled to focus, memories of ice-skating with Ødger dancing through her mind, as well as his smile when he'd opened her gift at Christmas, a set of Matthew Henry's Bible commentaries.

"You should not have spent so much," he'd said, shaking his head, while his calloused hands caressed the books' binding like a treasure. "I do not have something so dear for you."

But she'd thought him wrong, when he gave her a pencil box he'd carved himself, with flowery scrolls etched around her name on top. *Helen Primrose*. "Since both names are part of who you are," he'd said, making her love him all the more.

Ødger, how are you? It's only been a few days, but I miss you. Despite the assurance they'd been finding together, when she didn't see him, she found her certainty about their future quaking. Did he really feel sure he wanted to join his life and ministry to her, with her fraught history? And pragmatically, how would they manage to live, since she couldn't teach if married, and he would be a newly graduated seminarian with no parish of his own?

At the crunch of wagon runners on the packed snow outside, Helen glanced out the window to see the wagon sliding toward the barn, Absalom on the seat and bundles in the back.

"Onkel Absalom!" Ruthie jumped up and ran toward the kitchen to meet him.

Sarah Marie squalled, no doubt dismayed that her doting older sister had fled. Erik rose and bent over the cradle, lifting his niece into his big hands and cradling her close.

Helen smiled to see it, and Erik glanced at her. "Where's Amalia?"

"She's in the kitchen, I think. I can take her if you like." Helen stood and held her arms out for the baby.

Erik nodded and handed his niece over.

Helen nestled the weight of little Sarah against her shoulder. At nearly four months now, Sarah held her head up and stared around, wide-eyed. She grabbed at Helen's cameo brooch.

"You like that, do you, little one?" Helen pressed a kiss to Sarah's soft, chubby cheek, savoring her baby scent. A sweet ache throbbed in her chest. Would she someday hold babies of her own, after all? "Come, let's find your mor."

She found Amalia unwrapping packages at the kitchen table as Absalom and the children brought them in from the wagon, his first trip to town for supplies since the snowstorm. Once Amalia had taken her daughter to nurse, Helen opened the door for Absalom as he hauled in the last armload of brown paper bundles.

"Ah, Helen." Absalom set the parcels on the table and reached into his coat pocket. His eyes sobering, he withdrew an envelope and held it out. "This was waiting for you."

"Thank you." Helen reached for the letter, then froze. The envelope was edged in black.

With numb fingers, she took the letter and turned it over to slit the seal. Her hand trembling, though she knew down deep what this meant, she unfolded the single sheet within.

My dear Miss Helen,

You have doubtless guessed the sad reason for my writing to you. Your Aunt Ophelia has departed from this world. She passed in her sleep, quiet and easy, so far as we can tell. I think she had some hint of it a few nights before, for her coughing was bad, and she told me to make sure to send you the news myself. She has left all her affairs in your hands, and her money too. We hope you will come home soon and let us know what your wishes are.

I remain, your
affectionate servant,
Mathilda Hoskins

The lines blurred before Helen's eyes. She sniffed hard and folded up the letter.

"Your aunt?" Absalom's voice came heavy with compassion.

"Yes. She is gone. I must go to Ohio." She wouldn't say anything, yet, about the inheritance—she had known, certainly, in the back of her mind that that was a possibility, but to think of the implications in reality . . . Helen shook her head, her eyes blurring with tears again. For now, she must mourn. And pack her bags.

"When do you want to leave?" Absalom asked.

Helen blew out a shaky breath. "If I go and return quickly, I can still begin the term almost when I planned. I'd better take the first train tomorrow."

Cincinnati felt so much colder, bleaker, lonelier than when she'd visited in the summer. Partly from the snow-covered stillness of winter, but also the lack of Aunt Ophelia's presence. She'd filled that old house, filled it with the force of her love and her wit and her strength. Now she was gone, and Helen and the servants seemed to rattle around in it aimlessly.

"So you don't think you'll keep the house, dearie?" Mrs. Hoskins asked her the evening after the funeral, when Helen begged to eat in the kitchen with her and Mr. Faraday rather than in the long, empty dining room by herself.

"No. There's nothing for me here—except for you dear people, of course. But my home, my teaching job, my life is in Green Creek now."

Mrs. Hoskins nodded. "I think your aunt knew that too. She didn't expect you to keep this place. Already set it up for her attorney to take care of selling everything, if you so chose."

"But what will the two of you do? I don't want you to want for anything." Helen looked from Mrs. Hoskins's gentle face beneath her cap to Mr. Faraday's bright blue eyes behind his spectacles.

"Oh, don't you worry about us, love." Mr. Faraday gave a brisk nod. "Remember your aunt left us each a tidy little sum, bless her. Enough to set us each up nicely in a little cottage or somewhat of our own. And my old legs won't mind not needin' to fetch and carry for anyone but meself at my age. Think I might take up gardenin.'"

"And my sister has been pestering me to come and live with her for ages." Mrs. Hoskins laid her hand on Helen's and squeezed it. "As Mr. Faraday says, don't you worry about us. This place would never be the same without your aunt, anyhow. It's seen its day."

"I still can't wrap my mind around her leaving so much to me." Yes, perhaps Aunt Ophelia had no other likely heirs, but what was Helen to do with such a responsibility?

"You were her life, dearie. And you know she'd no children of her own, nor yet any close family left. Whether she told you or not, she was that proud of you. What was it she would always say to us, Mr. Faraday? 'That girl is going to make an imprint on this world. She'll make it a better place.'"

Helen's throat tightened as she pressed Mrs. Hoskins's wrinkled hand.

That night in her old, rose-covered room, Helen snuggled into bed in her nightdress and opened her mother's diary once more, which she'd tucked into her carpetbag at the last minute.

She opened to the last few pages and began to read.

November 1, 1874

My mind is slipping, I know it. Even Helen sees it. She looks at me with fear in her eyes, and it tears my heart. I try to be strong for her, to think clearly. But then the darkness comes in, and I seem powerless against it.

People are talking about sending me away. I know, I see the looks and murmurs on the days I manage to deliver laundry. The minister and doctor came by together the other day. Part of me is glad. I do not want this life for Helen. I do not trust myself anymore. She would be better off without me. She would be better off if I had never found her at all. And yet . . . she has been the one true joy of my life . . .

The line faded off into a blur and a blot there, as if tears had fallen on it. Then picked up again stronger, in darker ink.

I will send her to Aunt Ophelia. She will do for Helen what I would never let her do for me. Then, perhaps, my precious girl can have a real life.

Helen closed the book, sudden tears on her cheeks. Dear Aunt Ophelia. And indeed she had done much for Helen . . . so very much. She could thank Adelaide for that, perhaps. A sudden wave of weariness washed over her, and she turned down the lamp and cuddled under her down comforter.

Yet sleep proved elusive, dancing just out of her reach, mingled with muddled memories she struggled to untangle. Hazy images from her earliest days, ones that hadn't surfaced for years. A woman bent before her, urging her to toddle toward her with a gentle smile. Yet the face was not Adelaide's, but another one, with soft blond hair. Christiana? Then waking in the night as a tiny child, weeping inconsolably, and a different woman coming to comfort her. This time, Adelaide, rocking her in her arms, holding her close to her heart.

Helen woke—or had she been sleeping at all?—with tears on her cheeks. She turned on her side, face against her damp pillow.

Adelaide had taken her, yes. But not from her parents, not really—they were already gone, or nearly so. And if she hadn't, Helen would never have known Aunt Ophelia, not have had the opportunities she'd been given. Someone else would have found and cared for her, surely—perhaps the grandparents Knut had mentioned, or perhaps she would have ended up in a children's home, like Thomi. Would that have been better? If, of course, she hadn't been swept downriver and drowned, as had been thought.

She turned up the gas lamp over her bed again and opened to the final pages of the diary.

Only a few entries remained, scattered and confused. They spoke of loneliness, abandonment. Hinted at stark conditions at the asylum—her mother had been kept in a room with a woman who raved all day long, another with ceaseless weeping. Sometimes her mother was restrained.

Helen swiped away her tears in order to read the last lines. Downstairs, the parlor clock gave two low bongs.

I cannot think enough to write anymore, most days. But sometimes the chaplain visits, and when he prays, I sense that peace I have always sought. Perhaps someday I will find the land of that peace, where all things are made new. Perhaps I will be well there, where the trees bring healing. Perhaps Helen will forgive me . . .

No more entries lay in the book. Helen closed its cover and laid it gently aside. She blew her nose on her handkerchief and sipped from the glass of water Mrs. Hoskins had left by her bed, then lay back down.

Lord . . . She hardly knew what to pray. Yet He knew what was in her heart. *You have been there all along, haven't you? In that carriage accident that took my parents . . . when my mother, Adelaide, found me. Even through those hard years with her, and then bringing me to Aunt Ophelia. And leading me to Green Creek, to Forsberg House. To . . . Ødger. At least I want to believe so. And finally to learning the truth of who I am.*

"Fear not: for I have redeemed thee, I have called thee by thy name; thou art mine."

Tears blurred again then. Even when she hadn't known who her earthly parents were, or where she belonged . . . she had always been His. His child, His daughter. Held safe under the shadow of His wings. *Thank you.*

At last she shifted onto her side and closed her eyes, a new purpose beating in her heart. At least to begin with, she knew what she wanted to do. She must meet with Aunt Ophelia's lawyer tomorrow.

And she could hardly wait to tell Ødger her idea.

Ødger's heart thudded hard as he waited on the train platform, shifting his feet as he glanced at his pocket watch once more.

Would Helen mind that he was the one who had come to pick her up from the Decorah station? He had offered, to spare Absalom the trip. Though Hank or JJ could have come just as well. But they had let him, with knowing smiles that sent heat rising up his neck.

Everyone knew. Of course they did.

He turned up the collar of his coat against the frigid wind. Helen had made it a quick trip, that was certain, only delaying the planned start of school after the big snowstorm by a few more days. Whatever she'd had to do back in Ohio, she'd made efficient work of it. But what were her plans now? Would she return East after finishing this school term? Amalia said Helen's aunt had left her everything—her elegant home in Ohio, her entire estate. What did he have to offer, as a poor preacher, in comparison to that? Though Rev. Larsen had asked him to stay on as associate pastor for the foreseeable future, insisting on paying him a small salary even before his ordination would become official. But still . . .

Overhead gray clouds blanketed, hinting at more snow. At last the train whistle blew, and the engine chugged into the station, billowing smoke and soot.

Ødger coughed and waved his hand before his face, straining to see through the clouds of steam as passengers began to disembark.

And then—there she was, climbing down the train steps, the conductor handing her the bag. Searching the platform with her gaze. He knew the moment her eyes landed on him. The joy that sprang into her face set his heart pounding again, a foolish grin spreading on his face as he hurried toward her.

She met him halfway, smiling despite her black hat and coat. "I didn't know it would be you coming to fetch me."

"They let me. That is—I wanted to." His tongue fumbling, he reached for her carpetbag. "May I?"

"Yes, thank you."

Side by side, they walked to the boardinghouse wagon. Despite all he wanted to say crowding his mind, Ødger couldn't find any words. He set her bag in the back of the wagon, then helped her up onto the seat, the grip of her gloved fingers warming his palm. He swung up beside her and hupped the horses, turning off down the street.

"How was your trip?" The words seemed trite, inadequate, but he had to start somewhere.

"It was . . . enlightening." She cast him a glance. "Did you hear my aunt made me her heir?"

"Ja." His throat worked. "She chose well."

"I could hardly wrap my mind about it at first. I felt so unworthy. And yet the Lord has been showing me some things, these last few days."

Ødger cast her a quick glance. She did indeed hold a new . . . rootedness, a peace, in the always graceful set of her head and shoulders, the blue of her eyes. "Ja?"

"I still don't understand everything about my childhood, my mother, the tangle of all that. But I've begun to see that regardless, like Joseph in Egypt, the Lord was with me through it all. Working those tangled threads into a plan for good."

Ødger wished he could reach for her hand. "I am so glad."

"Also, I heard again from my uncle Knut in Independence."

"Ah, good. What did he say?"

"He sent his condolences—I'd written him of my aunt's death. He said he would like to see me often and will sometimes come to Green Creek, so I don't have to always make the trek to Independence."

"I am so glad to hear that." Ødger's chest warmed. How good the Lord was, to lead them to this connection with her birth family. And through Professor Amundson, of all things.

"But speaking of Independence, I've had an idea, of one thing to do with this trust I've been given. Remember when you talked about the mental hospital there, how you wanted to find a way to minister to the residents?"

He nodded. He'd scarcely ever heard Helen say so much at once—she usually measured her words with such care.

"I've been reading some about typical conditions at such places, and I spoke with Aunt Ophelia's doctor about it. Treatment methods and living arrangements can be truly atrocious, yet some are working for reform. I'd like to set up a charitable foundation seeking to improve conditions in mental hospitals, to help bring beauty and humanity there. We could provide more chaplains, private rooms, support new treatments that are being developed . . . I need to do much more research on just how to help. I've even dreamed we might someday fund a hospital in Decorah—a general hospital, but perhaps with a mental wing."

Ødger stared at her. "But that is wonderful." His mind retraced her words. "You said . . . we?"

"Yes." She glanced at him. "That is . . . I do not mean to presume. But I hoped . . ."

"No—I mean, ja. Of course I want to be involved."

"Just . . . involved?" Her voice wavered.

"Helen." He sighed, set down the reins, and turned on the seat to look at her. The horses could find their own way from here, down the familiar snow-rutted road toward Green Creek. "You *know* what I want. You know I want . . . you. I love you. I want . . ." He swallowed hard. "To marry you. But—you are a Cincinnati heiress, with all sorts of grand plans. You could travel the world, sing opera, become a famous benefactress. I am just a poor immigrant preacher."

"Ødger." She took both his hands in hers, sending a shock clear to his elbows despite their warm gloves. "Listen to me. Don't you see the answer, right before us? Aunt Ophelia has left me so well off. You can pastor and preach and shepherd, as God has made you to do, without having to worry overmuch about money. We can buy a little house in Green Creek, and I can teach music lessons from our home. And together . . . we can make a difference. For those who have so few to give them voice." She paused for breath, her cheeks flushed as if she suddenly realized what she was saying. "That is, if you are sure you truly want . . . me."

"Helen." His voice came husky. Her pulse thrummed against his, despite their gloved hands. "I have told you so, again and again. But is this really . . . I mean, do you?"

She gave a choked laugh. "I can't think of anything else I want more in the world."

He pulled off his gloves then, and cupped her face in his hands, so warm despite the snowflakes beginning to drift down around them. "I would like to kiss you right now. If I did not fear some school superintendent might be watching nearby."

Glancing at the snowy cornfield on one side and the dormant creek on the other, Helen smiled and lifted her face to his. "Then perhaps I should be the one to kiss you."

EPILOGUE

May 1893

"Are you all right?"

Helen looked to Amalia. "I will be when I can quit shaking." The two women smiled at each other in the mirror in the church dressing room. Helen wore her pearl-colored wedding dress—the one she'd loaned to Amalia, thinking never to wear it herself.

"I was beginning to believe this was just a dream, so much has happened. Just think, right here in this church two weeks ago Ødger was ordained. And Reverend Larsen was strong enough to walk down the aisle and be part of the service. Even he called that day a miracle."

They both turned at the knock on the door. "Yes?"

Rev. Larsen poked his head around the opening door. "About time to begin, although I could just sit and enjoy the concert."

His smile made Helen warm with gratitude. How close he had come to stepping into his heavenly home, a year and a half ago now. "I'm so grateful you are here for today."

"Me too." He laid a hand on each shoulder. "Let's pray. Heavenly Father, we thank thee for this day, for the glorious music from our new organ that Helen graced our church with. Bless now the union of thy dear children, this service that will begin their new life together. Thank thee for the friendship of these two women, now true sisters in thy son Jesus Christ. We rejoice in thy holy name. Amen." He stepped back and nodded. "Ready?"

Helen inhaled a deep breath. "Ready." The women picked up their bouquets of lilacs and waited until the music changed from organ to piano, then paused in the doorway to the sanctuary.

Rev. Larsen stood facing the guests. "Please rise." The congregation stood and looked down the center aisle. Amalia stepped out.

"Ma!" The little voice carried. "Ma-a-a!"

While the guests chuckled, Amalia smiled at her little daughter in Mrs. Miller's arms and kept on walking toward the altar.

Helen looked ahead to where Ødger and Absalom waited with the pastor and stepped out. Were those tears in her almost-husband's eyes? She sniffed and smiled and stopped between Amalia and Ødger. The music ceased and Rev. Larsen asked the guests to be seated.

"Dearly beloved, we are gathered here today to witness the marriage of Reverend Ødger Kristoff Gunderson and Helen Primrose Stenerson. Let us pray."

Helen bowed her head, the warm pressure of Ødger's fingers on her own. As the reverend's prayer washed over them, her thudding pulse settled, the trembling eased. Here—this was where her life had been heading, where she belonged. *Thank you, Father.*

"Amen." Rev. Larsen lifted his head and beamed at them, his eyes sparkling behind his spectacles. "Now we begin the part I've been looking forward to for, well—it seems like a long time."

Chuckles rippled through the congregation. Ødger squeezed Helen's hands, smiling into her eyes. How she loved him . . . and now, they were about to be joined as one.

"Ødger, do you take Helen to be your wedded wife, to love, honor, and keep her, in sickness and in health, as long as you both shall live?"

"I do." His voice resounded through the church.

"And, Helen, do you take Ødger to be your wedded husband, to love, honor, and keep him, in sickness and in health, as long as you both shall live?"

She met his blue-gray gaze and spoke loud enough for all to hear. "I do."

"Now, do we have rings?"

Erik stepped up to Ødger's side and handed him a slender circlet of gold, while Amalia handed Helen another. The ring slipped onto her finger, cool and smooth, and then she slid the slightly larger band onto Ødger's work-roughened finger. His mouth tipped in a grin, and she smiled back, squeezing his hand.

"And now"—Rev. Larsen glanced between them—"by the power vested in me, I pronounce that you are husband and wife. What God has joined together, let no man put asunder. Ødger." The elderly pastor smiled at him, a bit of a sheen in his eyes. "You may now kiss your bride."

Ødger gently laid his hands on Helen's shoulders and kissed her, gentle but sure, as the congregation broke into applause and cheers.

"And now," Rev. Larsen said, beaming over the gathering, "we have a gift for all of us from Reverend and Mrs. Ødger Gunderson. It gives me great joy to announce that since his ordination, Ødger has agreed to stay on at the Green Creek church, as official assistant pastor." More clapping. "To celebrate this day, the newlyweds would like to share a musical offering with us all."

Murmurs and rustles came from those seated. Only Amalia, Absalom, and the reverend had known their plan. Helen smiled as Ødger led her over to the piano, then seated himself at the new organ Aunt Ophelia's generosity had enabled them to gift the church.

Helen met her husband's gaze over the top of the piano, nodded, then rested her fingers on the keys and began to play Bach's "Jesu, Joy of Man's Desiring." After a few measures, Ødger joined with rich chords from the organ, and they played in harmony, alternating carrying the melody and providing soft accompaniment in the background. The music swelled, carrying Helen's heart with it up to the church rafters.

When they finished, the congregation broke into applause so thunderous little twenty-month-old Sarah Marie began to cry, quickly soothed by Amalia in the front pew. Ødger rose from the organ and held out his hand to Helen. She took it, smiling so big her face had started to ache. Slipping her arm through her husband's, they faced the rows of beloved faces.

Rev. Larsen clasped his hands. "May I present to you all the new Reverend and Mrs. Ødger Gunderson!"

Cheers and applause once again as they hurried down the aisle arm in arm, beaming and blushing. Hank, Thomi, and Ruthie fairly shouted themselves hoarse, along with the rest of Helen's former students.

After the reception on the church lawn and hours of greeting, well-wishing, and cake eating, Helen and Ødger finally slipped away to their own little house prepared for them down the lane, just as the springtime dusk fell and the evening birds began to chirp.

"I still can't believe we found a house so close to the church," she sighed, looking up at the leafy canopy of branches over the lane. "God is so good."

"Ja, He is that." Ødger squeezed her arm. "And I still cannot believe a Cincinnati heiress, with a voice like an angel, chose to be tied to a country preacher."

She patted his arm. "With you, I am the richest woman in the world—with or without Aunt Ophelia's money. But I'm glad we can do some good with it, I hope."

Ødger nodded. "Reverend Bakke in Independence wants to meet with me about our foundation for the mentally ill. He has connections with the mental hospital there and wants to introduce us." He hesitated, glancing at her, his bearded face understanding. "I can go alone, if you prefer."

Helen paused at the little white gate to the garden in front of their yellow clapboard house—what would be their home, now, where she would teach music and he would write sermons and they would welcome the community . . . and someday, God willing, children of their own. "I think . . . I'd like to go with you. I think I am ready."

He kissed her hair. "You know I would always rather have you by my side."

She turned toward him, lifting her face to kiss her husband properly. *Oh, Lord, I never thought you would have this joy in store for me—but I'm so grateful.*

Then Ødger took her hand, opened the gate, and led the way down the path to their new home.

DISCUSSION QUESTIONS

1. In the Home to Green Creek series, little had been revealed of Helen's backstory until this book. What surprised you the most about her story?
2. Despite learning she never knew her biological parents, Helen has many people who have become family to her, from Aunt Ophelia to the folks at Forsberg House. Who do you have in your life who is not related to you by blood but feels like family?
3. Ødger realizes that having an aunt with mental illness helped prepare him for avenues of ministry he hadn't expected—and even for his relationship with Helen. How have you seen God prepare you for aspects of the path He has laid for you, perhaps in unexpected ways?
4. Amalia struggles at first to tell Maya of her pregnancy, due to the loss her cousin experienced in the previous book. Have you ever hesitated to tell someone close to you good news of your own because you didn't want to hurt them? How did you approach it? What did you learn through that experience?

5. How have Ruthie, Thomi, and Hank's relationships changed and grown? How do you see each of these children developing and growing in this book?
6. Mental illness is a hard topic, in the past and still today. How do you think our contemporary approach has changed and improved compared to the past? Where do we still need to improve?
7. Helen struggles to think Ødger could truly want a relationship with her, and she also struggles to tell him her story. What advice would you have given Helen during the book?
8. Thomasina faces prejudice from some people in Green Creek due to her Italian heritage. Did you know Italian immigrants used to face prejudice? What lessons can we learn about showing welcome from the people at Forsberg House?
9. What does Helen learn through this book about the way God sees her? Have you ever sensed the Lord speaking similarly to your own heart?
10. Helen and Ødger both love music—it helps draw them together as well as soothes their souls, enables them to express emotion, and turns their hearts toward the Lord. What role has music played in your life, and why do you think music holds such power?

Coming Soon:

Look for Ruthie's story in the final book in the

HOME TO GREEN CREEK

series.

Available June 2027.

For more from Lauraine Snelling,
read on for an excerpt from

The Promise of Dawn

In 1910, Signe, her husband, and their boys emigrate from Norway to Minnesota, dreaming of one day owning a farm of their own. But the relatives they've come to stay with are harsh and demanding. As Signe's family is worked to the bone to repay the cost of their voyage, can she learn to trust God through this trial and hold on to hope for a better future?

Available now wherever books are sold.

One

April 1909

"Mor, a letter from Amerika!"

Gunlaug Strand Carlson looked up from the loom where she was weaving a rug for her son Johann's wedding present. "From Ingeborg?" Her heart leaped. If only she had not lost touch in the years since her cousin Ingeborg married Roald and moved to North Dakota. At least she got bits of news from Ingeborg's mor.

Ivar, her youngest at fifteen, shook his head. "This is from Minnesota, so it must be your other cousin."

"Is it to me or your far?"

"It says 'Mister and Missus.' The writing is hard to read." Ivar handed her the letter.

"Takk." She studied the envelope and then smiled at her son. "So how was school today?"

"Better. There aren't as many absent, but some of those who came back are still coughing like to blow up their chests."

"Uff da." The schools had been closed for a week due to the influenza that seemed to come through every year. Every day she thanked God for keeping her family safe. Of all her children, Ivar loved school the most. He was already dreaming of college and becoming a schoolteacher. How they would ever pay for something like that was beyond her comprehension. She tapped the letter on the edge of the loom.

"Aren't you going to open it?" Ivar glanced at the clock. "Far will be home soon. What's for supper?"

"Ask Nilda. She's cooking for us tonight."

"Not porridge again?"

"Nei, Johann is bringing Solveig for supper to talk about the wedding. We will read the letter at supper."

"We could read it real quick and pretend like we didn't."

"Get on with you." She fluttered her fingers, shooing him on his way. "I want to get a few more rows woven before I have to cover it." She wanted the rug to be a surprise.

Ivar left the room, whistling. Besides being her most scholarly child, he also seemed the happiest. Like her cousin Ingeborg, Ivar saw the good in things; even as a baby he'd smiled and laughed. If only there were some way his dream of becoming a teacher could come true.

That night, with everyone gathered around the supper table, Gunlaug slit open the envelope and unfolded the one sheet inside.

"Dear Cousin Gunlaug and Thor,

"I hope all is well with you and your family. I am finally in a position to write to ask for help. As you know, Gerd and I have never been blessed with sons to help us here in the new land. The section of land I have purchased from a homesteader is covered with huge pine trees that we log and send to the mills in Minneapolis. The money from those trees has made it possible for us to build a home large enough to house a family. We farm what land we have cleared, but we need help. Gerd is not well, so we are asking if Rune and his wife and sons would be willing to immigrate to Minnesota. I would pay for their passage with the understanding that over time those funds would be paid back.

"We live near a small town called Benson's Corner, with the nearest big town being Blackduck, Minnesota. There is a school for the younger ones in the winter. Once the trees are felled and shipped on the local railroad spur to the northern mills, we will clear the stumps and plant crops. We have one cow now, but I have always planned on a dairy herd when the land is cleared.

"We are hopeful Rune will agree to come. This is indeed a land of opportunity. I know we are grateful we came here when we did.

"Yours truly,
"Einar Strand and
Gerd"

Gunlaug laid the letter on the table and looked to her eldest son, who sat to her right. "What do you think?"

As she watched him ponder the news, she saw his slightly stooped shoulders stoop even more. His scalp showed through his thinning brown hair. *Oh, my son, I fear you are not built to be a logger. A farmer, yes, but . . .* It was the *buts* that hurt her heart. Her gentle son so far away. And his Signe? She looked frozen, like she might crack at any time. But she wouldn't. The light caught the gold highlights in her braided crown of long hair, but her lashes shielded her blue eyes. She sat erect, to scare off the fears Gunlaug knew were attacking.

Rune blinked in the kerosene lamplight. "Well, it is a surprise, but I have to say, I've considered emigrating more than once. But I planned to join the Bjorklunds in North Dakota. You know they've often sent letters asking for workers to come." He glanced at his wife, who stared down at her hands clenched in her lap. "What do you think, Signe?"

"I think we should say yes." Bjorn, their eldest at fifteen, could hardly sit still.

Rune frowned at him. "I was speaking to your mor."

Bjorn nodded slightly, but his excitement only dimmed rather than going out. He elbowed his brother Knute, to his right.

Nilda, the eldest of Gunlaug's three girls, set a plate of fritters on the table and went back for the coffeepot. "Warm-ups, anyone?" She nudged Johann. "Shame you don't have sons yet."

"Let us get married first, all right?"

"Well, I would go as soon as the ticket arrived." Nilda refilled Rune's coffee cup. "Come on, Signe, think of the adventure." She and Signe had been best friends since their school days and became even closer after Signe married Rune. Nilda had lived up to her reputation as a matchmaker.

Teeth clamped on her lower lip, Signe stared from her husband to Gunlaug and back. Shaking her head, she spoke softly. "If we go there, we will never see our families again."

Oh, you poor dear. Gunlaug patted her daughter-in-law's work-worn hand and nodded at her son. "I have always wanted to go find Ingeborg. How often I have wished we agreed to emigrate when they asked for more family to come."

"Why didn't you?" Nilda asked.

Thor interjected, "Because I have no desire to cross that ocean and then spend days on a train to North Dakota. I am content here in Norway." He looked to his wife, who shrugged. They never had agreed on this matter.

"Tante Ingeborg and her family have certainly done well," Rune commented. "At least that's what we've heard."

"Ja, they have." Gunlaug made sure her smile was back in place. No sense dreaming of what could never be. She looked at her children. "If you decide to go, know that it will be with my blessing and your far's also. Right, Thor?"

"Ja. If you want to go, so be it. But remember, not everyone who goes to Amerika does as well as Ingeborg and her family. There are heartaches aplenty there too." Thor nodded to Rune. "You must think and pray on this. You do not want to make hasty decisions and regret them later. Felling the tall trees is not only hard work but dangerous."

Gunlaug saw Signe shiver. Leaving her family—both families—would be especially hard on her, since she had already lived through such sorrow in her life. Her first husband died shortly after their son Bjorn was born. Nilda had brought her and the baby to live with the Carlsons and played a big part in bringing Rune and Signe together. Such opposites, she who loved to talk and he who made sure not one word was spent carelessly. He took after his father in that way.

How dear Rune and Signe's three sons were to the whole family. But tragedy had struck again and again as Signe suffered miscarriages. Then two girls died after birth, and after that, Signe began to believe she was barren. Sometimes life was harsh indeed.

And now that Gunlaug suspected Signe might finally be pregnant again, they might be leaving. Taking her grandchildren with them.

Gunlaug brought her mind back to the letter at hand. Einar had said Gerd was not well. Did that mean she was bedridden or just had a weak constitution? Either would mean a big load for Signe.

Rune looked thoughtful. "I know it is a big decision, but I am not afraid of hard work. Einar doesn't say anything about having land of our own. Does he expect us all to live in their house for the rest of our lives?"

"And what if we have more children?" Signe was frowning now.

"Did you know Einar and Gerd well when you were growing up, Mor?" Rune asked.

Gunlaug shook her head. "They didn't live close by. That family settled over on the mountain, and we hardly ever saw them. I never met Gerd. I know my mor stayed in touch with them, but she is so good about writing letters. That's probably where Einar learned you have sons. But surely he doesn't think Bjorn is old enough to fell trees. That's a man's job."

"I can handle a crosscut saw, can't I, Far?"

"Ja, but there is a difference between cutting up firewood and felling giant trees. Ach, we would have so much to learn. How old is Einar, do you think?"

"He was younger than I when they emigrated, probably in his late thirties. Just think—you can homestead in Amerika and earn your land free and clear."

Thor looked at his eldest son. "There are strict rules to be met. Remember Ole Sorenson? He gave it up and came back home. He said free land was all a lie. You might want to write Einar and ask him some of your questions."

Rune nodded. "Ja, that would be wise. Can we take the letter home with us so we have the address?"

"Of course." Gunlaug passed the envelope to him. "You might ask if there are any other family members near them. And when they would expect you to come."

"From the sounds of this, the sooner the better." Thor's scowl hadn't let up. If anything, the lines in his forehead had deepened.

"Remember, tonight we are supposed to be talking about our wedding." Johann raised his voice over the conversations breaking out. He smiled at his intended sitting next to him. "Do you have any questions?"

Solveig shook her head. "My brother Arne went to Amerika, then wrote back and asked for someone to send him a bride. He couldn't find a woman to marry over there and didn't want to be a lumberjack all his life. Even though he made enough money to pay for a ticket."

"And someone went?"

"Ja, he included a ticket, so the daughter of some friends agreed to go. As far as I know, they got married and now have a baby. Mail-order brides is what they're called, I think."

"I've heard of that." Nilda sat down in her chair. "Maybe that's what I should do, become a mail-order bride. After all, there are not many young men left in Norway."

"Don't be silly," Thor said. "It's not like you're an old maid."

"What a gamble." Rune rubbed his eyes. "I think we need to head home. You boys get your things together. Signe, I'm glad we got married when we did. Mail-order brides." Shaking his head, he tucked the envelope in his breast pocket and pushed back his chair. "When is the wedding to be, Johann?"

"Three weeks. You better not leave before then. You agreed to stand up with me."

Rune smiled. "We'll still be here, never fear. Solveig, how you'll put up with my brother is beyond me."

"My far said the same thing about me. I know I wouldn't mind emigrating to Amerika." Solveig looked at her intended. "Would you, Johann?"

"It bears thinking about." He slapped Rune on the shoulder. "You get us a place over there in a year or two, after we see how you do."

The next day, Gunlaug wrote Einar and Gerd a short, newsy letter—just a page—while Rune wrote a letter with his questions, the main one being when Einar would expect them to travel. To save postage, they sent both letters in one envelope,

Gunlaug worked long into the night in order to finish the rug, the monotony of throwing the shuttle and clamping the rug giving her too much time to think. If Rune and his family went to Minnesota, she would never see those grandchildren again, let alone her eldest son. Just like she'd never seen Ingeborg again. How could two cousins who were closer than sisters lose touch with each other this way? The break had happened when her far learned that the will of his younger brother did not deed any of the family land to him but all to Ingeborg's far. He'd forbidden them any contact with the family.

When the two families finally had contact again, it was not the same. Too much water under the bridge, as her mor would say.

She had written several letters through the years, but she'd not had an answer and had finally given up. Was it worth it to try again? That was the big question. Ingeborg did not even write to her own family very often. Mostly only when sending a request for help.

But Thor was adamant. He would not emigrate. The fact that he had so easily agreed to send Rune with his blessing was a shock.

She finished the rug a week before the wedding. After wrapping it in an old sheet, she tucked it away and restrung the loom for another rug, this one to go with Rune and Signe to Amerika. Even living in someone else's home, they would have a piece of her heart to lay by their bed. Einar must have a really large house to invite a whole family like this.

The day before the wedding, Rune and Signe brought the answer from Einar to the house. "He wants us to come immediately."

Gunlaug clasped her hands over her heart. "And you will go?" She looked at Signe, whose face wore tear tracks.

Signe nodded.

"And your mor?"

"She is so disappointed with our decision that she can hardly speak to me."

Gunlaug gathered her daughter-in-law into her arms. "I am so sorry to hear that. But perhaps she will relent as the day draws nearer."

"Rune says I must be strong, but where do I find the strength?"

"The only place I know is in the arms of our God. If this is His plan for you, He will provide the strength."

"Easy to say," Rune grumbled under his breath.

Having lived under her far's edict all those years ago, Gunlaug well knew the pain this was causing Signe. How could she help her?

What would it take to stiffen this young woman's spine enough to endure the voyage and a hard life in the new land? Not that life was easy here in Norway. Would that Gunlaug had had that spine years ago.

"So what will you do?"

"Answer him that we will be ready to leave within a week of receiving the tickets." Rune had obviously given this a great deal of thought. But he was the one fighting to support his family and keep food on the table in a land with few opportunities for the younger folk.

Gunlaug looked at the calendar. "How long did it take for his return letter this time?"

"Between two and three weeks. So I suspect we will hear by the first of June. Summer voyages are supposed to be much easier than winter ones." He looked at Signe. "Not so much seasickness."

Signe flinched, her sigh filling in the blanks. She obviously dreaded the voyage.

"If you send the letter by return post, then we will put this out of our mind for a couple of days and enjoy the wedding tomorrow. It's Solveig and Johann's big day, and it would not be fair to overshadow it with this news." Gunlaug hoped she sounded firm and positive and did not even hint at the cracking of her heart. Her oldest son and his family would be on the opposite side of the world. Somehow, reminding herself that they could write letters did not ease her sorrow.

After looking out the window the next day, Gunlaug stepped outside to enjoy the sunrise. It looked to be a clear day for the wedding, always a good omen. Johann was already out in the garden. With the extra-cold winter, it had taken longer for the soil to thaw out, which meant later planting.

"A good day for a wedding," she called out.

"Any day would be a good day for this wedding," he answered. "I've waited long enough."

She reached in the door for the shawl always hanging at the ready. Wrapping it around her shoulders against the early morning chill, she made her way to the outhouse and then to the garden. "Takk for your help."

"We all eat from this plot of ground." He leaned on the handle of the hoe. "I wonder if they grow the same things in Amerika."

"Most likely. I looked at a map. We aren't much farther north than Minnesota. But I hear in North Dakota the winters are worse than here, as there is nothing to stop or even slow down the wind off the northern plains of Canada. We have hills, mountains, and trees to protect us." *I want to go there!* The thought echoed in her mind like a trumpet call.

Johann walked to the fence. "When we go, Mor, we will take you with us. Both Solveig and I would go in a heartbeat."

"How you will save the money for that trip is more than I could do. I try to save against a rainy day, but something always eats it up." Last winter, when Thor had been without work because the cows were dry, had been a tough one. The porridge had been terribly weak at times.

"Ah, but we are young and don't have a family to feed yet. If the folks of Blessing—or in Minnesota—send out another call, I will go and send money back for a ticket for Solveig. Just the name of the town, Blessing, makes me want to go there."

"Why have you never said this before?"

"I've thought of it but never had someone else depending on me, like I will now. After today, I am no longer a free and easy young man. I will be a husband, a man with responsibilities." He laid his hand over hers. "But, Mor, I will see that you get to Amerika."

And find Ingeborg. But she didn't voice that dream, for after all, that was all it was.

Johann's words dug in and took root in Gunlaug's mind as they prepared to send Rune and Signe on their way. Their two trunks were tightly packed, and each of the boys had a rucksack of his own. Gunlaug hoped that keeping busy would ease the heartache, but when the tickets arrived, she felt like Signe looked.

Realization dawned. She drew the younger woman into the bedroom.

"Signe, is there any chance you are with child?" It had been eight years since Leif was born, and she had figured, as did Signe, that her childbearing years might be over.

Signe nodded. "I have not told Rune yet, but if I have no showing next week, well, I feel sure . . ." She blew her nose. "If I lose this one on that horrible voyage, how will I forgive myself? Or Rune?"

"For forcing you to go?"

The shake of her head was barely perceptible. "He wants to do this, and I cannot keep him from it. If there is hope for a better life there, we must try. But the thought of him out cutting down trees gives me nightmares. He has no experience like that." She blew her nose again. "And Mor is barely speaking to me still."

Gunlaug clamped her teeth together to keep her thoughts back. Forgiveness might be preached in church, but too often those listening didn't heed the words. "I am so sorry, but I feel my job as a mother is to encourage my children to do what is necessary for the family. I wish your mor felt the same. I pray she will see the light before you go."

"Ja, it better be soon. I cannot worry about her, this babe I am probably carrying, and keeping my sons and husband safe on both the voyage and the train rides."

"Keeping you all safe is God's provenance, and He promises to never let us go. Do you believe that?"

"Ja, I try, but this is all so unknown."

"True, but hanging on to His promise to be with us always is what keeps my mother's heart from breaking right in two." Someday. Someday she would see them again, if Johann could keep his promise to her.

Waving goodbye when the wagon took them to the train tested Gunlaug beyond belief.

LAURAINE SNELLING is the award-winning author of more than one hundred books, fiction and nonfiction, for adults and young adults. Her books have sold more than five million copies. She makes her home in Tehachapi, California. Learn more at LauraineSnelling.com.

KIERSTI GIRON grew up loving Lauraine's books. After being mentored by Lauraine as a young writer, she is now blessed to collaborate with Lauraine on new historical series together. A lover of history and story, Kiersti lives in California with her husband and young son. Learn more at KierstiGiron.com.

Sign Up for Lauraine's Newsletter

Keep up to date with Lauraine's latest news on book releases and events by signing up for her email list at the website below.

LauraineSnelling.com

FOLLOW LAURAINE ON SOCIAL MEDIA

Lauraine Snelling Author